Congratulations to RITA finalist Karen White!

A HAUNTING RESEMBLANCE

My hand flew to my throat. The portrait could have been me, except for the eyes. The eyes I saw in my own reflection were haunted and hungry, but still quite human. The ones in the portrait were cold and lifeless. If I had not known the subject of the portrait, I would even have called them malevolent.

A hot breath teased the back of my neck. I spun around and found myself staring up into the face of John McMahon.

I swallowed. "It was the dress, wasn't it?"

He nodded. Keeping his voice low, he said, "It was quite a shock for us. The resemblance . . . especially in that dress, with your hair done up that way . . ." His voice lingered.

His presence pinned me to the spot, draining me of the will to move away. "I don't understand. She is your wife! Why do reminders of her bring such terror to not only you but to your daughter as well?"

His gaze flickered across my face as he raised a hand. I didn't flinch as he lowered a finger to my neck and gently brushed away a lock of hair. I felt the heat of his touch long after he had removed his hand and half-wished he would touch me again. Still, I didn't look away.

"You are so much like her, and yet . . ." He stopped, his gaze regarding me openly. "You have such a gentle spirit. I'm left to wonder sometimes if I married the wrong sister."

Other *Love Spell* books by Karen White:
IN THE SHADOW OF THE MOON

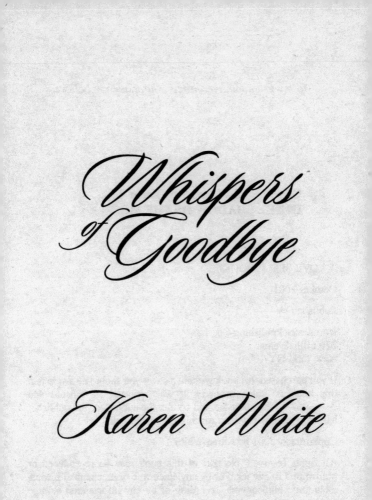

Whispers of Goodbye

Karen White

LOVE SPELL NEW YORK CITY

To my grandmother, Grace, who made me believe.

A LOVE SPELL BOOK®

October 2001

Published by

Dorchester Publishing Co., Inc.
276 Fifth Avenue
New York, NY 10001

ISBN 0-505-52455-4

Visit us on the web at www.dorchesterpub.com.

ACKNOWLEDGMENTS:

I'd like to thank my husband, Tim, for his patience, support and ability to know when to just nod and say, "yes, dear." And especially for all the cooked meals—your talents are limitless, and I love you for all of them.

Thanks also to my invaluable critique partners, Wendy Wax Adler, Susie Crandall, Jenni Grizzle, Vicky Harden, and Karen Moser. Not only are you critiquers *par excellence,* but also very good friends. And to Theresa White, Donna Michael, Ruth Reed and Nan Jackson—thank you for being fans. Your enthusiasm and encouragement made me want to sit down at the computer every day.

Whispers of Goodbye

Chapter One

Grief cannot be apportioned as if measuring flour for a cake. But when Jamie died, my husband claimed the lion's share of it, leaving me with only a handful to mull over and sift through my fingers. I was not entitled, he insisted, because I had killed our beloved son.

What was left of my husband after the war was quickly destroyed by Jamie's death, and I watched the destruction with pity and frustration until his final act of obliteration and revenge. I found him in his gray uniform, his sword still in its scabbard, his revolver lying next to him on the pillow in the bedroom. The blood seeped crimson into the white sheets of the bed, marring their purity. I gathered my grief and held it close to me, tucking it inside where I would never allow anyone to see.

My anger and the gnawing of hunger pulled me from my bed each morning. My fields, where the finest quality Sea Island cotton had once grown, now lay as barren and trampled as my own soul. The old house, the house in which I had lived first with my parents, and then my husband and son, lay in ashes. The odd fragment of brick or china shone like bone in the scorched earth, the only remains of my once happy life.

There were fewer friends and neighbors huddled around Robert's casket at Christ Church Cemetery than had been at Jamie's memorial service. I suppose that many, facing the same devastation as I, had left our beloved island of Saint Simons to seek refuge inland. Even as the pastor's words droned on to their inevitable conclusion, I knew I couldn't leave. My anger was as fresh as the newly turned dirt, and my leaving would be like a forgiveness—something with which I was not yet ready to part. But the hunger pangs gnawed on.

I thought often of joining Jamie in the surf off our island, of feeling the shifting sand beneath my bare feet as I walked slowly into the dark depths of the ocean. But perhaps akin to the stubbornness of my fellow countrymen who would not recognize defeat, I held firm to life. I would stare out over the ocean, the salty air stinging my cheeks, and refuse to look behind me. Whatever lay ahead did not frighten me. I had nothing left to fear.

I had sought shelter in the overseer's cottage. Mr. Rafferty had abandoned it in the first year of the war, leaving in the middle of the night. The Yankees who had encamped on Saint Simons had left the cottage intact, finding the simple furnishings not valuable enough to steal. As a result, I had a roof over my head and a place to lie down at the end of each day.

Two weeks after Robert's funeral, while scrounging around the overgrown vegetable garden for a forgotten or only half-rotten potato or onion, I heard the sound of approaching hoofbeats pounding down the road.

Will Benton took off his sweat-soaked hat when he saw

me, then gingerly slid from the saddle, his wooden leg not seeming to hamper him overmuch. His gaze flickered over me, and I was surprised to see sadness instead of the pity I was used to. Perhaps he, too, was remembering the old days when we were not too much younger, days when we danced in the ballroom of the old house, him with two legs, and me in a satin gown with ribbons in my hair.

I wiped my cheek with the back of my hand, realizing too late that dirt crusted my knuckles. "Hello, Will. This is a pleasant surprise."

A ghost of a smile haunted his face, an apparition of the boisterous smiles of his carefree youth. The youth he had been before the war came and robbed us all. "Hello, Cat. That's nice of you to say."

Will looked behind me at the crude structure of the tabby cottage, and then back at me, his eyes focusing on the faded black cotton of my dress. "I brought you a letter. I didn't know the next time you'd come to our side of the island, and I thought it might be important. It's from Louisiana."

My heart constricted slightly. I had not heard from my older sister, Elizabeth, during the long four years of the war. Three months after the firing at Fort Sumter, she had been bundled and packed away to her husband's home state of Massachusetts, leaving behind the beautiful home on the Mississippi that had been left to her and her new husband by our grandmother. I hadn't even sent news of Jamie and Robert, not knowing if my words would ever reach her.

I tried not to look at my dirty hands as I opened the envelope, too starved for news of my sister to worry about my bad manners in making Will wait.

My dearest Cat,
My situation here is intolerable, and I have no one

11

with whom I can share my thoughts and feelings. There is something evil here which I do not understand, something heavy in the air.

Oh, Cat, you have always been my constant, the one who helped steer me from trouble. It is hard to imagine sometimes that I am the eldest! I am afraid I may have made quite a mess out of things, and I need your guidance.

Please, if it is at all possible, do come to me. You can have your old room, and I will grant you as many favors as you request if you will just come. If your Robert is back from the war, I would welcome his presence, too. He's always given me a feeling of strength and security, as have you, and I need that now, more than you can know.

I have taken the liberty of sending a coach and funds for your journey. It should arrive within a week or so of this letter. I know how you hate to leave your precious island, but I have nowhere else to turn.

I need you, dear sister. I am so afraid.

Affectionately,
Elizabeth deClaire McMahon

My gaze met the concern in Will's. "Everything all right, Cat? You look like you've been spooked by a ghost."

I shook my head. "No, I'm all right. It's from Elizabeth. She wants me to come . . . for a visit."

Will's face was grim. "It's about time, if you ask me. No offense to your sister, but it's just not right for you to be living out here alone like this. It's a crying shame." He turned toward his horse, then vigorously closed up the mailbag. "I'm sure that Yankee husband of hers has been holdin' her back from askin' you to visit."

I didn't know much about John McMahon other than

that he was the second son of a wealthy Boston merchant. On a business trip to Saint Simons he had taken one look at my sister and decided that he had to have her along with the bales of cotton he was purchasing from our father.

Elizabeth had been transfixed by the dark, brooding eyes and tall stature of the Northern stranger. I had caught those eyes watching me several times, an unreadable emotion lingering in their dark depths, but he always turned away whenever I acknowledged him. I believe I hated him on sight with all the fierceness a fourteen-year-old girl could muster. It wasn't for anything he had ever done to me directly, but for the simple reason that he had decided he needed my sister more than I did. It did not matter that his inscrutable face softened and his cold ebony eyes warmed when he gazed upon her. She was as much a part of me as the island, yet John McMahon separated us for the first time in our young lives when he married Elizabeth and took her to Louisiana.

Too hungry and tired to disagree with Will, I said good-bye and watched him ride off in the late-afternoon sun. Buttery light pierced the trees and the veils of Spanish moss, and I sighed heavily. How could I ever leave this place? I stilled for a moment, straining to hear the quiet murmur of the ocean. I began walking toward it, needing to feel its tranquillity and contemplate whether my sister's letter would be my salvation or my ruin.

Puffs of dirt sailed out from under the wheels of the coach, like little whispers of good-bye. I stared down at my hands, not wanting to watch my life pass by outside the window. My mother had once told me that if you stared after somebody until they disappeared, you would never see them again. I refused to think of this parting as permanent, and so kept my gaze fastened on my worn black leather gloves.

My sister's words traveled with me each day of the long,

13

arduous journey. I knew in my bones that something was dreadfully wrong, and I had to reach Elizabeth as soon as possible. The driver, a Mr. O'Rourke, deferred to my comfort, frequently asking if I needed to stop. But I urged him on, only consenting to stop and rest when the horses were near exhaustion. My aching bones and muscles protested each mile, but my sense of urgency pressed us on. If I hadn't been worried about the driver needing his sleep, I would have demanded that we drive day and night, not stopping until we reached the welcoming arms of my sister.

My mother would have been scandalized by my lack of a chaperon, but my circumstances had changed. I simply didn't have the resources left to worry about social niceties. Patrick O'Rourke, a ruddy Bostonian, was courteous and protective, and I felt quite safe in his presence.

As we drove farther and farther inland, the heat and humidity pressed in on us, and I found myself missing the cool breezes of the ocean. The prick of tears began behind my eyelids, but I willed them away by pulling at my anger like an old wound, making it swell again inside me.

Twilight fell on us as we neared the outskirts of New Orleans and the final leg of our long journey. A smattering of rain slapped the roof of the coach as if small hands urged us on. The coachman pulled up on the reins and stopped on the road near a muddy swamp, visible in the dim light. He climbed down from his seat and opened the door of the coach to speak with me. Something screeched high in a tree.

"The road is very wet, and I don't want to risk going farther in the darkness. If it's been raining for a while, the river could have overflowed its banks and washed out the road. We'd do best to find a place in town to stay and start off again tomorrow morning."

I sat on the edge of my seat, listening to the croaking

tree frogs and creatures of the night. I sniffed deeply, but raised my hand to my nose when I smelled the murky miasma of the muddy river instead of the salty air of home. It had seemed so familiar for a brief, heartbreaking moment.

The rain fell harder as something screeched again, beseeching, pleading, crying. I felt my skin tingle with the sound of it, hearing in it a spoken plea for help. *I need you, dear sister. I am so afraid.* It was as if Elizabeth spoke to me through the wild animal, begging me to continue on.

Facing Mr. O'Rourke, I said, "No, we must go on. I'm afraid this is a matter of the utmost urgency."

His face, mottled with dark shadows and yellow light from the coach's lanterns, looked down at me. "No, madam. We are turning back."

I grabbed at his sleeve and leaned toward him, not caring about the rain soaking my traveling gown and cloak. "No. It is urgent I see my sister—tonight. And if you won't take me, then I shall rent a hack."

He stepped back, as if to gauge my seriousness. I grabbed my carpetbag from the seat across from me and stepped out of the carriage, nearly tripping on my skirts.

"Tell me the way to the city, where I might find somebody to take me."

The rain pelted on my hat and dripped onto my face, but I stood resolute.

The man shook his head. "Mr. McMahon will have my skin if I let you do such a thing. Please, madam, it's for your own good. Please get back into the coach."

I jerked my arm away from him, the night sounds pressing close, the pulsing beat a rhythm of urgency. "I'll get back in only if you promise to take me to Whispering Oaks. Otherwise I am walking."

He turned around to face the darkness that eluded the small circle of lantern light. A guttural growl echoed in the distant swamp, pressing an unseen finger of fear at the base of my skull. *I need you, dear sister. I am so afraid.* I made a move toward a lantern to remove it from its hitch.

Mr. O'Rourke stared at me, then pressed his lips together. "Fine, then. But don't say I didn't warn you if we get stuck on the road."

"Thank you, Mr. O'Rourke." Without waiting for his assistance, I stepped back into the carriage, afraid he'd see the abject relief on my face.

The rain continued its steady pace, making the carriage sway to and fro more violently than before as the mud greedily sucked at the wheels. I closed my eyes in a futile attempt at rest and clenched my jaw to still the chattering of my teeth. The humidity weighed on my person like a log, but my body shivered uncontrollably. From what, I could not say.

It happened before I had time to realize I was in danger. Mr. O'Rourke shouted, but before the sound had even reached my ears, a sickening thud came from the front left of the coach, followed quickly by the splintering of wood. The coach lurched to the side as the lantern light disappeared, sending me in a spiral through total darkness. I hit my head, felt momentarily disoriented and then realized I was lying on the roof of the carriage, my skirts and feet under about a foot of water.

I shouted for Mr. O'Rourke, but only the incessant patter of rain and the interminable night sounds of the river answered me. Something splashed in the water outside the half-submerged carriage and I called for Mr. O'Rourke again. This time I heard his voice very faintly. I struggled to the side of the coach and fumbled with the upside-down door handle. It turned, but the door could not be opened.

"Help me! I can't swim!" Mr. O'Rourke's voice sounded stronger.

My blood stilled. It was as if I were hearing Jamie's voice

again, crying for help from the water. I remembered jumping in to save him, feeling the pull of the water on my skirts, my arms cutting through the waves, strong and sure. But I could not save my son. And now the water taunted me, daring me to try again.

The two horses whinnied, stamping their feet in the water, and trying to pull away from the waterlogged coach. Something was out there. Something they didn't like. I willed myself to move. I had to get to Mr. O'Rourke. With trembling fingers, I removed my cloak and hat, then tore at my skirts.

Relieved of my cumbersome clothes, and wearing only my underpinnings, I slipped easily through the window and found myself in water up to my knees. Tall grass reached up to my shoulders, brushing against me with deceptive sweetness. A faint light shone above me, and I looked up what appeared to be an embankment. The light seemed to be coming from one of the coach's lanterns, which had fallen during our plunge downward.

The plaintive cry of the driver came again. "Help me!"

I struggled through the tall grass, the blades tearing at my skin, then up the embankment. I used my hands to claw my way to the top, the dirt caking under my nails. "Mr. O'Rourke—where are you?"

The rain had slackened, and I listened closely for his voice. Something moved behind me, and a large splash broke the silence. I ran for the lantern and held it high over my head. The light picked up something white in the darkness, and I realized it was a leg waving from a scrubby tree high on the other side of the flooded road.

I clamped my teeth together to cease their chattering, then spoke. "I'll come get you—don't move." My confident voice almost deceived me.

The earth reverberated with a muffled thudding coming up from the ground, racing up my legs, and matching the pounding of my heart. I strained my eyes in the darkness, my mind tricking me into seeing would-be rescuers.

Rushing water and swishing reeds sounded from below the embankment where the carriage lay upside down. The horses screamed, stamping up and down in the water. Thundering hoofbeats bore down on me as something slithered outside the realm of my lantern. A movement skittered past me and I started, dropping the lantern, the light disappearing as suddenly as if a hand had closed on the flame. The water tugged at me, pulling at me, rendering me useless, just as it had once before. The water had beaten me yet again, and I could not save Mr. O'Rourke.

Heavy clouds moved above, uncovering a three-quarter moon and lending the tall reeds and scrubby oaks a blue cast. Bobbing lights accompanying the thundering hooves grew larger, and I forced my legs to move, my feet slipping in the mud and mire as I ran toward the sound and lights.

"Elizabeth!" a man's deep voice called out as the large form of a horse and rider took shape.

I reached toward him and felt strong hands grab me under the arms and lift me onto the saddle in front of my rescuer. The horse snorted and reared as other men on horseback arrived. A gunshot, and then another, rent the air. I struggled against the hard chest I was being smothered against.

"We must get the coachman—he's in a tree. He can't swim." I pointed to where the white of Mr. O'Rourke's shirt shone in the darkness.

The man stiffened, then pulled me against his chest again and began barking orders. More shots were fired in the air as a horseman rode across the submerged road to rescue Mr. O'Rourke.

My rescuer's voice was hard and deep, as if used to delivering orders. The men followed his directives without question. My face was pressed against a smooth linen shirt, the smell of starch mingling with cigar smoke, leather, and the smell of man—a smell I had once enjoyed and now pulled away from like a skittish horse. But muscled arms held me fast, and I sat rigid, trying to limit the contact between our bodies. He twisted in his saddle and I found myself enveloped in a large wool cloak.

Another horseman pulled alongside. "It doesn't seem to be robbery. The coachman is our Mr. O'Rourke. Is the woman Elizabeth?"

My rescuer grunted. "No." His fingers worked their way around my jawbone and tilted my face to his. He raised a lantern and his breath hissed as he sucked it in, his face wearing the shock of a man who has seen a ghost. "Who are you?"

I recognized him then, the coal black eyes glittering in the lamplight: John McMahon, my brother-in-law. A small tremor passed through me. "I am Catherine, Elizabeth's sister. Where is she?" Running water moved under us, the small ripplings teasing my ears as I waited for his answer.

He lowered the light, casting his face in shadow. "She is gone."

I gathered the cloak under my chin. "What do you mean—gone?"

His warm breath brushed my cheek, making me shiver, and I felt those dark eyes on me again. "She has disappeared without a trace. No one has seen her for four days. She is simply . . . gone."

He reined in his horse and turned it around. Holding me tightly against him, he urged his mount on, the thundering hoofbeats resonating like a distant nightmare.

Chapter Two

Either the chill of the humid night or the slowing of the horse woke me from a brief doze. The rain had stopped, leaving a pungent scent of wet mud and grass in the air. I jerked awake with a start, aware of the hushed feel of the night. My grandmother's house loomed ahead like a brilliant ghost through the alley of live oaks. The eight Doric columns along the front of the structure gleamed in the moonlight. Long fingers of Spanish moss reached down toward us, the storm-borne breeze causing them to undulate like a hand beckoning us onward.

The darkness came alive as we neared the house, torches on poles illuminating the night and making it as bright as day. Despite the late hour, small groups of men approached on horseback, and small campfires brought the smells of coffee and food to us.

"Are they searching for Elizabeth?"

My brother-in-law said nothing, but continued to move

toward the house, coming to a halt at the foot of the wide steps. A young boy appeared and took the reins of the horse as my brother-in-law slid to the ground with me in his arms. As if I were a baby, he effortlessly carried me up the stairs and through the wide set of mahogany double doors and into the foyer I had not seen since I was a young girl in plaits.

But I was no longer a helpless girl. Life had certainly stamped her out of existence, and I refused to be treated as one. I struggled against him. "Please put me down. I am more than capable of walking."

Without a word he approached the wide, elegant staircase and proceeded to carry me up the stairs two at a time. With a booted foot, he pushed open a door at the top of the stairs, and proceeded to unceremoniously dump me in the middle of the bed. I recognized this room as the one I had stayed in as a child. I remembered the tall four-poster with red velvet hangings.

I scrambled off the side of the bed. "How dare you, sir! I am not a child. And I demand to know what has happened to my sister."

He stood in the doorway, the breadth of his shoulders nearly filling the space. "I will send Marguerite for you."

With that, he closed the door neatly behind him.

I flew to the door, flung it open, and stifled a scream.

A woman perhaps twenty years my senior stood close enough that I could smell the cooking smoke in her hair. Pale green eyes stared out of a face of light brown skin. Hair the color and texture of dried moss was pulled off her face and wrapped in a scarf, showing a cluster of gray at the temples. Her eyes widened in surprise when she saw me, as if in recognition.

I did not know this woman, nor did I expect to. In her early letters my sister had explained that her husband had freed our grandmother's slaves and brought in hired Irish help from Boston and a few local freed slaves to work the sugar plantation.

"I'm Marguerite," she said. "Mr. McMahon has asked that I see to you."

Her voice, low and soothing, surprised me. It was not the voice of a servant, but rather that of an educated white woman.

I tried to see past her, but she gently led me back into the room and closed the door. "We need to get you cleaned up and fed. After a good rest, Mr. McMahon will see you."

For the first time I became aware of the heaviness of John McMahon's cloak around my shoulders. Looking down I saw with dismay the muddy condition it was in and the unmistakable white of my undergarments showing beneath.

Reluctantly, I allowed Marguerite to help me bathe. She brought in a white cotton nightgown and robe for me to wear, and I caught the familiar scent of lavender on the robe as I put it on. It was my sister's scent, and I felt a stab of panic and worry course through me. Where was Elizabeth?

A steaming tray of food was brought to me, and I ate from hunger. I should have refused it on principle. My brother-in-law had been a major in the federal army, his rank no doubt protecting his land and property from the marauding armies of the North. But I had survived far worse than starvation thus far, and I was not about to succumb to something as unworldly and impractical as principle. I speared a steaming forkful of ham and stuck it in my mouth.

Marguerite reappeared as soon as I was finished, and whisked the tray away with a promise that Mr. McMahon would be in to see me as soon as he could. I crawled under the sheets and lay against the white linen pillowcases, a luxury I had not indulged in within recent memory. I closed my eyes to rest, and soon sank into peaceful oblivion.

When I awoke, I blinked in confusion. The candle by the bed was barely more than a wick, the sputtering flame wreaking havoc on the walls in the forms of shadowed beasts. I sat up suddenly, aware that I was not alone.

He sat in the wooden rocker by the fire, his coat gone and his white shirt lying open at his neck. His black hair, just brushing his collar, was swept off his forehead as if by agitated hands. Long legs, encased in knee-length black boots, were braced on the floor, and in his hand he held a glass of spirits. He stared at me with something akin to revulsion. An unseen energy seemed to hum around him, crossing the room to where I lay. My skin tightened, and I pulled the covers up to my neck.

"This is not acceptable, sir, for you to be in my bedchamber. Please leave. I will speak to you in the library after I have properly dressed."

"Why are you here?" He acted as if he hadn't heard me speak, his eyes never leaving my face.

"My sister sent for me." I almost mentioned to him her fear, and the sense of urgency I had felt, but I did not. Something about his demeanor alarmed me, and if there had been something for Elizabeth to fear, I had the suspicion that it very well could have been the man sitting across from me. "Didn't she mention it to you?"

He took a long sip from his glass, his eyes glittering in the faint light. "No. She did not. That's why when I saw you I thought . . ." He lowered his gaze to stare into his glass, his brow furrowed. He turned to stare into the flickering flame. "Do you realize how much you resemble Elizabeth?"

Despite our four-year difference in age, people who

didn't know us well would mistake us for twins when we were children. But as we grew, our faces and demeanors seemed to evolve into two quite distinct people: Elizabeth, the otherworldly beauty excited by new dresses and parties, and me, the reserved sister, the one satisfied to sit on a beach for hours, her bare feet stuck contentedly under warm sand. As we had reached womanhood, people no longer considered us to be quite so similar.

"Not anymore," I said. "I haven't seen Elizabeth in nearly seven years. Perhaps we've grown alike again."

He tilted his head back against the rocker, staring at the undulating images on the ceiling. "You could be one and the same." He took another sip, and in the still room I heard him swallow.

"Do you have any idea where she could have gone? Did she leave a note?"

He stood abruptly, the chair rocking in his wake. "No. We've searched the area and questioned our neighbors. Nobody has seen her." He strode to the door. "As for a note, there wasn't one. At least none for me."

He opened the door, but I held him back with a question.

"How did you know I wasn't Elizabeth when you found me on the road in the dark?"

He contemplated me for a moment, then took another swallow of spirits. "Because you showed kindness and concern for Mr. O'Rourke's welfare." He paused. "My wife would have shown neither."

As he closed the door, the draft extinguished the small flame of my candle, throwing me into complete darkness. I lay back on the pillows, listening to his footsteps disappearing down the stairs, and wondering at his words.

Brittle morning sunshine crept through the windows when I next opened my eyes. The sound of jangling horse harnesses and the low murmur of male voices brought me out of bed and to the window.

I looked out at the expanse of front lawn leading toward the alley of oaks, and saw several men and horses milling about, tin cups grasped in their hands. John McMahon stood in the middle of one group, and my gaze was irrepressibly drawn to him. He struck an imposing figure, even from a distance. He stood a good head taller than the next man, his form solid and lean but pulled taut like well-honed leather. As if sensing an unseen audience, he stopped speaking and twisted around, looking directly at my window. A current moved through me like a flash of light, filching the wetness from my mouth. I stepped back, aware that I was not only staring, but also wearing only a thin nightgown. I held the curtain panel tightly, willing it not to swing, and hoping I had not been spotted.

A dress had been laid out for me, and the pitcher filled with clean water. I picked up the gown, wondering if any scent of my sister might still linger. It was faint, but still there, and I closed my eyes, remembering the times of our childhood we had spent in this house. It had been one of the first plantation houses built on the river road. Despite the threat of the ever-encroaching Mississippi River, it had remained intact since its original construction in 1800.

Our mother had been born here, as had our grandmother. But deaths outweighed the births at Whispering Oaks, and I always wondered what we had done to be so cursed. Yellow fever had taken my mother's five brothers and then returned for another visit two years later, taking my grandfather when it left. The names on the mausoleum in the small cemetery in the woods behind the house were all that remained of my aunts and uncles. When we were children, Elizabeth told me stories of how the dead would rise from the crypt and come into the house to watch the living. I would lie awake far into the night, never doubting the veracity of her story.

Grandmother Delacroix had faced the withering sun of her grief, the petals of her strength refusing to shrivel and die. My mother said that I reminded her a lot of her mother, but I had my doubts. Grandmother's heart had remained soft, her love a constant in our lives until the day she died. But my grief had turned my heart into a cold, hard orb in the center of my chest, and I doubted I'd ever find the warmth to nourish it back to health.

I laid the dress back on the bed and went to the washstand to clean my face. As I poured the water into the basin, a peculiar sound reached my ears. I held the pitcher tightly, listening closely. It sounded as if a small child were humming a tune—a tune that was hauntingly familiar to me. I knew it—yet I didn't. Perhaps it was a song from my distant past, long since forgotten.

I walked to the door and opened it a crack. There it was again—that humming. It was definitely a child and it was coming from the L-shaped corridor to my right. I stepped out into the hallway, my bare feet padding gently against the wood floors as I followed the sound. The low murmur of a female voice accompanied the humming, and I followed the sound until I stopped at a closed door at the end of the corridor.

Curious, I pressed my ear against the door and listened. The humming became more frantic now, faster and higher-pitched. I recognized Marguerite's voice, soft and soothing, as if attempting to comfort a child. A sudden crash came from inside the room, and the humming turned into a loud and piercing scream. I jumped back and found myself pressed against a warm, firm body.

I jerked around and stared into the unreadable eyes of John McMahon.

His voice was gruff. "What are you doing here?"

"I . . . I heard a sound. I wanted to see what it was."

He released his hold on me. "This was Elizabeth's room. There is nothing in there that might interest you." I noticed his use of the past tense, and I took a step backward.

Straightening my shoulders, I attempted to still the shaking in my voice. "But perhaps there is. I am Elizabeth's sister, and I ask that you allow me to help find her. There might be letters, or a journal or something that might give us a clue as to where she is." I turned toward the door, my hand on the knob. "And there is somebody in there with Marguerite; it sounds like a child."

His hand closed over mine, and again I felt a current ripple from his fingertips and surge through my blood. "Please let go of me." My voice shook.

His gaze flickered over me and I was made aware once again of my undressed state.

"Go get dressed. I'll send Marguerite to help you. Breakfast is waiting for you in the dining room." His eyes were hard, making it clear that opposition to his wishes was not recommended.

Slowly his hand slid from mine and I released my grip on the doorknob. Being in a somewhat precarious situation, I decided not to press the matter. Not yet. I began to walk away, but turned back when I heard the door open without a knock. Inside I spied Marguerite on her knees, picking up small porcelain fragments, and a blond, wide-eyed child staring up at the man on the threshold. The door quickly shut, blocking the scene from my view.

I was alone at the foot of the long dining room table, mounds of food displayed on the polished surface. A young woman with red hair and freckles and a thick Irish accent introduced herself as Mary. She stood at attention by my chair and waited until I was seated before beginning to pile food on my plate.

Karen White

I wanted to turn away in disgust at the wasteful abundance, remembering my recent months on Saint Simons relying on the charity of friends and neighbors and whatever I could find in the abandoned gardens. My every waking thought had been concerned with where my next meal would come from.

Such thoughts were unnecessary here. Still, I had to eat to survive, and survive I would. I lifted my plate and allowed Mary to serve me.

As I worked my way through my second helping of grillades and grits, my brother-in-law strode into the dining room. Without a greeting, he moved with a panther's grace to the server and poured himself a cup of coffee. The small china cup looked out of place in his long, lithe fingers. I saw the power in the muscles and bones in the back of his hand, and pictured them shattering a cup with very little effort. I lifted my gaze to meet his.

"I've sent some of my men to salvage what they can from the coach. As soon as we can get all your things cleaned and dried, we'll have you on your way back to Saint Simons. There's nothing you can do here."

I dropped my fork with a clatter. "I beg to differ."

Mary, who had been in the process of pouring my coffee, began to shake so badly the teacup rattled in the saucer. I took them from her with a look I hope passed for understanding. She left the room with small, hurried steps.

He placed his cup back in the saucer with forced control. His gaze darkened as he regarded me. "You, madam, are in no position to differ with me. You were invited by someone who isn't here, making you an uninvited guest. I will be more than happy to see you are escorted safely home."

I slid my chair back, heedless of the scraping on the wood floor. I fairly shook with emotion as I faced him. "How dare you, sir. My sister is missing—and she may be

28

in grave danger. I cannot—and will not—return to my home before I know that she is safe." Tears stung my eyes, but I refused to give him the satisfaction of seeing me cry. "Even if I have to sleep on the front lawn, I will not leave." I swallowed thickly, forcing back the anger. "I have no one else, sir. I have lost everything. Even my home. I will not easily give up my sister, too."

Something passed over his face—pain? Regret? It softened his features for a moment, allowing me to see inside his soul, and what I glimpsed did not frighten me. For that brief moment I recognized something as cold and barren as my own soul, and I understood. I made a move to leave the dining room, but his words made me halt.

His voice was almost kind. "Don't go. Please finish your breakfast. You're looking too thin." I drew in my breath as he placed his cup and saucer on the sideboard. "You may stay—but you must keep to yourself as much as possible. I don't want you interfering in the search; nor do I want you making the servants nervous with any questions. If you do have questions, you are to bring them directly to me."

I lowered my head. "Agreed." I looked back up at the sound of his retreating footsteps. "Who was that child upstairs with Marguerite?"

He stopped without turning around. As if holding his breath, he said, "That is Rebecca, your niece." He began walking away from me again toward the front door.

"My niece? Elizabeth's child?"

His only answer was the slamming of the door.

Chapter Three

For the remainder of the morning and most of the afternoon, I was left to my own devices. I wandered through
the house, noticing the dust on the dark wood of the furniture and the scuff marks on the floors. The black marble
around the fireplaces looked pasty, as if the mantels hadn't
been polished in quite some time. I tried to listen for the
voices of Rebecca or the servants, but I heard none inside
the house.

The windows were covered with a thin coating of dirt,
muting the sunlight that tried to eke its way in through the
cracks between the closed velvet draperies. In the front
parlor I had opened them, only to find myself choking on
the dust I stirred up with the movement of fabric.

Despite my love for my grandmother, I had always hated
coming to this house as a young girl. The light here was
full of shadows, never quite making it inside the dark cor-

ners of the large rooms. It made it seem as if the house had no soul, only lurking secrets.

Elizabeth said it was because our great-grandfather had built the house on the highest piece of land he could find this close to the Mississippi River. Legend said the rise in the land was due to an ancient Tunica Indian burial mound. Some say he knew the legend, but built the white-columned mansion anyway, piling any bones they found in a heap and burning them. I had been told by my sister that an Indian woman carrying a crying baby was seen many times walking across the grass at the back of the house, toward the pond, then disappearing into thin air. I peered out the dirty window of the library at the murky water of the pond, wondering if my sister had shared the same fate.

Mary called me for supper, and I ate in complete silence, noticing again the piles of food. I wondered where it would go when I finished with my portion, and if the master of the house would be joining me. But my meal progressed without interruption, and when I finished, Mary cleared the table.

I wandered out into the foyer, my hands fidgeting against my skirts. I was frustrated at being idle when so much needed to be done. The front door opened, and I turned, surprised to see a man in the doorway.

He was slightly taller than I, with light blond hair and a heavy mustache. His clothes were simple, but well tailored, his black boots polished to a high sheen. He clutched a black felt hat to his chest as he slammed the door behind him. When he spotted me, he seemed to sigh with relief, then strode toward me.

"Elizabeth," he said, his voice more of a breath than words. As he neared, his steps slowed and he regarded me with curiosity. He stopped, examining me closely, his head tilted to the side.

"Elizabeth?" he said again, this time as a question.

His eyes were dark gray with black specks in them. They were kind eyes, and I warmed to him, in desperate need of a friend. Pale lashes blinked as if to clear my image.

"No," I said. "I'm Catherine deClaire Reed—Elizabeth's sister." I stared at him for a moment, wondering if I had seen him before. "Have we met?"

He took a step back. "No, I don't believe so." He gave me a deep bow. "Allow me to introduce myself. I am Daniel Lewiston, country doctor, gentleman farmer, former Yankee, and friend and confidant of John McMahon." A deep dimple appeared in his right cheek as he smiled at me. He took my hand and kissed it, his mustache tickling the skin.

I felt an unfamiliar smile creep to my lips. "It's a pleasure to make your acquaintance, Dr. Lewiston. But I'm afraid that if you came to see Elizabeth or John, neither of them is here at the moment."

A shadow seemed to cross his face before disappearing as quickly as it had come. "Then perhaps we should use this opportunity to become better acquainted. Shall we, Mrs. Reed?" He offered his arm.

I paused for a moment, looking closely at his friendly face. Needing someone to talk to, I took his arm. "Yes. Thank you, Dr. Lewiston."

He led the way to the front porch, where we settled ourselves into wooden rockers and eyed each other politely. Leaning toward me with his elbows on his knees, he looked up at me, his gray eyes lighter in the waning light.

It felt good to be outside the dreariness of the house. A cerulean sky had replaced the dark clouds and rain of the previous night, bringing with it a hint of temporary coolness, not uncommon for late spring in the delta. I stared past the lane of oaks toward where the great Mississippi River lay, breathing in deeply to catch the brackishness of it. I had hated the smell as a child; it was a constant reminder of how much I missed my faraway home.

To the east lay the wide fields of sugarcane and the sugar mill. I remember my father saying it took a very rich cotton planter to be a very poor sugar planter. I wondered at my brother-in-law's success. He had known nothing about planting until he had moved here with Elizabeth to take over the running of the former cotton plantation. My father said he had brought with him the luck of the Irish. Years without flood or frost, and protection against enemy invasion, certainly made John's success appear lucky. But if Elizabeth's disappearance was any indication, it would seem his luck had finally run out.

I turned toward my visitor. "I assume you've heard about my sister."

He nodded, a dour expression on his face. "I did. I couldn't come sooner because I was with Mrs. Brookwood delivering her twins. I'm afraid I do not know any more about the situation than you do."

I rocked steadily in my chair. "Mr. McMahon will tell me nothing. All I know is that my sister disappeared from here five days ago and hasn't been seen or heard from since. It would appear my brother-in-law has sent out search parties, but no one has found any trace of her."

Dr. Lewiston looked toward the ancient oaks and spoke almost absently. "That would have been Thursday. She came to my office that day."

I sat up. "Was she ill?"

He didn't look at me. "I'm really not at liberty to say. Everything between a patient and her doctor should be kept in strictest confidence." He turned to me with a smile that didn't quite reach his eyes. "I'm sure she will tell you all you need to know when she returns."

I placed my hand on the arm of his chair. "Do you really think she's coming back?"

He smiled reassuringly as he patted my hand. "Yes, I'm certain of it. And I'm sure there will be a good explanation for all of this. You'll see." He sighed heavily. "She has to. It would kill John to lose her. He loves her so much."

I wondered at the strange tone of his voice. When he didn't say any more, I settled back in my chair and diverted the subject. "You said you were a former Yankee. How did you come to be here?"

His mustache bristled as he smiled. "John and I were boyhood friends in Boston. We've known each other since we were in the nursery. Shortly after his marriage to Elizabeth, I accepted an invitation for a visit down here, and while at Whispering Oaks I met my wife. Clara and her father were visiting from their cotton plantation in Saint Francisville and were invited to dinner." His pale eyes looked down at his hand and the band of gold on his third finger. "I suppose it must have been love at first sight, for we were married within three months, and I had become a Southern planter."

He sent me a rueful grin. "To be honest, I'm not much of a planter. Clara's father had over thirty thousand acres in cotton and people to run just about all of it. Most of it survived the war, too, thanks to John's influence. But as far as I could see, my father-in-law didn't really need me. Besides, medicine's my calling, and I continued to practice in my field up until the war. I was conscripted into the Confederate Army, and became an army doctor. Which is a good thing, since I couldn't see myself taking up arms and firing on my own countrymen. I'm surprised John still speaks to me." There wasn't much mirth in his voice.

Dr. Lewiston seemed kind and affable, but his voice was so forlorn I took pity on him. It had been so long since I had been able to give comfort. I reached over and placed my hand on top of his.

A dark shadow fell over our hands. My brother-in-law stood towering over us, a cool expression on his face.

I released Dr. Lewiston's hand and he stood to greet his old friend. "John," he said, extending his hand. "Your lovely sister-in-law and I were just discussing this business with Elizabeth. I'm here to offer whatever help I can."

John took his hand and shook it. "Thank you, Daniel. But I don't think there's anything else anybody can do right now. I've got my men going all the way to New Orleans and Baton Rouge. I can only wait here for word of her." He concentrated on pulling the riding gloves off his fingers. "Clara tells me that Elizabeth came to see you last week."

Daniel's eyes widened in surprise. "Well, yes . . . yes, she did. But you could have asked me, you know, instead of my wife. I would have given you the same answer."

John appraised his friend with narrowed eyes. "I'm sure you would have. But you were with Mrs. Brookwood and I didn't want to disturb you."

"Yes. I was." The doctor clamped his teeth together, and I could see his jaw muscles working.

"Was my wife ill, Daniel?"

Dr. Lewiston looked his friend squarely in the eye. "I'm not at liberty to say. Elizabeth can tell you herself when she returns."

John took a step forward, but the doctor refused to step back. "And if she doesn't come back?"

The doctor squared his shoulders. "Then we will discuss it. But she will return. I know it."

John's eyes clouded as he stared out across his sugar fields. "I wish I were as confident as you, Daniel. But I have my doubts."

Despite the heat of the day, I shivered. I stood, ready to

demand his reasons for doubting Elizabeth's return. I paused in midbreath as the front door swung open with a crash, and a young girl, about four or five years of age and clutching a doll that was nearly as big as she was, ran out onto the porch, neatly colliding with Dr. Lewiston.

Unbound blond hair reaching almost to the child's waist hung limp and wet with sweat; the girl's cheeks were reddened with exertion. Marguerite followed her closely out the door, but pulled up abruptly when she saw the three adults.

"I'm sorry, Mr. McMahon. I'm trying to get Miss Rebecca to learn her letters, but she keeps running away from me."

The girl clung to the doctor's knees, refusing to relinquish her grasp. Dr. Lewiston stroked her hair and murmured comforting words while keeping a wary eye on his friend.

I watched as John's face softened, resembling the look I remembered him saving for Elizabeth when they had first met. He knelt, bringing his tall frame down to a more approachable level for a child, and held out his arms. Rebecca lifted her face, then ran with her doll to John with outstretched hands.

His transformation from a brooding ogre was completed as he kissed the bright blond head and lifted her into his arms. She put her head down on his shoulder and stuck a thumb in her mouth.

"Perhaps, Marguerite, you should attempt to make her lessons more stimulating for a child. For heaven's sake, she's running away from you, not her lessons. Play with her. Make her laugh. God knows there's not enough of it around here."

Marguerite's mouth tightened. "You are undermining my authority, Mr. McMahon. I've raised children before, and I know what's best." She stepped forward as if to take the child, but John held tight.

"Don't touch her—can't you see she's upset? It's time for her nap. I'll take her upstairs."

I raised my hand to stop him. "Please—wait. I'd like to see her." I walked toward the child, and brushed the blond hair away from her face. Her coloring was so different from Elizabeth's, but the eyes, almond-shaped and a vibrant blue, were identical. I touched the back of my hand to her cheek, then jerked it away. They were also Jamie's eyes. If her hair and brows were darker, she could have been my child.

She stopped sucking on her thumb, those eyes regarding me closely. And then she began to scream.

I stepped back, astonished at her reaction, wondering if she had sensed any of my sadness and disappointment that she was not the child I wished her to be.

John pulled Rebecca away from my reach, then entered the house without a glance back. I sat down in my chair, trying to catch my breath.

Dr. Lewiston spoke softly to me. "Don't worry, Mrs. Reed. Rebecca is a high-strung child and is overtired at the moment. I'm quite sure her screaming had nothing to do with you."

I nodded, still unable to speak, and wondered if my own animosity toward the child was a random event, or a personal reaction to a child who resembled my son so much that I could feel nothing but resentment toward her.

I continued to rock in silence as Dr. Lewiston approached Marguerite. "It's good to see you again, Marguerite. Clara still misses you and sends you her best."

Marguerite gave him a tight smile. "Thank you, sir. She knows I feel the same. But we do manage to see each other often enough, I suppose."

A subtle change flickered over the doctor's expression. "Really? Clara hasn't mentioned it to me."

Lids lowered over pale green eyes. "You're probably too

busy tending to your doctoring to notice such things." She reached for the door handle. "I must go. It was good seeing you, Dr. Lewiston."

With a small swish of her skirts, she disappeared inside.

The doctor leaned against a column, his arms crossed over his chest. "She raised my wife from birth. Clara considers her almost a mother." He pulled a gold watch out of his watered-silk waistcoat and looked at it for a moment before replacing it. "Had to sell her during the war—needed the money—and Elizabeth certainly needed the help. Your sister wasn't as . . . strong as she would have liked to be, and she needed another female here at Whispering Oaks. Soon after purchasing Marguerite, John freed her." He took a deep breath, his face sad. "I suppose she'll stay on for Rebecca's sake."

I rubbed my temples with the pads of my fingers, the start of a headache beginning to pound behind my eyes.

The doctor's voice was soothing. "Will your husband be joining you?"

I blinked at him in the sun, unable to find words. Finally I managed, "I'm . . . no. He won't be. I'm . . . I'm in mourning." I took a deep breath, needing sympathy from a kind soul. "For my son, too. He . . . he drowned."

He stood, swallowing, and I saw the kindness in his pale gray eyes. "I am sorry, Mrs. Reed. You, well . . ." He looked down at the celery green gown I had borrowed from my sister. "You're not dressed in mourning."

"My clothes were ruined in an accident. This is Elizabeth's dress."

"Yes, I just realized." He stood near me. "I'm sorry for your loss." I looked into his eyes and saw that he meant it. He took my hands and squeezed them.

"Yes, well . . ." I dropped my gaze and stared at his pale hands covering mine, the skin as soft and smooth as a girl's. Gently, he let go.

"I must be leaving. Would you please do me a favor?" He reached into his coat pocket and pulled out a short rope of licorice. "Rebecca loves these. I always give her one when I see her. Could you be so kind as to pass this along to her?"

I didn't want to, but I realized I could not avoid the child forever. Perhaps this would serve as a sort of peace offering. I nodded and took the piece of candy.

"Thank you, Mrs. Reed. It is greatly appreciated." He bowed, placed his hat over his head, and descended the steps. As an afterthought, he turned toward me as he reached the bottom. "Do call on us soon. My Clara would love to meet you. She and Elizabeth were great friends. We're straight down River Road in Saint Francisville. Barely thirty minutes by horse."

I smiled, ignoring his past-tense reference to my sister. "I will—thank you."

He waved as he walked toward the stables, and I turned back to the house.

I paused in the dim doorway, hearing the strange humming again. The tune vibrated against my own lips, so taunting in its familiarity, yet its identity still beyond my grasp. With the licorice held tightly in one hand, I slowly ascended the stairs, following the haunting melody hummed with such sadness by a young voice.

The door to Elizabeth's room stood open and I approached it with caution. Quietly I peered in, not sure what I would see.

Rebecca sat on a small chair in front of a dressing mirror, wearing nothing but her camisole and bloomers, her large doll leaning against her legs. I remembered that she was supposed to be napping, and wondered what she was doing in her mother's room.

She sat brushing her fingers through her long fair hair, staring transfixed into the mirror. The lingering scent of lavender made me turn my head, as if my sister had just walked through the room. Only dark corners and rose-colored satin bed linens met my gaze.

The humming ceased and I focused back on the little girl. Her blue eyes widened with fear as she spotted me, and she scrunched her shoulders as if trying to disappear into the dressing table. *Oh, Jamie,* I thought, the crushing sadness upon me again. I turned to leave, then stopped. She was only an innocent child, my sister's child. Perhaps she needed comfort now as much as I did.

Slowly I turned to face her. Not quite managing a smile, I approached, the licorice held in front of me. When I stood before her, I knelt, remembering her father's action.

"Dr. Lewiston asked me to bring this to you. He says it's your favorite."

Her head was down, dimpled hands folded on her lap. I touched the back of a hand with the piece of candy. She did not look up, but her pudgy fingers opened and took it.

I was so close, I could smell the sweetness of her. My heart broke again as I remembered holding Jamie, and burying my face in his little neck and crying with the joy that he was mine.

My voice faltered, but I swallowed, clearing my throat. "Do you know who I am?"

She shook her head, still looking down.

"I'm your aunt Cat. Your mama and I are sisters."

That brought her head up as two piercing blue eyes stared at me intently. I forced myself not to look away.

I patted the yellow yarn hair of her cloth doll. "What's her name?"

"Samantha." Her voice was clear and high-pitched. So much like Jamie's.

"She's beautiful. Where did you get her?" I lifted the doll

to get a better look and noticed the painted-on bright blue eyes.

"My papa. She's my friend." She grabbed the doll and hugged her close.

Abruptly she slid from the chair and ran past me and out of the room.

I stood to follow her, then halted. Turning around, I looked down at the dressing table. Except for a nearly empty bottle of perfume, it was empty. Dust outlined the spot where a hand mirror would have lain and long dark strands of hair littered the top. But there was no sign of my sister's comb, brush, or mirror.

I walked toward the large armoire and threw it open. Ruffles and flounces of every type of silk, satin, and linen filled the entire space, hiding the back of the armoire. It would have been impossible to determine if something were missing. I pushed two dresses aside and peered into the back of the armoire. An empty brass hook, made to hang a dressing gown, winked at me. I looked on the floor of the armoire to see if it might have fallen, but there was nothing there except a pair of evening shoes. The scent of stale lavender permeated the small space, almost gagging me.

The humming commenced again, so I closed the armoire behind me and went after Rebecca out the door.

I stood and followed her to a room down the hall, entering through the open door. She stood before a tall chest and was tugging on a bottom drawer. I knelt next to her and helped her open it. She looked at me with grateful eyes, imparting a tender thread of caring in me.

I gasped in surprise as I looked at the contents of the drawer. It was filled with licorice ropes, identical to the one I had just given her. With little aplomb, she dumped the latest addition to her collection.

"Are you saving them?" I asked, curious.

She shook her head, blond hair swinging. "No. I don't like them. But Mama says I'll hurt Dr. Lewiston's feelings if I say no. So I keep them here."

"I see," I said, brushing hair off her face. She didn't flinch.

We both turned at a sound from the door. Marguerite stood there, a frown on her face.

"Mrs. Reed, it is time for Rebecca's nap. It would be much better for the child if you would leave and let her rest." She came over and took the doll from Rebecca's arms and tossed it on the bed.

I opened my mouth for an explanation, then closed it. She was right—the child needed her rest.

I rose, resisting the impulse to pat the little girl on the head, and left. The door shut abruptly behind me, and as I walked down the hallway to my own room, I heard the haunting melody drift through the house once more.

Chapter Four

Marguerite had laid a deep blue silk gown on the bed for me to wear to the evening meal. I walked past it and opened the armoire where the cleaned and dried clothes from my trunk had been hung.

I stared in dismay at mended spots and uneven dye color, my gaze straying to the silk gown on the bed. With a sigh, I pulled the faded black cotton from the armoire, and called for Marguerite to help me dress before going down to dinner.

The smell of food drifted into my room, enticing my long-starved appetite. I paused in the gloomy hallway, the dusty lampshades mellowing the yellow flames, breathing shadows onto the walls. I descended the stairs, listening to the tread of my slippers, the only sound in the tomblike silence.

The dining room table had been set with three places, and Rebecca and her father were already seated at one

43

end of the table. Samantha must have been left in the nursery. John's gaze flickered over me, and he frowned as he eyed my dress. He stood and indicated the chair to his right.

He pulled the chair back for me, his presence somehow unnerving.

"Was there something wrong with Elizabeth's gown?"

I shook my head, embarrassed that he had noted the condition of my clothing. "No. But I'm . . . I'm in mourning."

He took his seat, then filled my goblet halfway with red wine. A drop stained the white linen tablecloth, spreading like a drop of blood. "I assumed you were in mourning from your clothes. I'm sorry for your loss." He stared at me unblinking for a moment. "The dark blue was the closest I could think of. Elizabeth didn't own anything black. Or anything very dark, for that matter."

I looked down at my plate, feeling my face color. It had never occurred to me that he had selected the gown.

Eager to change the subject, I turned my attention toward Rebecca, who sat silently in the chair across from me, thumb in mouth.

"Does Rebecca usually join you at table?" I watched as Rebecca slowly twirled a blond lock around her finger.

"Why do you ask, Mrs. Reed? Do you not like children?"

My host indicated to Mary that she should start serving the food. She came to stand by me with a covered silver dish, and lifted the lid. Candied yams, covered in sauce, swam invitingly inside, making my mouth water. I helped myself to a large portion, concealing the fact that his question had stilled my hunger pangs.

"That's not what I meant. My husband and I always enjoyed our son's presence at our table. But I know not all parents feel that way." I took a bite of yam, savoring the sweet taste.

Strong fingers wrapped around his goblet, obliterating the facets of light. "Elizabeth did not allow it. But she is not here, and I like Rebecca to dine with me." The same hand that had been grasping the wineglass so tightly now softened and reached for Rebecca's tiny hand. Palm upward, he closed his fingers around hers.

"Did your son remain on Saint Simons, Mrs. Reed?"

The candied yams seemed to stick in my throat, but I forced them down with a swallow of wine. I took another quick gulp, needing fortitude to find words to describe the loss of my son without communicating the depths of my grief. That was mine, and all I had left. I would not share it. Especially not with this forbidding man who would offer brittle platitudes that could never compare to the warmth of my son's hand in mine.

"My son is dead, Mr. McMahon. He drowned this past March."

Ebony lashes lowered over dark eyes. "I am sorry. I cannot fathom the loss of a child."

His voice caught, giving me a start, and I noticed how his hand closed even tighter over his daughter's.

I took my time cutting a piece of ham and then chewing it. "I'm sure you can understand my dedication to finding my sister, sir. She is all I have left."

His weary gaze brushed my face. "But surely you two weren't all that close. We haven't seen you since the wedding."

I pressed my napkin to my lips. After her marriage, Elizabeth had promised to visit, but never had. Even at my wedding and our parents' funerals, following so closely one after the other, Elizabeth's presence had been conspicuously absent. We assumed the reluctance lay on the part of her husband, which would also have been the reason why I was never invited to visit her at Whispering Oaks. And then the war came and Elizabeth was sent to live in

Boston, all contact had ceased. Until her last cryptic note.

"That was not my choosing, sir." I lifted my gaze to his, expecting to see guilt. But all I saw was confusion—and perhaps regret.

A black eyebrow shot up, oddly resembling a crow's wing. "Nor was it mine. You were always welcome in this house, as you are now. Even up north, Mrs. Reed, we are capable of extending hospitality. You are welcome to stay as long as you like." He took a long drink of his wine, his gaze never leaving my face, the sincerity of his words unclear. "I simply expect you to follow my rules in this house. And that would include staying out of rooms I have told you are off-limits."

I recalled Elizabeth's dresser empty of toiletries and her missing dressing gown. I wondered if that was what he didn't wish me to see.

Mary stood by my side again with sweetened corn bread, and I helped myself to two large pieces, remembering in time to use the serving utensil instead of my fingers. Starvation had been my companion for so long, I could only hope that my table manners would not desert me completely.

"Take all you want, Mrs. Reed. There's plenty more in the kitchen."

I dropped the serving utensil ungraciously onto the platter, feeling the flush rise in my cheeks.

"I'm sorry. I didn't mean it unkindly. I only meant to imply that we have plenty of food and I would like you to avail yourself of it."

I looked down at my hands resting on the snowy white napkin in my lap, the nails brittle and broken but mercifully now free of dirt. Humiliation simmered under my skin at the need to take this man's charity. He had worn the dreaded blue, and it was his ilk who had brought me so low.

I raised my napkin to the table in an indication that I was through with the meal, but my host appeared not to notice as he cut up meat for Rebecca. The child had sat silently since I had been seated, slowly chewing food her father cut and put on her plate. Her almond-shaped eyes seemed to miss nothing as her gaze shifted between her father and me.

Mary stood behind John with the bowl of yams and took the lid off the dish. He waved her away and she returned it to the server.

"Do you not care for candied yams, sir?"

His gaze met mine slowly, as if embarrassed about something. "No, actually. I do not."

"Then why have them at your table? Surely, as the master of the plantation, you can dictate what is served?"

He took a long drink of wine, then offered a smile to Rebecca before answering me.

"Elizabeth told me once they were a favorite of yours. I thought they might help you feel not so far from home."

I carefully studied my plate, unsure of my response. I was humbled, but at the same time could not help thinking he had an ulterior motive for showing such concern. Finally I said, simply, "Thank you."

Slowly I slid my napkin back to my lap, lifted my fork, and speared a bite of sliced turkey. "Any news of Elizabeth?"

He took his time chewing and swallowing, and I wondered if he was stalling for an answer. When it came it was short and abrupt. "No. I'm afraid not."

I leaned forward. "Don't you think you should be the one traveling to Baton Rouge and New Orleans to search for her? Why leave such an important task to others?"

His face appeared set in stone as his eyes narrowed. "I am needed here. If Elizabeth chooses to return, this is where she'll find me."

47

I slapped my fist on the table, making the wine dance in the glasses. "But what if she is in danger? What if she needs you?"

His face relaxed as heavy-lidded eyes regarded me. "That, my dear Mrs. Reed, is highly unlikely."

I sat back in my chair, stunned. I remembered Elizabeth's letter. *I need you, dear sister. I am so afraid.* What had she been so afraid of? And was it enough to send her away without a word to anybody?

Too late, I remembered Rebecca's presence. She had been quietly eating, but now I realized she had dropped her fork and was listening intently. My heart sank as I tried to recall what we had said and if she would find any of it hurtful.

John picked up a silver bell at the end of the table and rang it. His hands were so gentle when he touched his child, but their breadth and strong tendons told of the strength in them. I couldn't help wondering what those hands were truly capable of. Within moments Mary rushed in, her freckles prominent on her flushed face. "Yes, sir?"

"Tell Marguerite that Rebecca is through with her dinner and is ready to be put to bed." Mary left as the child slid from her chair and moved to put her head on her father's arm. He reached a hand around her shoulders as she stuck her thumb in her mouth and continued to regard me closely.

"Mama?" she said. I watched as she ducked under her father's arm and came to stand near me.

A warm, sticky hand reached up, hesitated a moment, then touched my cheek. Pain chilled my veins. I wanted so much to comfort this motherless child, to smooth away her fears. But I could not. When I looked into those familiar eyes I was reminded again of what I had lost. I averted my head, afraid she'd see the tears welling in my eyes.

Marguerite came and took the child, and only then did

I look up. My brother-in-law was looking at me coolly, his hands gripping the arms of his chair. "I see you have more in common with your sister than mere looks, Mrs. Reed."

Without explanation, he excused himself and stood, leaving me alone at the table.

Having no more appetite, I, too, slid back my chair and left the room.

Dusk had settled over the plantation, casting more shadows inside the dimly lit house. I wandered the downstairs, curious as to the obvious lack of a house staff. A cloudy chandelier, suspended on a velvet rope in the foyer, swayed gently in the hot breeze from the open windows. The candles flickered briefly, undulating like lovers.

I drifted into the front parlor, where a lone hurricane glass offered the only illumination. Long shadows followed me as I sat down at the piano in the corner, an old friend from the days I visited my grandmother. Sighing softly, I hit a few keys. I was surprised to find it in tune. My fingers touched each key, sliding up a chromatic scale and then down again. I began playing a tune with just my right hand, plucking out each note from memory. I realized I was playing the song I had heard Rebecca humming and stopped, the last note echoing in the dark room.

A movement in the corner twisted me around. The tall form of my brother-in-law stepped forward. The light was behind him, casting his eyes into dark circles of shadow. "Please, don't stop. This house hasn't heard music in a very long time." He stepped around me and lit three arms of a candelabra atop the piano. The breeze from his movement brushed my skin, making it tingle with a thousand pinpricks.

I turned around on the bench, self-conscious. "I'm not that good. Elizabeth was the one with all the musical talent, I'm afraid."

"I wouldn't know. She never played for me. I made sure

to keep it tuned, but she never showed any interest."

He stood behind me and the room began to feel incredibly small. Gingerly I stroked the keys, my hands finding their homes, and started a Brahms waltz. His presence unnerved me, causing my fingers to stumble like a small child learning to walk. I lifted my hands from the keyboard but didn't turn around. "I'm sorry—I'm a bit out of practice. My piano was demolished by the butt of a Yankee rifle. That made it quite difficult to play."

I regretted the words as soon as they left my mouth, but my anger still burned fresh. I let my hands fall to my sides. "Why was Elizabeth so unhappy?"

Only his soft breathing answered me. Then, after a moment, he said, "She alone could tell you that. She did not make me privy to her thoughts. And I eventually grew tired of asking." He remained behind me, close enough that I could feel his breath on the top of my head. I didn't turn around.

"Was it your decision to keep the birth of Rebecca a secret? I can't believe that was my sister's wish." I kept my gaze focused on the keys, watching the light dance with the shadows upon their surface.

He shifted away from me. I turned and watched as he walked to the window and stared out through the murky glass. "You were not the only one she kept in the dark. I did not know I was a father until my first furlough during the war. Rebecca was already five months old."

The sadness in his voice was palpable, tugging at my compassion. But I held back, wondering if this man was responsible for Elizabeth's actions. I smoothed the fabric of my dress. "This woman you describe is not the sister I remember."

He stared at me a moment, the house utterly quiet except for the breeze moving through the darkened rooms.

"Perhaps. People do change. Or maybe you never actually knew the real Elizabeth."

I stood. "I assure you, sir, my sister and I were very close. There were never any secrets between us. At least not until she married."

He tilted his head as he regarded me. "You're not the young woman I remember from seven years ago. The first time I saw you, you were dancing barefoot along the beach, impervious to the broken shells. I gather that it has been some time since you've felt carefree enough to do such a thing."

I flushed, embarrassed that he should recall such an intimate detail about me. "I suppose, Mr. McMahon, that a war can change people. I don't believe that girl exists anymore."

I moved to the doorway and he followed me. Turning to say good night, I found him standing very close. Something akin to panic flooded through me, and for a moment I could not find words. He spoke first.

"If Elizabeth never returns, would it be your desire to take Rebecca to her mother's family?" Penetrating eyes stared down at me.

"No." My vehemence showed in the one syllable. I recalled the small cemetery where the rest of my family lay, and the scorched and overgrown land that had once held so much bounty. "There is nothing left of our family on Saint Simons. And . . . and I don't think I could care for another child."

His eyes never left my face. "Good. Because I would never let her go."

"The child is yours, sir. I would not consider taking her from you." I looked for an answer to my unasked question in his eyes. "Elizabeth will return. She must."

I waited for a response but he remained silent. My heart thudded in my ears. Something about this man pushed at

51

my blood, making it rush through my veins in a hurried torrent. I stepped back. "I am tired and will retire now to my room. Good night, Mr. McMahon."

I reached the bottom of the stairs before he spoke. "If you will be staying here for an extended period of time, you might call me John."

My hand flew to my neck, where I felt the heat under my palm. I forced my voice to stay calm as I stared at my hand on the balustrade. "If you wish. And you may call me Catherine."

I took two steps.

"Good night, Catherine."

I paused, then turned around. "Good night, John."

The shadows hid his face, but I was quite sure I saw a glimmer of white. I hurriedly climbed the stairs, feeling his gaze upon my back until I disappeared from view.

My heart pounded as I entered my room. I had to lean against the door to catch my breath and recover from the heat that had suddenly pervaded my body. The bedside lamp had been lit, and it threw a circle of light over my bed, illuminating black spots on the coverlet.

Thinking they were insects, but wondering at their stillness, I approached cautiously. When I got close enough, I realized they were leaves. Gingerly I scooped a few into my hand.

They were thin, shiny, dark green leaves, about six inches long. I sniffed them, hoping for a clue, but I could only smell the night air.

The hair at the back of my neck stood up and I turned to the closed door, thinking I heard a footfall in the hallway. I flung open the door, but saw no one. Immediately I ran for the bell and pulled it urgently.

I waited for what seemed an eternity but was most likely only about five minutes until Marguerite appeared, wearing a cotton wrapper, her eyes heavy with sleep. "Yes, madam?"

I opened my palm to show her the crushed leaves. "I found these on the bed. Do you know what they are or how they got there?"

Green eyes widened and I saw fear in them as she gazed at me. "Those are oleander leaves. They can kill you if you eat them."

My hand shook a little. "How did they come to be on my bed?"

She shook her head. "I don't know. Maybe some of the other servants are playing a trick on you."

"Really," I said, sounding doubtful. "What other servants? I've yet to see any evidence of their existence."

Marguerite crossed her arms over her chest. "They're afraid of you. Those that didn't run off because of your sister don't like to show their faces too much."

"What do you mean? Why would they be afraid of Elizabeth?"

Dark lashes lowered, hiding her eyes. "There are some who take their unhappiness out on other people."

"Why do you think Elizabeth was so unhappy? What would make her so miserable?"

She shook her head, then fixed her cool green gaze on me. "People build their own prisons and then don't know how to find a way out. It made her angry—and she'd take that out on anyone who was about."

I swallowed, not quite believing that what she said of Elizabeth was true. "But why should they fear me?"

Her eyes seemed to flicker. "You look so much like her, they think you're one and the same. They think a voodoo priest has you under a spell and you have a nice spirit in you now, but the evil spirit will come back."

I raised an eyebrow. "That's nonsense." She continued to stare at me as if I were the one speaking irrationally.

"You may go now. I'm sorry to have disturbed your sleep. Good night."

"Good night," she muttered before leaving and closing the door quietly behind her.

I stared at the closed door for a long while. Then, opening my hand, I let the leaves fall slowly to the floor.

Chapter Five

I slept fitfully, waking throughout the night, sure I had heard a footfall nearby. Whispering voices moved from my dream to my waking, causing me to sit up in bed, my ears straining to hear what was being said. When I opened my door, I found more oleander leaves sprinkled on the threshold of my bedroom. Somewhere in the depths of the house a door closed, and I shivered in the warm air.

After twisting the key in the lock, I went back to my bed and lay down, not again closing my eyes until the white light of dawn peered through the windows.

I was awakened midmorning by Marguerite knocking on my door. I opened it and she bustled into my room with an armful of clothes. Following her was a young black girl, around fifteen or sixteen years of age, carrying a steaming breakfast tray. I tried smiling at the girl, but she kept her eyes averted from me the entire time she was in my room.

The girl set the tray on the bedside table as Marguerite spoke. "They're starting to harvest the sugarcane today, so you'd best stay out of Mr. McMahon's way. You'll be getting most of your meals in your room until the harvest is over." I nodded, my heart sinking slightly. I was already terribly lonely, and the thought of not seeing another adult for days on end, even if the adult was morose and not extremely pleased with my presence, was stifling.

Staring at the large bundle in Marguerite's arms, I protested. "I'm in mourning, Marguerite. I really cannot wear those clothes. But thank you anyway." I looked at the bundle closely. "Did you notice any of Elizabeth's things missing? Things she might have packed if she were going on a trip?"

She continued folding and placing the clothes in the large rosewood armoire—the same armoire I remembered Elizabeth locking me inside during a game of find-the-button. She was quiet for a moment, smoothing down fabric and ruffles. Then she said, "No, ma'am. I don't think so. And I would have noticed. Seems like she just ran off without a second thought."

I swung my legs over to sit on the edge of the bed. "Do you really think she ran off? What would have made her do something like that? She knew I was coming."

She regarded me coolly for a moment, but she didn't answer. Changing the subject, she said, "Mr. McMahon told me to bring these in for you. He also told me to burn your old things."

She glanced at me from the corner of her eye as I sat up straight with indignation. "They are the only clothes I own and you will not burn them."

She shook her head. "Mr. McMahon will not be very happy to find his orders are not being carried out. You'd best just let me have them."

I slid out of the high bed, my feet slapping the wood floor. "I will not."

Marguerite turned toward me, her hands on her hips. "He's ordered some new dresses for you." Her green eyes narrowed. "I wasn't supposed to tell you that, so keep it to yourself. If I were you, I'd just accept it and leave it at that. Mr. McMahon doesn't like to draw attention to himself."

Who did the man think he was, orchestrating something as personal as my own wardrobe? He could order dresses without my knowledge as much as it contented him. But I would never wear any of them.

Marguerite picked up what looked like a black serge skirt. I raised my hand. "Wait. What's that?"

She held it up for me to see better. "It's Miss Elizabeth's riding habit."

"May I see it?"

I held the soft fabric in my hands, noting the exquisite workmanship. Small grosgrain-covered buttons ran up the front, and a large pocket decorated the left side of the skirt. The collar and cuffs were of fine cream linen. A blue grosgrain cravat completed the ensemble. It was simply exquisite and carried the mark of my very elegant older sister. I slid my fingers over the fabric. It had been many years since I had been privy to such a beautiful thing. Every stitch of clothing I owned had been taken by the soldiers before they burned my home, leaving me with only what I had on my back. I had been given two more dresses by kind neighbors, who helped me dye them black when it became necessary for me to wear the mantle of mourning.

"I'll wear this," I said, holding it up to myself. "I'd like to go riding this morning."

She nodded and helped me dress.

I felt almost foolish wearing such high style. It had been much more my sister's desire to be fashionable than mine.

She had waited with anticipation for the day she could put up her hair, lower her skirt lengths, and wear a corset. I had dreaded it, knowing how the auspices of womanhood would restrict me in ways not just physical.

As Marguerite stood behind me, putting the final pins into my chignon, our gazes met in the mirror. "I found more oleander leaves outside my door last night. Do you know how they got there or what they mean?"

I studied her reaction closely, looking for some clue. There was something about this woman that made it clear she didn't like me. Whether or not it was because of my resemblance to Elizabeth, I couldn't say.

She studied my hair. "I don't know who would do such a thing, Miss Catherine. It could be bad gris-gris. Or maybe somebody just wants to warn you."

I knew what gris-gris was, having spent time in my girlhood at my grandmother's plantation. There had been a young slave, Rowena, who had been about my age and whose mother secretly practiced voodoo. I had been fascinated, if not wholly convinced, by her potions and charms, but I knew there were more than a few who believed in such things.

Marguerite's hands rested on my shoulders near my neck as our gazes clashed again in the mirror. "Maybe somebody's just trying to warn you. Maybe they think that whatever happened to your sister could happen to you if you stay here much longer." She shrugged. "I don't know. It's not my business to know." She stuck a hairpin firmly into my hair, pricking me in the back of my skull, and filling me with a sense of foreboding.

My toilette completed, I went outdoors. The thick odor of the river pervaded my first breath of morning air as I stepped outside. My nose wrinkled and I wondered if I would ever get used to it. As I walked toward the stables, I looked out toward the sugar mill and the fields, the tall cane swaying from unseen hands. On the outskirts of the field I saw dark men, their torsos shirtless in the heat of the morning, carrying long wooden-handled blades with hooks on the end. They were slicing at the cane near the ground where it grew, leaving patches of bristling cane that resembled the fur on a frightened cat.

I recognized Mr. O'Rourke inside the stable, spreading fresh hay. He looked startled to see me, then visibly relaxed when I spoke.

"Hello, Mr. O'Rourke. I see you've recovered very nicely from our little mishap." I forced a smile to my lips but it was not returned. "I hope you'll accept my apology for getting us into that mess. You were right. We should have stopped. But I knew my sister was in trouble. . . ." My voice trailed off, my fingers fiddling with my riding gloves.

"Can I help you with something?" He closed his mouth, stingy with his words.

A horse whinnied in a back stall. "I've been meaning to ask you a question. When my sister sent you to me, did she say anything about where she might be going?"

He glanced at me quickly, his eyes resentful, before going back to his job of spreading hay. "No. She gave me my instructions and indicated that I needed to follow them as soon as possible." He paused for a moment, his lips pressed tightly. "I believed that Mr. McMahon knew of her plans, which is why I didn't question them." Looking at me with narrowed eyes, he said, "I do as I'm told, and nothing more."

I nodded, uncomfortable with the news of my sister's deception. I recalled Marguerite's words regarding the servants who thought I was Elizabeth but with a temporary gentle spirit inside. I wondered if Mr. O'Rourke was of the same school of thought.

I doubted my host would easily accept my asking the servants about Elizabeth, but I had no other recourse if I was to solve the mystery of my sister's disappearance. My brother-in-law certainly had no intention of enlightening me further. "Mr. O'Rourke, did anything Mrs. McMahon tell you give you any idea that she was planning a trip or where she might be going?"

He squinted up at me, the sun illuminating the bristles on his cheek. "No, ma'am. She didn't make a habit of chatting up the servants." With a reproachful look, he went back to spreading hay.

I swallowed, embarrassed, then changed the subject. "I would like to go for a ride. Does my sister have a mount?"

He straightened, dropping a handful of straw. "Yes, she did. But she didn't like to ride her. Preferred to take Rebecca out in the buggy instead. Never wanted a chaperon, she said. Was content with just her daughter."

"Is her horse still here?"

The first smile erupted on Mr. O'Rourke's face. "Oh, she's a fine filly. I ride her myself just to give her exercise. The mister bought her for his wife, but I don't think she's ridden her but once or twice."

"What's her name?"

I was amazed to see a flush appear on his broad cheekbones. He looked at his feet and kicked at the newly strewn hay. "Mrs. McMahon named her Jezebel."

"I see," I said, understanding Mr. O'Rourke's discomfiture. "May I ride her, then?"

"Yes. Just give me a few moments to get her saddled for you."

"Thank you." I moved my hand to the skirt intent on brushing away a stray strand of straw. When my fingers touched the fabric, I felt something hard and unyielding within.

I thrust my hand into the pocket and pulled out a small brass key. I held it up, examining it closely. The key was too small to be a door key, yet big enough to serve another purpose. Perhaps it was for a desk or writing box? I slipped the key back into the pocket, intent on pursuing the matter later.

Jezebel was a bay with smooth chestnut hair and a black mane. A calm horse, she gently nuzzled my neck as I stood near her and rubbed her nose.

"She's delightful," I said, glad to have finally made a friend at Whispering Oaks. I wondered why my sister had not ridden her. Elizabeth had been a fine rider at home on Saint Simons. But even then she had preferred riding in the phaeton. She claimed she could spread her dress prettily and avoid the dust that way. I had preferred the exercise of galloping on the beach and the narrow lanes of the island, racing the ocean-borne breeze and feeling the wind pull at the pins in my hair.

Mr. O'Rourke helped me mount. "I'll return in a moment to escort you. Mr. McMahon would not want you riding unchaperoned. But I can only be gone for half an hour. I'm needed at the field to help bind the cane and cart it over to the mill."

"Really, Mr. O'Rourke. That's not necessary—and I hate to cause you any trouble. I promise I won't go far, and I'll rub Jezebel down myself when I return. It will be all right. I promise."

He cupped his hand over his eyes to shield them from the piercing morning sun. I felt drips of perspiration slip down between my shoulder blades as I sat still in the saddle. Finally he spoke.

"If you promise not to go far, I don't suppose Mr. McMahon would mind. But stay close, you hear? Go toward the river—you'll find bridle paths there. Keep out of the swamp on the other side of the property. It's not safe even for those of us who know it."

I remembered well the area he spoke of. It had been one of my favorite places until Elizabeth had told me it was haunted by the ghost of the Indian lady and her baby. The horse shifted, and I held the reins tightly. It had been Elizabeth's favorite place, too, and I wondered if it would hold any clues to her disappearance. I coughed, the cloying smells of hay, horse, and humid air pressing in on me.

Nodding, I pulled Jezebel away. I adjusted the small hat on my head, waved good-bye to Mr. O'Rourke, and headed toward the river.

My own horse on Saint Simons had been a gelding named Persimmon, and our favorite pastime had been riding along the beach at low tide, the spray of water kicked up by his heels shimmering in the island sun. But he, like so much in my life, had been taken from me. Along with most of the livestock on our plantation, he had been confiscated as enemy contraband by the Yankees. I missed Persimmon more than I cared to admit. But there was so much to be missed, I dared not think of any of it at all. Otherwise I'd stop in my tracks and suffocate from the thoughts just as if a heavy blanket had been wrapped around my face.

Jezebel cantered down the dirt lane between the ancient oaks. At the end of the drive I pulled up and looked back, making sure we were no longer in view of Mr. O'Rourke. Slowly I turned her to the right, running parallel to the river and toward what Mr. O'Rourke had referred to as the swamp. It was really nothing more than a bog, with ornamental gardens that had been planted by my grandmother, complete with a grotto and whimsical brick bridges. It had been a magical place for me at first, before Elizabeth had told me about the ghost and I found myself looking for an apparition behind each tree.

I skirted the pond at the back of the property, then headed toward the cover of trees surrounding the bog before anyone in the tall canefields could spot me.

Nothing looked familiar as I ducked under the shade of

the trees. Things were hushed in there, as if I had entered another world. The horse whinnied, stepping back, but I urged her on. The barely discernible path was strewn with sticks and rocks, making it hard to stay on solid ground. Choked reeds of swamp grass hovered in their shifting garden, the alluvial sand moist and sucking. We edged forward until we reached what was left of Grandmother's clearing, and my heart sank with sadness. Nothing here resembled the magical world of my girlhood. It appeared as if this last refuge from my old life was gone.

Moss covered a stone bridge, its color a deep, mottled gray. Weeds grew in profusion at the base of the grotto, which was almost completely disguised by ivy. A small gecko, its tongue whipping in and out in a furious manner, darted its head in my direction, then disappeared over a slime-covered rock.

A cloud of gnats lifted from the still water and enveloped both me and Jezebel, causing her to move her tail with a frenetic swish. I swatted at them with my arms, almost sliding off balance as Jezebel stepped back to get away from her tormentors.

A small splash diverted my attention for a moment. Only swirls of water eddying out toward the path remained of whatever creature had made the noise. I leaned forward to get a better look when Jezebel reared, throwing me completely out of the saddle. I hit the ground hard, my leg landing on a rock and bearing the brunt of my fall. The horse reared again, nearly catching me underneath her hooves. I hunched over, my arms crossed over my head, not looking up until I heard her running down the path from whence we had come.

I sat up, trying to catch my breath, an icy finger of foreboding brushing the back of my neck. A thick, black snake lay coiled only inches from my hand. Its tail vibrated as it

63

raised its head, opening its mouth to reveal a white interior.

Cottonmouth, I thought calmly. I didn't move; even my breath remained stilled in my chest. The snake's obsidian eyes watched me closely as its head swiveled in the air, but I felt no fear. Perhaps the lack was due to a primal act of survival. Or perhaps my life had left me immune to fear. Regardless, my only thought in the first moments after I spotted the serpent was, *Let it be quick.*

Leaves crackled on the path behind me, but I didn't turn my head. As the scaly body reached me, the air was rent by the sound of a shotgun, and the snake exploded into bits of skin and gore. I turned my head away, feeling pieces of the animal land in my skirt and hair.

A man's harsh voice spoke beside me. "Rufus—go get Dr. Lewiston and tell him to come to the house."

John knelt by my side. "Are you hurt?"

His voice was anything but solicitous. I shifted away from him and tried to stand, but my legs buckled under me. John caught me and lifted me in his arms.

I tried to push away. "Please. Let me down. I can walk."

Ignoring me, he made his way down the path. He addressed the man Rufus again. "What's wrong? I asked you to get Dr. Lewiston. Now go!"

I lifted my head and stared at Rufus, a large black man whose broad shoulders strained the buttons on his red-and-white-checked shirt. The man's eyes were wide with fear, the whites showing around the black irises. He stared at me as if he were looking at the devil incarnate.

He spun on his heel and fled down the path in front of us. Shortly after he disappeared, I heard a horse riding away. My leg throbbed and I began to see spots in front of my eyes. Reluctantly I laid my head on John's chest, finding the warmth of him cold comfort.

I was vaguely aware of him lifting me onto his horse and

mounting behind me. I slumped against him and didn't protest when his arm came around my waist to hold me steady.

His voice was low but forceful when he spoke. "Did not Mr. O'Rourke give you explicit instructions to stay by the river?"

I didn't lift my head. "Yes, he did. Please don't fault him for this accident. I simply wanted to explore my grandmother's plantation. I'm not a stranger to this place, you know."

He stiffened and I shifted my head, pressing it against the linen of his shirt. My cheek brushed against soft flesh, and I realized his shirt lay open. I heard his intake of breath and looked up at his unreadable eyes. I ducked my head again, taking care to rest it on cloth.

"If my overseer had not seen you, you would be dead by now. There is no cure for a cottonmouth's bite." He took a deep breath. "I am master of this plantation now, and I expect everybody to follow the rules that I have set. I can't have people disobeying me. I've got much more important things to take care of than playing nursemaid to a silly woman who won't listen to directions."

I bolted upright, causing him to tighten his hold on my waist. "I am not a child who needs instructions and discipline."

"I beg to differ. Perhaps you're not so unlike your sister after all."

I stayed where I was, not touching him. "It has been more than six years since I've seen her." My voice caught, and I looked down at my hands. His hold on me loosened. "And it would seem that there was quite a lot about Elizabeth that I wasn't aware of." I looked directly into his eyes. "I'm beginning to doubt that we are very much alike at all."

I leaned back against him again as we continued our

ride in silence. Finally he said, "Elizabeth never knew how to give proper thanks, either."

His words brought back the memory of a Christmas when I couldn't have been more than twelve and Elizabeth sixteen. I had received the gift of my dreams, a rabbit-fur muff to keep my hands warm on chilly winter days. Elizabeth, despite having received an entire roomful of gifts, threw a tantrum because she had not received a muff, too. Upset to see her so distraught, I had given it to her. She wore it every Sunday to church during the winter season, and it gave me great joy to see it bring her such happiness. I didn't recall her ever offering me a word of thanks, but then, she didn't have to. She was my sister and I loved her.

"What do you mean?" I asked, too lulled into complacency by the warmth of his hard chest to take affront at his suggestion that I was ungrateful.

He didn't speak for a moment. Then, "I understand that your life has been difficult these last few years. If I had known of your plight, I would have offered help sooner. I don't know how much Elizabeth was aware of your situation. She never discussed it with me." He paused, looking out toward the canefield. "I do feel responsible for you, and I would appreciate it if you would accept my help without complaining. It would make it easier for both of us."

"I never asked for your charity," I said, not sure whether I should be angry or grateful. "I fully intend to return to Saint Simons when Elizabeth is found. I doubt I will require your assistance after that." I sincerely believed that I would rather starve than ask this man for help.

"Then you could at least say thank-you. Surely your Southern pride doesn't override common courtesy."

We entered the shade of the oak-covered lane leading to the house. My cheeks flamed, and I was glad my mother was no longer alive to witness my lapse in the manners she had instilled in me from the cradle.

"Thank you," I said, my voice low. "Thank you," I said again, louder this time. "For the new clothes. Marguerite told me not to mention it to you, but I don't want you to fault me again for deplorable manners."

His voice sounded puzzled. "Really? I wonder why she'd say such a thing. If something makes you happy, I would like to know about it. If it makes you smile, I would double my efforts to repeat it. I would venture to say that your lips haven't smiled much in the recent past."

I bent my head, attempting to hide the flush I felt rising to my cheeks. This man unsettled me greatly, and I did not want him to.

I was spared from saying anything else by our approach to the house. Once again he lifted me from his horse and carried me inside and upstairs to my room. As he placed me gently on the bed, his arms seemed to linger. My skin burned through the fabric of my dress where he touched me, causing an ache I had not felt in years. I looked into his dark eyes, the pain in my leg and the day's adventure making me reckless. I made a stab at imitating Elizabeth's flirtatious nature. "I'm starting to make a habit of needing your rescue, aren't I?"

He released me and stood. "Yes. It would appear that you are."

His solicitous manner had changed suddenly into one of wariness. "I will send the doctor up when he arrives. In the meantime I'll have Marguerite see to your needs."

I heard a quick swish of fabric and the muffled sound of running feet out in the hallway. John appeared not to have noticed.

With as much suddenness as his change in mood, he left the room.

Marguerite came and dressed me in one of Elizabeth's

nightgowns and laid me against pillows on the headboard. She examined my leg, pressing on the sore spot, and pronounced it not broken. Then she left, too, and I dozed.

The eerie melody seemed to creep into my brain as I slept, nudging my memory. All I knew for certain when I opened my eyes was that it had something to do with Elizabeth.

I saw the child Rebecca and her doll sitting at the foot of my bed, humming the melody, and I started.

"Hello, Rebecca," I said, yawning. "Where have you been all morning?"

Grass was stuck in her hair, and her wayward braids were almost completely undone. A tear in the hem of her dress hung open. Her doll had fared no better, with dusty smudges on her face and pinafore. I imagined she'd been attempting to hide from Marguerite again.

I wondered at her sudden appearance at the foot of my bed. Then a thought occurred to me. "Did you know Dr. Lewiston is on his way over?"

She looked at me shyly, and her pixie face brightened with a grin. Her blue eyes sparkled, and I caught my breath. I sensed the spirit of my son within her and felt a small portion of my heart begin to thaw.

I recalled the sound I had heard out in the hall when John was placing me on the bed. "Do you like to spy on people, Rebecca?"

Her thumb plopped into her mouth as the fingers on her other hand twirled Samantha's yarn hair. She nodded solemnly, as if she expected me to scold her.

"What interesting things you must see."

Before the child could reply, a sharp rapping sounded at the door. It startled me, as I had not heard footsteps. I called out for whomever it was to enter, then greeted Dr. Lewiston.

He smiled, giving Rebecca an odd look. I wondered

how much of our conversation he had overheard. He smoothed Rebecca's hair, then rested his hand on her shoulder as he addressed me. "I understand you've had another accident."

"It was silly, really. My horse got spooked by a snake and I fell off. I hit a rock, and I hurt my leg."

"I see," he said, setting down his black bag on the bedside table and opening it. "Let me make sure it's not broken; then I'll have a poultice made to reduce any swelling. I'll have you good as new in no time."

I turned my head as he examined my leg and pronounced it merely bruised. I thanked him, and prepared to say good-bye when Rebecca began humming her mournful tune again.

The doctor paled, turning his head toward Rebecca. The child caught his movement and stopped.

I pushed myself up against the pillows. "Perhaps you can help me, Doctor. I'm so sure I know that tune, but I can't quite place it. Do you have any idea what it could be?"

He shook his head, forcing a smile, but his face blanched. "No. I don't believe I've heard it before. It is very beautiful, though."

He snapped his bag closed. With another pat on her blond head, Dr. Lewiston handed Rebecca a stick of licorice. She looked down at the piece of candy, then stole a glance at me, a glance so full of childish humor that I had to wink at her. The rush of pleasure I received from that one little act healed a small part of the great wound inside me. It would take much longer to heal completely, but I recognized then that the road to recovery did indeed exist, and that I might have found my way to that meandering path.

Chapter Six

The same young girl who had brought my breakfast came to my room after the doctor had left. She entered, visibly trembling, her gaze darting about and landing on everything but me.

I slid from the bed and approached her, noticing how she flinched as I neared. "What is your name?" I kept my voice low so as not to frighten her further.

Her jaw shook so badly it was difficult for her to force out the words. "Del . . . phine." Her gaze stuck to the floor.

"Delphine. That's a pretty name. I'm glad to meet you."

The girl stood quietly shaking, her dark skin matching the cocoa color of her dress. I was beginning to lose patience. Superstitions or not, I couldn't manage with an entire household of servants frightened of me.

"I'm Mrs. Reed—Mrs. McMahon's sister. I understand we look quite a bit alike."

Amber eyes flickered up to my face, then back down

again. "Yes, ma'am," she mumbled. Still studying the floor, she forced out, "Dr. Lewiston's stayin' for supper. Mr. McMahon wants to know if your leg's feelin' better and if you wants to join them."

My leg was sore, but walking on it posed no difficulty. "Tell Mr. McMahon that I will be there. Please send Marguerite to help me dress."

She gave a quick curtsy, then scurried from the doorway. I hobbled to the window seat and sat down. I moved aside the lace curtains and looked out upon the lawn. This had always been my favorite part of the day, the time when the sun gave way to the gathering dusk, its thin fingers of light holding on to the earth as they clawed their way to the edge and disappeared.

Oh, Elizabeth. Where are you? What were you so afraid of? A heavy breeze moved the curtains, brushing them against my face. A soft tapping sounded at the door, and Marguerite appeared with a gown over her arm.

It was beautiful—a midnight silk that shifted from blue to black as the light moved over it. The neckline was uncomfortably low, but I recognized it as a favorite cut of Elizabeth's. Marguerite offered to do my hair, and stood behind me at the dressing table as she brushed out my long, dark curls. Her eyes sparkled in her reflection, as if she held something back, something she couldn't wait to share. But she kept silent, the rhythmic strokes of the hairbrush almost hypnotic.

When she was finished, I checked my reflection in the cheval mirror, surprised at what I saw. Years of near-starvation had hollowed out my cheeks, adding a bit of mystery to my face, and making my eyes appear even larger. The dress, like most of Elizabeth's clothes, fit me well, if just a bit loosely around the waist and hips. After all, she had been well fed in Massachusetts during the long years of the war. But the gown hugged my bosom like a glove, displaying more of my chest than I thought proper. I searched in vain for my shawl, then had to be content with just tugging at the neckline to pull the dress higher.

I followed the male voices to the parlor and found Dr. Lewiston and John speaking companionably, with little Rebecca perched on her father's knee, giggling as he bounced her up and down like a horse. The doctor, while replying to his friend, never looked away from the child, his face aglow with affection.

The moment I stepped into the room, all movement and words ceased. I stood, hovering on the threshold, unsure. The doctor stared, his voice suspended midsentence. Something sparked in his eyes, then disappeared again. John merely glowered, his lips clamped shut.

Rebecca stopped in midchortle and began to scream the wailing sound of a banshee. It chilled me to the bone that such a small child could hold that much grief and pain inside. Dr. Lewiston stood, his face devoid of color and his mouth open in abject surprise. "Elizabeth," he whispered, his voice rasping the word.

John stood, too, holding his daughter against him while she buried her streaming face in his neck. "It's all right, sweetheart. It's just Aunt Catherine." He held the back of her head as she ventured a look at me. She stopped screaming, then stuck her face back into her father's neck, still sniffling.

I took a step forward, then stopped. "It's Aunt Cat. Remember?" I spotted Samantha lying prone on the floor and picked her up. Cautiously I approached Rebecca again, handing her the doll. She took it and buried her face in the doll's chest with a huge sniffle.

I looked at John. "What's wrong?" I felt as if I had walked undressed into the room. I pressed my fingers to my neck, feeling the rapid pulse of my blood. Why had Rebecca acted so frightened? What—or who—had terrified her so in the past to cause such a reaction? I wanted to leave, back out of the room unnoticed, anything to stop the terror in the child's eyes and the shock on the faces of the two men.

Dr. Lewiston approached, his smile warm but his face strained. He offered his arm to me. "Nothing, my dear. I believe we are all hungry and ready for supper. Please do me the honor of allowing me to escort you to the dining room."

With a glance back at Rebecca, who seemed to have calmed down considerably, I placed my hand on his arm and accompanied him to the dining table.

I don't recall what food I stuck in my mouth and swallowed. The air in the dining room was stifling, despite the slight breeze creeping through the tall windows. Three sets of eyes regarded me intently, as if I were the evening's entertainment.

Dr. Lewiston watched me with a look I supposed a man would give a beloved object he had lost and then found again in the most obvious place.

John left most of his food untouched, drinking glass after glass of wine, his cool dark eyes watching me, then watching Dr. Lewiston's close appraisal of me.

When Mary brought in dessert, I pleaded a headache and excused myself. Welcoming my escape from the dining room, I ran quickly upstairs. As I reached the landing, I leaned against the banister trying to find my breath, my heart hammering in my chest from the exertion. I was not used to wearing stays, my life of the last year making them unnecessary and absurd, and I was finding myself constantly out of breath and on the verge of fainting.

The door at the end of the hallway stood open, spilling light onto the dark floor. This had been my grandmother's room, and I knew that it now served as the master bedroom. I faced the door for a moment, and spotted an intense splash of color on the wall: a splash of midnight blue.

Slowly I approached the door and pushed it open, the hinges moaning a protest. There, hanging on the wall opposite a huge four-poster bed, was a full-length portrait of Elizabeth. She wore the same silk dress that now clung to my frame. Instead of comforting me, the sight made me feel unclean.

My hand flew to my throat. The portrait could have been me, except for the eyes. The eyes I saw in my own reflection were haunted and hungry, but still quite human. The ones in the portrait were cold and lifeless. If I had not known the subject of the portrait, I would even have called them malevolent.

A hot breath teased the back of my neck. I spun around and found myself staring up into the face of John McMahon.

I swallowed. "It was the dress, wasn't it?"

He nodded. Keeping his voice low, he said, "It was quite a shock for us. The resemblance . . . especially in that dress, with your hair done up that way . . ." His voice lingered.

His presence pinned me to the spot, draining me of the will to move away. "I don't understand. She is your wife! Why do reminders of her bring such terror to not only you but to your daughter as well?"

His gaze flicked across my face as he raised a hand. I didn't flinch as he lowered a finger to my neck and gently brushed away a lock of hair. I felt the heat of his touch long after he had removed his hand, and half wished he would touch me again. Still, I didn't look away.

"You are so much like her, and yet . . ." He stopped, his gaze regarding me openly. "You have such a gentle spirit. I'm left to wonder sometimes if I married the wrong sister."

My eyes widened and he stepped back, breaking the spell. He walked toward the portrait and stood before it.

"Elizabeth seemed always to be searching . . . searching for something more. Whatever would make her happy. I'm afraid that whatever it was she required, I couldn't supply. It didn't matter where she lived. She was miserable in Boston and here. And when Elizabeth was unhappy, she made sure everybody around her was unhappy, too. Even an innocent child."

My gaze wandered to the looming portrait, but I found I could not look at it. Small snatches of memory came at me, making his story ring true. Even as a child, Elizabeth had been full of mischief, always goading me into one of her adventures. But her mischievous behavior never seemed to take the form of simple playfulness. Rather, it stemmed from her desire to experience things new and dangerous. Her vivaciousness always seemed to mask something darker, something unsettled about her. Yet her persuasive charm was something few could resist. I grew comfortable in her shadow, sharing the center of attention with Elizabeth only when I could be dragged along clinging to her skirts.

He sighed, still absorbed with the portrait. "There is something within me that almost wishes she were gone forever. There were certainly times when my anger at her was so great I could have—"

He stopped speaking and turned, as if he suddenly realized I was there. A cold chill gripped me as I stared at his hands. I had felt how gentle those long, powerful fingers could be. But I wondered at what else they might be capable of. My husband had had gentle hands, too. Yet they had committed such a vile act of revenge, an act tantamount to destroying a part of me. The evil that lurked inside a man's heart was rarely visible to the naked eye, yet I knew enough never to put any man above suspicion.

As if he sensed my thoughts, his entire demeanor shifted to the cold, brooding manner I had grown used to.

I suddenly realized I was in his bedchamber, alone with him. "I . . . I shouldn't be here. I'm sorry. . . . I saw the portrait . . ." I backed out of the room. Looking down at my feet before turning and retreating, I stammered, "Good night."

I felt his gaze on my back as I walked down the hallway to my room.

I sat at the writing desk in my room, dressed in one of Elizabeth's nightgowns and my own wrapper, nearly overwhelmed by the cloying sent of lavender that clung to her clothes and stationery. Unable to sleep, I had tried to write a letter to my closest neighbor on Saint Simons, but had held pen poised over paper for nearly an hour with only the greeting spelled out.

I did not want to discuss Elizabeth's disappearance as yet, nor her enigmatic husband. I wasn't sure what I thought of him, and certainly couldn't relate it on paper.

The doctor had left shortly after dinner, and I was disappointed that I had not had the opportunity to talk more with him. I found his company entertaining and peaceful—completely the opposite of my host.

When I heard his buggy being brought around, I had peered through my window. Dr. Lewiston had not seen me, but as the buggy drove down the drive, I looked down to find John's dark eyes staring up at me from the front entrance steps. I had quickly let the curtain fall.

I laid the pen down and rubbed my eyes, finally ready to seek the comfort of my bed. The room was stifling, with no hint of a breeze coming from the open window. I slapped at a mosquito that had found its way inside, thankful once more for the netting hung around the bed.

I stood and opened my door, trying to catch a cross breeze. As soon as the door opened, I heard scurrying feet at the end of the hallway. I stuck my head out in time to see the bottom half of a small white nightgown disappearing around the corner of the hallway.

Grabbing my bedside lamp, I sped toward the fleeing figure. As I reached the corner and looked down the hallway, I was surprised to find it deserted. Baffled, I raised the lamp higher to see if anyone could be lurking in a corner. This portion of the house contained guest bedrooms that were barely used in my grandmother's day. Elizabeth and I had played hide-and-seek in them, and I had been locked inside more times than I cared to recall. Servants rarely came to this wing of the house, and I had once been left in one of the rooms until supper. Elizabeth had been my rescuer, hailed by our parents as the heroine of the day. I had waited for her to mention that she had also been my jailer, but I don't believe she ever did. I so enjoyed seeing her revel in all the attention that it never occurred to me to mention it either.

I called for Rebecca and listened. A clock chimed softly from the depths of the house. I was about to call for her again when I heard the distinct sound of bare feet running upstairs. I recalled that the door to the attic was on this corridor and I hurried to it. Flinging it open, I shone my light into the dark space. I thought I saw another flash of white at the top of the steps and raised the light higher. Nothing but uninterrupted darkness touched the circle of light.

"Rebecca?" I called again. Something rustled up the stairs and I quickly followed the noise into the attic.

I remembered the large space from childhood: exposed beams and stacks of old trunks and furniture pushed against the perimeter walls. It was hot and stifling, a breeze stealing its way through a broken window the only relief. A movement sounded overhead in the rafters, something different and not at all like the sound of a young girl's footsteps. "Rebecca?" I said, my voice quiet and not too steady. Something fluttered near the roof and I jerked my light to see. Straining my eyes, I could see only blackness.

A huge crash from behind spun me on my heels. I gasped, spotting Rebecca standing not two feet away, holding the ubiquitous Samantha. There was a dark, heavy shape at her feet. "What are you doing?" My voice was lost in my throat as I regarded her.

Without a word she dashed away in the direction in which I had come and disappeared down the dark and silent steps.

With my heart knocking loudly in my chest, I bent down to discover what had been knocked over. My hand touched something smooth and solid. Wood, I thought. I set the lamp down to get a better look.

It appeared to be a box-shaped object and it was lying on its side, having probably fallen from a nearby low chest. Using two hands I picked it up and turned it over, ecstatic at my discovery. It was obviously a writing box, and the brass keyhole winked at me in the dim lamplight.

The key! My hand fell to the pocket of my wrapper. The key had been left in the skirt of the riding habit. Had Marguerite taken it to be laundered? Eager to discover if the key and this box belonged together, I lifted it and tucked it under my arm.

I felt a breath of air near my cheek, and then a light form touched the top of my head and subsequently disappeared into the blackness of the ceiling. I screamed, dropping the box. The sound made the attic erupt into motion as a dozen fluttering objects propelled themselves from the rafters and dove at me, whipping at my hair and touching my clothing. I abandoned the lamp and the box and crawled toward the steps. The sound of small bodies whipping through the air surrounded me. I swallowed the bile in my throat and concentrated on crossing the short distance to the stairwell.

I stumbled down the wooden steps, my knees and hips taking the brunt of my fall. Struggling to stand, I fumbled for the doorknob in the pitch dark, feeling relief flood through me when my hand grabbed the cool brass. I turned it and pushed, but the door held fast. I tried again with no success. The door was locked.

Panic spread through my veins like a raging fire as I pounded on the door with the flats of my hands. "Let me out!" I shouted, the air around me roiling with unseen tormentors. High-pitched squealing assaulted my eardrums, reverberating in my head.

The door swung open and I fell through it and into the arms of my sister's husband. He slammed the door behind me, creating an immediate silence. I clung to him with both hands, my body shaking, but my will still strong enough to prevent tears. No man would ever see my tears again.

His arms fell around me, pulling me against him in the hushed hallway, pressing my head against his chest. He smelled of his own unique scent of soap, cigar, scotch, and something else. Something raw and powerful and as enticing to me as blood to a mosquito.

His fingers threaded their way through my unbound hair and I felt him bury his face in it, breathing in deeply. I needed to move away, to step back and stop. But, God help me, I couldn't. Nor did I want to.

"Are you all right?" His voice vibrated in his chest.

I nodded, not daring to look up.

"Why were you in there?"

I swallowed. "I was following Rebecca, but she ran away. I was attacked by bats, and when I tried to escape the door was locked."

He didn't say anything. Finally his fingers touched the edge of my jaw and brought my mouth to within inches of his. His breath teased my skin, making me tremble anew. I should go back to my room. Now.

His mouth brushed the air in front of mine. He pressed my body against his, our lips almost touching, but I could sense his reluctance to move nearer. Our gazes locked, speaking of desire and longing and things that I had not allowed myself to feel in so long.

And then I remembered who he was: Elizabeth's husband. I jerked back, my hand on my lips. He let me go, but remained where he stood, his eyes flickering in the light from the wall sconce. I backed away, not able to break his gaze.

"Papa!" Rebecca ran down the hall and past me, into her father's arms.

As he lifted the child, I backed away, finally turning on my heel and disappearing into my room.

I sat on the edge of my bed in the dark, watching the sultry sway of the curtains in the damp breeze. It was only much later, as I lay half-awake, that I wondered why John had been close enough to the attic door to rescue me so quickly.

Chapter Seven

When I awoke the following morning it was with the vague feeling that I had forgotten something. The mood persisted as I bathed and dressed in one of my black dresses.

Again I ate breakfast alone in my room, thankful I did not have to face John. What would I say? I should have been appalled by his behavior and by my own response to it. I had every reason to be, yet I was not. He stirred something long dormant in me, something I had been quite content to leave slumbering until the end of my days. And he was my sister's husband.

The canefield was alive with people, and I spotted John from a distance, his towering height making him easily visible. Heat teased at my cheeks and I turned away. Marguerite had told me that the harvesting and processing of the cane in the mill would occupy John for a good many weeks, keeping him away from the house. I prayed fervently that Elizabeth would return before then, thus releasing me to go back to Saint Simons.

Idleness did not come easily to me after my years of running a house and plantation and then finding myself responsible for my very survival. I needed to do something to fill my time. In search of Marguerite, I walked through the back door to find the kitchen at the rear of the house.

I recognized Delphine, leaning over to take biscuits out of the bread oven. She dropped the tin on a sturdy wood table when she spotted me. A woman, not much older than me and with a clear resemblance to Delphine, turned from a mixing bowl to see what was making the young girl's eyes go round.

"Good morning." I watched the woman wipe her doughy hands on an apron, her eyes as wide as Delphine's. "I'm Mrs. Reed, Mrs. McMahon's sister." Inexplicably, she made the sign of the cross.

I thought it odd, but held on to my composure. "I was looking for Marguerite, but I suppose you should be able to help me." I looked around at my audience, suddenly nervous. "In my sister's absence, I was hoping to assist with her duties. The food has been wonderful since I've been here, but I was thinking I could help with the menu planning. I've also noticed that the housecleaning is not what one might expect and would like to speak with the housekeeper if I could."

The older woman finally stepped forward, standing between Delphine and me. Her eyes were wary as she spoke. "I'm Rose, Delphine's my chile." She looked back at the girl as if to make sure she was still there. "There ain't no more housekeeper. No housemaids neither except for Mary. Miss Elizabeth done let them all go. Well, all thems that didn't leave themselves."

"I see," I said, feeling uncomfortable in the heat of the kitchen. Nothing was making sense. My sister hated housework. The Elizabeth I had known couldn't have cared less about housemaids, just as long as her house was clean. I hardly recognized this person I called my sister anymore.

"Well, then. You'd best show me where the beeswax is. The floors are in dire need of attention."

The door to the kitchen opened and Marguerite entered. "Miss Clara is here—Dr. Lewiston's wife. She says she's come with news of Elizabeth."

Before I could turn, I caught Rose making another sign of the cross. Thanking Marguerite and asking her to bring us tea, I left the kitchen to meet Mrs. Lewiston.

I almost overlooked the small woman sitting on the settee in the parlor. She wore beige, with no other color to accent the drabness. It matched her skin tone and the back of the settee so well that she blended into her surroundings.

She smiled timidly when I entered, her mouth opening only slightly as if from years of practice at hiding slightly protruding front teeth. I had the oddest urge to ask Marguerite if she had announced the proper visitor, for this woman did not match the doctor's vibrant personality in the slightest. He had told me it had been love at first sight, and I examined her closely to see the same spark he had seen.

Rising, she extended a small gloved hand to me. At full height she came only to my shoulder, and her voice was so quiet I had to bend my head to hear her.

"I'm Clara Lewiston—but you may call me Clara." She studied my face intently. "You look so much like Elizabeth, I would have known you anywhere."

I smiled, relieved to have found somebody who did not mistake me for my sister. "Yes, several people have mentioned that." I took her hand. "I've already met your charming husband. I'm Catherine deClaire Reed, but please call me Catherine."

83

Clara nodded. "I shall call you Catherine, then. Daniel has told me so much about you." Her expressionless face left me with no clue as to the content of such conversations.

Marguerite entered with the tea service and set it down on the small table at my side. As I began to pour, I felt Clara's steady gaze on me.

I handed her a cup and noticed that her fingers shook as she took it.

She kept her eyes down as she spoke to me. "I actually have a twofold purpose for my visit. I wanted to meet you, and I also have news for John of Elizabeth. My father has just come from Baton Rouge and is quite certain he saw her there at a party at the governor's mansion." She took a sip from her cup, a rather unattractive position for one with protruding teeth. "I knew that John would be eager for any word."

I sat up quickly, the hot tea sloshing onto my hand. "He saw Elizabeth—he's quite sure?"

She sent me a timid smile. "Yes, he's quite sure." She set her cup down on the table. "Where is John? I'd like to tell him in person."

The back of my neck tingled even before I heard his voice. "Hello, Clara. I saw you arrive."

He stood just inside the room dressed in a rumpled white linen shirt and fawn-colored pants tucked inside black knee-high boots. His face appeared anxious as he patently ignored me, turning his complete attention toward Clara.

Feeling heat in my face, I found I could not look in his direction. Instead I focused on Clara. She didn't smile at him, and she held her lips over her teeth primly. "As I was just telling your sister-in-law, my father is quite sure he saw your wife at a ball at the governor's mansion in Baton Rouge." She patted her lips delicately with a napkin. As she lowered her pale lashes, I noticed how her hand shook and I wondered if she was always as nervous as a rabbit.

She looked almost apologetic as she spoke with her quiet voice, her gaze never quite making it to John's face. "She appeared to be in the company of a young man whom my father could not name."

The shock of her words held back my breath. I forced myself to look at John. His skin, bronzed by the sun, had turned a murderous shade of red, his fists clenched at his sides. "Is that so." The words came out practiced and precise. "Did your father approach her?"

Clara blinked, then swallowed, her gaze focused on a chair. "No. You know my father is . . . Well, he hasn't been well. The shock of seeing her weakened him, and he walked outside to the gardens for a breath of fresh air. By the time he returned, she had vanished."

Thin, pale lines showed in the skin around his mouth. "And he's quite positive it was Elizabeth?"

Her small hands twisted in her lap. "As sure as he can be. Again, he is easily confused—he is of that age—but he seemed quite sure."

"I see." He bowed stiffly. "Then I must go see about leaving for Baton Rouge. I have things to take care of first, but I hope to be off tomorrow morning. Please thank your father, Clara." His gaze rested on me for a moment, and I colored again. I lowered my eyes, staring at the blue veins crisscrossing the white skin at my wrist. "Ladies," he said in farewell, then left the room.

Clara shifted in her seat. "My husband told me how much you resembled Elizabeth. He was quite right." Her light brown eyes met mine. "She was quite beautiful."

"Yes. She is." I didn't continue, not wanting to share my thoughts and doubts with a near stranger.

She compressed her lips and appeared to be deep in thought. "I wonder . . . I wonder why she left. I can't understand why she would leave her husband."

"Or her daughter," I added almost absently.

She blinked rapidly. "Oh, yes. Rebecca."

I glanced at her sharply. There had been something about the way she had said Rebecca's name.

Clara continued, her fingers clutching the teacup tightly. "She's an odd child. Difficult enough to raise a child like that, and now . . . this."

"What do you mean, a child like that?"

She smoothed her hands on her skirts and tilted her head. "I know she's a sweet child, but I just recall everything that Elizabeth told me. Rebecca's a bit high-strung, I think. Her mother even called her a clingy, needy child."

I bristled. "Most children her age are. She will undoubtedly grow out of it. All she needs is a mother's love."

Clara shook her head and tucked her chin to her chest, making it even more difficult to hear her. "Elizabeth didn't really . . . understand children. She didn't spend a lot of time with the little girl, I'm afraid."

"How can that be? I understand that they used to go for frequent rides together—just the two of them in Elizabeth's little phaeton."

My question seemed to disturb her, the pallor of her skin lightening one degree. "Well, then. Perhaps I am mistaken."

"Do you have children, Clara?"

Her face grew pinched as she looked down at her fingers, busily plucking at the sturdy fabric of her dress. "No. The good Lord has not seen fit to bless us with children."

I softened. "I'm sorry. Perhaps you will. You're still quite young."

She didn't answer but looked away, her gaze resting on a small daguerreotype of Rebecca sitting on the end table. Picking it up, she rubbed a finger over the glass, brushing off dust.

I cleared my throat. "Why do you think Elizabeth left? Do you know if she was unhappy?"

She placed the small frame back on the table. "We were quite close, you know, and the only thing she ever told me was . . ." Looking up, her gaze met mine, her face stricken. "But perhaps I shouldn't share confidences."

My interest had been piqued. I placed my hand on her arm. "If you have any information concerning my sister's state of mind before her disappearance, I think it should be shared. Please. Tell me. What did she say?"

She grabbed hold of both my hands, her fingers cold, and her lusterless eyes sought mine. She lowered her voice to almost a whisper. "She was afraid of her husband."

I raised my eyebrows, hoping to encourage her to say more.

Her gaze flickered toward the doorway where John had stood, then back at me. "She was afraid he might . . . he might hurt her somehow."

I gripped her hands tightly. "What did she mean? That he might strike her? Had he struck her before?"

Shaking her head, she dropped my hands. "She didn't say." She leaned toward me, her voice earnest. "But I do know he has a fiery temper. They say he shot a man in Boston in cold blood. His family is rather powerful and they claimed it was self-defense. He never was charged. But I can't help wondering what else a man capable of murder could do. . . ." Her voice trailed off, the silence full of implications.

"Why do you think John would want to hurt Elizabeth?"

She pursed her lips as if contemplating the right words. Finally she said, "I'm not privy to what might have transpired between them as husband and wife. But servants talk." She kept her voice hushed in a conspiratorial manner. "They say they had awful arguments—things being thrown and mirrors broken. Even smashed furniture. Lots of shouting and screaming. Foul language, too. They're not exactly sure what all the fighting was about. They never stayed close enough to find out." She sat back in her seat, closing her eyes, her face drawn. "I hope I haven't offended you by this gossip." She opened her eyes again. "But I suppose you should know."

"Thank you for telling me." It was hard to force the words out. I felt as if I had suffered a blow to my chest. I could hardly breathe. I recalled how John had courted Elizabeth, the quiet looks, the soft words, the restrained touches. I couldn't help wondering if my recollections had been colored by the eyes of a fourteen-year-old. Perhaps I had seen only what I wanted to see. One striking memory floated back to me—the memory of Elizabeth packing her trousseau before her wedding. Even at the time I had thought it odd that she made no mention of her soon-to-be husband. Her biggest excitement at the time was not that she would be getting married, but that she would be leaving Saint Simons. To see the world and have real adventures, she had said.

I poured another cup of tea for the two of us, my thoughts in turmoil. Sitting back to sip the fragrant brew, I studied the room around me, with its dark woods and heavy fabrics. I somehow doubted that Elizabeth had found the adventure she craved in our grandmother's plantation in the backwoods of Louisiana.

My guest placed her cup in its saucer with a small clatter. "I hope I haven't upset you. It is my sincerest wish that perhaps something I've said to you today might assist you in locating your sister. We all miss her, you know."

I nodded and stood with her. She offered me a tight smile. "I hope that you will do us the honor of a visit. Since the war, we don't get very many visitors, and it would be lovely to have a friend to chat with. Perhaps you and John would care to join us for dinner soon?" Her gaze dropped to my black dress. "My husband has told me you are in mourning, but I think it would be acceptable to a have a small dinner amongst friends, don't you think?"

I wanted to tell her no, that I couldn't bear the thought of sitting alone in a carriage with John for the time it would take to reach their plantation. But I couldn't turn down her invitation without seeming rude. "Yes, I would like that. I'll mention it to John."

"Wonderful. Daniel will be so pleased to hear it. He has developed quite a fondness for you, you know."

"That's very kind. It will be nice having friends close by. It can get rather isolated here during the day."

The light changed in her eyes. "Yes. I believe it can."

I watched as she was helped into her carriage and waved good-bye from the porch as she took off down the oak lane. I felt incredibly lonely all of a sudden.

The sky darkened, swallowing the shadows on the ground. The air reeked of rain, of summer grass and the pungent scent of the river. I looked up at the sky to see fat, billowing black clouds moving quickly toward us.

I heard a footfall behind me and I stiffened, knowing instinctively who it was. My skin tingled, betraying me, but I did not turn around.

His voice was close to my ear. "Don't believe everything she tells you. She's a horrible gossip."

"Really?" I said, pressing myself against the front railing in an attempt to move away from him. "Do you give any credence to what she tells us about her father seeing Elizabeth?"

He sighed. "Her father is quite old and Clara says he is senile. It is anybody's guess as to what he really did or did not see. But I am compelled to find out for myself."

Fat drops of rain began to fall from the sky, exploding in the dry dust of the ground below us. "Then you'll be leaving tomorrow morning?"

"Yes. I feel I must." He paused for a moment, then said, "I'm sorry for last night. I should not have touched you as I did."

Heat inflamed my cheeks as I recalled every last detail—the feel of his body against mine, the coarseness of his shirt under my hands. It was wrong, and I wanted to be sorry for it. But I could not.

"Turn around."

Reluctantly I faced him. His eyes mirrored the storm clouds above, dark and roiling and full of pent-up energy. I couldn't speak.

"Will you accept my apology?"

I nodded, unable to find my voice.

He took a step closer. "I want you to know what I'm sorry about. I'm sorry that what I did was inappropriate. I am not sorry that I wanted to kiss you."

I gasped, swallowing my breath.

He touched my arm, then dropped his hand as if realizing we were in full view of anybody who chose to look. I lowered my gaze so I could no longer see the lit fire in his eyes. "I can understand how you must miss your wife, and our resemblance must have confused you."

Leaning down, he whispered, "No. I knew exactly who you were the moment you fell into my arms."

"You are my sister's husband." My voice was barely audible.

"There is much you do not know." He stepped back then and walked down the porch steps, his legs lean and powerful in the formfitting pants. He strode all the way to the barn without turning around once.

As I went back into the house, the sky erupted in a torrent of rain, echoing the turbulence in my heart.

Inside, I stood in the middle of the foyer amidst the gathering gloom. I turned this way and that, restless, wondering what I should do. Suddenly I remembered: *The key!*

I dashed up the stairs, into the darkened hallway, and then into my room. The wind blew the rain at the window with force, the trees outside bowing to its strength. I threw open the armoire, my hands hungrily grasping each fabric, looking for the riding habit. My fingers recognized the soft wool and I snatched it from the armoire and threw it on the bed.

A loud clap of thunder shook the window, making me jump. I lit the lamp with shaking hands, eager to get on with my search. I found the pocket and reached my hand inside, only to come up empty. I stuck my hand inside again, stretching my fingers into every corner, but found nothing. It was simply not there.

I remembered Marguerite helping me out of my clothes on the day of my accident. She must have found it and put it elsewhere. I would just ask her where it was.

A door slammed downstairs, followed by the distant wail of a child. I ran back down the stairs looking for the source of the crying. Lamps had been lit in the foyer, casting a yellow light and reflecting off something on the floor. I stooped to look and saw it was water.

Clinking silverware brought me to the dining room and I found Marguerite, her hair shimmering with raindrops, setting plates and silverware on the table with force.

"What's wrong?" I asked, still hearing the distant wailing. "Where is Rebecca?"

Marguerite braced her long, slender fingers on the back of a chair. Her green eyes coolly appraised me. "She is being punished. For stealing."

"But she's only a small child. Surely there's been some misunderstanding. What did she take?"

She continued to regard me with brittle eyes. "Something of mine. Something she had no business touching."

I wanted desperately to let the matter rest. This child

might be part of my blood, but she had no claim on my heart. I would not allow the attachment. I moved to leave the room and had reached the threshold when a flash of lightning threw an eerie blue light into the dim foyer, quickly followed by a loud crash of thunder.

The wailing became a shriek and I stopped. Jamie had been petrified of storms and would without fail run to my bed at the first crack of thunder. I could almost feel his small, shivering body in my arms as I attempted to soothe him. If Rebecca were frightened, and alone, I could not ignore it.

I turned back to Marguerite with alarm. "Where is she? She sounds petrified."

She had resumed setting the table. "Leave her be. I will see to her discipline."

I rushed forward, the impulse to strike someone stronger than I had ever known it. "Tell me where she is!"

The woman looked at me with an insolent smile. "It is no concern of yours." She turned a china plate on the table, making sure the pattern matched the one next to it.

I ran out of the room, listening to the crying to orient myself. It sounded so far away, almost as if Rebecca were outside.

My mind reeling, I headed toward the back door, then raced off the back porch and into the rain, my ears picking up the sound of the shrieking, now louder. I ran past the kitchen garden and into the grassy field behind the house and toward the pond.

I saw her then, a forlorn waif in sodden pale yellow, a withered buttercup felled by the rain. She was hunched over in the grass, her small hands over her ears, and by the time I reached her, the shrieking had stopped.

I called her name and she jerked her face up. Like a drowning soul, she reached her arms up to me and I lifted her, holding her tightly against my body. She pointed back to the ground and I spotted Samantha, as sodden as Rebecca. I leaned over and handed her to Rebecca. She hardly weighted more than a puppy, and I easily carried her through the grass and back toward the house, my skirts heavy with rain.

We met John at the back door, his expression questioning. I walked past him into the house and waited for him to shut the door. "Marguerite left her out in the storm as a punishment for stealing. She's just a child." I hissed my words at him, thinking he had somehow condoned Marguerite's behavior.

"Oh, my Lord," he said, his voice breaking. He stepped toward us and reached for his daughter.

The little girl lifted her head from my shoulder and peered at her father. "Papa," she said, then buried her face again.

"She's still scared. Let me bring her upstairs and put her in some dry clothes and I will bring her to you."

His face darkened. "No. I want her now. I am her father."

I looked at him coldly. "And I am her aunt. She has just had a terrible fright and she wants to stay with me. Unless you want to terrify her further, I would suggest you leave her with me."

He looked taken aback, but didn't stop me as I carried Rebecca upstairs and into her room.

I pulled a blanket off the bed and dried her and Samantha with it as best I could before wrapping it around Rebecca's small body. It took a while to calm her, but I sat in the small rocker and sang to her all the songs that I had used to calm Jamie. They were hard to force out at first, but after a few stumbles the words came more easily.

Eventually I dried her hair and changed her clothes, hiding my tears from her as I touched her sweet white skin and thought of Jamie. About the same age as Rebecca, he had just begun to grow out of his babyhood, his bones pushing through the layer of baby fat on his arms and legs, giving him a new, angular look. The image of that emerging boy was the only thing I had left of my son.

As I brushed out her hair I marveled at its silkiness and its blond paleness, so different from Jamie's black hair, but similar, too. It had the same thickness and even the same wave at the back of the head that forced the hair to stick up regardless of what I did with the brush. I impulsively bent and kissed that little part of my son, causing Rebecca to turn around quickly, looking at me with those eyes. It was almost as if she knew I wasn't seeing her, but wishing that perhaps I would.

A nagging question forced itself into my head, and I knew I had to voice it. "Rebecca? Remember in the attic, how you showed me that writing box and then you ran away? Were you the one who locked me inside?"

Again those bright blue eyes studied me carefully, an understanding far beyond her years clearly visible in their depths. She shook her head.

"Do you know who did?"

She shook her head again and buried her face in Samantha's hair, which now smelled like wet wool.

I held Rebecca's hand and led her to the door, preparing to bring her down to supper with her father. She slid her hand from mine and ran back into her room. I watched as she took a china doll off the bed. Instead of bringing it to me, she turned the doll upside down and shook it.

Something clattered on the floor and Rebecca stooped to pick it up. With a mischievous grin on her face she walked back to me, her arm poised as if she wanted to give me something.

I opened my palm toward her, my curiosity aroused. The small brass key bounced into my hand before coming to a rest, the bright metal winking at me again in the lamplight.

Chapter Eight

I knelt in the foyer, my sleeves rolled up, my hands covered in beeswax. I had been working for nearly an hour and had yet to cover even a quarter of the floor with wax. My back ached at the thought of going back over it with a buffing cloth, but it felt good to be busy again, to be doing something useful. It was much more desirable than worrying about Elizabeth or letting my thoughts settle on her husband. Rebecca sat on the bottom stair, mimicking my silly alphabet song. Every once in a while she would stop, and I would look up at her and find those blue eyes watching me intently.

I bent my head back to my task, only to jerk it up suddenly as the child began to hum the old haunting tune again. I listened for a while, then resumed my task while the little voice repeated the simple melody over and over. Although I still could not put a name to it, I found it strangely comforting, as if I had heard it as a child, during a period of my life when all was well and safe.

The night before, I had sat down at the table with John, glad of Rebecca's presence. He had informed us that Marguerite would continue with her household duties and assisting me, but that she would no longer be serving as Rebecca's nanny. That responsibility was being handed over to me. I resented being told, rather than asked. Then, peering at Rebecca's waiflike face, I realized the good judgment behind his decision. Anything would be better than leaving her in the care of someone who would put a small child out in a thunderstorm as punishment for a minor infraction.

I questioned him as to why he didn't let Marguerite go. He had regarded me with hooded eyes before explaining that Elizabeth was very attached to Marguerite and that they would decide what to do with her once Elizabeth returned. There was also an obligation to the Lewistons. Marguerite was like a member of the family to Clara, but Clara, like most of the families in the county, could not afford to rehire her if she ceased working at Whispering Oaks. She would have no place to go.

I brought my head up at the sound of the doors to John's study sliding open and Rebecca's joyful cry of "Papa." John, dressed for traveling and carrying a valise, approached. He dropped the valise and bent to pick up his daughter, his hand absently stroking her blond plaits.

I stood suddenly, the blood rushing from my head. Dizzy, I put out my hand to steady myself and clutched John's coatsleeve. His strong fingers gripped my arm. "Are you all right?"

Nodding, I pulled away. "I'm fine. I must have stood too quickly."

He and Rebecca stared at me with the same penetrating gaze, one dark blue, one obsidian. "Did you eat enough at breakfast? I've noticed how very thin you are, and I feel it's my duty to see that you get enough to eat while you're here."

"I . . . I can take care of myself. I don't need you to nurse-maid me."

"Perhaps you do." He looked at the smudge of wax I had left on his sleeve. I did not apologize.

He glanced at the wadded rags and thick paste con-gealed on the wood floor. "And Rose or Delphine should be doing this—not you."

"I'm used to keeping busy, and this needed to be done. I want the house to be in order when Elizabeth returns."

We shared a moment of silence as I watched his face. He seemed unsure of a response. Finally he said, "I doubt your sister would want you cleaning floors. Don't you have a hobby or some other ladylike pursuit to occupy your time?"

I crossed my arms in front of me. "I did. I used to paint. Before the war. Before the Yankees burned my house and my studio and all my paints and canvases. Besides"—I looked down at my hand and scraped a clump of wax out from under a fingernail—"there wasn't anything left to paint."

Patrick O'Rourke appeared at the door, a hat crumpled in his hands. "If your bag is ready, sir, I'll pack your horse." His gaze flickered uncomfortably to me, then moved to Rebecca. Slowly he raised his eyes to John.

"Thank you, Patrick. I believe I have everything . . . ex-cept for my pipe. I can't seem to find it, and I'm starting to think somebody may have made off with it." He patted his coat as if hoping it might appear, then handed his car-petbag to the coachman. The man, with a look that was almost like relief, touched his forelock and left, sliding his hat back over dirty hair.

John kissed his daughter on the cheek and let her slide from his grasp. Addressing me, he said, "I'm going to Baton

Rouge. I plan to be back with or without Elizabeth in three days. I expect you to keep an eye on Rebecca and see to her well-being."

"Sir, that is something I need not be told. She will be well cared for, I assure you."

His mouth turned upward in a smile, and I was amazed at the transformation. John McMahon was a handsome man, despite his brooding, dark nature. But when he smiled, he was devastating. "I am quite sure she is in capable hands."

He picked up his hat from a hall table, then turned to leave.

I squared my shoulders, snatches of my conversation with Clara coming back to me with full lucidity. "But was my sister in capable hands?"

He turned slowly to face me, his black eyes glittering in the morning light streaming from the windows. "That would depend."

I waited for him to continue. Rebecca moved to my side and wrapped her fist in my skirt. I broke the silence. "On what?"

"On whose hands she put her trust in." He placed his hat on his head and opened the door. "Good-bye, Catherine. I will see you in three days. Perhaps Elizabeth can answer your questions better than I can. I'm afraid she's as much a mystery to me as she is to you."

He strode across the porch and I followed.

"I never did ask you. Why were you so near the attic the night I was locked inside?"

A dark eyebrow arched over an eye. "My daughter is wont to wander the house at night when she should be in bed." He glanced briefly at the child, who stood as if attached to my skirts. "I went to check on her and when I found her bed empty, I went in search of her. I heard the noise in the attic, which brought me to the door. If you are asking me if I locked it, no, I did not." His eyes sparked. "If you are through with this interrogation, I must be leaving."

I stepped forward. "What if you don't find Elizabeth? Then what?"

He looked down at his daughter and his face softened for a moment. Then a deep scowl covered his features. "Then my daughter and I will resume our lives. I daresay the absence of her mother will not have a detrimental effect on either one of us."

Without another word, he strode down the steps and toward his waiting horse.

I stood, watching him walk away, wondering once again at his words. But the one person who could answer my questions had disappeared. I stopped my thoughts, realizing that I needed her presence more to reassure me that her husband had not harmed her rather than to be assured that she was safe. I bit my lip, ashamed, then looked down at the little girl who was tugging at my skirts. I wiped my hands as best I could with a clean cloth, then lifted her in my arms. "Come on, little peanut. Let's go find that box in the attic."

I walked up the stairs slowly, trying to get Rebecca to talk to me. She rarely spoke, but I suspected she saw everything that went on in the house. I needed to earn her trust so that she would be more willing to share confidences.

"How did you know that box was in the attic? Did your mama show you?"

Those incredible eyes stared back at me, and she plopped her thumb into her mouth.

I reached the landing and headed down the corridor. I recalled the sound of stealthy footsteps in the hall, and her confession earlier about how she liked to watch people without their knowing.

"Did you used to see your mother in the attic? And she didn't know you were there?"

Without removing her thumb, she gave me an impish smile.

We reached the attic door and I stopped. I put Rebecca down on the floor and knelt in front of her. "I need you to stay here while I go up, just in case there are still bats. I don't think so. Mr. O'Rourke promised me he chased them all out and mended the window. But I want to make sure you're safe, all right?"

She nodded, her luminous eyes wide.

I opened the door slowly, feeling a ghost of the apprehension I had felt the previous night. Pushing the door as far open as it would go, I headed up the stairs.

The new boards in the window made the attic dark, and I hadn't thought to bring a light. I waited a moment for my eyes to adjust, then moved to the spot where I recalled dropping the writing box.

It wasn't there.

I moved forward, my gaze searching the dusty floor, sure I was in the right spot. I saw the trunk it had fallen from and my extinguished lamp, and the dust appeared disturbed on the floor in front of it, but the writing box was conspicuously absent.

I lowered myself to my hands and knees, determined to find it, and refusing to accept the implication if, indeed, it were missing. I crawled amongst the trunks and old furniture, disturbing years of accumulated dust, making it rise from the floor like a cloudy phoenix, sparkling in the sliver of light from the boarded window.

Worry and a nagging fear tugged at me. I knew where the box had been and it simply wasn't there. I stood, ready to give up, when a small object caught my attention. It lay not three feet away from where I searched, its obvious position in the middle of the floor indicating that perhaps it had been dropped rather than hidden. Stooping, I picked it up and held it between my fingers. It was a gentleman's pipe.

I tapped the bowl against my palm and let the tobacco sprinkle into my hand. The scent rose to my nose—a pungent, leaflike smell that suddenly reminded me of my father. A pang of homesickness engulfed me for a moment, weighing heavily on my spirit. I shrugged it off and let the tobacco fall to the floor.

Somewhere in the house a door shut, the sound reaching me almost like a jolt of air. Putting the pipe in my pocket with the key, I walked toward the top of the steps and called down. "Rebecca? Are you still there?"

After hearing no answer, I walked down the steps to the hallway, looking for my niece.

"Hello? Is anybody home?" a female voice called from the foyer. I was quite certain I recognized the voice.

"Clara? Is that you? I'll be down in a moment."

I closed the attic door behind me, then brushed the dust off my dress before heading for the stairway. I patted my pocket and felt the outlines of the key and pipe as I descended the stairs.

Clara Lewiston waited for me in the foyer, breathing heavily as if she had just walked a great distance. She dabbed at her forehead with a handkerchief, blotting away perspiration. Her eyebrows lifted as she caught sight of me with my sleeves rolled up on my forearms like a cleaning woman. Her gaze moved to the wax and rags pushed against the wall and the half-waxed floor. Like any wellbred Southerner, she ignored the implication completely.

I had to still my breath so I could hear her quiet voice. "I apologize for letting myself in, but there doesn't seem to be anybody here to answer the door. And it's so hot outside." She snapped open a fan and fluttered it in front of her face.

I flushed, taking her comment as an insult directed toward my sister. Before I could stammer out an excuse, she continued.

"Please, you need not apologize for Elizabeth. She told me all about her problems with the servants. Their superstitions are quite silly, but they do take them seriously."

"What do you mean?" I recalled Marguerite mentioning the servants and their belief in the supernatural, and wanted to hear more.

Her pale eyes shifted as she surveyed the room as if to ascertain that we were alone. "Perhaps we should take a walk outside. These walls might have ears."

My curiosity piqued, I excused myself for a moment to find Rebecca. She was in the kitchen being plied with sweets by Rose. Her doll, Samantha, was conspicuously absent. "Where did you go, peanut? You were supposed to wait for me in the hallway."

Her wide blue eyes stared up at me, a hint of mischief making them sparkle. "It's a secret," she said, taking another bite of peanut brittle.

I felt Rose's gaze on me and dropped the subject. I gave Rose instructions to keep my niece occupied and within her sight until I returned.

I found my visitor on the porch. As we walked, she slipped her hand companionably into the crook of my elbow. Watching her from the corner of my eye, I studied her appearance. Again, she was awash in an unflattering monochromatic beige. She did have beautifully smooth skin, but the sallow color was even further emphasized by the shade of her clothing. Pale eyebrows nearly disappeared into her forehead, and her lashes were almost nonexistent, lending her the appearance of a blank canvas on which the artist had yet to apply color.

Again, I wondered as to what had sparked the attraction of love at first sight for Dr. Lewiston. Even Clara's personality seemed timid and drab compared to his warmth and charm. But I was no expert on what lay inside a man's heart. I had been married for four years to a man I later learned I didn't know at all.

We walked in silence down the avenue of oaks, a light breeze teasing the tops of the trees, making the leaves whisper like a hushed conversation. I waited for Clara to speak, but she seemed content to walk by my side, avoiding mud puddles and ignoring the heat that swallowed us as completely as a wave from the ocean.

"Clara, please tell me. What happened to all of the servants?"

She clucked her tongue, reminding me of an old woman I had known on Saint Simons. She had no teeth and had been wont to snap her tongue against her empty gums at the most inappropriate times. "I hope you don't think I'm gossiping, but as Elizabeth's sister I suppose you should know." She squeezed my arm in a reassuring manner and I nodded for her to continue. "It all started innocently enough." She looked down at our feet, as if wondering if this would be called gossip. "It began at the Blackmores' annual masquerade ball. I suggested she rethink her costume, but I'm sure you know how stubborn she could be. Elizabeth dressed up as that Indian princess who's supposed to haunt the pond in the back of your property. She even carried a doll to portray the poor dead baby. Her gown was absolutely shocking . . . it didn't appear as if she wore stays or any petticoats at all. Just a doeskin sheath and her dark hair in plaits with feathers."

She stopped walking for a moment and looked at me, her eyes blinking in the bright light. "She was very beautiful, and the men couldn't take their eyes off her. I daresay most of the female population of the county was scandalized. But the servants thought she really was the ghost, and fled the house that night after seeing her."

We paused again, tilting our heads back to gain access to the faint river breeze that moved amongst the oaks and down the lane. "Of course, that wasn't the only problem dear Elizabeth had with servants."

She closed her mouth, as if she were finished speaking. I cleared my throat. "What other problems did she have?"

Her watery eyes looked into mine as a thin line of perspiration beaded her upper lip. "Well, some of them felt the need to approach her husband with problems they had with her. She felt they should do whatever she asked them at the drop of a hat, regardless of whatever other jobs they were expected to do." She sniffed. "If they complained to John, Elizabeth made their lives so miserable that they were soon compelled to leave."

I stopped, tilting my head, straining to identify the odd sound coming to us on the breeze. "Elizabeth and I weren't raised that way, Clara. I don't know what could have made her change so. But I love her, regardless of what she may have done, and I will welcome her back. And Rebecca needs her mother."

I watched Clara as she pursed her lips and then turned her head, hearing the same sound I did. Her eyebrows knitted together, forming a parenthesis of wrinkles on the bridge of her nose.

"Do you know what that is?" I closed my eyes, concentrating on the faint musical chiming.

She dropped her hand from my arm and began walking briskly to the end of the lane. I followed her, noticing how the sound grew louder. She stopped under an oak and looked up under the veil of Spanish moss. I came and stood next to her and raised my eyes to the tree.

Five empty bottles, in an assortment of colors, hung by thin twine ropes from a tall branch. The breeze whistled over the mouths of the bottles, creating an odd melody. I found them enchanting and turned to my companion to tell her so, but stopped.

Clara's face had stiffened as she stared at the wind chimes with disapproval. "I would have your man Mr. O'Rourke or somebody else take this down immediately. It's pagan and shouldn't be allowed on your property."

I looked up again at the bottles, trying to find anything ominous about them. "Don't be silly. Clara. It's just a wind chime."

Her eyes widened to form perfect little circles. "Oh, no. They're used to ward off so-called evil spirits." She nodded her head knowingly. "Marguerite told me all about those African beliefs when I was growing up. It's dangerous and sacrilegious and is not allowed on my property. I doubt John knows about it." She placed a trembling hand on my arm. "You don't suppose—"

She stopped talking, then looked directly into my eyes, but didn't speak.

Finally I spoke, my voice strained. "You don't suppose this has anything to do with Elizabeth's disappearance, do you?"

She glanced away as I looked furtively back at the bottles, which began to moan again in the wind.

She shook her head quickly, causing the thin ringlets on the sides of her head to bounce. A forced smile crept over her face. "No, of course not. I'm sure everything is all right and this doesn't mean anything. Elizabeth will come home. You'll see."

The sky darkened suddenly, carrying with it a humid breeze, thick with the scent of rain. The bottles clanked against each other with reckless abandon, the sound filling me with apprehension.

A heavy drop of rain slid against my cheek. Turning around, I grabbed Clara's arm and began to lead her quickly back toward the house, the eerie sound of the lost wind in the bottles following us. As the tall columns of the house came into sight, I turned to Clara to ask her to clarify what sorts of evil spirits might need warding off. I opened my mouth to speak, only to be silenced by an ear-piercing scream from somewhere behind the house.

I lifted my skirts, not caring what kind of undergarments I might be displaying, and ran as fast as I could around the house. I paused near the kitchen and saw Rose and Delphine coming out the kitchen door, their eyes wide with fright.

"Where is Rebecca?" I shouted. My stays pressed tightly into my chest, making it difficult to catch my breath.

They both looked past me, toward the pond. Delphine pointed. "She went to get her doll."

Spots danced before my eyes, but I sucked in as much of a breath as I could and ran in the direction of the pond.

Something floated in the middle of the water. Something with a head and arms and legs. My head seemed to explode as I reached the edge of the pond, the water just licking at my shoes. Raindrops dotted the water's surface, making it move and sway like a living thing. I couldn't seem to breathe in enough air, my lungs refusing to expand. The body continued to float in and out of my vision, my mind screaming to me to put a foot in the water and to dive under the cool depths and rescue whoever it was.

But I couldn't move. Huge black circles now hovered before my eyes, obliterating my sight. I fell to my knees and somehow registered the piercing wail again. *Jamie, don't let me fail you again*, I thought, sinking into the grass. The sweet smell of oranges filled my nostrils, so thick I could taste the fruit. Was I in my grandmother's orange grove? The image of the body in the water flitted through my mind again. *Rebecca?*

Another voice cut through my consciousness. A man's voice. "Catherine!"

Strong hands moved under my head. I gulped in air, calmed enough that I could fill my lungs again, clearing my vision. My eyes flickered open and I stared into John's worried face.

"Catherine?"

I nodded my head to show I had heard him, then pointed toward the pond. "Rebecca . . ." Rain pelted my face, soaking it, dripping inside the collar of my dress.

He bent his head close to mine and said, "Rebecca's fine. Somebody threw her doll in the water, that's all." Warm hands brushed the rain and matted hair from my eyes as the fear gripping my belly eased its hold. But there was something in his eyes that told me all was not well.

"Why are you here? I thought . . . you were in . . . Baton Rouge." I laid my head back against his arms, exhausted.

"I was on my way but hadn't gone very far. Patrick O'Rourke rode out to call me back."

His jaw clenched, and I raised a hand to touch his cheek. "What's wrong?" I whispered.

His arm trembled beneath me. "They've found Elizabeth." He looked away for a moment, then gazed down at me again, his eyes hard. "She's . . . she's dead."

Chapter Nine

The wind moaned through the oaks that surrounded the house and slapped the windows and roof with rain. A full day had passed since Elizabeth had been found, and she now lay in a hastily made pine coffin in the front parlor, lit candles burning at her head and feet and around the room. The house accepted her presence without even a stir, as if nothing could make the pall in the old rooms darker.

The pinched, waxlike face of the woman in the pine box bore no resemblance to the beautiful sister of my memory. No wind teased her hair; no sun brightened her eyes and highlighted her hair—nor would it ever do so again. The sister I had known and loved was gone. But she had been gone long before her last breath had left her. The person who lay before me was a stranger, and I had no more grief to give.

I need you, dear sister. I am so afraid. I leaned over the edge of the coffin and whispered, "What were you so afraid of, Elizabeth?"

A hand closed about my arm and I stifled a scream. I looked up into the steely gaze of Elizabeth's husband. He abruptly dropped his fingers. "Why do you think she was afraid?"

I swallowed, the sound audible in the still room. "She . . . wrote me. She said that she needed me. That she was afraid of something . . ." I let my words drift away as my eyes strayed back to the woman in the coffin.

"Do you think it was me she feared?"

My head jerked back to regard him. I paused for a moment, searching for an answer. Finally I said, "I don't know. She didn't say. And now her secrets will be buried with her."

He stepped toward me and I flinched. Something heavy and foreboding filled the room, not all of it due to the open casket. Leaning toward me, he whispered, "Perhaps some secrets are best buried."

I held my ground, my back pressed against the smooth pine box. "Are you saying that the circumstances of her death are best kept secret?"

John took a step back, allowing me room to move away from him. He looked down at his wife, his face hidden in shadow. "Perhaps they are." His eyes met mine again, and a chill tiptoed up my spine. "But not for the reasons you might think."

I briefly wished for some semblance of fear to hold my next words back, but life had beaten that emotion out of me. "Did you have anything to do with Elizabeth's death?"

He stared at me and said calmly, "No."

I didn't say anything, afraid my doubt would show in my voice. The rain continued to punish the house, reverberating on the windowpanes. I touched Elizabeth's cold hand, the bones small and fragile, and so much like my own. "Why is her skin still so perfect? She was left lying in the canefield for so long. . . ."

John turned to stare out the window, the shadows of raindrops covering his face. "I saw Elizabeth . . . there. Nobody would go near her. There wasn't a mark on her—not even bugs crawling in the vicinity of her body." He turned his head toward his wife for a moment. "It was so odd. And then Rufus became hysterical and had to be taken away, mumbling something about her being fixed with a curse." He faced me, his expression unreadable. "There's to be an inquiry. They will be taking her body tomorrow morning to determine the cause of death before we can have her burial service. I hope that it will not upset you overmuch."

I shook my head, mute for a moment, the image of Elizabeth's pale, sightless eyes staring up from a sea of sugarcane vivid in my mind. "No. It will be a relief to be able to find some answers."

A clearing of the throat brought our attention to the doorway. Dr. Lewiston stood there, his hat in his hands, his eyes fixed on the dark box in the corner. A candle at the foot of the coffin fluttered, then died, leaving the acrid scent of burned wax.

"Your man O'Rourke sent for me. My condolences, John, Catherine, for your loss." He seemed to visibly struggle to move his gaze from the coffin to his old friend. "If there's anything I can do . . ." His voice died in the heavy silence.

John turned his back to the doctor and faced the coffin again. "Yes, Daniel. There is something. And I'd like to speak to you in private."

I nodded, understanding the implication, and left the room, closing the door behind me. I stood in the darkening foyer, listening to the murmur of voices behind me and the windows rattling from the assault of the rain. The candelabra above had been lit to chase away the gathering gloom. With a start, I noticed that the large mirror over the hallway console had been covered with a white sheet. I moved to stand in front of it and saw Marguerite hovering in the alcove below the stairs. She had been avoiding me ever since I had been given the responsibility of seeing to Rebecca's needs, and she must have stepped back in hopes I would not see her.

"Why has the mirror been covered?"

Marguerite stepped forward, the whites of her eyes almost glowing in the dimness. "To protect the soul of the dead. If a soul sees her reflection, then she'll be trapped in the mirror forever."

A shutter banged against the front of the house like a disembodied shout. The crystal beads jostled each other as the flames on the chandelier sputtered from an unseen breath.

"That's nonsense," I said, trying to keep the edge of unease out of my voice. I reached up to try to pull the sheet off the mahogany acanthus leaves at the top of the mirror. They held fast and I heard Marguerite's throaty chuckle.

"They don't want you to take off that sheet, Miss Catherine."

My hands stilled. "Who's 'they'?"

Marguerite stepped closer to me, her voice almost a whisper in my ear. "The undead. They don't want you messing with what's theirs."

I resisted the urge to move back. "My sister's soul is with her Lord and savior. All of this talk is superstitious nonsense, and it will serve no purpose except to frighten Rebecca." I gave another tug to the sheet but it remained unyielding.

Her eyes flickered. "Then you'd best get down on your knees and pray for her soul. But I think you'll be wasting your time. Only repentant souls are saved." She stepped back. "I need to see about supper."

I listened as her soft footsteps padded across the foyer. The men's voices in the room behind me grew steadily louder. John's voice, deeper, more stern, seemed to be asking the same question over and over while Daniel answered in a strained tone, his voice escalating each time he spoke. The one word I understood was *no*.

I left the sheet on the mirror, making a mental note to take care of it later. Quickly I walked toward the stairs, not wanting to be privy to their conversation. The fleeting temptation to stay and listen inflamed my cheeks, and I hurried up the steps, longing for a brief nap.

As I reached the top of the stairs, a high-pitched keening sound struck my ears. I stopped, my hand clutching the railing as I listened closely. It wasn't keening. Instead it was the old haunting tune that Rebecca favored, and my skin crawled as I heard the odd tune hummed at such a high pitch as to be almost a cry.

The sound stopped almost as soon as it had begun. With hesitating steps, I walked toward the child's bedroom and the direction of the sound. I pushed open her door slowly and found myself staring into her empty room. A lamp had been lit, and I stayed on the threshold for a few moments listening to the dying rain.

"Rebecca?" I called out softly.

The only answer was the running of small feet and a slamming door somewhere down the corridor behind me. I rushed out of the room and stopped suddenly. The doll Samantha lay sprawled on the floor at the end of the long hallway, her legs caught in the opening of the attic door.

Ignoring the blood thumping in my temples, I approached the attic door with purposeful footsteps. "Rebecca!" I called again. "Come here this instant. This is not the time for playing."

Approaching the door, I picked up the doll, still damp from its adventure in the pond, and peered up the dark steps. "Rebecca! If you are up in the attic I ask that you come down now or I will have to punish you."

Somewhere, deep in the recesses of the great house, I heard the humming again, faint and liquid, oozing up the walls toward me. It seemed to come from the very plaster. Clutching the doll tightly against my chest, I stepped back and into a rock-hard chest. Strong hands held my arms. With a deep breath I turned.

John's eyes regarded me calmly. "Catherine, what is wrong?"

I swallowed and kept my voice steady. "I'm trying to find Rebecca. I think she's playing tricks on me."

He looked past me and up the attic stairs. "Do you think she may have run into the attic again?"

"At first I thought so, but I just heard her somewhere else in the house." I indicated the doll. "But she had to have been here just a moment ago because I found this at the bottom of the stairs. She must be very fast, because she was able to run down the corridor and down the steps before I could even turn around."

John took the doll. "I think I'll take a look in the attic anyway."

He stepped past me and took the stairs two at a time. The wood floor creaked as he walked overhead and softly called his daughter's name.

I heard him at the top of the steps and watched as he slowly descended again. His brow was furrowed as if he were deep in thought.

I wondered at his expression. "Is everything all right? Did you see Rebecca?"

He shook his head. "No. I didn't see anything." He stepped past me, still holding the oversize rag doll. It reeked of wet wool and pond water, and the old feeling of panic settled in my veins again. I placed my palms flat against the wall behind me, trying to steady myself.

John looked at me. "Are you all right?"

I nodded, forcing my breathing to return to normal. I searched for something to distract my thoughts. "I heard raised voices downstairs. Does Dr. Lewiston know anything more about Elizabeth?"

He turned his back to me as if preparing to leave, but remained where he was, his attention on the damp doll in his hands. "Yes, actually. He did."

I moved closer to him, my hand raised to touch his arm. I let it drift back to my side. Being this near to him affected my senses in ways I could not control, and to touch him might be disastrous. "What did he say?"

He tilted his head, an ebony brow cocked like a crow in flight. "I told you that some secrets are best buried with the dead. Perhaps this would be one of them." He started to walk away, his boots thudding softly on the carpet runner.

I walked quickly toward him. "If this concerns Elizabeth, then I demand to be told. I'm stronger than you seem to think and . . ." My words died in my throat as it constricted, and I thought for one horrifying moment that I might cry. Perhaps it was his brief look of sympathy as he turned to face me, or perhaps it was the shock of my sister's death that suddenly paralyzed me, but I found myself standing in front of John, unable to speak a word.

Inexplicably, he reached a hand to my face and I didn't flinch. He wiped away a tear and let the back of his hand caress my cheek. "My dear Catherine. You have already been through so much." His hand stilled as I trembled at his touch. "I am loath to add to your burden."

I turned my head aside, making him drop his hand. "My burdens are not your concern. Tell me what Dr. Lewiston told you. I need to know."

His eyes darkened as he stared dispassionately at me. "Elizabeth was with child. That was the reason she went to see Dr. Lewiston before she died." He turned from me once more, the doll hanging limply at his side.

I raised my hand to touch his shoulder but let it fall. "I'm . . . sorry. This is a double loss for you."

He shook his head and stepped away. "The child was not mine."

His words reverberated in my mind as I watched him approach the stairs.

I followed on his heels and clutched at the railing. "Wait." I nearly screamed the word. "What do you mean?"

I watched his jaw work, as if he were negotiating a difficult mouthful. "I do not wish to sound indelicate, but you have been a married woman and understand the affairs between man and wife. Suffice it to say that I know, without a doubt, that I could not possibly be the father of her unborn child."

He paused for a moment, as if to gauge my reaction. Seemingly satisfied that I would not faint and take a plunge over the banister, he turned and continued his descent.

I stood at the top of the stairs, looking down at him, my mind reeling from the implications and trying to think clearly. "But that would mean . . ." My face flushed hotly.

He turned to stare up at me, his eyes hard. "Yes, Catherine. Your assumptions would be correct." He bowed slightly, then turned away. "If you will excuse me, I must go find my daughter and return her doll."

I listened until his footsteps faded away. My gaze strayed to the closed parlor door, the still body of my sister lying behind it, and I wondered, not for the first time, what other secrets might have died with her. I fled for my bedroom. Lying on my bed, I stared up at the canopy until the beat of my heart had returned to normal and I could fill my lungs with air again. Finally I turned onto my side, my sister's name whispered on my lips. *Was this why you were so afraid? And would this be reason enough for your husband to end your life?* I listened to the dying winds as they blew good-bye to the old house by whistling under the eaves, the sound eerily like that of a crying baby. I blinked, feeling the tears run down my face. *Who were you really, Elizabeth? I don't seem to recognize you at all.*

I let the tears fall until none were left. My gaze roamed the room, searching for what, I did not know. Finally I settled on the gown I had worn the previous day. Delphine had hung it outside the armoire to dry thoroughly before putting it away. I sat up quickly, the room spinning for a moment. Slowly I slid from the bed and approached the dress. My fingers slowly crept to the large patch pocket and pulled out the gold key. Reaching in again, my hand closed over something smooth and hard, and I lifted it out. I opened my palm and stared at the pipe, the smell of tobacco still fresh. I recalled John's puzzled expression as he descended the attic stairs and felt with certainty that I knew what had caused it.

I need you, dear sister, I am so afraid. The pipe fell from my hand, landing with a small thud, and sprinkling dark tobacco on the cream-colored carpet like spots of blood.

Soldiers came at dawn the next morning to take Elizabeth away. I did not venture downstairs, but watched from my bedroom window. I saw John speaking with familiarity to the captain. The captain squeezed John's shoulder, and I wondered if they knew each other from the war and if their friendship might have some bearing on the proceedings.

I listened as the soldiers scuffled their way into the parlor and began carrying out the coffin. A man cursed and something crashed to the floor. With a sickening feeling in the pit of my stomach, I raced to the top of the stairs, clutching my wrapper tightly about me.

One end of the coffin had dropped, a deep gash in the freshly polished wood floor bearing testament to what had happened. The lid had slipped, revealing Elizabeth's face, her sightless eyes now open and staring directly at me. I turned my face away, more from respect for the dead than from any fear I might have felt. Despite the vagaries of my life over the last few days, I stubbornly clung to my fearlessness. If war, starvation, and grief had not yet killed me, then surely they had made me stronger. For seeing the corpse of my sister, her clear blue eyes coldly appraising, did not scare me. But what had put her in her coffin certainly did—if not for my own sake, then for that of her child, Rebecca.

I turned back to see John placing coins over Elizabeth's eyes to keep them closed. With impatience, he instructed the soldiers to seal the coffin again. They hesitated, and more than one remarked on the incredible preservation of the body. If not for the still chest, she appeared to be sleeping.

With the cloying scent of freshly hewn pine heavy in the air, they lifted the coffin once more and carried it out the door to the waiting wagon. I stayed where I was at the top of the stairs, listening until I could no longer hear the wheels rolling down the long drive. Before I could turn to go, John reentered the house and stood at the bottom of the steps, looking up at me with a shadowed face.

"You look like an avenging angel." His gaze swept over me, lingering on the almost transparent white fabric of my wrap and then moving slowly upward until our eyes met.

Unbidden, my pulse raced faster. I clutched the fabric tightly under my neck. "Perhaps I am."

His eyes darkened as he put one booted foot on the lowest step. "What do you mean?" He climbed another step toward me.

117

I did not back away. "I meant that perhaps I am here for a reason."

He did not drop his gaze but continued to climb the stairs. When he reached the step below me, we were at eye level. I didn't blink under his close scrutiny. "Tell me then, Catherine. What do you think happened to Elizabeth?"

I dropped a hand from my wrapper and reached for the banister behind me. "I . . . I don't know. I think we all must wait until we learn the cause of death." My pulse raced and skittered, but not from fear. What I felt was much more of a curse.

He was close enough that when he spoke, his warm breath pushed at the fine hairs lying on my forehead. "Do you think I had anything to do with her death?"

I could feel my own heart beating. The need to ask him again pressed down on me. "Did you?"

His black eyes stared directly into mine. "As I told you before, and as I will doubtlessly be forced to say repeatedly, no. I did not."

He stepped past me and into the upstairs hallway. I faced his retreating back. "Clara Lewiston said you shot and killed a man in cold blood in Boston."

Stopping, he turned around. "It was self-defense—which was proven in a court of law. It is public record, if you should choose to question my word. As for idle gossip, you are bound to hear quite a bit. Unfortunately, speaking ill of the dead is not something the people around here shun. I would ignore it all. Although some of the rumors might hold a grain of truth, I won't justify them with any remarks and cause a scandal. I want Rebecca to hold her head up high when she's old enough to care about such things."

As if she'd been summoned, a door opened down the hallway, followed by the quick scampering of small feet.

"Papa!" John reached for Rebecca and scooped the child up in his arms, holding her closely to him. His face softened as he held her, the love and adoration he felt clearly etched on his usually forbidding features. He was undoubtedly the same darkly handsome man who had the disconcerting habit of stealing my breath away, but he was almost unrecognizable when with Rebecca.

He faced me. "You need to get dressed, Catherine. They want you down at the courthouse for questioning. I told the captain we would be there before noon."

I nodded and watched as he carried Rebecca back to her room. His broad shoulders cradled her head, his strong fingers gently patting her hair. Could a man who loved a child as much as he obviously did also be capable of the ultimate act of violence?

A movement from downstairs caught my attention, and I found my gaze drawn to the large mirror in the foyer. I had taken off the sheet and had heard no more about the subject from Marguerite. Something dark and shadowy flickered in the depths of the glass, and I started. Surely it had been a trick of the eye or the reflection of a bird flying outside the window.

I leaned over the banister to get a better look and spied Marguerite standing in the dining room doorway and watching me with a smug expression. I straightened and went to my room without acknowledging her, the sound of Rebecca's humming suddenly flooding the house with its melancholy and mournful tune.

Chapter Ten

John helped me into the buggy and then slid in next to me, taking the reins. The roads were full of puddled ruts from the recent rains, the air thick and heavy. Navigating the road took most of John's concentration, and I used the opportunity to scrutinize him closely.

He wore an elegant coat of black wool broadcloth, and a light gray silk waistcoat. A gold chain hung from the pocket. I recalled that Elizabeth had purchased him a watch for their wedding and wondered if it was the same one. Being tall and broad shouldered, he wore his clothes well, his taut muscles discreetly covered but as obvious as if he were shirtless. I recalled how he had turned heads on his visit to Saint Simons. As a child of fourteen, I had been immune, but now, as a woman of almost twenty-two years, I found it impossible to ignore the physical force of his presence.

Staying as far away from him on the single seat as I

could, I allowed my gaze to travel the length of his powerful body, watching the shift of his leg muscles through the fine cloth of his pants. I lifted my gaze to his hands, which were bare of gloves. I had felt the gentleness of his touch but knew also of their hidden strength. The fine muscles moved under the skin as he handled the reins, and I imagined those same fingers touching Elizabeth as a man would touch his wife. How would those hands have reached for her if he were confronted with evidence of her infidelity?

My gaze shifted to his face. Lean and tanned from his daily work on the plantation, it hinted of brutal strength and unforgiving words. But I had seen it soften as he looked at his daughter, and fleetingly wondered what it would be like to be the object of such a gaze. The brim of his hat covered his black hair and shaded his eyes to such an extent that I didn't realize at first that he was watching me closely.

Flushing, I turned away, an apology ready on my lips as the wheel hit a rut and sent me skidding over to him, my hands greedily clutching his coat. He pulled me to him, my face pressed momentarily into the shoulder of his coat.

I lifted my head with a sudden motion, oddly disturbed by a scent lingering on his coat. I looked into his dark eyes and realized what it was: freshly turned earth. It wasn't an odor I would ever forget, having buried so many loved ones in such quick succession, as well as having tended the barren earth of a garden that would not grow for me. I pulled back and his hand fell from my side.

Flicking the reins, he stared ahead. "Do I repulse you so much, Catherine?"

I looked down at my hands, covered in the soft gray kid of my sister's gloves. Squaring my shoulders, I faced him again. "On the contrary, John, you're an enigma to me." I took a deep breath, wondering if I should be thankful for my newfound confidence—a trait hard-won and not without its terrible price. "I have glimpsed a kind and warm soul in you since I arrived. But there's something else in you—something that battles with the goodness. It's like a dark shadow on your soul that you go to great lengths to hide."

His hands tightened on the reins, the skin over his knuckles pulling taut. "I don't recall your being so outspoken the last time we met."

I settled my back gently against the seat. "I was only fourteen when last we met. I have changed a great deal since then. Not that I think you took much notice of me with Elizabeth near."

He faced me for a moment, something flickering in his eyes. He turned away again before speaking. "You wore your hair loose down your back regardless of your mother's pleas to tie it back or put it up. You would walk barefoot on the beach every day with your sketch pad and your paints and spend hours painting the birds and the ocean. Your smile was open, honest, and genuine, and your laugh was like an ocean-borne breeze. I found you intoxicating."

I stared at his broad back for a moment as he leaned forward, imagining the play of muscles under his coat. "I . . . I had no idea . . ."

"No, you wouldn't have. You were fourteen and completely without guile. Since Elizabeth looked so much like you, it was not hard to imagine that perhaps she held the same blithe spirit."

"And did she?"

He flicked the reins again before settling a dark look upon me. "No. She did not."

I waved away a swarm of gnats that had surrounded my bonnet, hovering in the heavy humidity. "I loved Elizabeth—worshiped her, almost, as only a younger sibling could. Despite our age difference, I always believed that we were quite close." I closed my eyes, recalling the look on John's face when he told me the child Elizabeth carried could not have been his. "I can't help wondering if I inherited my parents' adulation of her. She was so beautiful, it was hard to imagine her capable of doing any wrong. I . . . I wanted to be more like her."

John reached out suddenly, grabbing my wrist, his expression firm. "Don't. Don't ever say that." His gaze flicked downward toward his hand and he quickly let go. "Elizabeth was very clever and very charming. She let you see only what you wanted to see. Until it was too late."

I turned away and stared at the scrubby trees along the road, not wanting to look at John or hear the truth in his words. There had been times in my childhood when Elizabeth had frightened or hurt me with her sharp words, but her charm and beautiful smile always made her easy to forgive, or at least made one believe that her actions held no evil intentions to harm or deceive.

Finally I said, "Perhaps we're all like that."

He leveled black eyes on me. "I think you may be right."

The buggy climbed the road to the levee, the murky water of the Mississippi moving thick and lazy below us, chunks of leaves and debris from the recent storm dipping and twirling in a watery dance. It was so different from the salty blue ocean of my Saint Simons. For a brief moment I felt a stab of nostalgia, a deep longing for the way things used to be when I was free from grief and Elizabeth stood high on a pedestal to be admired and adored.

The town of Saint Francisville remained relatively unchanged in the years since I had last seen it. Because it had not been in the direct line of marching troops, it was virtually unscathed by the recent war. However, as was evidenced by the boarded shops and flaking paint on some of the buildings, the fortunes of many of the townspeople had changed. Because of the new military rule descending on Louisiana, soldiers wearing the dreaded dark blue of the federal army marched around the town square, the weathered storefronts frowning darkly down upon them.

The Stars and Stripes flew over the town hall, filling me temporarily with dread. I held tightly to John's hand as he helped me down from the buggy, feeling strangely relieved that he was here with me. Our gazes met briefly as he placed me on the ground, and I thought I recognized relief in his eyes, too.

While John was escorted into another office, I was led into the chambers of the town magistrate, an officer with kind brown eyes and a warm countenance that calmed me despite the navy blue uniform. He waited for me to be seated before seating himself and calling for refreshments. I wondered briefly if John was being afforded the same treatment. I recalled the respectful greetings of the other officers in the building, many of whom seemed to recognize John and hold him in high regard, and I knew that he was among friends. I only wished that I could feel the same way.

The interrogation lasted almost an hour, each question asked with a gentle regard for my feelings. I answered each as best I could, explaining that I had not been in contact with my sister in almost seven years. I didn't imagine I had been able to help much with the investigation, and wondered at my own hesitation to offer possible reasons for Elizabeth's death.

As Major Brody stood to dismiss me, he asked one last question: "Mrs. Reed, how is it that you found yourself at your sister's house? I believe you live on Saint Simons Island."

"Yes, that's true. But since I hadn't seen my sister in so long, I was quite desperate to see her." *I need you, dear sister. I am so afraid.* I shut out my sister's words, seeing instead the dark eyes of John McMahon and listening to his denial that he had anything to do with his wife's death.

Major Brody nodded. "I see. So you wouldn't have known that she harbored thoughts of taking her own life."

I held my breath for a moment. "No. Never. My sister would never have contemplated such a thing." I hoped that my doubts at my own words were not apparent. Elizabeth's heart harbored many shadows, and I would never know how dark some of them had been. I held the man's gaze. "She . . . she was expecting a child. Dr. Daniel Lewiston told us yesterday. Elizabeth had been to see him the day before she vanished."

"A double tragedy for your brother-in-law, to be sure."

I could do nothing but nod. Would the mere existence of an unwanted child have been enough for Elizabeth to end her own life? Or could having proof of a wife's infidelity drive a man to murder? I could not point an accusatory finger at John. Nor could I sully the reputation of my dead sister. Perhaps John was right: there were secrets best buried and forgotten.

The major showed me to the door. "If you think of anything, please don't hesitate to contact me. I am most sorry." With a gallant bow, he dismissed me.

John stood waiting for me in the corridor, his tall frame nearly blocking the light from the tall, smudged window at the end of the hallway. Without a word, he offered me his arm and led me down the steps and outside into the hot afternoon sunshine. He helped me into the buggy and then we set off, the silence between us almost palpable.

Just as we cleared the outskirts of Saint Francisville, the buggy jolted over a rock. Something, presumably tucked under the seat and out of sight, was loosened and cascaded into the back of my shoes. I looked down and picked the object up, holding it gingerly between my fingers.

It appeared to be part of a wasps' nest mixed with long strands of dark horsehair. It lay on a small square of red silk, the fabric marred with small smudges of dirt. It seemed to carry with it the scent of sun-scorched earth and grass as I held it, feeling the brittle weight of it in my hands. "What is it?"

His gaze swept from my hands to my eyes before he pulled off the road, parking the buggy behind an ancient live oak, obscuring us from any possible passersby. Before I could question him further, he reached under the seat and pulled out a man's leather glove.

His eyes darkened as he regarded me, and I shivered in the heat as if a dark cloud had covered the sun. "I found it clenched in Elizabeth's hand when I found her. I think that's what made Rufus so crazy—he called it bad gris-gris."

Lowering the bundle into my lap, I began to cover it in the red silk. "Who do you think put it there?"

He paused for a moment before answering. "Elizabeth."

I stared at him. "Elizabeth? Why would she do that?"

He held up the glove. "For the same reason she placed my glove near the spot where her body was found. The red silk is from a handkerchief of mine, and I have no doubt that the dark horsehair came from my horse. She wanted it to look as though I had been involved or at least responsible for her death."

I blinked in the strong sun, noticing the stillness of the trees around us. No breeze stirred a single leaf nor teased my cheeks. The air sat heavily on my shoulders and I could barely move. "So you also believe that she took her own life."

He sat as still as the air around him, the heat swirling over his broad shoulders like an aura. "I am quite certain of it. A week before she disappeared we had one of our arguments. We were standing in Rebecca's room arguing over something I can't even remember." He took a deep breath. "She told me she would rather die than live another day here with me. She said she would leave this place even if she had to take her own life to do it."

I thought back on Elizabeth's note to me. Was this what Elizabeth had been so afraid of? That whatever desperation had grabbed her soul was bringing her to the brink of suicide? I clenched my eyes shut, unwilling to look at the despair that had hovered so close to my own soul since Jamie's death. I could not blame Elizabeth for her desperate act; I knew the temptation far too well.

We sat in silence and breathed in the heated air, watching the gnats flit around us. Finally John looked down at the red-wrapped bundle and held out his hand to show me the glove. He gave a short bark of laughter. "Her final act of revenge against the man who could never give her what she really wanted—whatever that happened to be.

"It is presumed she took poison—something that is hard to detect and had some sort of preservative qualities. That would explain the condition of her body. Your sister was known to dabble in . . . such things and would know which one to use." He shook his head. "So vain—even in death. But I wouldn't have expected any less from her." He looked at me closely, and I didn't flinch. "I've convinced them to list the cause of death as unknown. That will be easy to accept, since nobody had any real motivation to kill Elizabeth. Except for me, of course."

I swallowed but didn't look away. "And what of the father of her child? Would he have had a motive?"

John shrugged, staring off into the distance. "It could have been anyone. Elizabeth traveled to Baton Rouge quite frequently. I was not aware of any one lover in particular. Besides, his secret would have been carefully kept.

Elizabeth had too much to lose if the truth were known."

A stab of guilt assailed me. "Why did you hide this from the authorities? Don't you think they should know?"

He raised a dark eyebrow. "Know for certain that she killed herself and implicated her husband? I could not do that to Rebecca. I believe the authorities know all they need to."

Our gazes met, and I'm not sure if what he saw in my eyes was a look of accusation or an offer of collaboration. With a sudden movement, he grabbed the evil charm from my lap and threw it far from the buggy. It landed in a patch of dried brown grass, the red silk glaring a reproach.

I stood, but he pulled me down with his arm. "It's foolish nonsense, Catherine, and I won't allow my family to be tainted by it. It had nothing to do with Elizabeth's death, and I will not give it any credence by bringing it to the authorities." He placed his face so close to mine, I could feel his hot breath on my cheeks. "I have Rebecca's future to consider. I will not let what has happened spoil her chances for a happy life. Her mother is dead. Let us bury her and move on with our lives."

Shaking off his hold, I shot back at him, my words harsh, "You forget sir, that Elizabeth was my sister. I shall not bury her and forget her as you would wish me to."

His voice softened. "That was not my intent. I expect you to grieve. I'm merely thinking of Rebecca's happiness. As her father and as her aunt, I believe we both need to do whatever we can to make things go easily for her. Having it be known that her mother committed suicide would be detrimental to her. She has not had an easy childhood so far."

I sat back on the seat, recognizing the truth of his words and wondering, too, at how easily he allayed my doubts. He grabbed the reins again and I found myself mesmerized by his hands, unable to turn away. Beneath the bronzed skin lay a gentleness hidden by incredible strength.

I stared straight ahead as the buggy made its way back onto the road. "You seem to know my weaknesses, don't you? You know that I would do whatever possible to protect a child. How very clever of you."

The buggy lurched and I found myself again pinned to his side. He reached his arm around me, his hand pressing into my shoulder. "I'm not trying to be clever. I'm merely protecting my interests, my daughter being the primary one."

I pulled away, strangely reluctant to leave the warmth of his touch. I recalled again the scent of freshly turned earth on his coat, and I wondered at my willingness to so easily place my trust in him.

We rode in silence for a short while before John spoke. "You didn't flinch when you saw the gris-gris. You're not afraid of much, are you?"

Splaying my hands wide on my lap, I stared at the fine leather and perfect seams of Elizabeth's gloves. "Water. I seem to have developed a fear of deep water."

He turned to me, his face compassionate, and I looked away. "My son, Jamie . . . he drowned, you see. I was with him, painting on the beach. He wasn't supposed to go into the water . . . he was too young and not yet a strong swimmer." Closing my eyes, I could almost feel the sand beneath my feet and hear the gentle lapping of the ocean. "I had taught him to swim, against Robert's wishes, and Jamie thought he could go by himself." I forced a smile, recalling my beautiful boy with dark hair and vivid blue eyes, so much like Rebecca's. "He was so strong-willed. He thought he'd show me himself what a good swimmer he was." I stopped speaking, trying to find my breath, my lungs constricting tightly.

John placed a hand gently on top of mine. The reassurance restored my voice, and I continued. "He was so far out when I heard him shout. I dove in as quickly as I could, but my skirts were so heavy, and I couldn't move. He shouted for me one more time, and then I heard nothing else." I clenched my eyes shut, willing the tears to go away. I wanted to be through with them. They stole my soul and sapped my will for living. John squeezed my hand and I continued. "We never found his body. The currents can be so strong and . . ." My voice disappeared, caught in the dark undertow of haunted memory. I focused on the creak and groan of the buggy, waiting to find my voice again.

Quietly I said, "All I have to remind me of him is a small marker in Christ Church Cemetery in Saint Simons."

I pulled my hand away from John's and stared out over the unforgiving waters of the Mississippi River. "When Robert returned home from the war and found out what had happened I think he went slightly mad. I almost felt as if his anger at me for letting it happen was even greater than his grief at losing his son." I took a deep breath, seeing again the growing red stain on the bedsheets. "He took his own life."

John swore under his breath, causing me to lift my eyes to his face. It was covered in a dark scowl, and for a moment I believed it to be directed at me. Flicking the reins harshly, he said only one word: "Coward."

The buggy rumbled at the increased pace, and I found myself clutching John's sleeve until we reached the lane of oaks approaching the house. The suspended bottles in the trees sparkled with new meaning as they tinkled against each other in the humid breeze. We came to a stop under the porte cochere, and Mr. O'Rourke approached to fetch the buggy.

I found myself weary down to my bones and craving nothing more than to lie down in my darkened room. I stared up at the house, wanting to feel reassurance or at least a welcoming, but felt nothing except an unspoken foreboding as I looked up at the empty windows. We climbed the steps, each one a real effort. As we approached the front door, my arm was jerked back and I found myself pressed against John.

I turned to question his behavior and saw him staring at the floorboards in front of the door. There, glistening in sun filtering between the oak leaves and Spanish moss, lay a cross molded out of what appeared to be salt.

I wanted to take a step back, but John held my arm firmly. With an oath, he swiped his booted foot over the cross, scattering the white crystals. The sound of scurrying feet came from beyond the door and he jerked it open, letting it crash against the wall. We stood in the threshold of the empty foyer, waiting for our eyes to adjust to the dimness. It was then that I saw her. I blinked, staring at the mirror in the foyer and into the eyes of my dead sister.

Chapter Eleven

"My God." John's voice held in check a burning animosity, and I reached for his hand.

He took it, then pulled me close to him, but I pushed away, mesmerized by the frozen image in the mirror. I blinked, marveling at the vivid blue of her eyes—the same shade as the midnight blue of her dress.

Swiveling on my heels, I turned to face the full-length portrait of my sister, now inexplicably leaning against the wall in the foyer.

John swore under his breath, then moved swiftly across the floor. With both arms he gripped the top of the frame and pulled the portrait from the wall, stepping back to let it fall, facedown, onto the bloodred rug. It landed with such force that thick clouds of dust puffed out of the carpet, rising like a specter in the filtered sun from the open door. A large fissure appeared in the gilded wood of the frame, neatly splitting it in half. Yet the canvas seemed undamaged.

"Marguerite!" John's voice bellowed up the stairs and throughout the house, and I prayed that Rebecca was not near to see her father's fury. I had never witnessed such anger, nor did I wish to ever be on the receiving end of it. I thought briefly of Elizabeth and wondered, not for the first time, if she had ever borne the brunt of her husband's wrath. Without being aware of it, I pressed myself against the console, the mirror at my back, as I watched Marguerite approach.

She lowered her gaze as she came to stand in front of John, but not before I noticed those strange green eyes full of knowing and completely without remorse, flouting his anger. Watching him closely, I saw him struggle to curb his emotions. His hands clenched and unclenched at his sides while he took deep breaths, his jaw working furiously.

A deep red stain on his face belied the calmness of his words as he spoke to her. "I thought I asked you to get Rufus to remove this portrait from the house. Why is it here, of all places?"

Her tone didn't match her apologetic words. "I'm sorry, sir. You just told me to get it out of your room, and I did."

John closed his eyes as if getting his anger in check. "I want it out of the house. In a barn or cellar, I don't care—just get it out of this house!"

"Yes, sir. I'm sorry, sir." Marguerite bowed her head, but I could see that her lips were upturned in a smile.

John took a step closer. "And are you the person responsible for the salt cross on the porch?"

She lifted her head, her proud chin raised, her expression blank. "Yes, sir. To keep the evil out of this house."

133

With deliberate slowness, she leveled her gaze on me. "Evil is easily disguised sometimes."

John closed his mouth, his lips a straight, unforgiving line. "You are employed here solely as a favor to the Lewistons. But your refusal to do as you are asked could very well be cause enough to send you packing. Consider this a warning. I won't hesitate to dismiss you should you disregard my orders again."

Marguerite stayed firm, her voice calm. "I don't think so, Mr. McMahon. We both know it's in both our best interests that I stay here."

His long, bronzed fingers clenched and unclenched again, his fury close to the surface. "Get out of my sight. Now."

With a mocking bow, Marguerite left the room.

My fingers hurt, and I realized it was from clutching the edge of the console. Ignoring John, I walked over to the broken portrait and knelt on the floor, my finger tracing the jagged tear in the wood.

"She's not even buried, yet you're erasing her presence already. Have you no compassion?"

I felt his shadow upon me, but I did not look up when he spoke. "I wish I could tell you . . ."

I looked up then, but found his face guarded, his black eyes hiding his emotions. "Tell me what? That Marguerite knows something that you do not wish for others to know? You're hiding things from me."

He lowered himself next to me, and our gazes met. "Whatever you suspect my motives to be, be assured that protecting you and Rebecca is my highest priority. I could not save my wife from the demons that haunted her, but perhaps in you and my daughter I have been given another chance."

I brushed my hand over the damaged wood again, and

stabbed my finger on a long golden sliver, making me gasp.

John took my hand and held it close to his face. His skin was still warm, nearly burning my own, and I shuddered at his touch. He looked at me with the knowledge of what his nearness did to me, and my gaze retreated to my hand.

Gently he slid the splinter from my finger and we watched as a small circle of blood pooled on the white surface. He raised my finger to his lips and I watched, spellbound, as he placed it on his tongue and sucked. My blood gushed through my veins, heating my skin as I suppressed a moan. I tried to pull away, but he held fast to my arm.

Slowly he removed my finger from his mouth and reached into his pocket for a linen handkerchief. With steady hands, he wrapped it around my wound. "Press tightly on it and it will stop bleeding."

I couldn't speak. I merely placed my hand in my lap and pressed the handkerchief tightly against my finger, waiting for the throbbing of my pulse to return to normal. He hovered near me, and the desire to ask him about Marguerite's words was strong. But I hesitated. Perhaps there were things that were best left unsaid.

John stood abruptly at the sound of the front door knocker. I stood, too, on shaky legs while he opened the door to let in a large gentleman who oddly resembled a pear in shape, and wore green pants and jacket to complete the image. When he was introduced as the mortician I was sure I had misunderstood. The man who had seen to the removal and burial of my parents and of Robert had worn solid black, with a dour countenance to match.

Mr. Cumming greeted me warmly and with genuine sympathy in his eyes. I welcomed his presence and his intrusion. The atmosphere in the foyer had become charged with unseen energy. His gazed raked over the fallen portrait, but he refrained from comment.

I excused myself and went to find Rebecca. The child had just lost her mother and would need comfort. I found her on the back porch with Samantha, having a pretend tea party. I sat on the steps, smoothed my skirts, and watched.

Rebecca didn't acknowledge my presence at first, and I remained quiet, waiting until she was ready. As she poured the tea she began humming the old familiar tune. I leaned forward on my elbows, feeling a haunting sadness as I noted the odd similarity she bore to my Jamie. They even had the same hands, small and square, and so unlike mine or Elizabeth's. I wondered absently which ancestor had given them this unique trait.

She stopped suddenly and looked at me, her dark blue eyes wide. "Why don't you like my song, Aunt Cat?"

I drew up, surprised at her astuteness. "Why do you think I don't like it?"

She picked up Samantha and held her on her lap. "Because your face looks all sad."

"It's not the song, child. It's just that you remind me so much of . . . of someone. Someone I miss very much." I brushed long strands of blond hair off her face.

Rebecca resumed her tea party, holding a pretend cup to Samantha's mouth. "I don't miss my mama. I'm glad she's gone."

I moved closer, wondering at this vehemence in such a small child. "You don't mean that, Rebecca. I know I miss her."

She looked at me with those innocent eyes again, and said, "Then you must not have known her very good."

I straightened, unsure how to respond, and searched for something else to say. "What is that song that you hum so beautifully? It sounds so familiar to me but I can't quite give it a name."

She said nothing, but began to hum the tune again. I watched as she methodically placed a girl and a boy doll next to each other on the small blanket that was being used as a tea table. Abruptly she stopped singing. "Mama liked it, too. But she told me not to tell."

I moved closer to her. "Told you not to tell what?"

She shook her head, her blond hair flying. "It's a secret. My mama would be angry if I told you."

Gently I lifted her onto my lap, and she didn't resist. "Rebecca, your mama has gone to heaven. There's no anger in heaven." I held her tightly, wishing briefly for the respite of heaven instead of the residual anger and hurt living in those left behind.

"My mama's still here. Marguerite told me so." She stuck her thumb in her mouth and rested her head on my shoulder.

I would deal with Marguerite later. No matter what secret she held over John's head, surely its revelation would pale in comparison to the torment she inflicted on his beloved daughter.

I brushed Rebecca's silky hair with my hand, feeling the soft slope of her skull, so small and perfect—like Jamie's. I closed my eyes and buried my face in her sweet-smelling hair. "I'd like to take you back home with me sometime— to Saint Simons. Your mama and I grew up there, you know. It's so beautiful." I could almost smell the salty air and hear the incessant rhythm of the waves on the sandy shore. I made no mention of the water. It was no longer a refuge for me, but the sounds and the memories of it were.

"Maybe, when I've found a home to live in again, you can come stay with me for a long time. I'll show you how to dig for clams and where to find the beautiful great blue heron. He's very shy, you know, but I know where he likes to hide." I smiled at the memory of lying in a shallow-bottomed boat on the edge of the marsh with my Jamie, and seeing his eyes widen in wonder at the glorious bird.

A footstep sounded on the bottom step, and I jerked my eyes open to see our visitor.

"I beg your pardon, but my daughter is not leaving this plantation. She is mine, and nobody will be taking her anywhere."

Without further preamble, John lifted Rebecca from my lap and held her close to him. She reached in my direction and I took heart, until I realized she was reaching for Samantha. I handed the doll to her and stood.

"I would never take her without your consent, of course. I simply thought that a visit to her mother's home could be therapeutic—" I stopped, the cold expression in his eyes halting my words.

"It doesn't seem to me that you found Saint Simons therapeutic in the least. When you arrived here you were as pale and skittish as a rabbit."

I sucked in my breath at his cruel words and his eyes softened with remorse. "I'm . . . I'm sorry," he choked out. "I didn't mean . . ." He closed his eyes briefly. "I shouldn't have been so harsh with you. But when you spoke of taking Rebecca . . ."

I stepped back, feeling the pinpricks of tears. "I . . ." I couldn't think of a thing to say. He knew of my circumstances, yet he could slap me in the face with them. I slipped past him off the porch steps and ran across the yard toward the orange grove, intent on getting as far away from John McMahon as possible.

Elizabeth's funeral was held on a wet Saturday morning. The family mausoleum was unsealed, waiting with gaping mouth to receive its next coffin. I had been inside it once when I was eleven during one of our summer visits—on a dare from Elizabeth. It had been opened to inter the remains of a distant cousin who had died overseas. It was Cousin Peter's wish to be buried at Whispering Oaks, and so his coffin had been shipped across the Atlantic and down the Mississippi toward its final resting place. Cousin Peter had died in Egypt, and it was rumored that he had been mummified to preserve his body on its long trip home. Elizabeth had had a wonderful time wrapping herself in strips of sheets and frightening me and our friends. She had made amends by allowing me to dress as the mummy while she transformed herself into Cleopatra. That was so very much like her; she always made sure that everyone had what they thought they wanted.

The mausoleum had been built into a sloping hill, covered on three sides by grass and the opening sealed with a heavy metal door and a locked gate. The door had been opened and the gate unlocked in preparation for Cousin Peter's burial, and the dark opening seemed to beckon to my sister with a call to mischief.

Elizabeth had given me a small stub of a candle to light my way and then told me to stay inside until the candle burned out. She had shut the door behind me, and I had sat shivering inside the oddly cool cavity, staring at the flickering candle, watching each undulation with breathless fear. When it began to fizzle and burn my fingers, I had dropped it, finding myself suddenly swallowed by suffocating blackness. I waited for Elizabeth to call for me, to congratulate me on my bravery, and to let me wear her red cape to church, as she had promised.

But no one came for me. After waiting for countless minutes, I dropped to my hands and knees, praying I wouldn't bump a shelf with a dusty coffin, and crawled out of the enclosure. The sunshine blinded me momentarily. When I could see again, I saw Elizabeth and Philip

Herndon, from nearby Bellevue plantation, sitting on the ground behind the grassy slope of the mausoleum, and he was holding her very close. When he spotted me, he pulled away and stood, yanking Elizabeth with him. Her clothes were rumpled and covered with grass, and her lips were red and swollen. Philip flushed with embarrassment but Elizabeth only gave me a crooked smile and then merrily announced that I had earned her red cape—an object I had been craving—but only if I promised not to mention that Philip had been by for a visit. I agreed, too excited to have the lovely cape and not realizing the precarious position in which I could have put my sister had I told Grandmother.

And now, as I turned my face to the steady drizzle, Elizabeth would be placed into the crypt herself. All of her beauty and wit would be hidden forever under the green slopes of the mausoleum.

Just a few close friends came to the interment. I kept my somber thoughts at bay by studying the faces of those around me. Rebecca stood solemnly, clutching her Samantha close, and holding her father's hand. Clara and Daniel were there, as well as an older couple and an elderly gentlemen I thought I recognized from my visits to my grandmother's.

Following the funeral, a larger group gathered at the house for the wake. Daniel seemed drawn and reserved, Clara always at his side. At one point, as I leaned against a dining room chair for support, Daniel sought me out. I was surprised to find him alone.

He kissed my cheek, then held my hand. "I can't imagine how devastated you must be right now. Please know that my shoulder is always available for you. I . . . had great affection for Elizabeth."

He looked as if he were about to cry and I patted his shoulder. It was at that moment that Clara appeared and promptly claimed Daniel's arm, steering him away from me. Again it struck me how incongruous the two of them looked together, like a mismatched pair of bookends.

The late arrival of a tall man and an older couple caught my attention, and I studied them closely trying to remember how I knew them. The young man looked vaguely familiar, and his soft hazel eyes flickered in recognition when he spotted me. He dipped his head in a brief greeting before turning his full attention to the reverend.

I spotted him again much later. He stood in a corner of the dining room scouring the crowd as if searching for someone. When his gaze alighted on me, he approached with a singular determination.

He stood in front of me and looked down at me. "Cat? It's me, Philip. Philip Herndon. An old summer friend."

Now I remembered. And I recognized the older couple as his parents—old friends of my grandmother's. "Yes, of course. I thought you looked familiar. It's good to see you again."

His face sobered. "It was a shock to hear about Elizabeth. My deepest sympathy for your loss."

I studied his handsome face, now fully matured without the softness of his earlier youth, and saw true remorse. "Thank you, Philip. I shall miss her deeply." I felt better, somehow, speaking to him. Just seeing him brought back memories of my carefree youth, the time of my life when death and loss were not my constant companions.

He looked down for a moment before speaking. "I'd . . . if you don't mind, I'd like to call on you sometime while you're here. I feel there's so much catching up to do. And I'd like . . . I'd like to talk about Elizabeth. Perhaps that would bring us both some healing." He smiled a small, faraway smile. "You know, I thought for a long time that she and I might marry . . ." His voice trailed away and his eyes seemed lost in thought.

His smile faded as he caught sight of something behind my shoulder. I turned and watched John approach, his face a mask of restrained thunder.

"Mr. Herndon," he said brusquely, giving a brief nod. "I must say I'm surprised to see you here. I thought I made it quite clear that members of the White League are not welcome in my home."

Philip flushed deeply. "I don't know what you mean, sir. I'm here with my parents to show our respect to our closest neighbor and old friend."

John gave him a mocking smile. "I see. Well, consider your duty done, sir, and see yourself out. You may wait outside until your parents are ready to leave. But you are not welcome here, and if you don't want to cause a scene, I suggest you do as I ask."

The red flush on Philip's cheeks quickly faded to a pale white. Anger flickered in his eyes and I thought, for a brief moment, that blows would soon fall. Instead, with a brief nod in my direction, Philip excused himself and I watched as he let himself out the front door.

Angrily I turned to John. "What was all that about? You just insulted him gravely. He was here with a sincere offer of sympathy, you know. He was a friend not only to Elizabeth but to me as well."

John gripped my elbow, pulling me close to him so he could speak without others hearing. "The man hasn't a sincere bone in his body. Even if it weren't for my personal dislike of him, I'd dislike him on principle. He spent the entire four years of the war in Europe, miles away from the battlefields where his friends and neighbors were being slaughtered. And now he's involved himself in the White League with men whose main purpose is to take the law into their own hands and harass freedmen and Republicans. That group alone is responsible for over a dozen lynchings in the last year."

We were interrupted by the appearance of an elderly gentleman whom I recalled to be Judge Patterson, a contemporary and old friend of my grandmother's. My heart leaped at the recognition for this man had been like a grandfather to both Elizabeth and me. We had always suspected that more than friendship lay between him and my grandmother, but they had never married. Regardless, he had loved and spoiled us like his own grandchildren, and I had loved him deeply in return.

Leaning heavily on a cane, he bent to kiss my cheek, his lips dry and withered against my skin. The judge offered his condolences and we spoke of my grandmother for a while until John excused himself to find Rebecca. I turned back to the judge to find his warm brown eyes examining me closely. His hand, with gnarled fingers resembling claws, grabbed hold of my forearm, and he leaned close to my ear.

"I want you to know . . ." His next words were lost in a spasm of coughing. Still gripping my arm, he continued. "I've missed you all these years, my dear. You've grown into a beautiful young woman."

I blushed, but thanked him and smiled.

"I remember you always telling me what lay in your heart—all your wishes and fears. If you ever need someone to tell your heart to, know that I am still here to listen."

I wondered if I should dismiss his utterance as the rambling of an old man, but when I looked into his eyes I knew the sentiments were real and sincere. Patting his hand, I said, "Yes, Judge Patterson, of course. It's reassuring to know that I have friends who care about me."

"There might be some unpleasantness regarding Elizabeth's death. I'm sure it's been kept from you, but you need to be aware that there's talk that John may have gotten away with something because of who he is and who he knows. You and I know this isn't true, but the gossip is there. Just remember that I'm here to help you if you need me." He squeezed my arm, then left to go. I watched the bent figure of the old man as he walked away and felt no small comfort in knowing that I had a friend.

I seemed to be the focus of attention and braced myself for the inevitable onslaught of neighbors and friends who sought me out to introduce themselves and examine me closely. From their curiosity, I feared that I must have grown three heads. But every so often I would look up and find John's eyes on me, and he never failed to send me a reassuring smile.

The scrutiny and constant attention left a throbbing headache at my temples. At the first opportunity I slid out of the room and hid myself in John's library. I felt completely numb. I wanted to grieve for my sister in private, and to relegate my memories of her to some sort of sanctuary while allowing the truth of who she had become to slip through the thin fingers of my memory and evaporate into the firmament.

Taking off my shoes, I curled up into John's desk chair and rested my forehead on my knees. I let my eyes flicker as the droning voices behind the door lulled me to a dreamless sleep, an enviable place where there were no mysteries or unanswered questions.

When I awoke I noted that the sun no longer shone through the window and the purple cast of dusk had settled into the corners of the room. The guests must have left, because I heard no voices. The house nearly shouted its silence.

I sat up, my neck stiff, and knew instinctively that I wasn't alone. I slowly lowered my legs and stilled, my eyes struggling to focus on a dark shadow by the door. The steady rhythm of somebody breathing pulsed in the still room as I widened my eyes to see better. The shadow moved closer and my breath caught in my throat.

"Catherine."

John's voice did nothing to still the hammering of my heart. "I've been thinking about you. Your future, to be exact."

I searched my sleep-muddled brain for words. "My future?" Something in the tone of his voice heightened all of my senses.

"Yes, Catherine. Your future. I've been thinking about it quite a lot lately."

I straightened, feeling suddenly that I could read his mind. I wanted to reach up and put my hand over his mouth before he could continue. But I remained where I was.

"I think that you and I should marry."

145

Chapter Twelve

A door slammed somewhere in the house and I think I must have said something. John approached and leaned toward me, but I didn't move. He lit a lamp on the desk and straightened. His black eyes flashed in the lamplight with an emotion that I couldn't read but which made my skin heat as if I'd been burned by the sun.

I tried to stand but realized my legs couldn't bear my weight and sat back down.

John raised an eyebrow and spoke. "I know this is sudden, but after today I have found that your presence in my house has led to a great deal of speculation and that your reputation is at stake."

I gripped the edge of the desk. "I assure you, sir, that my reputation does not concern me at this juncture of my life. And I don't plan to remain here at Whispering Oaks, so it doesn't much matter."

He paused, his eyes raking over me, my every pore tingling from the intensity of his gaze. I pushed the chair back, putting distance between us.

He took note of my movement and smiled. "There's another matter I wished to discuss with you. It concerns Rebecca. She needs a mother, and it seems that you two are growing fond of each other. I can't imagine that you would wish to leave and not see her again."

I forced myself to stand, leaning heavily on the desk for support. As much as I wished for the solace of Saint Simons and to be away from the child who so reminded me of the one I had lost, John was right. I had no wish to abandon Rebecca here in this house of dark shadows. But his proposal was not to be considered.

"You seem to forget that your wife is barely cold in her grave. If your acquaintances are gossiping about my mere presence here, imagine what such a hasty marriage would do to your own reputation."

He studied me with those black eyes that held so many secrets. "It is not my reputation that I care about. I know that there is nothing left for you on Saint Simons. And I want you to stay—for your sake as well as Rebecca's. The only way that can occur is if you marry me and live here as my wife."

My heart seemed to stutter, skipping a beat. "I have no desire ever to wed again. I tried marriage once and found it lacking."

That infernal eyebrow shot up again. "Then perhaps you were simply married to the wrong man."

I heard myself sucking in my breath before I realized what I was doing. "You go too far."

He stepped around the edge of the desk until he stood directly in front of me. "Robert treated you badly, Catherine. Don't you think that you are due a husband who will treat you with nothing but kindness and respect?"

I jutted my chin. "Like you did Elizabeth?" I regretted the words as soon as I had uttered them.

He gripped my shoulders, pulling me closer. "You don't know the truth of what was between your sister and me. I hope, for your sake, that you never do."

His eyes burned with controlled passion and I craved, just for a moment, to see it unleashed. This man fascinated me. As much as I wished to pull away, I wanted to feel his touch on me and let his heat burn away the coldness that had resided in my soul for so long. But he was like a fire: uncontrollable and dangerous.

He released me and let his hands fall slowly to his sides. His gaze dropped to my mouth and then, deliberately, to my throat, where he could see my quick breathing and rapid pulse. I raised my hand to hide my traitorous lips, but he reached and took my fingers.

My palm stung where he had touched but he would not let me pull away. His voice was low and seductive, the tremulous notes warming places inside me that had not been touched in so long. I closed my eyes for a moment, trying to shut him out, but his presence overwhelmed me.

"Catherine, let me take care of you. You will never lack for anything: certainly not food, nor clothing, nor a dry roof over your head. Can you honestly tell me that you have any of those things waiting for you back on Saint Simons?" He spoke softly into my ear, his warm breath sending goose bumps down my neck and arms. "Can you?"

I found myself leaning into him, and put my hand on his chest to stop myself. "Why would you want to marry me? I have nothing to give you."

His eyes became hooded, his emotions effectively locked away from my view. "I have always held you in high regard, Catherine. You had such a brightness of spirit about you, a joy for life that was very captivating. I—"

Abruptly he dropped my hand and turned away toward the window. "And Rebecca needs a mother—desperately. I think you two would be good for each other."

I stared at his broad back, foolishly imagining placing my face against it and finding rest. "Then you . . . you are speaking of a marriage of convenience."

He whirled on his heels, the grace of his movement reminding me of an encounter I had once had with a catamount. So sleek and beautiful, so deadly. Back then I had my father and his rifle for protection. Now I had only myself.

A flash of white appeared as he smiled. "No, Catherine. I have no desire for another cold marriage bed. I would fully intend to claim my marital rights."

I was glad for the dim light to hide the flush I felt creeping over my face. "I . . . I see."

He walked toward me, his footsteps muted by the carpet. I held my breath and forced myself to look at his face.

"I don't think you'd find my bed wanting." He leaned down, his lips hovering over mine. "Let me show you how it should be between a man and a woman."

When I spoke his lips brushed mine, taking away the intended sting of my words. "Sir, you are being presumptuous."

His fingertips lightly swept down my arms, and for the first time in my life I felt completely and utterly helpless. I hardly knew this man, and what I did know was incomplete. There were too many unanswered questions, too many hidden emotions, for me to want him the way that my body demanded. But when he was near me, even barely touching me, reason abandoned me.

His lips touched mine gently and I tasted him for the first time. When he pulled away for a moment, I closed the gap between us like a starving person craving sustenance. Our mouths collided in an unnamed hunger and

149

my body melded into his. His arms pulled me closer to him, his tongue invading my mouth and my body betraying me by welcoming the intrusion.

I found myself floating in an ocean of warmth and passion, the waters threatening to suffocate me but their lure of refuge and heat impossible to resist. I wondered if this was what drowning would be like, and the thought brought a return of reason to me. Like a person coming up from a deep slumber, I pulled away.

He didn't step back but continued to hold me close. "You're not indifferent to me, Catherine. We've both felt this thing between us since that first night when I rescued you from the swamp."

I shook my head, swallowing thickly. "No, I'm not indifferent to you." His expression remained guarded, but I could feel the steady beat of his heart beneath my palm. I was aware of every place on my person that he had touched and felt a small pulse of anger at myself for allowing him to see how he affected me. Who was this man? What secrets did he hide? I needed to remove myself from his presence so I could think. It was nearly impossible to do so clearly with him so near. And he was well aware of it.

I pulled back and stepped away from him. "I . . . I need time to think." I walked clumsily around the desk, putting it between us, my legs wanting to buckle under me.

He stood rigid by the desk, regarding me intently. "Yes, do think about it. Think about your life these past months on Saint Simons and then think about your life here. I doubt you'll have to think much further."

"But marriage! Surely there's another way." A new thought budded in my brain. "For what reason could you possibly want me as your wife?"

He raised an eyebrow. "I've already mentioned my reasons."

"No, there has to be more to it. What do I have that you could possibly want enough to acquire by marrying me?"

His gaze darkened. "Do not insult me, Catherine. Perhaps, in due course, you'll understand. But for now, suffice it to say that I need a mother for my child and a companion in my bed. And you, my dear, will lack for nothing."

"It is you now, sir, who is being insulting. This transaction you are proposing is only slightly better than selling myself. I may have lost everything, but I still have my pride."

"Forgive me. I did not mean to insult you. You know that I hold you in the highest regard." He began to walk around the desk toward me. "And I find your pride one of your most attractive assets. One of many, I might add." His gaze flickered over me before returning to meet my eyes. "I merely meant to imply that a marriage between us would be mutually beneficial."

He now stood within arm's length of me, and I knew I had to escape before I agreed to anything just to have him touch me again. "I need time." Without another word, I turned on my heel and left the room.

I ran to my bedroom, feeling faint from the pressure of my corset as I closed the door. I sat down on a small settee by the window and waited for my breathing to return to normal. My thoughts were in turmoil—torn between grieving for my dead sister and this remarkable proposal from a man who I could admit intimidated me as much as he excited me.

I thought of my barren existence on Saint Simons, the constant gnawing of hunger and grief, and knew that John was right: there was nothing there for me except for more of the same, and with no end in sight. At least, if I stayed here, I'd have food and shelter and no more worries. And I'd have Rebecca. She wasn't Jamie, but I knew, in due course, that I would come to love her as my own. She was all that I had left, a final connection, somehow, to the family I had loved and grown up with.

But marriage to John! The thought thrilled and repulsed me in equal measure. The physical intimacies of my marriage to Robert had been mechanical and painful, but I could only imagine that sharing a marriage bed with John McMahon would be anything but.

I shivered, my body at war with my mind. What did he know of Elizabeth's death? And what wasn't he telling me? He had sworn to me that he was innocent of any wrongdoing, and I had believed him. It was so easy to believe his words when standing in his presence. But now, away from him, I had doubts. How could I marry a man I wasn't sure I could trust?

A niggling thought teased at the back of my mind. Kneeling before my dresser, I pulled out the bottom drawer and reached into the back, feeling with my fingers until I grabbed the pipe that I had found in the attic. I stared at it in my hand, and then, without really knowing why, I placed it in my pocket. I supposed I carried it on my person for the same reason I now wore the key on a chain around my neck and securely tucked inside my dress.

I paced the room, unable to come up with any answers to my predicament. I heard John leave the house and I opened my door, feeling relieved that I wouldn't run into him. My steps took me outside to the back porch, where I heard voices from the kitchen. Hoping to find Rebecca, whom I had left in Delphine's care, I entered the small brick building.

The pungent aroma of old smoke mixed with freshly baked bread touched off my memory and sent a wave of nostalgia through me. I stood in the doorway and waited for my eyes to adjust to the dimness. Rebecca sat at a small table in the corner, Samantha on her lap, eating a thick slice of bread liberally smeared with butter. Delphine and her mother, Rose, stood silently, their gazes watching me with open curiosity.

I smiled. "I'm sorry to disturb you, but I wanted to read to Rebecca and put her down for her nap."

Rose knotted her thick, dark eyebrows, staring at me intently for a moment before speaking. "Delphine do that. I needs to speak with you, Miss Catherine."

Rebecca finished her last bite of bread, then willingly took Delphine's hand, allowing the young servant to lead her and Samantha away to bed.

"Is there a problem, Rose?" I had once run a plantation, and I relished the thought of becoming useful at Whispering Oaks.

She placed a cup of tea on the wooden table recently vacated by Rebecca and motioned for me to sit. "Have some of this green tea, Miss Catherine, while we chat."

There was something ominous in her voice, and I did as she asked. A sizzling and popping sound came from a large black kettle hanging above the fire, and I jerked around to see Rose throwing a yellow powder into the pot.

"What is that?"

She didn't respond, but instead wafted the smoke in her own direction, sniffing deeply of the sweet and pungent odor. I looked down into my tea, but doubts assailed me, and I could not bring myself to drink it. I should have left then, but I'd always had a stubborn curiosity and I found that I couldn't.

Rose dipped a long-handled ladle into the pot and poured it into a tin cup. This she placed across the table from me and stood by it expectantly.

"Sit, Rose, and tell me what it is you need."

She sat across from me, still silent, then lifted the dented tin cup and drank slowly from it, her eyes closed. She sat motionless and breathing deeply for several moments. I was growing impatient but didn't want to say anything to break the spell she seemed to be under.

Finally she opened her eyes, the black pupils in the centers enlarged. When she spoke, her voice was foreign to me, the words sounding old and withered and full of thick black smoke.

"You're not like the other one. They says she your sister, but blood is the only thing you share."

She looked directly at me, but her eyes didn't seem to see me. Rose continued, her words without inflection. "You have suffered through much sadness. And it's not done with you yet."

I drew in a breath sharply, but she appeared not to notice. "There be two men in your life—two men you share your life with." She shook her head slowly, her eyes still not seeing. "But one of them is not who you thinks he is. He betray you in a terrible way."

She paused, and I used it as an excuse to try to stand, but her hand snaked out to hold my arm, knocking over my tea. It splattered over the table, unheeded, the dark liquid creeping slowly to the edge. It seemed to thicken first before hurtling off and hitting the hard-packed dirt floor. I longed to ask her about the two men, but didn't want to give any credence to her words, despite the effect they had on me.

Her grip on my arm tightened, hurting me, but she seemed oblivious to my struggle to free myself. "But there's a great love to be found. A man who loves you like you deserve. You're soul mates—you were together in a past life and you've found him again." Her gaze settled on my face and her eyes seemed to clear. "Your lives are like the roots of an old oak tree—they runs deep and they cross over each other again and again. Don't you fight this love. It will save your life."

Slowly she released her hold on me. Rubbing the spot

recently relinquished by her fingers, I asked, "Why would my life be in need of saving?"

Shrugging, she said, "It's not for me to see the why of it. I jus' see the way it will be."

I tried to lighten the mood. "But I'm sure your prophecies are only meant for those who believe in such things."

She smiled broadly, a gap of missing teeth prominently displayed. "No, ma'am. They's for everybody who listens." She pushed back from the table and walked over to a rough-hewn box sitting by the fireplace. Opening it, she reached in and pulled something out before returning to the table. She spread her palm wide, and a shiny black stone rolled onto the table's surface.

"This lodestone be for you. It pulls in all the good luck while pushing away the evil. You needs to carry this with you wherever you go."

I stared at it for a long time with some loathing, not wanting to touch it. But neither did I want to insult Rose. What would be the harm in taking it? With a smile, I reached across the table and took it, sliding the smooth stone into my pocket. My hand brushed against the pipe inside and my skin chilled. There was so little I knew, but so much I had to learn. I thanked Rose and left.

I had my supper sent to me on a tray, unable to face John as yet. Luckily the cane from Whispering Oaks and that of local tenants needed to be processed at the mill, and John was kept busy for most of the following week. When he was home, I managed to avoid him, but knew he was waiting for my answer.

I had done nothing but think about our discussion. The more I thought about it, the more sense it made. I had nowhere left to go and he was offering me sanctuary. It was surely not a reason I would have hoped for to marry, but I had few options left. I could not admit to myself that the prospect of marrying John excited me. My common sense continued to tell me to leave, to run away as fast as my legs could carry me.

And there was Rebecca to consider. My heart remained wary, its scar tissue still raw, but the child had begun to find a place within me. Her sweet smile and joyous laugh touched me in ways I could not name, but for which I was grateful. I was a long way from healing, but she was bringing me there, her little hand tucked securely into mine. We needed each other, and I knew I could not bear to be parted from her.

The Sunday following Elizabeth's funeral, I dressed with care for supper. Marguerite selected a dark amber silk from Elizabeth's room for me to wear, and I shed my black and donned the beautiful gown before I had a chance to think about what I was doing. Marguerite swept my hair up, fastening it with tortoiseshell combs, and I sent myself a frail smile in the mirror, pleased with the results.

I felt John's appraising eyes on me the moment I entered the dining room. With a gallant bow he seated me, his fingers brushing the back of my neck. I pretended not to notice, but was sure he could see the flush that crept over my neck and shoulders.

Rebecca had eaten her dinner earlier, at my orders, and John did not seem displeased to have my undivided attention. We talked of mundane things, avoiding any topic that was close to the heart. The only reminder of the reality of our lives was the sweet, cloying smell of flowers left over from the funeral. Most of the blooms had withered and died, dropping their petals on the floor. Lack of direction for the servants had allowed them to remain, their weeping stems the only sign of grief in the house.

When dinner was over and he stood behind my chair, I wondered if he could hear the thudding of my heart. I knew that the time to tell him of my decision had arrived, but I somehow couldn't find the words. He offered his arm to me, and I took it, our eyes meeting for a brief moment before I turned away.

Stalling for time, I walked slowly toward the parlor. When we reached the hallway console and the old mirror, he stopped, his movement turning me around to face him. The chandelier above cast shadows on his face so that only the spark from his eyes was visible. "I've waited long enough for an answer from you, Catherine."

I felt my chest rising and falling with each breath. Turning my back to him, I faced the mirror. I couldn't stand so close to him and look in his eyes and be able to think coherently. "I . . . I think I've come to a decision."

His hands gripped my shoulders, but I didn't turn around. "But I first must ask you something."

I opened my hand in which I had been clutching my handkerchief all evening, letting go long enough to let it rest in my lap while I ate. Slowly I unfurled the corners, displaying the pipe I had found in the attic. "Is this yours?" I faced him but stepped back, making sure no part of me touched him.

He seemed unusually calm as he took the pipe from me. "Yes. It's the one I've been missing." Something flickered in his eyes as he raised his gaze to me.

I took a deep breath. "I found it in the attic—when I went back to find the letterbox. The box was gone, but this had been left."

He raised an eyebrow. "And?"

I was taken aback. "I want to know how it got there—if you were the one who removed the letterbox."

A dark shadow seemed to pass over his face and I looked up, expecting to see something large obliterating the light from the chandelier. But all I saw was the ornate crown molding and the brass chandelier, each flame making a valiant effort to shine light into the darkness.

John laughed. "You have quite an imagination, don't you, Catherine? It's another one of your admirable qualities." He sobered slightly. "But I can't tell you how the pipe got in the attic because I don't know. I've been up there quite often in recent weeks trying to locate a box of papers pertaining to the plantation. It could have fallen from my pocket on several occasions. You just didn't notice because you were so absorbed in your find."

His words soothed me but I knew that as soon as I was alone, my doubts would assail me once again. Taking yet another deep breath, I pressed on, my future hanging in the balance. I looked directly into those black eyes, daring him to look away. "What do you know about Elizabeth's death that you're not telling me?"

He placed his fingers under my chin and lifted my face up to his. "I am going to say this only once more and then I never want to discuss it with you again. I had nothing to do with Elizabeth's death. I am not saddened by her passing, except for any grief that it might have caused you and Rebecca. I truly believe that she died at her own hand." He lowered his face closer to mine, his scent overwhelming and addictive. "But I will admit that I don't think she could have pushed me much further before I would have been forced to take matters into my own hands to get what I want."

I turned away again, facing the mirror, trying to find the will to resist him. But I was like a bee drawn to nectar and I was afraid I had gone too far already. My voice sounded far away. "What is it that you want?"

His eyes met mine in the glass. "I want you."

I closed my eyes as he bent his head, placing his lips on my neck. A low moan escaped me and I pictured myself turning in his arms and succumbing to the passion I knew we both felt, letting him make love to me there, on the floor in front of the haunted mirror.

"Marry me," he whispered in my ear.

I opened my eyes and stared at our reflection. My voice sounded breathless when I answered. "Yes. Yes, I will marry you."

Our gazes met again in the mirror but a distortion in the glass seemed to change John's face into a malevolent mask, and I wondered if the spirits inside were trying to tell me something. I shut my eyes once again to block out the image and surrendered to the passion John's mouth and hands evoked deep inside me.

Chapter Thirteen

I wanted a long engagement, to observe a proper mourning period for Elizabeth. But John was impatient and I knew he was a man used to getting his way. I didn't fight him on the matter, although I refused to admit even to myself the anticipation I felt. It was anticipation tinged with alarm—not the usual emotions of a soon-to-be bride. I found now that I could not be in a room with him without watching his hands and wondering how they would feel touching me. He'd catch me staring and I would flush, causing a devilish grin to spread over his face.

My doubts would consume me once I was out of his presence. I spent many a night tossing and turning, mulling over all the missing pieces in the puzzle of Elizabeth's existence at Whispering Oaks and of her death. John had allowed two weeks before we announced our engagement, and I intended to use that time to truly consider my alternatives.

On a warm afternoon while Rebecca napped, I found myself in the old grotto once again. Despite my deep musings, I kept a wary eye out for snakes, not ready to replicate the disaster of my last visit. I could see that someone had been there clearing out the underbrush and removing debris that many years of neglect had brought. Heavy foliage created a verdant screen from the wilting sun, and I sat down on a crumbling bench nestled against an ancient oak tree, and turned my face up toward the subtle warmth.

A crunching of dead leaves alerted my senses. I looked around, wondering who was near, but saw no one. I heard another footfall and stood, peering through the overgrown foliage. "Hello—is anybody there?" Irrationally, I thought of the ghost of the Indian woman and her baby, and felt a chill of apprehension creep up my spine.

A tall figure pulled back the thick fronds of a fern and stepped into view. I smiled with relief, recognizing Dr. Lewiston.

He gave me an apologetic grin. "Sorry if I frightened you. I was just riding up for a visit when I saw you coming here, so I followed. I hope you don't mind."

I was genuinely glad to see him. "No, of course not. Come sit over here with me. It's quite cool in the shade."

I made room for him on the bench and he sat next to me, removing his hat. A shard of sunlight glinted off his head, making it shine like gold. I remembered longing for hair like that as a child and grinned to myself, thinking it wasted on a man's head.

With a gallant gesture, he pulled a bloodred tea rose from his lapel and offered it to me. "I brought a beautiful flower for a beautiful woman, hoping it would make her smile in her sadness. She does have the most ravishing smile."

"Thank you," I said, blushing at his compliments. It had been so long since anyone had made me feel pretty, and my mere words of thanks could not adequately describe my gratitude. Instead, I reached toward him and squeezed his hand where it rested on his knee.

He squeezed mine back, then let go quickly. His eyes, so cool and gray, studied me closely. "It's amazing, you know, how much you resemble her."

"Elizabeth?"

He nodded. "Yes. She was so beautiful." He looked away for a moment. "It's hard to imagine her taking her own life."

I studied him. "I've learned, since coming here, that Elizabeth showed a different face to everyone who knew her." I leaned back against the ungainly oak, whose monstrous roots had been rerouted to make room for the small creek that oozed from the bottom of the grotto. "I remember one summer when our grandmother took us to a carnival in New Orleans. They had a house of mirrors and Elizabeth was captivated by it. I was rushing along the hallways, trying to find her. I'd see her face and run toward her, only to find it a reflection." I sighed into the tepid air, the distorted image of Elizabeth haunting my memory. "She was vastly amused by my pursuit. I think that's how she pictured her life—sitting back and laughing at those of us who tried in vain to find the real Elizabeth. I wonder if she's laughing at us now as we try to sort this out."

His eyes hardened to a steel gray, reminding me of the sky over the ocean before a storm. "How different you are from her—but you have that same ethereal beauty. It's almost like . . ." He paused, as if realizing he had spoken aloud. Covering my hand with his, he faced me with a concerned expression. "I hope you don't find this forward of me, but if you should be afraid of staying here . . ."

"Afraid? Why should I be afraid?"

He patted my hand. "Nothing I can really say, but with Elizabeth's death, despite the coroner's verdict and John's suspicion of suicide, there seems to be things here at Whispering Oaks that just aren't right. Besides, there's the matter of a lack of chaperon. In your grief you might not have noticed how . . . improper it is for you to stay here. I really feel, as a close friend of the family, that a move to our home would be the right thing to do under the circumstances."

His concern warmed me, and I placed my other hand on top of his. "Thank you, Daniel. I really cannot express how much your concern for my well-being touches me." I squeezed his hand. "But I don't think—"

"Daniel!"

We both started at the sound of Clara Lewiston's voice. For such a small woman, her voice could be loud and commanding. Standing directly behind her was John McMahon, a scowl darkening his features and his gaze focused on our entwined hands. Not knowing why, I guiltily slipped my hands from Daniel's and stood.

Daniel stood, too, and I could feel the tension in the thick air as he spoke. "Clara, John. This is a surprise. What brings you here?"

Clara's nose twitched, like that of a small rabbit, but her voice was level as she answered her husband. "My father told me you had come to call at Whispering Oaks, and it seems that you have forgotten our dinner plans with the Herndons. John was helping me find where you might have run off to." She sent a reproachful look to Daniel.

The doctor forced a laugh as he approached his wife. "My dear, I haven't forgotten anything, nor have I run off anywhere. I was just following Catherine into the grotto. I've invited her to stay with us."

Clara's pale mouth had formed itself into a perfect O. "I . . . well . . . of course Catherine is welcome at Belle Meade. And I must apologize for not thinking of it first." She smiled at me, and I judged her offer to be sincere.

John had come to stand by me, and I felt his hot gaze. Without acknowledging him, I spoke. "It is very kind of you both, but I must decline. With Marguerite and the other servants, I find myself adequately chaperoned. And I do feel that it's best for Rebecca if I stay here with her."

John placed a hand on my shoulder, my skin heating at his mere touch. "I must agree with Catherine. It is best for Rebecca to stay amongst familiar surroundings and equally important for Catherine to remain close by."

Out of sight of the Lewistons, John's thumb traced circles on my back, caressing the thin fabric of my dress as if it were my bare skin. I couldn't pull away without making it obvious, and I was almost glad of it.

I heard the hint of amusement in his voice as he added, "And I promise, as a gentleman, to behave as one."

Dr. Lewiston flushed. "Really, John—acting as a gentleman has never been your forte. I find I must insist, for the sake of Catherine's reputation, that she return with Clara and me to Belle Meade. And I invite Rebecca, as well, if that is your wish."

John's hand stilled on my shoulder, but he didn't remove it. In a very controlled voice he said, "No. Rebecca stays here and Catherine with her. I will hear no more arguments—the matter is settled."

John placed his hand on my arm to lead me along the path out of the grotto, but I held back. I felt uncomfortable with John's dismissal of their offer and felt I needed to smooth any ruffled feathers. "Why don't you join us for some refreshments? We would very much enjoy your company."

Clara spoke first. "Thank you, Catherine, but we must be getting back. I left in the middle of doing an inventory of my spices and I hate to leave them out from under lock and key for so long. Not to mention that we have dinner plans for later. But thank you very much. I hope to return the invitation as soon as your mourning permits."

I nodded. "Thank you. I shall look forward to it." I found myself frowning, and quickly straightened my features. But I couldn't help wondering why she hadn't sent a servant to fetch Daniel—and why it was so important to remind him of dinner plans now. It was barely past noon. I studied her plain face for a moment and the way it nearly glowed when she looked at her husband, and thought I knew the answer.

As John turned to allow us to pass in front of him, he stopped before the tea rose, its brilliant red an odd splotch of color against the cream-colored bench. He retrieved it and held it up. "Clara, this looks like it came from your renowned rose garden." He sniffed it and smiled, but there was nothing pleasant about the gesture. "Here. Let me return it to its rightful owner." Ignoring Daniel's outstretched hand, John approached Clara and affixed the wilting flower to a button. "I hope, Clara, that you will do us the honor of letting us use some of your beautiful roses for our wedding."

I turned to him with a look of anger, but he ignored me. He seemed intent on watching Dr. Lewiston.

Both of the Lewistons appeared startled, but good breeding quickly changed their expressions to polite interest. Clara's light brown eyes seemed to shrink despite her smile. "Then let me be the first to congratulate you. I'll be happy to have you as our neighbor." She laid her hands on my shoulders and brushed her lips against my cheek.

Dr. Lewiston stepped forward. "Yes, of course. Congratulations are certainly called for. It's just a bit of a shock, especially after . . ." His words fell away, but each of us understood his meaning.

John inclined his head. "I thank you for the congratulations. The wedding will be small, under the circumstances, but you will be receiving an invitation soon."

Without further comment, John placed his hand at my elbow and led me out of the grotto. I asked the Lewistons again if they would stay, but again they declined. I don't know why it was so imperative not to be left alone with John, especially since I had agreed to be his wife. But the feeling persisted.

After the Lewistons left, John turned to me, a knowing look in his eyes. "I'm hoping your eagerness for guests has nothing to do with there being something lacking in my company."

Heat inflamed my cheeks at having been read so accurately. "Not at all. I merely enjoy their company."

He raised an eyebrow but made no further comment. Instead he bowed slightly and said, "Please excuse me. I have business matters to attend to. I look forward to seeing you at dinner." With an amused glint in his eyes, he raised my fingers to his lips. Instead of kissing the top of my hand, he turned it over and let his lips brush the inside of my wrist. The sensations that swirled through my veins at his touch nearly undid me. With a knowing glance, he turned and left. I tried to force myself not to stare after him, but found I could not.

I retired to my room and tried to read, but my thoughts were too easily diverted. I tried to gauge the Lewistons' reaction to John's announcement, and wondered if it was because it was simply too soon after Elizabeth's death. But then there was Daniel's veiled warning to me, and even Judge Patterson's, and it was clear that both men believed there to be something unknown and possibly dangerous at Whispering Oaks. It wasn't clear to me, however, if both warnings had been referring to the same thing.

Absently, I picked Rose's lodestone off of the dressing table and felt its cold smoothness against my palm. I recalled the older woman's words about the two men in my life and of a great betrayal, and wondered anew at her meaning. Had she been referring to Robert? His suicide had been the greatest betrayal I had ever faced, the bullet that had killed him having shattered my own life, leaving me with mere fragments to piece together again. But who was the other man? I was contemplating sharing my life with John, but could she have been speaking of him? Or was she referring to someone else—someone whom I would love and want to share my life with?

But I was afraid my battered heart had no room for such a fickle affection—an emotion that acted like waves on one's life, raising a woman up to the highest frothy crest, and then plummeting her below, creating a frantic struggle for air beneath the surface. I set the lodestone back on my dresser, determined not to let such silliness affect my reasoning.

The window in my room had been opened to let in the late summer air, bringing with it the heavy odor of the river. I watched as the sky took on darker hues, an unseen hand painting strokes of magenta and burnt sienna across the horizon. It reminded me of the sunsets at home, and I surrendered myself to the glory of it. It was time to dress for dinner, but the lovely image of the sunset transfixed me, and I sat in peace for the first time since my arrival. The irony that my first moments of serenity had come only with a memory of home did not evade me.

I sat up suddenly, my ears straining to hear the faint notes of music that crept in through the window. The fine hair at the nape of my neck bristled as I recognized the odd tune and Rebecca's voice. I stood and left my room to find my niece, even though the humming had stopped abruptly.

I stopped in front of Delphine, who was waxing the foyer floor. "Have you seen Rebecca?"

"Yes, ma'am. She be in her room resting afore supper."

I shook my head. "But I just heard her singing and it was

most definitely not coming from her room."

"That's where I put her, Miss Catherine, and she cain't get by me without me seeing her, so she must still be there."

Confused, I stepped past Delphine until I reached the rear door. I found Rebecca on the back steps with Samantha on her lap. She didn't look up as I approached but stared out at the gathering gloom. I sat down next to her and began smoothing her hair with my hand.

"How did you manage to sneak past Delphine?"

I saw her cheek crinkle in a smile but she still didn't look up at me. Night had completely descended, leaving only the moon and the stars in the sky, like a queen with her court. "It's a secret."

"A secret? Does that mean I can't know?"

She looked at me finally, her bright eyes shining like two more stars in the moonlight. "Not yet, Aunt Cat. It's got to be a surprise."

I nodded, not wanting to press her. "It's too dark for you to be outside, Rebecca, and I don't want you to catch a chill. Why don't you come inside now and get dressed for supper?"

She shook her head vehemently, her coiled curls shaking in agreement. "No—not yet. It's too dark in there."

I put my arm around her small shoulders and drew her closer. "But it's darker out here. Inside we have the lamps lit."

I felt her shiver under my hands. "No, Aunt Cat. Inside there's dark places I'm afraid of. There's shadows that live in the corners and I don't want them to get me." Her wide eyes shone as she raised them to mine. "Like they got my mama."

I wanted to refute her words, but I couldn't. I knew the dark shadows she spoke of, had felt them even as a child, and couldn't deny them now as an adult. As much as I wanted to dismiss her fears as a child's fancy, I could not. They were all too real to me. Instead I held her close and patted her head.

She pointed a chubby finger up at the moon, full and round like a ripened peach. "Marguerite says that on nights with a full moon the Indian lady walks with her baby." She tilted her head, as if trying to hear a far-off sound. "If you listen real good you can hear the baby crying. Marguerite says the baby cries because she and her mama were buried under the house and they want to get out."

I raised my ear to the slight breeze, listening intently, and I heard it: a high-pitched cry, shifting in and out at the whim of the wind. I stood and moved down the steps to hear it better. I heard it again and I started, a mother's first reaction to the sound of a crying child. My own child's cries were forever stilled, yet the plaintive cry reached out to me with silent fingers of need.

"Do you hear it, Aunt Cat?"

I nodded and stepped slowly off the bottom stair. Then I remembered the glass bottles and realized where the sound was coming from. I turned to Rebecca. "It's the wind blowing through those old bottles that are hung on the trees. It sounds just like a baby crying."

Her wide-eyed look was one of disbelief, but she didn't say anything. Taking her hand, I said, "Come on. Let's go get dressed."

She placed her hand inside mine and followed. As I guided Rebecca up to her room, I thought of the Indian woman and her child buried under this house, their spirits crying to be free. And I thought of Elizabeth, her spirit just as wistful and strong, and wondered if her time here made her feel as if she had been buried within the four walls of this dark house, desperate to be set free.

The evening meal passed slowly. I felt John's constant gaze upon me and was grateful for Rebecca's presence.

169

The child charmed me and I found myself seeing more in her than just the things that reminded me of Jamie. Her blue eyes would still suddenly catch me off guard at times, causing a cascade of grief that I struggled to keep hidden. But her indomitable spirit and sweet hugs had begun to take the chill out of my cold heart.

When Delphine arrived to take Rebecca to her room, I rose, too, eager to excuse myself.

But John stayed me with his hand. "Please wait. I have something I wish to give to you."

I nodded and allowed myself to be led into his library. He strode over to his desk and, after unlocking the top drawer, took out a rectangular black velvet box. He returned to stand in front of me again, but made no move to either present the box to me or to open it himself.

"I first met your father in New Orleans. It was at my club there, and he had been invited by an associate of mine to discuss business. I found him a very charming man, and was especially enthralled with his stories of beautiful Saint Simons. I think that he loved it almost as much as you do."

He smiled at me gently, as if he knew that he must use great care when speaking of my father and my home. "But I soon realized that what he loved most of all were his two daughters. He spoke of you both, but the one he spoke most about was the daughter who loved openly and freely, was beautiful both inside and out, and whose nature was as wild as the waves she liked to race into with bare feet. She was an artist who painted the natural beauty of her island with a lover's touch." He lowered his eyes, staring at the box. "I think I fell in love with that girl. She seemed so foreign and exotic compared to the prim Bostonian misses my mother had been tossing in my direction since I had grown out of boyhood." His gaze met mine and I caught sight of an emotion I thought I recognized before he hid it again from me.

Holding up the box, he opened the lid. "I had these made for that girl before I had even met her, knowing I wanted her for my wife."

I looked inside and held my breath. The double-strand necklace was composed of the most perfectly formed pearls I had ever seen, faultless in their round, creamy beauty. They circled the strand, each in graduating size before coming to an end in a large, tear-shaped ruby. I didn't move, but continued to stare at the necklace.

He continued, "I pictured these on her flawless skin and against her long black hair." He reached behind me and began to loosen the pins in my hair. I heard them fall one by one to the floor behind me, each one a fallen drop of my resistance.

"Did Elizabeth ever wear it?" I held my breath, awaiting his answer.

His eyes darkened. "No. I never gave them to her."

I waited for him to continue, my lungs filling with air and a distant hope.

"Your father never told me how young you were. It wasn't until my visit when I saw you that I realized. But it was too late, then. I had come for a wife, and I wasn't a man used to disappointment. And Elizabeth . . ." Slowly he raised the pearls from their black box. "Elizabeth used all her charms on me, making me believe that she and you shared more than just appearance."

I didn't move as he placed the pearls around my throat, leaning over me to clasp the necklace in back. He lifted my unbound hair and placed it about my shoulders, then studied me closely, his warm breath brushing my neck. "Yes," he whispered. "This is how I pictured you."

I stepped back, my defenses rallying. "I'm no silly virgin to be so easily seduced."

He moved toward me and bent his head near my ear. "Neither was Elizabeth."

I looked up at him in shock. "You lie!"

"I am no liar, madam." He took a deep breath, his gaze locked with mine. "And that's the last I shall speak of it." He moved his lips down to my throat, almost making me forget the implications of his words.

"Why didn't you press for an annulment?" I had to force the words out, my lungs gasping for air.

"Because I fancied myself in love with her." He lifted his face to look into mine, his emotions completely hidden from me. "But for you and I, Catherine, our motives for marrying are much more tangible, aren't they?"

My hope fell with the hairpins at my feet. I tried to push away, but he wouldn't allow me to.

"My dear Catherine. We've made our decision; now let's make the best of it."

He lowered his mouth to mine and I discovered I had no more will to fight him. I eagerly opened my lips to his, letting him devour me with a passion that seemed to fill us both. His hands swept down the bodice of my dress, pulling me closer in an intimate embrace. His hands teased my hips, sliding upward to my waist. I felt as if I should stop him, but my traitorous arms wrapped themselves around his neck instead, pulling him even closer as I waited for his hands upon my breasts.

Suddenly he stopped, and he lifted his face to give me a mocking look. "Madam. It would seem that you are as impatient for our wedding as I."

Ashamed to have to admit the feelings that he stirred in me, I said nothing.

Abruptly he stepped back, only a sheen of perspiration on his forehead betraying his true emotions. "I won't be bothering you any more this evening. You are free to retire."

He bowed, then left the room, but not before I caught sight of a satisfied smile on his face. I wasn't sure what his game was, but I was quite certain I did not like being a part of it. Perhaps he was testing me—to see how much alike I was to Elizabeth. I wondered at his abrupt dismissal of me, and if my physical response to him had been an affirmation or a warning.

My hands reached up to the beads on my neck, their touch like cool fingers of warning. Slowly I undid the clasp, then dropped the pearls into their coffinlike box, leaving them on his desk to find in the morning. Turning down the lamp, I climbed the stairs to my room, ignoring the deepening shadows that seemed to reach out to me from the darkened corners of the house.

Chapter Fourteen

I awoke the following morning feeling as if I hadn't slept at all. I could tell from the brilliant white-yellow glow of the sun peering in between the wooden slats that it was late morning. Slowly I sat up. It was then that I noticed the black box on my night table.

Reaching over, I picked it up and flicked open the lid. Inside lay the pearl necklace, and I didn't doubt for one moment how it had come to be in my bedroom. I wondered how long he had stayed, watching me sleep, if he had stayed at all. But I knew why he had felt compelled to leave the box instead of waiting until morning. He wasn't a man accustomed to having his wants and desires curtailed in any way. If he wanted me to have the necklace, then have it I would.

I rang for Marguerite to help me dress. While outwardly she continued with the appearance of the dutiful servant, I watched her closely. According to Clara Lewiston, Marguerite had been Elizabeth's confidante, and I wondered how much Marguerite knew of Elizabeth's secret life and of her death. I felt I was a mouse, and Marguerite a cat—toying with me while I tried to pry loose a morsel of truth.

"Marguerite, how well did you know my sister?" I sat at the dresser, waiting for her to fix my hair, and watched her in the mirror.

She smiled faintly. "I was her maid. I suppose I knew her no more and no less than other maids know their mistresses."

"Did she . . . did she ever tell you anything personal—something only you were privy to?"

She lifted my hair off my shoulders, smoothing it down my back with her hand. "She told me lots of personal things."

I waited for her to continue, but when it was apparent that she would not, I said, "Did she ever tell you anything that might have been some clue as to why she would want her life to end?"

Her eyes glittered in the mirror with an indecipherable emotion. I turned to look at her. "Miss Elizabeth was not a happy woman, no matter what she had. There wasn't anything that could make her happy. She was like a child crying for the moon, and even if Mr. John had roped it and brought it down for her, Miss Elizabeth would have quickly tired of it." She pulled the brush through my hair in a long, slow stroke. "And she didn't care whose life she made miserable while she was searching for her happiness."

"Do you mean John? Was their life together really that unbearable?"

She shrugged. "There's some that bears it better than others and some who just look until they find a way out."

She fixed my hair in silence, allowing me to mull over our conversation and John's words of the previous evening. If it were true that Elizabeth had not been a virgin on her wedding night, then Elizabeth had been set in her ways long before she married John. I felt no little relief at the thought. I didn't want to think that my soon-to-be husband had had anything to do with Elizabeth's restlessness. Then again, since she and I had been raised in the same home, would I, too, be susceptible? Or were Elizabeth's demons hers and hers alone?

Due to the lateness of the hour, I ate breakfast alone. The quiet darkness of the house smothered me, and I made a mental note to do something to brighten the interior soon. I listened for Rebecca's voice, but only the brooding silence of the house answered.

After eating, I found Rebecca and took her for a jaunt along the levee in her mother's small buggy. I enjoyed listening to her laugh and hearing her stories of her life on the plantation. It didn't escape my notice that she never mentioned her mother at all.

When we were through, I placed her in Delphine's care while I retired to John's study to attend to some personal correspondence. Since my arrival at Whispering Oaks I hadn't yet written to my friends and neighbors on Saint Simons. I had been putting off telling them that I would not be returning, but the time had come. John had given me a wedding date two weeks hence, and I needed to adjust myself to my new situation. Writing our names together with a wedding date in a letter seemed to be a prudent way to go about it.

I had been writing for more than an hour when I heard the front door open. Heavy footsteps approached the library, and I chastised myself for the excitement I felt when I recognized who it was.

John seemed surprised to see me at this desk, but his surprise was quickly replaced by a smile. He clutched a medium-sized traveling trunk he held in his arms.

"I'm afraid I've been caught."

"Caught?" I raised an eyebrow.

He stepped forward and placed the trunk on the floor by the desk. "Yes. I drove into town to pick up your wedding present. I asked for these from an artist friend in New Orleans shortly after your arrival here. And now I have a reason to give them to you."

I stared at the trunk, unsure of my response. "I thought the necklace was my wedding gift."

He sent me a knowing look, as if realizing we were both thinking of the box sitting on my night table. "No—seeing you wear it is your gift to me. This is my gift to you."

I stood and walked around to his side of the desk, trying to give all my attention to the trunk. But it was hopeless. Whenever he was near me, I could scarcely remember to breathe, much less take note of anything else.

"Here—you'll need to do this first."

He reached down and flicked one of the latches with his fingers.

"Oh, yes. Of course." My fingers fumbled as I tried to unlatch the two metal loops on the front of the trunk. I managed the first, but I couldn't seem to get my fingers to do the second.

John seemed amused, as if he knew the source of my discomfiture. He stooped to help me. "Why don't I do this for you?"

With ease, he flicked open the latch and lifted the lid. Stepping back, he indicated the open trunk. "Shortly after you arrived here, you mentioned that the Union soldiers had destroyed all your canvases and paints. And that there was nothing left for you to paint. I hope that my gift will soften your heart for at least one Yankee."

Cautiously I peered inside. When I recognized what it was, my first instinct was to cry. Cradled inside wadded mounds of newspaper lay an artist's palette and an array of small glass jars filled with different-colored paint. Rolled and fitted neatly in the corners of the trunk were canvases of various sizes.

John stood close to me, studying my face as if to gauge my reaction. When I didn't speak, he said, "I had some of the paint pigments already mixed for you—and I hope I chose the colors you would have selected. I tried to re-create the colors of your home—of the ocean and sand and marsh."

I waited for a moment, trying to find my voice. "This . . . this is extraordinary." I found it hard to find the appropriate words.

"I want you to be happy here."

I looked in his eyes and wondered if he was thinking of his first wife and her desperate unhappiness. I felt hurt that he would again confuse me with my sister. I gently closed the lid of the box, not wanting him to see the longing in my eyes as I contemplated painting again. "I am not Eliz-abeth, John. You don't need to bribe me to keep me here."

He stiffened, and the hope I had seen in his eyes was quickly hidden by his usual sardonic smile. He took a step away, as if to distance himself from me. "My dear, I thought the offer of my bed was enough of a bribe to get you to stay. This gift is merely gravy."

I stepped back, the gift nearly ruined for me. He had cut me deeply and I didn't want him to see it. I moved to walk past him, but he grabbed my arm.

"I'm sorry, Catherine. I shouldn't have said that."

I faced him, trying to keep my fury under the surface. "I am not my sister and I do not expect you to treat me as if I were. Whatever was between you two, it is past. And if you expect a marriage between us, then you had best re-member that."

He pulled me closer to him, and my desire for him nearly consumed me. He angered me, yet still I could not resist him. "Forgive me," he said, and before I could con-template what he was asking forgiveness for, he covered my lips with his, obliterating all thought.

The world seemed to spiral out of control for a moment as my hands grabbed his hair and pulled him closer. He pressed me backward against the desk, our bodies touch-ing intimately. With visible control, he pulled himself back, disentangling my arms from around his neck. His eyes burned as he watched me try to find my breath. "I could never mistake you for Elizabeth. Only a fool would do that."

Embarrassed again by my easy acquiescence to his touch, I backed away from him and then fled up to my room. I paced for a few moments before my gaze caught sight of a piece of Elizabeth's riding habit stuck in the doors of the armoire. Yanking off my clothes, I pulled on the habit, struggling in my haste with the row of tiny buttons up the back. I desperately needed to burn off the energy that John's presence created in me. Perhaps then I could be calm and impartial when next he ap-proached me.

As I pinned the riding hat to my hair, I recalled the glim-mer of hope in John's eyes when he had given me the paints. John McMahon was a difficult man to fathom, but the very gesture of the gift told me that perhaps within the dark depths of his soul lay a kind and tender heart—a side to him that, if it existed at all, he was not at all comfortable letting others see.

Not sure why I did it, I slipped the lodestone into my pocket before walking quickly to the stables. I spotted Mr. O'Rourke and greeted him warmly. He still treated me with aloofness, due to the accident on the flooded road, no doubt, which was why I always gave him my biggest smile. I had the strong feeling that I would need as many friends as I could find if I were to make a home for myself at Whispering Oaks.

He saddled Jezebel for me and allowed me to go by myself only after I solemnly promised to stay on the levee road and not venture anywhere else. I gave Mr. O'Rourke a bright smile; then Jezebel and I took off at a brisk walk.

I kept a sedate pace as we passed through the lane of weeping oaks, then gave Jezebel her head as we raced toward the levee. I loved the feel of the wind kissing my face and tugging at my hair. I was a little girl again, with no concerns or worries, my future laid out ahead of me as sparkling as the sun-dappled river.

Slowing my mount, I allowed her to trot along the levee road as I stared into the murky depths of the Mississippi. How tranquil the water seemed, yet I knew of the strong undercurrents that could sweep one under without warning. Unlike my ocean, which showed his wrath with froth-tipped waves, the river was an insidious thing; so unassuming on the surface, yet turbulent and deadly underneath.

As I turned my horse to head back, I caught sight of another rider approaching me. The rakish angle of his hat and foppish dress gave away his identity before I even recognized the face of Philip Herndon.

His face seemed unusually pale as he drew alongside me, and for a moment he didn't speak. Finally, as if remembering his manners, he doffed his hat and bowed low. "My dear Cat, forgive my manners. I was so struck by your beauty that I was paralyzed for a few moments."

The stunned expression on his face made me almost believe his words until I recalled that I wore Elizabeth's riding habit. From a distance, I must have resembled her greatly.

"Hello, Philip. This is an unexpected pleasure."

He nodded, his smile wary. "Are you alone?"

"Yes, I am. But only because I promised not to get into trouble." I smiled, but it was not returned.

He leaned close to me. "Forgive the impudence, but I'm glad to find you alone. I need to speak with you and I would not be able to speak candidly if you had company." It was clear from his implication to whom "company" referred.

Jezebel stepped forward to nuzzle Philip's mount as if they were old friends. He continued. "I heard from the Lewistons that there is to be a wedding soon at Whispering Oaks."

I lifted my chin. "Yes, there is. John and I are to be married."

His face darkened. "How could you, Cat? Especially after what he did to Elizabeth!"

"Whatever happened to Elizabeth, Philip, was her own doing. I do not hold him responsible."

He scoffed, looking up to the sky momentarily. "Not responsible? But she's dead! Can you honestly tell me that you don't believe he had anything to do with it?"

"Yes, I can." I realized with a start that I was telling the truth. Despite all the unknowns, I had believed John when he claimed innocence in Elizabeth's death.

Philip grabbed Jezebel's bridle and leaned close to me. "Don't believe him. He's a dangerous man, Cat. And a Yankee. He's not to be trusted."

Growing impatient, I pulled away. "It is none of your concern, Philip, and I would appreciate it if you wouldn't be intent on spreading unfounded rumors. I have Rebecca to think of."

His eyes softened. "Yes—Elizabeth's child. Thank God you are here to see to her upbringing." Somber again, he said, "If you are intent on marrying him, just remember that I am only a short ride from you. Do not hesitate to call on me if you should need anything. Anything."

I wondered at his words as he bowed again and replaced his hat. "It's best that I leave now. Good day, Cat." To my surprise, he reached for my hand and held it to his mouth, his lips lingering longer than necessary. Jezebel stepped back, and I pulled away. His eyes darkened as he regarded me, but there was something in them that told me he wasn't seeing me but some distant vision from his memory. I wondered if it had anything to do with Elizabeth. He looked past my shoulder, and then, without another word, he bowed again, and took off at a quick pace.

In a contemplative mood, I stared after him until he was out of sight, oblivious to the pounding of hooves approaching me from the rear. At the last moment, I turned to see John approaching, his face a mask of fury. He drew up his horse quickly, making it rear.

"So we are not yet married and you are already having assignations. If you are to meet with men other than your husband, at least have the decency to choose a worthier adversary. That fop isn't even worth the energy of pulling out my pistol."

I was dumbfounded for a minute as I contemplated his implication. In an unaccustomed rage born of weariness and anxiety over the recent and dramatic turns in my life, I raised my hand to strike out at him. He leaned back, avoiding the blow, and I lost my balance, tumbling over the neck of my horse and down the embankment toward the swirling river below.

An abject terror of touching the water consumed me, and I acted as a wild woman, scraping and clawing at the grassy mud, trying to find something on which to grab hold. My struggles were rewarded when I managed to grasp a withered root, its frazzled ends reaching out from the dark mud like a groping hand. With a desperate strength, I hung on with all my might.

"Catherine!"

It was then that I remembered I was not alone, and I clung to John's voice with hope. The relief nearly weakened me, but I dared not let go.

"Hold on—I think I can reach you and pull you up. Just don't let go." I saw his gaze travel to the slurp and splash of the river below me. He disappeared for a moment and then returned.

"I've tied myself to my horse so there's no danger of my falling in and taking you with me." He lay on his stomach and inched himself slightly over the precipice, his hands reaching toward me, his fingertips nearly touching mine.

"Give me one of your hands."

I hesitated, thinking back on Philip's words. Could I trust this man?

"Cat—give me your hand."

His dark eyes bored into mine. With a deep breath, I let go with my right hand and placed it in John's strong palm. His fingers closed about mine in a firm grip and I had no more doubt. Without waiting for him to ask, I let go with my other hand and placed it in his other palm.

His face contorted with strain and concentration as he began to pull me up. I scrambled with my feet to find footholds, using them for leverage as John slid back toward his horse. Slowly but surely I inched my way up to the top, and when we were both safe, we lay on our backs panting.

John sat up and reached for me, pulling me into his lap. I didn't resist and allowed him to cradle me in his arms, much the same way I had seem him holding Rebecca, and I felt him tremble. I was warm and safe in his care, and my doubts about marrying him began to fade. "You called me Cat," I said foolishly. Only my family and those who had known me since childhood called me by that name, and I found his use of it oddly comforting and familiar.

"Yes. I did."

I felt his lips on my hair as we huddled together, his arms tight around me.

We rode back together on his horse, leading Jezebel, as John would not be separated from me. When we arrived, Mr. O'Rourke took the horses, and John insisted on carrying me up to my bedroom.

Despite my assertions that I was quite all right, I was still surprised that John did not suggest we call for Dr. Lewiston. As he settled me on the bed, he said, "There is no need to send for Daniel. I am quite capable of taking care of you, and he would only look upon your accident as another reason for you to stay at Belle Meade." He tried to force a grin but failed. "It wouldn't do to have the neighbors thinking that you might be in some sort of danger from me."

I found his words odd, especially after having spoken with Philip and Judge Patterson. But John had possibly saved my life, and I now knew their concerns to be unfounded.

Marguerite helped me undress and settled me into bed with an herbal tea to help me sleep. I felt like a child, but acquiesced, realizing that the afternoon had taken a toll on my nerves. The soothing brew settled in my brain like a warm blanket, and I was soon fast asleep.

It was near dark when I awoke and I knew instinctively that I was not alone. John sat on the edge of my bed, watching me. His expression was grim, his face pale.

"I came close to losing you today, and know I am partially to blame." He took a deep breath, and it almost sounded like a sigh. "I wanted to offer you an apology."

I sat up, pulling the blankets along with me to cover my nightgown. I was all too aware that I was barely dressed and alone in my bedroom with this disturbing man. "I met with Philip today simply by accident. It was not planned." I took a deep breath. "John, I am learning to trust you, and you should be doing the same toward me. I don't know if I can marry you if you're going to interpret every innocent action or remark as something suspect. A marriage without trust is like a prison for the soul."

My heart clenched as I recalled the painful weeks following Robert's return from the war when he had learned that our Jamie had drowned. Robert had gone to his grave believing that the woman to whom he had entrusted the care of his only son had betrayed him. And his harsh words had had me almost believing him. I met John's troubled gaze. "I would rather return to my destitution on Saint Simons than to live in such a prison again."

He took my hand and held it to his lips. My pulse leaped at his gesture, my breath quickening. "There are reasons for my behavior, some of which you understand and some of which I hope you never try to fathom. But I swear to you that I will do my best to be more trusting." His dark eyes bored into mine. "And you must do the same. I am not the evil man that some are eager to make me appear." His thumb stroked the top of my hand and I wondered if he could hear the erratic beating of my heart. "I can be quite gentle, if given the chance."

Reluctantly I pulled my hand away. "Don't try to seduce me with your words. I will pack my bags and return to Saint Simons tomorrow if you have no intention of building trust into our marriage."

"Then I give you my word."

I bowed my head so he could not see the hope I knew must be shimmering in my eyes. "Then I will marry you as we planned."

He took my hand again and squeezed it. Bending close to me, he kissed me chastely on the cheek. My skin burned where his lips had been and I looked up as he stood. "I'll have a tray sent up for you. I think you should remain in bed until morning."

I nodded. "Thank you."

He raised an eyebrow.

"For saving my life."

"Then I must thank you for the same reason. Sometimes I think that you may have saved mine as well."

With a brief bow, he turned on his heel and left. My hand went to my night table, where I had placed the lodestone when getting undressed. I rubbed its cool, smooth hardness as I contemplated his words until Marguerite arrived with my tray.

Halfway through my meal, I looked up to see the door of my room slowly being pushed open.

"Hello?" I called.

I saw Samantha's head first, shortly followed by Rebecca's, her face covered by her doll. Without answering or waiting to be invited in, Rebecca climbed up on the footstool by the side of my bed and plopped herself down at its foot, Samantha in her lap.

I stopped chewing, noticing the doll's face. It was completely covered in dirt; the yellow yarn of her hair had fared no better. Rebecca's hand rested in Samantha's lap, her nails caked with dark earth. When the child peeked around her doll's head, it was hard to tell the two apart, so filthy were the usually rosy cheeks.

"Rebecca—what has happened to you?"

She giggled, that high, appealing child sound that I had come to love. I tried to look stern and admonishing but it was so difficult when faced with so much guileless charm. I pressed my napkin to my mouth to hide my smile.

She pretended to pout. "Samantha's all dirty. She made me get dirty, too."

I nodded solemnly. "I see. And how did she make you get dirty?"

Rebecca pursed her lips into a perfect rosebud shape

and placed her little finger against them. "Sshh. It's a secret."

I tilted my head. "I promise not to tell."

She shrugged, her gaze wandering around the room, apparently losing interest in the direction of our conversation.

I continued. "Well, whether or not you tell me your secret, you shouldn't be getting yourself and Samantha so dirty. Wasn't Delphine watching you?"

She shook her head, her blond curls bouncing, a mischievous smile on her lips. "I ran away from her when she wasn't looking."

I put down my fork, feeling anxious. I remembered the cottonmouth snake and knew that dangers lurked everywhere for small children. Even under the serene waters of the ocean—or a pond. "Promise me, Rebecca, that you will never do that again. I don't care that you're all dirty—but I do care if you get hurt. That's why you must never run off by yourself. Do you understand?"

She looked at me as if she were about to cry, and I realized that my tone had taken on a sense of urgency. I reached out and took her hand. "I care about you, Rebecca, and I don't want anything to happen to you. Can you understand that? And can you promise me that you won't run off again?"

With a small sniff, she nodded. I patted her hand, noticing again the dirt-encrusted nails. Gently I asked, "Are you sure you won't tell me where you and Samantha have been?"

She looked up at me with those clear blue eyes, and my heart skipped a beat. I fleetingly wondered if I'd ever be able to look at this child and not see the one I had lost. "Somebody's buried under the orange trees, and me and Samantha was trying to dig up the body."

Something hit the floor, and it took me a moment to

realize that it was the lodestone that had slipped from my hand onto the wood floor and now lay cold and still. I thought I saw a movement by the door and imagined the sound of stealthy footsteps walking down the passageway outside. I hastily moved aside the tray and slid from the bed. When I stepped outside my bedroom door, all was still and quiet in the darkening house.

I walked down the passageway, not caring who might see me in my nightdress. I continued down the corridor toward John's room, but saw no one. I returned and peered down the hallway toward the attic door, but nothing stirred.

I returned to my room to find Rebecca gone. I had not heard her leave, nor had she passed me on the way to her room. When I bent to look for the child under my bed, I noticed that the lodestone was missing from my floor. Looking up, I spotted it on my night table like a diminutive statue full of secrets and hidden meaning, surrounded with a sprinkling of dirt.

Chapter Fifteen

I had no time to pursue the absurdities of Rebecca's claims. The preparations for the wedding consumed my time and energy. To assuage my curiosity, I would soon have to take her with me to investigate her mysterious place in the orange grove. Then perhaps I could put it out of my mind. But for now, the child's secretive smile and earnest words ensured that it was never far from my thoughts.

John's work on the plantation and at the sugar mill kept him out of the house from sunrise to sunset. But I always knew when he was near, as if something about him had heightened all my senses, creating an awareness of his presence.

Despite his long absences during the day, he would join us for supper in the evenings. I enjoyed his company, his intelligent conversation, and even his smoldering looks. But I was also glad of Rebecca's presence. The days in which I could make the excuse to retire to the privacy of my own room alone were dwindling, and I mourned the passing of each one. I had been my own woman for a long time, and the thought of answering to a man again was not appealing. Especially this man, whose mere touch could make me forget all reason and agree to anything he wished. I hated myself for this one weakness, while at the same time I enjoyed the tiny flashes of heat he created inside me every time our eyes met.

Our relationship seemed to have progressed since my accident at the levee. We no longer spoke of Elizabeth, and he seemed to have stopped making comparisons. It was as if Elizabeth were truly gone and buried, leaving us alone to start a new life together. I had no illusions as to our marriage. It was not a love match, but perhaps, in time, the bond between us could grow into something even stronger than that elusive emotion. If not, I would at least have the comfort of food and shelter, and old memories. My bargain with John still made me feel at times like a compromised woman, but I had done what I did in order to survive. I had not made it through the war and my grief to die of starvation.

My one consolation was that I would have Rebecca—and any other children I might bear through our union. The thought always made me flush like a virginal bride. But I was hardly that, and chastised myself for my foolish notions and the weak knees that appeared every time he entered the room.

We were married on the last Friday in September. In addition to the new clothes that John had ordered for me shortly after my arrival at Whispering Oaks, I had had several new dresses made, including a wedding gown of dove gray silk as I could not imagine wearing either one of my own or one of Elizabeth's. The dresses John had ordered for me were brightly colored reds, blues, and yellows, making a travesty of my mourning. I had thanked him, then put them away in an armoire in one of the guest rooms.

At the dressmaker's, I had felt like a child in a candy store, choosing between the multihued bolts of cloth. Still clinging to my mourning, I picked out only muted colors of gray and brown, but when I looked at my reflection I felt almost beautiful.

The clouds dripped halfheartedly on the small wedding party, anointing our hair with tiny kisses of rain. I stood on the church steps and smiled at my groom, intent on casting off any dark thoughts brought about by the weather. Marguerite, pausing earlier while helping me dress, had clucked her tongue as she looked out the window of my bedroom. "It's a bad sign for it to rain on your wedding day."

I had shrugged, determined not to let her words sour my wedding, but a little shiver of apprehension crept down my spine, settling in my stomach. I had stared at the reflection of the pearl necklace about my neck, and couldn't help remembering Elizabeth's wedding day, when the clouds had blackened, unleashing a torrent of rain that had saturated the earth and turned the roads into muddy creeks.

Whenever I smell the odor of wet leaves and moist earth, I remember the day when I stood at the altar of Grace Episcopal Church in Saint Francisville next to John and exchanged vows intended to last until death did us part. His kiss burned my lips, as if branding me his.

We were to honeymoon in New Orleans, and after extracting promises from Delphine and Mary not to let Rebecca out of their sight, we set off in a closed carriage driven by Mr. O'Rourke.

John sat next to me and took my hand. Slowly he drew off my glove and moved my fingers to his lips. "So. It is done."

191

I looked into those dark, unfathomable eyes, and wondered what he meant. "I would not say it is done, but rather that this is the beginning."

He gripped my hand tightly. "But all endings are the beginnings of something new."

I nodded, then leaned against the back of the seat, suddenly tired. He moved my head to his shoulder, and I must have slept, for when I awoke we were on the outskirts of the city.

I had always loved New Orleans, with its brash mixture of French and American customs and the grand mansions of the Garden District and Vieux Carré. The intricate iron balconies and balustrades delighted me with their foreign appeal, and I had thought as a child that they always made the buildings appear gift wrapped.

We checked into a small hotel on Royal Street, the accommodations intimate yet exquisitely furnished. Our suite consisted of two rooms, a sitting room and a bedroom, and I paused with trepidation on the threshold of the room with the large four-poster bed with heavy silk drapes.

After the porter had delivered our bags, John came to stand behind me and kissed me on the neck. "All in good time, my dear," he said. "But alas, I have reservations at Antoine's for a late supper. Shall I help you dress?" He removed my traveling cloak while I tried to breathe calmly.

All of my senses seemed sharpened somehow; every color, every sound, every touch seemed brighter, louder, or more sensitive. "No." My voice shook. "I would like a maid sent up, please. I need help unpacking and selecting a gown."

He nodded, his eyes once again hiding his thoughts from me. I turned away, thankful for his compliance. I needed time to fortify my mind before he touched me and all rational thought fled.

At Antoine's we sat in the glow of the candlelight eating and drinking and talked intimately. I don't recall what was said, or what we ate, but I do remember how I felt. The way he looked at me and the way he held my hand made me feel more whole than I had since I had lost my son. The grieving mother and destitute widow was not the woman in the dark amber silk gown, with her hair piled high on her head and pearls glowing at her throat. This woman was new to me; she was a woman desired by the man across the snowy white table linens, a woman equally capable of the same desires.

The ride back to the hotel was quiet, but the darkness inside the coach was filled with a heady anticipation that was thick enough to fill my lungs. John lifted me out of the carriage in front of our hotel, his touch solicitous and chaste, but my response was the same as if he had touched my naked flesh.

He opened the door to our room and allowed me to enter first. Before I could turn around, his hands were on me, the pins from my hair pulled out and scattered on the plush rug at our feet. With quick hands he expertly undid the myriad buttons of my gown, leaving it in a pool of silk at my feet.

His lips ravaged mine as his hands efficiently disrobed me, his fingers adept at every nuance of a woman's clothing. I stood trembling, wearing only my chemise, as he knelt in front of me to remove my stockings. Strong fingers slid up my nearly bare legs, coming to rest on my exposed thighs. I felt the heat jump from his hands and travel in a ball of flame to the core of my being. We said nothing, but each of us knew the steps to this primal dance and no words were needed. Slowly he slid the stockings down one leg, then the other, his eyes never leaving my face. Without letting go of me, he placed his hands on the backs of my thighs and drew me forward, pressing his face between my legs.

I wanted to push away at this intimate touch, but my rebellious body was intent on responding, rubbing myself against him, feeling his lips through the thin muslin of my chemise. A moan burst forth from my throat, like the steam from a long-simmering pot: rich and potent and full of promises yet unfulfilled.

He stood, bringing the hem of my chemise with him, carefully lifting it over my head. He reached his hand out to my neck and I realized that I still wore the pearls. "Yes," he whispered. "This is how I saw you."

He bent his head toward me, his lips brushing my neck, and then moving lower. I clung to him as his mouth covered my breast, swirls of light exploding beneath my clenched eyelids. I had never felt this wanting before, this need for a man. It frightened me, yet it exhilarated me, too, awakening the woman in me that had lain dormant for so long. I shed the skin of the grieving widow and became John McMahon's wife: cherished and desired, a woman of passion.

John lifted me and carried me to the bed, laying me down on the turned-back covers. He began to undress and I sat up to watch him, a craving rising within me such as I had never known. The lamps burned low, casting deep shadows on the walls. But instead of being foreboding, they warmed the room, creating the impression that we were in a cocoon. My bare feet sank deeply into the sheets on the bed and I arched my spine in a luxurious stretch, feeling his eyes upon me.

I lay back, my arms reaching for him, and he came to me, pressing his warm flesh against mine. There was no tenderness between us in our hunger. It was as if we knew we would have a lifetime for discovery, but this first time would be to claim each other.

My response to him was frightening, and I found myself clawing at his broad shoulders and pushing him into me as a drowning woman would search for air. The ball of flame that had been hovering inside of me whirled and expanded, finally exploding into a fissure of light and heat I had never experienced before. John shuddered as he finally stilled on top of me, our bodies coated in a fine sheen of sweat.

He rolled to my side, but held me close. His eyes shone in the light of the street lamp outside the window, and the look in them made me catch my breath. He had claimed my body, and now he seemed intent on claiming my very soul. Had he ever looked at Elizabeth in the same way? And was that what had driven her away?

He must have felt my slight withdrawal, for he reached for me, pulling me on top of him. "I knew it would be this way between us."

I turned my face away, my cheek against his bare chest, embarrassment at my wanton behavior flooding over me.

Lifting my chin, he raised my face to his. "Don't be ashamed, Cat. This is the way it's supposed to be between man and wife. What has gone before no longer matters. It's just you and me now."

His hands slid down my bare body, coming to rest on the dip of my waist. Raising his head, he ran his tongue along the sensitive skin of my neck, making me shudder. I felt him harden beneath me and I arched my back, my breasts grazing his chest. I heard his quick intake of breath as my gaze sought his.

"I don't . . . I don't want this to be all there is between you and me." My skin shivered as his hands caressed my bare back while his eyes continued to glitter in the darkness.

195

His hands moved behind my neck, brushing the pearls and lifting my hair, bringing my face closer to his. "My dear, there was never any question of that." He pressed his lips against mine, and I soon forgot all of my questions and concerns, lost as I was in the riptide of his lovemaking. It didn't matter whether I was drowning or swimming, and as the hours of our first night together ticked on, I simply did not care.

Ours was an idyllic honeymoon. We ate in wonderful restaurants, strolled along the river, and spent hours in the shops purchasing things for the house and gifts for Rebecca. I still had the suspicion that there were matters John preferred to keep hidden from me, but in our time spent together I learned that he was capable of great thought and feeling. He made me laugh again, a sound that had become foreign to my ears. For that, I was grateful.

He expressed concern over my thinness and questioned me closely about the condition of my home in Saint Simons. He seemed to be storing away the information for future use, but when questioned about it, he only smiled and diverted my attention to a street vendor selling pralines.

I no longer feared the night, but instead looked forward to sunset with breathless anticipation. John had awakened a passion in me I had not known existed, but which he insisted he had always known dwelled within. We would make love through the long hours of the night, then sleep in each other's arms until late morning. The hotel maids seemed to know not to disturb us, and let us sleep. It was terribly decadent, but John's touch consumed me, erasing all other concerns.

It was inevitable that I should compare John's lovemaking to Robert's. I had never felt anything akin to passion with Robert. He would crawl into bed, then roll on top of me without even removing my nightdress. Then the grunts and moans would start as he moved between my legs while I clenched my teeth, waiting for him to finish. When it was over, he would roll off, depleted. I, too, would be depleted, but for a far different reason. The thought of another child had made it bearable, but even that hope had died with Robert's infrequent furloughs.

Throughout my days and nights with John on our honeymoon, I would think back to that girl I had once been: Robert's wife and Jamie's mother. When I looked at myself in the mirror, it seemed she was no longer there. I still bore grief for my son, but I could now regard Robert's absence in my life as a gift of freedom, and felt very little remorse at the thought.

On our last night in New Orleans we dined at the St. Charles and we were both surprised when we looked up during the main course and saw Philip Herndon approaching.

John didn't stand to greet his neighbor, but placed his fork deliberately on the white tablecloth with a snap.

Philip bowed to me, then turned to John. "Allow me to congratulate you both on your recent nuptials. I've been in town for a while and I missed the big celebration."

I thanked him while John merely stared at him with barely concealed dislike.

Philip continued. "I can only hope that this marriage has a much happier ending than your last, John. I have a great fondness for Cat, and I'd hate to have her dead, too."

John stood suddenly, his chair wobbling but, blessedly, not falling over. Heads had already begun to turn. "I demand an apology for that remark, Herndon."

Philip stared at him insolently. "So you can call me out and kill me, too? Everyone knows you're a crack shot, John. But what's one more murder on your hands?"

I knew I had to intervene before matters disintegrated further. Standing, I put myself between them. "Please," I whispered urgently to both men. "Don't cause a scene. Surely this matter can be settled when you've both had a chance to cool off."

John looked at me and must have read the pleading in my eyes, for he stepped back. "My wife has uncommon good sense. But I don't wish to speak with you later—or ever. I have no use for irrational men."

I clasped John's arm, hoping to create the impression of a united front. We were husband and wife, and I wanted Philip to understand that attacking John would be akin to attacking me.

Philip leaned close so that only John and I could hear. "I will not forget what you have done. You have taken away the most precious thing in my life, and I will see that you, too, shall lose that which you hold in the highest regard."

With a brief glance at me, he turned and left, oblivious to the heads turning to follow his departure.

Shaking, John sat down. The meal was ruined for both of us and we soon left the restaurant, not even waiting to finish the last course.

His lovemaking that night was fierce; his touch was tender yet his passions boiled under the surface. When I touched him, he was like a man with fever, and I found myself arching toward him, trying to match his heated ardor. Afterward, he cradled me in his arms, making me feel more cherished than I had since I was a small child. I laid my head on his shoulder and slept.

Our honeymoon ended after only a week. John promised me an extended European honeymoon the following year, but for now he was needed at the plantation and mill, and he didn't want to leave Rebecca so soon after her mother's death.

I didn't argue, as I was also anxious to return to Rebecca. I only wished that we would be returning to Saint Simons instead of Whispering Oaks. When I thought of my new home it was always with apprehension. Its dark shadows, unseen footsteps, and haunted past seemed to follow me like a ghost—a ghost that refused to be exorcised.

We were both subdued on our return journey, John's brow furrowed with dark thoughts that he did not share with me, and me with my own. I thought back on Philip's words and wondered at his threats. He obviously still believed that John had something to do with Elizabeth's death. I did trust in John's innocence. He had given me his word. Then why the small shadow of doubt that threatened to obscure my new happiness?

I looked up suddenly to find John watching me closely. I colored, imagining that he could read my mind, and looked away. Whether or not he guessed my thoughts he didn't say. We had promised not to speak of Elizabeth's death again, for it was a topic we both preferred to avoid. My reasons were obvious—I simply didn't wish to be reminded of the person my sister had become. But John's reasons went unexplained to me.

Rebecca ran out to greet us, enthusiastically hugging us each in turn. She greedily unwrapped the porcelain doll with yellow hair and blue eyes, then put it aside with the fickle nature of small children when she saw the sweets we had brought. I had deliberately avoided buying her licorice, knowing how she disliked it, and enjoyed her cries of pleasure when she spotted the peppermint sticks.

After greeting his daughter, John went immediately to the sugar mill, leaving me alone with Rebecca. While my bags were brought up and Marguerite unpacked for me, the child and I went for a walk. She sucked on a peppermint stick as we walked, her words garbled. I smiled at her attempts to speak and suggested she remove the candy so I could understand her better, but she stubbornly refused.

I held her hand, now sticky from the candy, as we walked along the perimeter of the pond, staying a safe distance from the edge. She paused on the far side and pointed toward the orange grove. "Do you want to see my secret now?"

Her fingernails were filthy, and it was clear that she had been digging near the orange trees again. Feeling I should humor her, I agreed. It was late afternoon, and the early autumn sky was beginning to darken. The trees in the grove had been severely damaged in a storm several years before and had long since given up their fruit. Now the naked limbs reached up to the sky in silent supplication like the arms of barren mothers.

I realized for the first time how quiet it was in the grove. Even the screech of insects seemed to bypass this place, as if they, too, respected its peaceful solitude. Elizabeth had once told me that the orange grove had been the site of another burial mound, smaller than the one on which the house had been built. I thought again of Rebecca's claims of finding a dead body and wondered with trepidation if indeed she had.

She ran to the farthest corner of the grove, an area completely out of sight of the main house, and knelt down beside a tree trunk. "Over here, Aunt Cat." Even from where I was, I could see where new dirt had been replaced by old, the topsoil removed and then scraped back. A deep indentation in the middle of the small rectangle of dark soil showed where small fingers had diligently been digging.

I stood looking down at the disturbed earth and was about to suggest we go find help to finish the digging when a glimmer of something shiny caught my attention.

Kneeling down, I placed my hands on the cool earth

and peered into the hole. I stared hard, not really believing what I saw until I reached out and touched it. It was a brass hinge—an identical hinge to the ones on Elizabeth's letterbox. The same box that had disappeared from the attic.

My heart thumping, I stuck my hands in the dirt and began frantically scraping away. I sent Rebecca to go find a couple of sharp sticks and she returned, excitedly holding up our new digging instruments.

Knowing the size of the box, I easily outlined the shape with one of the sticks, making the process easier. It hadn't been buried deeply, and it took less than half an hour to release it from its grave. The sky had almost completely darkened by now, leaving only thin traces of glowing orange to guide us back to the house.

I sent Rebecca to the kitchen to wash up while I went to the front of the house, knowing that the servants would be mostly by the kitchen at this time. I had no idea who had buried the writing box, but whoever it was had obviously wished for it to remain hidden.

Cautiously I opened the door and entered. As I reached the bottom step I heard movement in the dining room. Peering over my shoulder I spied Marguerite setting the table. Our gazes met but I kept my back to her, only nodding as I proceeded up the stairs. As I pushed open my bedroom door I noticed behind me a trail of dirt and I made a note to sweep the steps before anybody saw.

I quickly hid the letterbox under the bed, then stood, taking note of my surroundings with dismay. All of my things were gone. The armoire doors stood open, exposing empty shelves and hooks, and my dressing table had been completely stripped. I realized with a mix of excitement and apprehension that my things had been taken to the master bedroom.

But where was the key? When I had left for my honeymoon, I had hidden it in the back of my dresser drawer, tucking it among stockings and chemises. I walked quickly over to the dresser and yanked open the drawer. My heart slammed in my chest when I saw the gaping cavity.

Calming myself, I left the room and walked to the end of the corridor to John's room. The door stood partially ajar and I waited for a moment before pushing it open. To my relief I found the room empty, but I still felt uncomfortable advancing further. This was John's room. My gaze strayed to the empty spot on the wall where Elizabeth's portrait had been, and then to the great mahogany bed. I flushed, imagining what we would be doing beneath its sheets later in the evening.

Elizabeth had had her own room, but her ghost seemed to be everywhere in this one. Even as I looked at the bed, I wondered if she had ever passed the night there, wrapped in John's arms and enjoying his caresses. I turned away, trying to avert my thoughts, and saw the trunk of paints and supplies John had given me. It sat in the corner, untouched, and I smiled again, remembering his thoughtfulness. One of the first things I would do to become settled would be to set up a place in the house for my painting.

I closed the door quietly behind me and leaned against it, contemplating where my things would have been placed. I was reluctant to go around blatantly opening drawers, still feeling like an intruder in somebody else's room. A large chest-on-chest occupied the space between the windows, and I was fairly certain it contained John's personal items. My gaze strayed to a lowboy against the far wall, and I thought that it would be the ideal place for my things.

With my breath held, I slid open the first drawer and to my delight found my underpinnings. Wiping my hands on my underskirt, I began digging into the drawer, hoping to feel the hard brass key under the light fabrics of my clothing. I almost cried out when my fingers found it, wrapped in a pair of stockings as I had left it, and I pulled it from the drawer.

I had started sliding the drawer closed when I spotted something unfamiliar in the back. It appeared to be a large linen handkerchief, certainly not one of my own, and when I pulled on it, it seemed stuck. I realized it was caught on the back of the drawer and would have been easily overlooked had I not had the drawer pulled all the way out.

I held it out to the light and saw the embroidered initials JEM and knew it belonged to my new husband. I had seen him in possession of several identical to this one. It was filthy, covered in dirt, with long streaks of mud bisecting the cloth. It was as if somebody had wiped very dirty fingers on it and then stuffed it in the back of the drawer to be hidden and forgotten.

My gaze strayed to my own dirty hands and they began to tremble as the realization of why it was there struck me. I remembered the ride to the inquest at town hall and how I had smelled freshly turned earth on John's jacket. I raised my eyes to the mirror over the chest and saw John standing in the doorway, watching me closely.

I turned quickly to face him, my hands behind my back and pressed against the lowboy. He approached with long strides, his eyes holding a dangerous spark. He stood so close to me that I couldn't move away without pushing against him.

His voice was like dark velvet when he spoke. "What are you hiding, Cat?"

"Nothing," I stammered. "I was simply cleaning and my hands are filthy. I was embarrassed to let you see them."

He placed his hands on my shoulders and slowly let them slide down to my elbows. "There is nothing about you that I don't think is beautiful." His eyes bored into mine. "Let me see."

I felt like an animal in a trap, with nowhere to run and hide. Without preamble, I moved my hands out from behind my back and raised them in front of me. One finger at a time, I opened my hands, revealing the key in one and the handkerchief in the other.

His eyes darkened and the first flash of fear I had experienced in over a year coursed through me. The key hit the floor with a small thud as the handkerchief drifted out of my fingers. John lowered his face to mine, those obsidian eyes glittering, and I clenched my own eyes tightly, waiting for what was to come.

Chapter Sixteen

"Why are you hiding these from me?" His voice was low and thick, like a dam holding back the words of accusation I knew he wanted to hurl at me.

I opened my eyes and faced him, forcing myself to raise my chin. "I should ask you the same thing. Why was your dirty handkerchief hidden in the back of your drawer? Did you use it to wipe your fingers after burying Elizabeth's letterbox?"

I waited for him to answer, my fingers clutching the lowboy behind me. To my surprise, he gave a low chuckle, but there was no mirth in it.

"Do you mean to say you're standing here acting like a hunted fox because you found a dirty handkerchief belonging to me?" He threw back his head and laughed. "I'm a planter, my dear wife. I get my fingers dirty quite often, which is why I always carry a handkerchief. Feel free to interview the laundress and she will inform you that yes, I always have dirty and muddy handkerchiefs that need her attention."

He narrowed his eyes at me, all traces of laughter gone. "Now you might answer a question of my own. Why is that key on a chain and why would you hide it from me?"

I felt suddenly foolish and found myself staring at him dumbly, unable to find any words to defend myself.

He leaned closer to me and I felt his heat. "I thought we had an agreement between us. An agreement to trust. It was even you who said you couldn't have a marriage without it."

I nodded, my eyes stinging at his chastisement. He moved his head lower, his lips close to my ear. "I want you, Cat. But I want your trust even more. Can you understand that?"

"Yes," I said, my voice barely audible. He was pressing me against the chest while his hands slowly raised my skirts. I wanted to protest but I wanted him as much as I wanted his forgiveness for doubting him.

His moist lips moved to my neck as his fingers deftly raised my chemise. "I want you . . . now," he whispered against my throat.

I was too aroused to tell him to stop, too inflamed by his passion even to want him to, but something in the back of my head told me that propriety should make me ashamed and disdainful of what we were about to do.

Instead I spread my legs for him as he lifted me on top of the low chest and stepped between my thighs. I was ready for him but still gasped as he slid quickly inside me, filling me completely, reducing my existence to the feel of him inside me and the loud beating of my heart.

"Cat," he whispered into my ear as he moved his hands to my hips and slid me closer.

I wrapped my legs around him and pressed my lips to his, his tongue penetrating my mouth in the same rhythm as our coupling. I moaned into his mouth and as he whispered my name again, time seemed to stop. He pressed me backward until I felt the wall behind me, my hair tumbling about my shoulders. I should have been ashamed, but all I could think of was my need for this man, and his desire for me, and I pulled him closer.

I felt him shudder at the same time as my passion consumed me, leaving me trembling as I fell back down to earth. We held each other for a long moment, he with his lips on my hair and my fingers clutching his shirt. Finally he lifted me off the chest and my legs slid down to the ground. He didn't let go of me, and I was grateful for his support because I was sure my legs would have buckled otherwise.

He looked honestly chagrined as he studied my face. "I'm sorry," he whispered, his voice hoarse. Gently he pulled me toward him, kissing me softly on my forehead. "I'm sorry," he said again. "I didn't mean for that to happen. But this wanting I have for you . . ."

I felt the sting of tears in my eyes—but they weren't tears of shame. The fire we had shared was new to me, new and liberating, and he had made me feel wanted again. I knew, that once I was alone, I would be shocked at our behavior, but now I was simply grateful. He had made me a woman to be desired, not pitied, scorned, or accused. Robert's suicide had done all those things to me, had, indeed, deadened all emotions in me. Yet John made me feel alive again, allowed me to feel passion and heat, to see colors where I had once seen only black and white.

He saw my tears and looked stricken. With the pads of his thumbs he gently wiped them away. "Forgive me, Cat."

I grabbed his wrists, stilling his hands. "There's nothing to forgive." I kissed his palm, then rested my face in his hand.

He placed his lips on the hair at my temple, now damp

from the sweat of our lovemaking. "I'll send Marguerite to help you dress."

Drawing back, he adjusted his clothing, then left the room. As I watched the door close I realized with a start that he had never actually denied burying the box. He had certainly implied it by giving an explanation as to how a dirty handkerchief would come to be shoved in the back of his drawer, but that wasn't a claim to innocence. I felt his seed warm and wet on my thighs, reminding me of our passion, and was ashamed at my doubt. I wanted to trust him but I knew asking him would never allay my suspicions. I would need to discover the truth on my own before I could lay to rest all of my doubts.

I stooped to pick up the key, intent now on finding the contents of the box and why somebody was so determined that I not discover it.

As I moved to the door, it opened and Marguerite came in, her strange eyes regarding me dispassionately. "I've ordered bathwater to be sent up."

"Thank you, Marguerite."

As she moved to the armoire to lay out my dinner gown, I slid the key into a drawer, then turned around and asked for her assistance unbuttoning the back of my traveling costume. When she didn't approach, I faced her. "Is there something the matter?"

Her face remained impassive, but her eyes were alive with a hidden light. "I brought you a message from Dr. Lewiston. He asked me to tell you to keep it private and away from Mr. McMahon."

I looked at her, startled. "For me? Are you quite sure?"

Her eyes narrowed slightly. "Yes, ma'am. I'm used to delivering messages for Dr. Lewiston."

"Thank you, Marguerite." I took the sealed note and left it unopened on my dressing table, waiting to open it in private. I was baffled by Daniel's actions, but from what I

Join the Love Spell Romance Book Club
and **GET 2 FREE* BOOKS NOW–
An $11.98 value!**
Mail the Free* Book Certificate
Today!

Yes! I want to subscribe to the
Love Spell Romance Book Club.

Please send me my **2 FREE* BOOKS**. I have enclosed $2.00 for shipping/handling. Every other month I'll receive the four newest Love Spell Romance selections to preview for 10 days. If I decide to keep them, I will pay the Special Members Only discounted price of just $4.49 each, a total of $17.96, plus $2.00 shipping/handling ($20.75 US in Canada). This is a **SAVINGS OF $6.00** off the bookstore price. There is no minimum number of books I must buy and I may cancel the program at any time. In any case, the **2 FREE* BOOKS** are mine to keep.

*In Canada, add $5.00 shipping and handling per order for the first shipment. For all future shipments to Canada, the cost of membership is $20.75 US, which includes shipping and handling. (All payments must be made in US dollars.)

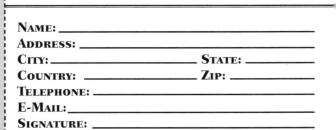

NAME: _____

ADDRESS: _____

CITY: _____ **STATE:** _____

COUNTRY: _____ **ZIP:** _____

TELEPHONE: _____

E-MAIL: _____

SIGNATURE: _____

If under 18, Parent or Guardian must sign. Terms, prices, and conditions subject to change. Subscription subject to acceptance. Dorchester Publishing reserves the right to reject any order or cancel any subscription.

knew of the doctor, felt confident that he would have a sound explanation.

I bathed and dressed for dinner, waiting until Marguerite left before I opened the note. It had tested the limits of my patience to wait so long, and I ripped it with a savage tear and took the note from the envelope. It read, *I am concerned for your welfare and would like to speak to you in private. I will be in the grotto tomorrow at two-thirty.* It was signed simply *DL.*

Thoughtfully I folded the note and placed it under a tray in my jewelry box. Then, sliding open my drawer, I spotted the key I had hidden earlier and took it out. Ascertaining that I still had a few minutes before supper, I walked down the hallway to my old room and pushed open the door.

The blinds had been left down and no candle had been lit. Still, I was familiar enough with my surroundings to be able to feel my way to the bed and kneel beside it. As my fingers brushed the hard wood of the box, I heard John calling my name from downstairs. I froze, then stood quickly, hiding the key under the mattress. Confident that no one would be entering the room, I left as quietly as I had come in, walking slowly down the stairs, my calm demeanor belying the fluttering of my heart.

Supper was a peaceful affair, with Rebecca chatting excitedly the entire time about her new presents and about everything she had done while we were gone. I watched her animated face, and for a moment I saw my Jamie, telling me about the size of a fish he had caught or how fast he had gone on his pony. But the image faded quickly, leaving me only with the vision of this beautiful little girl, happily sharing with her parents the precious things of her life.

She still called me Aunt Cat, and I didn't ask her to change it. It hadn't been so long since she had called Elizabeth "Mama," and I had no intention of erasing that. If she chose, in the future, to call me by another name, I would welcome it, but it would have to be in her own time.

After we ate, Mary came to take Rebecca to bed, and John and I retired to the parlor. I played the piano for him, and he stood behind me, not touching, but near enough that I could feel his heat. I smelled brandy mixed with his male scent, and I found the combination to be intoxicating. I missed a note but continued playing. I had chosen a Chopin nocturne, its melody haunting.

He touched the pearls about my throat, then bent to kiss my exposed shoulder. My fingers collapsed on the keyboard, unable to continue. I turned on the bench and looked up at my husband, and I knew the desire in his eyes mirrored my own.

Without speaking, I rose from the piano and allowed him to escort me up the stairs. His hand never left my arm, and I burned from his touch. When the door to our bedroom closed, it was as if the afternoon's events had inspired us both to a new height of passion. My need for him was as fierce as his need for me, and we were still partially dressed when he pressed me on the bed and took me the first time. It wasn't until after we were both completely sated that he began to make love to me slowly, taking off my remaining clothes bit by bit, and loving my body with his hands and mouth until I shouted out with the pleasure of it.

We lay in each other's arms long after the lamps had been turned down and we could no longer hear the stirring of the servants. The room was in almost total darkness, and I rested with my back pressed up to John, staring out at my new surroundings. Moonlight lent an eerie cast to the various pieces of furniture, and, like a glaring reproof, illuminated the large empty space on the wall where Elizabeth's portrait had once hung.

I waited until his breathing slowed to a deep and heavy pace before I stealthily slipped from the bed and put on my nightdress. I paused for a moment to stare down at my sleeping husband, feeling an unfamiliar tenderness. At that moment, I thought of my actions as a betrayal, but I quickly dismissed the feeling. This was simply to ease my mind and to help me pack my doubts away forever.

After tiptoeing across the room, I let myself out and scurried down the quiet corridor to my old bedroom. Finding my way to the window, I opened the blinds, letting in the soft glow of the moon. In a yellow shaft of light I slid the box out from under the bed and sat on the floor with it in my lap. Fumbling my way around the bedspread, I found the key and, with no little effort in the murky light, fit it into the keyhole.

With my breath held, I felt the key slide into place and then the latch click as I turned it. I waited for a brief moment for the pounding of my heart to settle before slowly opening the lid.

I blinked twice, wondering if the moonlight was playing tricks on my eyes, but was rewarded with the same vision each time—the sight of an empty box, just the dusty brown wood staring blankly up at me.

I leaned back against the bed, disappointment flooding me. I don't know what I had hoped to find—evidence of Elizabeth's descent into depression and desperation and of the thing she feared enough to write to me? Or perhaps evidence of John's innocence? I no longer knew which was more important to me—all I knew was that I had nothing now but John's words and my own suspicions of Elizabeth's true nature.

I placed the key inside the box, the chain making a hollow clatter, before closing the lid and replacing it under the bed. With a heavy heart, I stood and went back to my own room, moving quietly so as not to awaken John.

I slid back into bed, trying not to touch him, then turned to watch his face. His breathing remained slow and steady as I studied his dark shape. He was still an enigma to me, his strange allure all-consuming. I told myself I trusted him, and ignored the small doubts I harbored deep in the recesses of my mind. *Who buried the letterbox and why? And where are the letters?*

I ignored the questions pressing into my brain and continued to watch my husband. His heavy breathing continued, a sign of deep sleep. Slowly I lifted my hand and touched his cheek, the heavy stubble from his beard rough on my fingers. I traced the line of his jaw lightly with my finger, coming to rest on the sensual curve of his lips. John was usually so aloof and stoic in public that those lips seemed almost incongruous on his stern face. I doubted I was the only woman who had known the passion behind the man, and his mouth was certainly a hint of his true nature. I moved forward to press my lips against his and felt his hand grasp my wrist.

"Where have you been?"

I tried to pull my hand away, embarrassed not only that I had opened the letterbox in secret, but that he had caught me touching him when I thought he was asleep.

"I wanted to check on Rebecca. She kicks the covers off frequently and I didn't want her to catch a chill." The lie came easily, although I was not quite sure why I hadn't told him the truth. I again smelled the odor of fresh dirt in my memory, and a small doubt that had been hidden deep inside me wriggled free.

He let go of my wrist, his fingers sliding under the sleeves of my nightdress. Goose bumps rippled up my arms. He propped himself up on an elbow. "You seem to have caught a chill yourself. Let me warm you." He kissed me, his hard body moving over mine, and I soon forgot all about doubts and trust and the stale smell of loose dirt.

*   *   *

I spent most of the following morning making a few steps forward in organizing the household. I interviewed the servants to discern what their assigned duties were, reassigning them where responsibilities overlapped. I devised a cleaning schedule, including a long-overdue spring-cleaning that would involve taking down all the drapes and beating them outside. I wondered how the old house would react to having the drapes down and all the sunlight creeping inside, trickling into its dark corners.

The hall clock chimed twice, alerting me to the time. Daniel's note had said two-thirty and I didn't want to be late. His secrecy seemed odd to me, but I was sure he would explain it once we met. I knew that his objective was to speak to me without John being present, so I took pains to avoid being seen as I left the house and skirted the pond before heading out across the back lawn to the grotto.

I was there before he was and sat upon the bench to wait for him. As I waited, I thought I heard rustling in the bushes behind me, and jumped up, remembering the cottonmouth. But I saw nothing, and settled back down to wait.

It wasn't long before Daniel appeared on the grotto path, his friendly smile warming me. I hoped that I would soon be able to claim Clara as a close friend. Because of my fondness for her husband, I wanted to be equally comfortable with both.

He kissed my hand as he had done on the last occasion when we had met at the grotto. "You are a picture of loveliness, Catherine. Marriage suits you." He tilted his head, an odd look on his face. "I remember many times seeing Elizabeth sitting here just like that. The resemblance is uncanny, you know."

A shadow passed over his face, drawing away the

warmth of his smile. He sat down next to me and I turned to him. "You miss her a great deal."

Nodding, he looked away toward the thick greenery blocking our view of the house. "Yes. We were good friends." His voice trailed away and he didn't say anything else.

I touched his shoulder, feeling his sadness. "Is that why you brought me here today—to talk about Elizabeth?"

He faced me, his clear gray eyes dimming. "Not exactly. I wanted to talk about you." His lips turned up in a slight smile. "And please forgive my secrecy. I love John like a brother, but he's rather possessive when it comes to you. I wanted to speak to you in private and I could think of no other way." He pressed my hand, then let it go. "Thank you."

Daniel stood, as if preparing for a speech. "I've known John for a long time, and I know him to be a good man." Bracing himself with one hand against a tree, he leveled his gaze on me. "There might be . . . aspects . . . of his personality that you're not aware of, but perhaps should know." He took a deep breath. "John has a fierce temper—I've certainly witnessed it myself growing up with him in Boston. But here . . . well, you must know how servants talk, and there were stories brought to us about the arguments he and Elizabeth had."

I felt my blood cool in my veins. "Did he ever hit her?"

Daniel shook his head. "No—not that I ever heard. And Elizabeth never mentioned it either." His eyes clouded. "But she was afraid of him—she told me that much." He began to pace, his boots crunching the dead leaves and pine straw underfoot. "Elizabeth wasn't as strong as you, Catherine. She was emotionally . . . vulnerable. She craved love and attention, and when she didn't get it from John, she sought it elsewhere."

Again I imagined I heard a soft crunching of ground

cover behind me, but when Daniel showed no sign of noticing, I dismissed it. Lots of small animals lived in the pine forests that dotted West Feliciana parish, and even though I would have avoided the dark and shadowed woods surrounding Whispering Oaks, the deer and raccoons would not.

I shifted uncomfortably on the bench, feeling myself flush at the mention of Elizabeth's infidelities. Daniel came and sat down next to me again. He took my hand, holding it in his warm palms. "I'm sorry to be indelicate, but I thought you should know. Even if it's only to understand why John is so possessive of you." He smiled again, his eyes brightening. "It's amazing how much you resemble her. But one has only to be in your presence for a few minutes to know that the similarities end with your beautiful face."

I pulled my hand from his, and pretended to rearrange my skirts as I slid to the edge of the bench. He seemed to notice and his demeanor sobered considerably.

"Catherine, I'm sorry. I didn't mean to make you uncomfortable. I just wanted to warn you."

"Warn me? About my own husband?"

"Yes—and to offer you refuge. I know I've said this before, but if there is ever a time that you need to seek sanctuary, please know that you have a place at Belle Meade. I will welcome you there without questions."

I noted his omission of Clara's name. "I thank you for your concern, Daniel, but I can assure you that I am not my sister and I have no intention of raising my husband's ire. And, as you mentioned, I am stronger than she was. I can handle his temper without fleeing to the nearest neighbor."

He studied me carefully for a moment before speaking. "You defend him so readily."

"He is my husband."

Daniel dropped his head and stared at his hands. His fingers were long and slender, almost delicate. They were the hands of a doctor, unused to physical labor. So unlike John's, whose hands were strong and powerful, hiding their remarkable tenderness. "And he was Elizabeth's husband, too, and now she is dead."

I stood, anger flooding me. "What are you implying, Daniel?"

He stood, too. "I'm not making any accusations, but in Boston I witnessed John kill a man. I couldn't say he wouldn't do it again."

"It was in self-defense!"

He raked his fingers through his hair. "Yes, it was. But if John had left the man alone instead of inciting his anger, the man would still be alive."

I shook my head. "But that's in the past and has nothing to do with Elizabeth or me."

I thought of the baby Elizabeth had carried and John's knowledge that it wasn't his, and could only imagine his anger. With a steady gaze, I said, "You were her doctor and knew of the baby she carried. Did she tell you the identity of the child's father?"

His face blanched and he stared at me for a moment without speaking.

"I'm sorry," I said. "That was rather rash of me. Then I assume you didn't know?"

"Yes, of course I did. I was her doctor, and everything she told me was held in confidence. I just didn't expect you to know."

"John told me—before we were married. I suppose it was his way of letting me know that the Elizabeth I had known was not the same Elizabeth she had become."

"I'm sorry. It must have been a great shock for you."

"Yes, it was. But I'd rather know the truth."

He turned away for a moment, studying the small trickle

of water under the dilapidated bridge. "So does John know the identity of the child's father?"

"He said she had many lovers and that it would be difficult to name the father." I took a deep breath. "We've put Elizabeth to rest—there's no need to continue delving into a past that no longer matters."

He smiled again. "Yes. I'm sure you're right. I just want you . . . and John . . . to be happy." He came toward me and placed both hands on my shoulders. "And you certainly are a picture of happiness. I'm glad. You both deserve a helping of contentment in your lives."

I warmed to him. "Thank you, Daniel. We are lucky to have such a friend as you. And please don't worry about me. I appreciate your concern, but I am not afraid of my husband, and there's no cause for you to worry. Remember, I am not my sister."

He dropped his hands from my shoulders, his face sobering. "No, Catherine, you certainly are not." He studied me for a long moment, his eyes narrowed. "I don't even know if I should tell you this, but I think it is important for you to know. As much as Elizabeth's behavior is reprehensible to us both, there was a reason for it." He continued to study me, making me shift uncomfortably. "Never having met you, I didn't understand it at the time, but now I do. She was extremely envious of you."

I stepped back, shocked. "Of me? You must be mistaken."

Daniel shook his head. "Oh, no. She all but admitted it to me. She envied your happiness—or should I say your ability to be happy. You didn't need material things to be content. She said a blue sky or a smile from your father would set you adrift on a sea of happiness, as she put it." His face darkened. "But it was never that easy for her. She needed things—not just material things, but the undivided attention of everyone she met. I don't think it was easy for her growing up in your household and having to share your father's affections."

I shook my head. "I still can't believe it. Elizabeth had everything . . ."

"Everything but happiness. It hurt her deeply that that which she sought so vainly came so easily to you."

"I never knew . . ."

His voice was gentle. "But now you do. It certainly doesn't excuse her behavior, but perhaps it will help you to understand it."

I nodded and thanked him, then allowed him to escort me to the edge of the grotto. Taking my hand from his elbow, he faced me. "I think it best that we not be seen together. I've hidden my horse over by the levee, and I can walk through the forest to get to her."

As he was saying good-bye, I happened to look toward the lane of oaks and spotted a man sitting on a horse. The man's mount stomped the ground, then stilled. Squinting my eyes, I realized the man was looking in our direction. There was something familiar about him, and I pointed him out to Daniel.

Daniel stepped back into the shadow of the grotto while staring hard at the man on horseback. After a moment he said with distaste, "It's Philip Herndon. If he knows what's good for him, he'll get off of John's property before he's spotted."

"I'll go see what he wants."

Daniel stilled me with a hand on my arm. "No, Catherine. That would only fuel John's anger. I'll go get my horse and approach the lane as if I'm just arriving here for a visit. I'll see what he wants and get him to leave."

I nodded, seeing reason in his suggestion. "All right. Just tell me later what he's up to."

He bent to kiss my hand. "I will be sure to do that. Good-bye, Catherine. Take care of yourself, and I will see you soon."

Feeling fortunate to have found such a good friend so quickly, I turned and began walking back toward the house, my skirts brushing the brittle summer grass. My good spirits dimmed as I approached the looming white structure, the windows like foreboding eyes warning me away. But I had no intention of fleeing. Instead my determination to change the house deepened, and I marched toward the front porch with confident steps.

John met me in the foyer, a look of concern on his face. "Where have you been? I've been waiting for you. I have something to show you."

"I went for a walk," I said, hating my half lie. I pushed aside my guilt, justifying it by assuring myself that when our marriage wasn't so new, our relationship would be strong enough to handle unpleasantness. But for now I was reveling in our honeymoon period, and I didn't want to cast any shadows on it.

I went to him and reached for his hands. He immediately pulled me into an embrace, and I was lost in his touch completely.

"You're overheated. Perhaps you should go upstairs and change first."

I looked into his face and saw his mocking smile. "John," I said, pretending to be shocked. "It's the middle of the afternoon."

"Mrs. McMahon, I'm insulted that you could think I would be such a cad as to be suggesting anything other than changing your clothes." He bent to kiss my ear. "Of course, what I want to show you is upstairs in the bedroom . . ." His voice was smothered as he rained kisses down my neck.

Footsteps in the back passage made him straighten in time to see Marguerite approaching with two freshly polished candelabra in her hands for the dining room table. She sent me a knowing look, and I flushed. I wasn't sure if the look was intended to remind me that she knew of the note from Daniel, or if she knew what John and I had been discussing.

I headed up the stairs, John following close behind. When we reached the bedroom, he closed the door behind him, then locked it.

"John . . ."

He held his finger to his lips. "Sshh. Let me show you your surprise now."

He went to a door on the far wall that had led to a small sitting room in my grandmother's day. I had not yet been inside, assuming it to be unused. He held the door open and indicated that I should enter.

I held my breath as I walked in, my face flushing with pleasure. The windows had been stripped of their heavy drapes, leaving them bare for the sunshine to pour in through slatted blinds. A large armoire stood open on the opposing wall, its shelves displaying my paints and brushes. In the middle of the room were two easels, each holding a blank canvas.

John came to stand behind me, his hands on my arms. "I had Mr. O'Rourke and Marguerite fix this room for you while we were in New Orleans. I put in the paints and brushes myself today, seeing as how they were still in a box on the floor of the bedroom."

I couldn't speak, afraid that I would burst out crying if I did. Instead I walked toward the window and raised the blind. The view was of the long stand of pines that hid the grotto from view. I knew that if I turned to look out of the right corner of the window, I would see the pond, its dark, placid waters still a place I didn't willingly visit.

I turned to John, wrapping my arms around his neck, happiness flooding my spirit. "This is the most precious gift anyone has ever given me. How can I ever thank you?"

He reached for me, his powerful hands caressing my back. "Let me show you."

I felt his fingers beginning to undo the buttons on the back of my dress and I pressed myself against him. Unbidden came Daniel's words to me about John's temper and his penchant for violence.

As John's hands found my bare skin, Daniel's words faded into nothingness, lost as I was in my husband's gentle touch, thoughts of his anger long forgotten in the heat that flooded my veins and drowned my soul.

Chapter Seventeen

My days passed serenely as I settled in as the new mistress of Whispering Oaks. I felt proud of my ability to organize the household and to understand the ebb and flow of the workload on a sugar plantation. John took great pride in taking me for long rides and showing me the lay of the land. He showed respect for my intelligence and took pains to explain the problems of the encroaching Mississippi River and the never-ending battle to shore up the levee.

John spent a great portion of his day out of the house, and I came to know in time that it had nothing to do with me but, rather, with the house. As much as he loved the rich, fertile earth and the things he was able to coax from it, the house held no appeal for him at all. I had brought a measure of brightness to it with new draperies and furnishings, but for all the sunshine that now lapped at the creamy white walls, a pervasive darkness lingered over the old rooms, like a nightmare that followed one into the waking hours.

I had begun to paint again, and it wasn't until I first put my brush to canvas that I realized how much I had changed in the last years. Whereas before all I had painted had been flora and fauna and the blue ocean of Saint Simons, now I wanted to paint people. I wanted to study these new inhabitants of my life, examine each feature separately as if they were puzzle pieces that might add up to the sum of this new existence of mine.

My first subject had been, remarkably, Rebecca. Perhaps it was the desire to capture Jamie's eyes on canvas, but her pixielike face called to me, insisting that I paint it. I hoped that one day I might find the strength to paint Jamie from memory, but for now I reveled in capturing his endearing little cousin on canvas. I looked forward to our painting sessions on those early fall mornings that I can remember with a vividness of thought and color that is foreign to most of my memories. Perhaps it's with the knowledge of hindsight now that I recall those happy times with such clarity. I cling to the memory so as to block out the events that would soon change our lives forever.

On a bright October morning I sat painting Rebecca. It was still warm, as fall in the delta only rarely brought cold weather, but the heavy humidity had lifted. Rebecca sat on a blanket with Samantha by the pond, the sunlight spinning her hair into gold. I wasn't comfortable being this close to the water, but the child had insisted and I knew she was right. The sun reflecting off the water and the big house in the background were perfect for a portrait.

Still, I felt uneasy, as if the restless spirits of the Indian woman and her child were watching us. The breeze teased at my neck, making my skin prickle like little breaths of warning, and I found it hard to focus on my task.

As I mixed my paints for her hair, I realized with a start

223

what I was doing. It was the same combination of golds and yellows I had once used when painting a miniature portrait of Robert. It was as if he were mocking me now, calling to mind his beautiful hair, and the thick red river of blood running through it. It was as if that one gunshot had not ended his life, but merely perpetuated his existence to haunt me forever.

I realized my hand was shaking, and I went to sit next to Rebecca until I could calm myself. I sat with my back to the water and the little girl laid her head in my lap, her small arms clutching her doll. I ran my hands through her glorious hair, reveling in the thick texture of it. It was not baby-fine, like most children's hair, but more like that of an adult. My hand stilled, an unbidden memory assaulting me—a memory of Robert and me on the beach for a picnic, with his head in my lap and me stroking his hair, so full and rich and gold.

I let my hand fall to my side, clutching at the grass and dirt as if to ground my thoughts. I had come to the point that I could almost bear the memories of Jamie. Even though they were still tinged with great sadness, his conjured image could sometimes make me smile with remembered joy.

But memories of Robert were not allowed. John had helped me banish Robert from the marriage bed, but at other times thoughts of him caught me unawares. And each time it brought back the terrifying memory of a gunshot and red blood on white sheets. I closed my eyes, trying my best to focus on the smell of the earth and grass, and the feel of the beautiful child in my lap.

Rebecca began to hum her strange, haunting melody, her eyes transfixed on the still waters of the pond.

I listened for a while, still trying to identify where I had heard the music before. It was so familiar, yet so elusive. Finally I asked, "Rebecca, where did you learn that song?

I feel I should know it, but I can't seem to recall where I've heard it before."

She turned her head in my lap to face me, her eyes squinting in the bright sunlight. "It's a secret and I'm not supposed to tell."

I leaned forward to block the sun from her face. "Who told you that you weren't supposed to tell?"

She faced the pond again and didn't answer.

"Was it Marguerite?"

She shook her head vigorously.

I prodded again. "Was it your mama?"

"You're my mama now."

My heart lurched at this declaration, but I restrained myself from lifting the child high in the air and swinging her about. The thought was obviously as new to her as it was to me, and I wanted us both to get used to the idea.

Gently I continued. "It's such a beautiful song and I'd like to learn it, too. I promise I won't tell anybody you told me."

She furrowed her pale brows for a moment, as if in deep thought. Then she turned back to me, her face stricken. "But then I wouldn't get any more candy."

I looked down at the cherubic face of my niece and wondered momentarily if her mother's neglect had had any negative effect on her developing person. Leaning over, I kissed her forehead, determined not to press the matter further for the time being.

We sat in silence for a long time, enjoying the soft breeze and the crisp smell of the approaching autumn. Our fickle climate would allow the heat and humidity to return for brief periods of time, but for now the clear air was a welcome respite.

Rebecca continued to gaze out at the pond, her brows puckered. Finally she said, "I think they're down there."

I sat up with alarm. "Who's down there?"

"The Indian mama and her baby. They buried them under the house but when their bones were found, the people threw them into the pond."

I kept my voice calm. "Who told you this, Rebecca?"

She didn't speak for a moment but eventually turned her face to stare up at me. "They did. And they want me to get them out."

A frigid finger of dread slipped down my spine as I stared at the wide-eyed innocence of this child. I continued stroking her hair. "Who do you mean by 'they,' Rebecca?"

"They come to talk to me at night—after my lamps are turned down and it's all dark. Sometimes they scare me, but not a lot." She turned away from me and sighed, her fingers restlessly plucking at her dress. "It's the Indian lady and her baby. The mama does all of the talking. She tells me how lonely they are and how much they want me to come with them."

My hand stilled on her hair. "Where do they want you to go?"

I watched her profile as her long golden lashes closed over her eyes. "To the bottom of the pond. Then they'll be free."

Dread gripped my heart. I reached down and lifted her, sitting her on my lap to face me. "Rebecca—you must listen to me. These . . . voices are not your friends, do you hear me? They are in your imagination and you mustn't listen to them. The pond is a dangerous place for you to go alone and you must never, ever go there without me or another grown person. Do you understand me? Do you understand?"

The child's bottom lip began to quiver and I realized how harsh my voice must have sounded to her. I felt ashamed at having scared her, but the heaviness in my heart would not dissipate. I clutched her close to my chest, not hearing her cries of protest. It was only when her hands began to push me away that I let go.

She sat on my lap, gazing at me, her blue eyes questioning. I touched her soft cheek, brushing away fat tears. "I'm so sorry. I didn't mean to make you cry, but you scared me so. Can you understand that I don't want anything to happen to you? You mean so much to me and to your papa, and I just want to keep you safe from harm. I didn't mean to frighten you."

Rebecca touched my face. "You're crying."

I reached up and pressed my fingers to my own cheek and realized she was right.

In the next instant she was leaping at me, throwing her small arms around me and burying her face into my neck. "I don't want to make you cry. My old mama would cry and say it was my fault and that she was going to leave. And then she went away. Does this mean you're going away, too?"

I cradled her head on my shoulder, my heart breaking for this motherless child. "Oh, no—I will never leave you. If you make me cry, they'll be tears of happiness, for there is nothing that you can ever do that would make me go away. You bring so much joy to my life, Rebecca, and I will always want you in it." I realized with a start that I had meant every word.

She pulled back to contemplate me, her puckered brows telling me she hadn't understood everything I'd said, but perhaps enough. "You're not leaving?"

I shook my head vigorously. "Not ever."

She threw her arms around me again and squeezed tightly. Then she laid her head on my shoulder, putting her thumb in her mouth, and I felt her pat my back, just as I had done to comfort her. We sat like that for a long while, watching the sun slide lazily across the pond. Then, very softly, her voice heavy with drowsiness, she said, "I love you, Mama."

Tears pricked at my eyes. It seemed like an eternity and more since I had last heard those words. I began to cry in earnest now, recalling how I had emotionally pushed this child away, thinking of her only as a reminder of the child I had lost. Instead she had become a large piece of my salvation, warming a corner of my heart that I had considered forever dead. I placed my cheek against hers and whispered, "I love you, too, Rebecca."

She fell asleep in my arms, and I held her close, reveling in the joy of being a mother again, and vowing to myself that the bond would never be broken.

After I put the sleeping Rebecca into her bed for a nap, I passed Marguerite in the hallway outside my room. I was still unsure of her position in the household, and unsettled about her seemingly permanent place in it. I knew John would balk at any suggestion to dismiss her, so I tried my best to assert my authority.

"Marguerite, I need to speak to you for a moment."

She inclined her head slightly in acknowledgment of my request, but her expression lacked any semblance of servitude.

"I'm enjoying my art room very much and I wanted to thank you for helping Mr. McMahon surprise me with it."

She regarded me evenly. "I always do what I'm asked."

I was taken aback by her response, but tried not to show it. Instead I said, "Yes, well, thank you anyway. The room has proven to be a real pleasure to me."

Bobbing her head, she moved to pass me, but I called out to her. "I also wanted to speak to you about Rebecca."

She turned slowly, her eyes narrowing. "She's not my responsibility anymore."

"That's true, but I thought you might know who's been

putting ideas into her head. She's told me that she hears the voices of an Indian lady at night after she goes to bed. I know it's all in her imagination, but somebody has to be planting the seeds for her to be thinking such things."

Her odd green eyes widened. "And what makes you think that it's not real?"

I was at a loss for words. Finally I said, "Well, of course it's not real. The story of the Indian woman and her child is only a legend. And I don't want Rebecca to hear any more of those stories—they'll only frighten her."

"There's things you don't understand, but that doesn't mean they don't exist."

I tried to remain calm. "Such stories are irrational and frightening, and I don't want Rebecca hearing any more about them. I will speak to the other servants and make sure my wishes are clear, and I expect you to help enforce my orders."

Her eyes regarded me calmly. "If that's what you want."

"That's what I want, and I expect my orders to be obeyed. If you find that you can't, then you will be dismissed."

She lifted her chin. "You'll have to talk to Mr. McMahon about that."

I squared my shoulders. "Don't be too sure of that, Marguerite. I'm in charge of the household staff."

"Maybe with the others. But Mr. McMahon hired me, and only he can fire me."

Bristling, I walked past her. "We'll see about that. If you cannot accept my authority, then I don't feel you should be working here."

"I'd think twice about that, Mrs. McMahon. I know what a temper Mr. McMahon has, and I don't like to think how he'd react when he hears that the doctor sent you a note and you met in private."

I froze, my back to her. "That is not your concern."

"Maybe it is, and maybe it isn't, but it's certainly your husband's concern to know that his wife's been meeting with another man."

I turned quickly, my skirts whirling about my ankles, to face her. "You wouldn't dare."

She simply raised an eyebrow and silently walked past me.

My heart hammered in my chest as I ran to my room, taking the time to shut the door calmly. With my breath held, I opened my jewelry box and lifted the tray where I had thrown Daniel's note. It was gone. I threw everything out of the box, leaving it in a tangled mess on the dresser, but there was no note.

I shoved everything back in the box, too agitated to take the time to put it away neatly. I tried to force my breathing to slow down, rationalizing to myself that all I needed to do was speak to John and everything would be sorted out.

But I thought with longing of the weeks since our marriage, of the bonds of trust that we had forged, and I thought also of his anger when I had discovered the dirty handkerchief in his drawer. I closed my eyes, clutching the edge of the dresser. Marguerite had to be dealt with—but I was loath to create any ripples in the river of my new marriage just yet. It could wait.

Slowly I took everything out of the jewelry box again and replaced it inside neatly.

A brief tapping on the door made me look up. Marguerite appeared, a knowing smile on her lips when she saw what I was doing. I didn't acknowledge it, but simply asked her what she needed.

"Mrs. Lewiston is here to see you. I showed her into the parlor and will ask Rose to bring tea."

"Thank you, Marguerite." I stared after her long after she had gone, then smoothed my hair and went downstairs.

When I entered the parlor, Clara stood by one of the

windows, her pale hands clutching the draperies, staring out toward the front drive. She didn't appear to have heard me come in, so I moved to stand next to her.

"She's a beautiful child."

Clara's voice startled me. I followed her gaze to where Rebecca played on the front lawn with Delphine. They each had a large wooden hoop with a stick and were racing each other down the drive, seeing who could roll hers the fastest without making it fall over.

"She's supposed to be napping. But she is beautiful, isn't she? I'm afraid I can't take any credit for that. We must thank her parents."

Clara gave me an odd look, then returned to gaze out the window. "How are you finding the child? Does she seem . . . normal and healthy?"

I stared at Clara's profile, the pale skin and nearly lashless eyes. "She's a wonderful child—unique amongst most children I've known, but very typical of a girl her age. She's intelligent and loving, and very charming—especially when she wants to get her way." I smiled but it wasn't returned. "Why do you ask?"

Rose appeared with a tea tray and we seated ourselves on the sofa. As I poured tea, Clara said, "I'm just concerned. There have always been . . . rumors concerning Rebecca, and I was just wondering if you had noticed anything out of the ordinary."

I thought momentarily of mentioning the voices Rebecca said she'd been hearing, but I kept it to myself. I did not want my daughter's name dragged through the rumor mill. Despite any assurances, I doubted Clara would be able to keep a tidbit like that a secret. Instead I shook my head. "No, I've noticed nothing unusual. What sorts of rumors have you been hearing?"

She concentrated on putting sugar into her tea and stirring it slowly, her eyebrows tightly knitted. "Just that she has imaginary friends—that she sees people who aren't there and speaks to them. Daniel even mentioned to me that Rebecca has spoken to him of her mother as if she were still seeing her. As if she still lived."

Tepid brown eyes focused on me, and I returned her stare without blinking. "Clara, having imaginary friends is quite common for children Rebecca's age. My own son had an imaginary friend, too—an old fisherman." I laughed, trying to add levity to our conversation. "Perhaps it's in our blood—for I know not every child has such an active imagination as Jamie and Rebecca."

There. I had done it—used Jamie's name in a sentence without falling apart. In fact, it was good to hear his name spoken. It was as if I had buried his existence at his memorial service, never to be brought into the light again. How wrong I had been.

Clara smiled warmly. "I'm sure you're right—and you would know more of these things than I. After all, you've been a mother and I've not been so blessed. Yet." She smiled again. "I only wanted to broach the subject with you so that you'd know I'm more than happy to discuss it. I can only imagine how hard it must be for you here—far from your true home. It must be so lonely."

I took a sip of my tea. "We've had so many visitors since we returned from our honeymoon. I feel as if I know the whole parish by now. And Daniel's become a dear friend, too. It is my hope that we can all spend time together."

She looked down into her cup, hiding her expression. "Yes, I would like that, too. When Elizabeth was alive . . ." She paused, glancing up at me. "John and Elizabeth were our closest friends, and I sorely miss the companionship."

I placed my hand on hers and squeezed. "As soon as our mourning is over we can be more social, and I hope to see you and Daniel as frequently as possible."

"Yes. That would be nice." She took her hand away and

reached for a tea cookie. "How are you adjusting to being the new Mrs. McMahon?"

I chewed on a cookie, trying to will away the flush I felt creeping up my cheeks. "Very well, thank you. John has been nothing but kind in answering all my questions and helping me learn everything there is to know about the plantation. He's been very patient with me."

Clara put her teacup down in its saucer. "I don't think I've ever heard John McMahon's name and the word 'patient' used in the same sentence."

"Really?"

Her lips pulled over her teeth for a moment as she contemplated her next words. "I just recall certain aspects of Elizabeth's behavior that John was not so patient with."

I held my teacup loosely, afraid that I might snap the fragile handle. "Like what?"

Clara stood, walked back over to the window, and stared out. "Elizabeth had . . . friends . . . that she liked to visit. She would just take off without a word, returning when the whim took her. John would go into a fury when she returned—something I'd never seen the likes of before. He was so insanely jealous. . . ." Her voice trailed off as she turned to face me.

She continued. "He didn't even like her visiting Daniel. I knew there was nothing untoward about their friendship, but John couldn't be reasoned with when it came to Elizabeth. She infuriated him, and he was powerless to do anything about it. I understand she was the same way when she lived in Boston during the war." Almost as an afterthought, she added, "I always wondered why she stayed with him."

I sat up straight, feeling heat pervade my cheeks. "Perhaps, like me, she had nowhere else to go." I heard the acrimony in my voice, but her frivolous gossip regarding my dead sister had raised my ire.

Clara held her hand to her mouth and looked truly chagrined. "Please forgive me, Catherine. I didn't mean . . ." She looked down at her lap for a moment, studiously straightening her skirt. "And please don't think that you have no place to go. There's always Belle Meade, and if you need to get farther away, I would help you return to Saint Simons."

My voice was cool. "That won't be necessary. And I must resent the implication that I would have need of leaving my husband."

Clara's pale brown eyes blinked rapidly. "I've wounded you, and I am deeply sorry. It's just that Elizabeth and I used to be so frank with each other, and I suppose I forgot you were not she."

A booming voice sounded from the threshold. "Catherine is most definitely not Elizabeth." John entered the room and strode toward me, then placed a lingering kiss on my cheek. I was sure it was for Clara's benefit, but his touch thrilled me nonetheless.

John greeted Clara with a deep grin that made her squirm. I suppose he was using a little revenge to repay her for her gossiping.

"My, my. Where does the time go?" She stood hastily, knocking her teaspoon on the floor in a fluster. "I really need to be going but I wanted to extend to you both a dinner invitation at Belle Meade. I realize you're still in mourning, so it will be a very small affair, but I feel it necessary to introduce you into our society. Of course, many remember you from your grandmother's days, but they need to meet you as the new mistress of Whispering Oaks." She glanced from me to John, like a child seeking approval. "How about Wednesday evening in two weeks? We'll dine at eight."

My anger toward her lessened somewhat. I knew from John that Belle Meade had suffered greatly during the war and that it would be a struggle to entertain graciously, as Clara would have been used to. Still, she was making the effort to bring me into her social circle and for that I was grateful.

"Thank you, Clara. We would be delighted to accept. Thank you so much for your kindness." I took her hand and held it, hoping she'd realize it was an apology and an offer of a truce.

She smiled warmly at me. "No, Catherine—thank you. Thank you for putting up with my gossiping, and thank you for accepting my invitation. It will be a real pleasure." She moved to leave, then turned back to add, "For me and for Daniel, I'm sure."

John and I saw her out. After she had gone, I turned to John. During my conversation with Clara, my thoughts had been in turmoil. It had become very clear that my concern for Rebecca far outweighed any anxiety I might suffer at my husband's anger.

I took a deep breath before I spoke. "We must talk about Marguerite. I don't feel as if she should stay here—she is insolent and rude and does not take well to my direction. And somebody has been feeding Rebecca nonsense about the ghosts of the Indian woman and her baby—that they're under the pond and she needs to save them."

He looked at me intently. "And you think Rebecca believes it?"

I nodded. "She's young and impressionable—but I think I convinced her that it's not true and that she should never go to the pond without an adult. But still . . ."

He spoke gently. "Catherine, I understand how this is all very upsetting to you, but as you said, it's nonsense. We will speak to the servants and make it clear that no one is to mention the legend to Rebecca again—and that she must not be allowed near the pond by herself."

"But John, I feel Marguerite is behind it—that she wishes

Rebecca ill for some reason. I cannot forget the time she left Rebecca out in the thunderstorm as punishment. It chills me to the bone."

I saw him grit his teeth, his jaw working furiously. "I'll speak to her, but I'm sure you're mistaken. I've known Marguerite for years. Yes, her ways are strange, but I have never known her to wish evil on anyone."

I touched his sleeve, fighting to keep the desperation out of my voice. "I don't want her in this house. Please— send her away. Give her a large severance and a good reference if it will make you feel better, but please, John. Dismiss her."

He looked away, avoiding my eyes. "I said I would speak to her. But I will not dismiss her for ungrounded reasons. I know your concerns are real—but perhaps they're born of being uncertain and in a new situation rather than any real wrongdoing on Marguerite's part." He turned and kissed me on the cheek. "I've got to return to the mill."

I watched his retreating form, bristling at how easily he had dismissed my fears. But maybe he was right and I was being foolish. Maybe I had imagined harmful intentions on Marguerite's part. Perhaps I should trust John and try harder to accept Marguerite's presence in my house for the sake of harmony.

And then I recalled the note, and Marguerite's veiled threat. I shrugged—it didn't matter. I could only tell the truth, and the truth had nothing to hide.

I stared after John as he walked toward the mill, finally admitting to myself that the heady rush I felt whenever I saw him was perhaps more than fascination. The soft smiles that he reserved for Rebecca and me belied his stern demeanor, and made them all the more special for their rarity. Our tender bond had taken root in deep hurt and grief, and now I could only wonder if such fragile beginnings could blossom into something more.

I returned to the house, closing the door quietly behind me. The bright afternoon sun had begun its descent into the twilight sky and I stood in the foyer for a long moment, watching the play of light on the walls.

A shadow caught my attention, and I spun on my heels, wondering if I had seen something move in the mirror. I stared into the murky glass, watching with unblinking eyes. I turned around to see if what I had seen had been a reflection, but found myself staring at the empty wall on the opposite side of the foyer.

I approached the old mirror slowly, marveling at the newfound fear I felt lodged in my throat. Could it be that my new sense of contentment, now that I had something to lose, had resurrected my sense of fear?

Reaching out, I allowed my fingertips to graze the cold glass of the mirror. I dropped my hands, watching them as I slowly lowered them to my sides. I gasped as the top of the hall table came into view, then blinked to clear my eyes in the dim light.

Scattered over the table's surface lay a handful of oleander leaves, their tender corners lifted as if waving goodbye. I stared at them for a long moment before gathering them in my fists, squeezing tightly as if to choke the life out of them. I shoved them into my pockets, obliterating them from my sight, as if they, and the threat they represented to my newfound happiness, had never existed at all.

Chapter Eighteen

I awoke with a scream on my lips, the room of my dream still surrounding me, the pool of bloodred oleander leaves drowning me. I reached for John, but his side of the bed was empty, the pillow ice cold.

I sat on the edge of the bed, my teeth chattering, waiting for my eyes to adjust to the dark shadows of the furniture. Softly I called out, "John," but there was no reply. Sliding to the floor, I felt the cool wood touch my feet, sending more shivers up my spine. Carefully I walked to the door and opened it, the hinges singing a faint protest.

A thin triangle of light fanned the far wall of the corridor, and I followed it like a lost ship guided by a lighthouse beacon. I hesitated at the bend in the hallway when I realized the light came from Elizabeth's room. Slowly I approached the door, my feet padding softly on the carpet runner. I had not brought my wrapper, and I trembled in the cool night air.

My fingers, seemingly disembodied in the dark, bisected the illumination, making them glow before I pushed gently on the door.

John sat at Elizabeth's dressing table, a glass of scotch not far from his hand. He was fully dressed, and I recalled how I had retired before he did. His jacket was missing, his hair mussed as if he had spent many wretched moments sweeping his hands through it.

With a start, I noticed that her hairbrush, comb, and mirror sat on her dresser top. Had I imagined they were missing when I had first come into this room? Or perhaps they were merely someplace else in the room and had been put back.

I turned my attention back to John. He did not see me right away, and I stayed where I was, watching as he picked up her hairbrush and held it idly in his hands, then lifted it to his nose to smell deeply. He turned his head away quickly, as if the scent from the brush was not that which he wished for.

He lifted his eyes and spied me in the mirror, but did not act surprised to see me.

"What are you doing, John?"

Taking a drink of scotch, he remained silent. I entered the room and closed the door behind me. I had already grown used to the knowledge that these walls had ears, and I had no intention of fueling the gossip mill any more than I had already. "What are you doing?" I asked again.

He dropped the brush, the clatter loud in the quiet room, and stood to face me. "I'm not sure," he said slowly. "Perhaps I'm simply trying to ascertain that you and Elizabeth are not one and the same."

I smiled, thinking he was jesting until I caught sight of the crumpled note on the dresser. I knew without asking that it was Daniel's note, and I realized Marguerite had made good on her threat. Still, I wasn't sorry I had spoken to John about dismissing her. Rebecca's welfare had to come first.

I sobered quickly, the blood draining from my head. Nausea rose to my throat and I had to sit down on the corner of the bed for fear of fainting. "I can explain that," I said weakly.

Silence pervaded the room for a long moment as we watched each other warily. "I'm sure you can. Elizabeth always had good explanations, too. Until she felt that she no longer needed to bother with such trivialities."

I tasted bile and grimaced as I swallowed it down. I stared up at him, my anger rising. "So, that's it, is it? I'm guilty regardless of the truth, and you are judge and jury. How dare you." I struggled to stand, clutching one of the bedposts for support.

His face was ragged, his torment plain to see. "What else am I supposed to think, Catherine?"

"That your wife is innocent." I glared at him, struggling to ignore the nausea that threatened to engulf me. "This wife—not Elizabeth. What about trust, John? Can one simple misunderstanding erase everything we've worked for?"

He stared at me for a long moment, his face hidden in shadow. Slowly he put his glass down on the dressing table, the small clinking sound an intrusion in the heavy silence.

I leaned against the tall bed, pressing my forehead against the bedpost, seeking something cool. I heard the resignation in my voice. "I told you before we were married—I'd rather have my freedom and starve on Saint Simons than live this way."

He took a step toward me, out of the shadows, and I raised my face to his. "Daniel was simply concerned for my welfare, and he didn't want to raise your ire by questioning my well-being in your presence. Your mistrust and jealousies are building a prison for me. Is this how it started with Elizabeth? Did your jealousies imprison her, too?"

The words I hurled at him hit their mark and I closed my eyes, unable to look at the hurt in his. I took long, deep breaths and felt the cool wood of the bedpost against my face. I opened them again to look into his inscrutable eyes and spoke the words that I had never intended to utter: "If only you knew what is in my heart."

Dark eyes stared at me, unblinking, a flash of hope flickering within. "How can you expect me to know what is in your heart when you are meeting with other men without my knowledge, when my best friend is sending you private notes? Elizabeth . . ."

"I am not Elizabeth, John. If you have any question as to my behavior, ask me and I will tell you the truth. I have nothing to hide. And what lies is my heart is worthless if you cannot trust me with your secrets. You say that it's to protect me, but I'm telling you that it is killing me—little by little. It is leaching the strength and energy from my blood. It is starvation of the soul, which is far worse than starvation of the body. And I have experienced both."

I shook as I spoke and felt my knees weaken beneath me. He crossed the room in two long strides and lifted me in his arms. Gently he sat on the bed with me in his lap, cradling me like a child. "I'm sorry," he whispered. "I'm sorry."

Soft lips brushed my forehead, and it must have been a healing kiss, for the wave of nausea vanished. I still felt cold and clammy, though, and I snuggled deeply into John's arms, closing my eyes and relishing his scent.

His words fell softly on my ears. "What is really in your heart, Cat?"

I didn't open my eyes. I had no desire to banish my hope by not seeing what I wanted reflected in his. Instead I tilted my head to face him, but kept my eyes tightly shut. "I feel weak whenever you walk into a room. And my blood seems to move faster and my heart to beat louder when you look at me or when you make Rebecca laugh." I took a deep breath, still not daring to look at him. "And when you touch me, I feel as if I've found a part of paradise here on earth. I would die for your touch, for I find myself living just to have you pull me toward you each night."

Small kisses touched my eyelids, and I opened them in surprise.

His eyes darkened as he gazed down at me. "And I feel as if I've always known you, as if there has never been a time in my life when you weren't a part of it."

I kept my eyes open as he kissed me, his lips caressing me, his mere touch arousing all of my senses.

I struggled to sit up, clutching his sleeves for support, intent on speaking before I lost my will and allowed my being to dissolve under his fingertips. "Then let us start anew. Let us pretend that all that has gone before us never happened. That there was no pain, loss, and betrayal—that there was simply us, waiting to find each other."

His face stilled, his voice heavy and dark when he spoke. "If only I could share in your optimism—that it is possible to forgive and forget old betrayals. That it is possible to pretend they never happened, despite the fact that the evidence of their existence is before us." He pressed his lips to my forehead, holding me close. "I swear that I will do all that I can to help you remain so innocent and forgiving. I would preserve those qualities in you even if I am incapable of forgetting or forgiving."

I struggled to read his eyes, but he had once again masked his true emotions, hiding his thoughts and tucking whatever secrets he kept from me far back into the recesses of his mind.

I felt emboldened by his words and I turned to him with confidence. "There is already something you can do."

He raised an eyebrow. "What is it?" Those impenetrable dark eyes flickered.

I kept my voice low, the sound of it rasping into the dark night. "Dismiss Marguerite. There is something . . . unholy about her. She is working against my authority here, and I'm afraid of her influence on Rebecca." I made no mention of the oleander leaves or the obvious way John had received the note from Daniel. The one sure way to elicit his cooperation would be to invoke Rebecca's name.

His arms stiffened around me. "It sounds as if you're suggesting blackmail. You'll stay if I dismiss Marguerite."

I shook my head vehemently, a sick feeling churning in the pit of my stomach. "No, I'm asking for your trust. You're keeping Marguerite here for a reason that you will not divulge to me. Trust me, John, with your secret. Whatever my reaction to it, it cannot possibly be worse than the damage should Marguerite stay."

To my astonishment, John moved me from his lap, settling me onto the bed, and then he stood, turning his back to me. I watched as he brushed his hands over his head, sweeping the hair off his forehead in uncharacteristic agitation. "I can't. With all your talk of trust, why can't you trust me in this matter?" He shook his head, then turned to look at me with haunted eyes. "And the matter is not to be discussed further."

I slid off the bed and approached him, my hands on his sleeves. "What do you mean, you can't? If it's due to a promise you made to the Lewistons, I'm sure they'd understand if you'd just explain—"

His words cut me off. "I said I can't, and nothing will change that. The matter is closed."

He resembled a madman, his hair looking storm-tossed and his face ravaged. I very quietly said, "Then everything you have said to me tonight, in this room, has been a lie."

I waited for him to refute my words, to apologize or

make some move of reconciliation, but he did not. Slowly I turned from him and left, waiting until I was safely behind the closed door of my old room to let the tears fall.

The next few days were difficult as relations between John and me remained strained. I had slept in my old room the first night and had continued to do so in the ensuing days. I made a show of retiring to the room I shared with John to ready myself for bed, but would return to the room down the hall as soon as the servants had gone to sleep. I was too angry and hurt to make love with him, and I knew all he would have to do would be to touch me and I would forget all his empty promises and the damage they had caused in our blossoming relationship.

We ate our meals together and I sensed his gaze resting heavily on me. I spoke civilly to him, for Rebecca's sake, but refused any intimate conversation or contact. He accepted my withdrawal coolly, never acknowledging it outright, but aware nonetheless. He would watch me as a cat might watch a mouse, waiting for the first show of weakness to catch me.

On the third night, I excused myself with Rebecca, and helped her get ready for bed. Since her revelation of her conversations with the dead woman and her baby, I had been seeing to Rebecca. I dressed her in the morning and put her to bed each night, sitting in a chair by her bed until I was satisfied that she was sound asleep. I would sit in the darkness and strain my ears for voices or a baby's cry, but would hear only silence.

I fought fatigue as I slid her nightgown over her head and tucked her into bed, and when she was asleep, I gratefully walked down the corridor to the master bedroom to change for bed. I rang for Mary and began pulling the pins from my hair, the dark strands falling past my shoulders and almost to my waist. It was the one feature Elizabeth and I had in common that I had not resented. We would spend long hours braiding each other's hair into elaborate twists and styles, each one more beautiful than the next.

I paused for a moment at the memory, relieved that it had been a good one. I leaned toward the mirror at my dressing table, the candlelight making my hair and skin glow, and saw the smile on my lips.

The door swung open behind me, making the candle flame shiver and swirl. I swiveled in my seat and stood to watch John enter the room.

I cleared my throat. "I rang for Mary."

"And I told her not to come. I'll see to your needs to-night."

"No, John. I'd rather not."

I could see his visible effort to control his impatience. "You cannot keep me from your bed forever, you know."

I stepped back. "It's just that . . . I need time away from you. To think."

He took a step forward, tension evident in his face. "To think about what?"

I realized I was wringing my hands and stopped. "The way things are between us."

His face relaxed, as if he had been expecting another answer. "We are married. I already told you that I did not want a cold marriage bed. And my bed has been very cold these last few nights." He held out his hand. "Come back to me."

As he spoke he approached, and I retreated until my heels hit the wall behind me. "No, John, not until this is settled between us."

He reached me and I had nowhere else to go. "Avoiding me and my bed will not settle anything." With a light touch of his finger, he stroked my cheek, the gentle touch nearly undoing my resolve.

I turned my head, making him drop his hand. "You treat my concerns lightly."

"And I tell you that you have no reason for concern. I have promised you that I will learn to trust more freely. You know it isn't easy for me and that I am only learning. Be patient with me."

"What of Marguerite?"

His face darkened. "That is still a subject not open to discussion." He placed his palms on the wall behind me and leaned in closer. "I have sworn to protect you with my life, Cat. You need never fear anything as long as I am here. And I will do all that I can to give you the gentle life you so deserve." His warm breath fell softly on my skin, making me sigh. "Surely there is nothing more you could ask of me."

He kissed my cheek, his lips and deep voice the final caress needed in banishing my resolve. I turned my head to face him, feeling the change in the air between us. I almost felt that if I lifted my finger to touch him, a great ball of fire would erupt, burning us to ashes.

"Let me love you, Cat. Let me show you that all is right between us."

I hated myself at that moment. I hated myself for putting my arms around his neck and pulling him closer. And for allowing his fingers to undress me and for his lips to arouse me. I willingly succumbed to self-loathing and denial just to be in his arms again.

When we were undressed, he lifted me in his arms and carried me to the bed. His lovemaking was sweet and tender, reminding me of our honeymoon before the realities of our married life together had intruded. I clung to him, forgetting all that had gone between us, and cried out my passion for this man as he loved me into oblivion.

He turned to me several times that night, and each time I welcomed him. It was as if we had been starved of food and now could not be sated. As dawn approached, I lay in his arms, our bodies cooling under the thin cotton sheet, the other bedclothes thrown in rumpled heaps on the floor.

Stroking my bare shoulder, he kissed my temple and moved me closer to his side. "Tell me about Robert."

I stiffened, startled at his request. "Why would you want to know about my first husband?"

"It's only natural curiosity. You know about Elizabeth, and I feel the desire to know about Robert. I want to know everything about you, Cat."

I pressed my cheek against his chest and sighed. "There's not much to tell, really. We were married only a short time before the war. But we had known each other from childhood. Our mothers were great friends, so we saw quite a bit of his family even though their cotton plantation was on the mainland."

I shut my eyes tightly against the memories that were assailing my heart—the memories of happy childhood days on warm sunny beaches and of sand beneath bare toes and the stirrings of what I had thought to be love.

"Elizabeth was always our leader—she was quite bossy. Even though Robert was Elizabeth's age, he always agreed to follow. I was the younger sister and had always been the little soldier for Elizabeth. I suppose both Robert and I were in awe of her. She would get us into scrapes and we would let her. I rarely remember her getting punished for them, either. She would feign illness or true remorse, leaving Robert and me, who were far less clever, to face our fathers' switches. Not that we ever learned our lessons, of course. We'd be up to the same old tricks as soon as our bottoms had healed."

I felt John's cheek as he smiled against the top of my head.

"I always thought that she would marry him, and I think

our parents did, too, even though she never treated Robert any differently than she would have a little brother." I slid my hand underneath the sheet as I talked, smoothing John's taut chest, my fingers curled in the thick black hairs.

"I don't believe she paid any attention to him at all until he started courting me." I recalled then the look of rage on Elizabeth's face when she had caught Robert trying to steal a kiss from me. At the time I had thought that she had been angered that he would take such liberties with her sister, who was barely fourteen. But now, for the first time, I looked back on that memory anew.

"It was during your visit—when you and Elizabeth became engaged. I suppose Robert had realized that Elizabeth was forever lost to him, so he turned his interest to me." I rolled over, placing both arms on top of John's chest, my chin cradled on my hands. "She became the most outrageous flirt. Even though she was engaged, she sought Robert out at every opportunity. I heard other mothers and their daughters calling her fast, but it didn't stop her."

He pushed the hair away from my forehead with gentle fingers. "Did you love him?"

I laid my head down on my clasped hands and closed my eyes for a moment, opening them quickly at the remembered sight of bloodstained sheets. "I think I did—at least in the beginning. I thought what I felt for him was love. But what does a young girl really know of love? We were good friends, and I thought that would be a fine start to a marriage. And he was going off to war and looked so handsome in his uniform—we were just all caught up in the excitement of it. We were young and happy, with no idea of the harsh realities of life or of the devastation of war. And it never occurred to us that perhaps whatever we had based our marriage on wasn't strong enough to help us survive the bad times."

I looked up at him again and he used a roughened thumb to wipe away the wetness on my cheeks. "No, I don't think I really loved him. He gave me my beautiful son, and I was grateful to him for that, but I can't say that I loved him."

His large hands closed about my waist and lifted me on top of him. My hands spread on the pillow behind his head to support me, my long hair brushing his face and chest. I felt him harden beneath me and the blood thumped and raced at my temples.

"I'm glad," he said, lifting me and sliding into me quickly. I arched my back, matching his rhythm and forcing myself to breathe. "I have no intention of sharing your heart with another man."

Our passion was frenzied this time, as if the heat and rising tide of our emotions were needed to negate the past and forge new, stronger bonds. I lost myself in his arms and when he shuddered, he called out my name. The image of sandy beaches and bloodstained sheets evaporated in a sea of feeling and need for this man and for the refuge he offered my bruised and battered heart.

It was only later, when his breathing had slowed to the deep and heavy rhythm of sleep and I watched the dawn light the sky, that my doubts returned. His reluctance to dismiss Marguerite alerted me to a secret that had been kept hidden from me. But I was powerless against his will. My last thought before I lapsed into a deep sleep was that perhaps I was being unreasonable by not accepting his word that he would protect me. And that, indeed, there were some secrets best kept hidden.

Chapter Nineteen

I kept Rebecca close to my side, her dreams of ghosts and voices haunting me. I had spoken to all of the servants and threatened them with dismissal if I ever heard that one of them had mentioned the Indian woman and her baby to Rebecca. Still, I wanted the child with me, trusting my own protection more than any promises.

With the heavy heat of summer gone, we spent a great deal of time out-of-doors. I would speak soon to John about buying a pony for Rebecca and teaching her to ride, but for now we would go for long drives in the small buggy that had been Elizabeth's favorite. We'd race along the lane of oaks in front of the house and beyond, but I would slow the horse as soon as we reached the levee road.

I was still uncomfortable on the levee after my fall, and would have avoided it altogether if the child hadn't clamored for it. She loved the view of the water and could never be convinced to try a different route.

On an overcast morning, just as Rebecca and I approached the levee, we were hailed by a lone rider. With dismay I thought at first it was Philip Herndon, but I soon realized that it was Dr. Lewiston. I smiled warmly and waved back.

He bowed grandly to both Rebecca and me, wiggling his golden eyebrows as he did so, and making her giggle. "What a lovely surprise to find two such beautiful ladies out for their morning ride. I would be flattered to accompany you, if only so I can bask in your beauty."

Rebecca laughed harder and I had to smile, too, despite my trepidation. I could only imagine John's anger were he to find out I had seen Daniel again without my husband's presence.

Daniel pretended to be hurt, and pressed his hat to his heart. "You wound me, ladies. I am merely trying to brighten this terribly cloudy day, yet you laugh at me."

He winked at Rebecca, then reached into his jacket pocket and pulled out a string of licorice. "And this, my dear, is for you. I always carry it around in case I am lucky enough to see you."

Rebecca reached up to take it, her smile never fading. Then she placed it in her lap, one of her gloved hands on top lest it should fall off. I assumed she was protecting it to make sure it made it to her collection in the bottom of her bureau drawer.

Despite my wariness, I couldn't help showing my genuine gladness to see him. "It's good to see you again."

I smiled up at him and he grinned back, but his eyes were serious. "You're looking as lovely as ever, Catherine."

I looked down at my gloved hands, attempting to hide my discomfiture. I knew Daniel was simply being gallant, but I doubt John would have considered his compliment innocent. The thought of John sobered me considerably, casting another cloud into my day. I thought of Daniel as

251

my friend and felt I should not be made to feel guilty for spending time with him.

"Thank you, Daniel. Your flattery goes too far, but it's always nice to hear. I'm afraid we need to be returning home."

Daniel looked disappointed. "But surely you could spare a little bit of time for me to show you Rebecca's secret place."

Intrigued, I looked at the little girl beside me. She jumped up and down on the seat, her eyes pleading. "Please—let's go. There's my own little waterfall and sometimes I find bird eggs and rocks for my collection. I haven't been there since my other mama went up to heaven." Her blue eyes shimmered. "Please?"

Reluctantly I nodded, hoping that our extended excursion would not be noticed. "All right, Rebecca. But just for a little while."

Daniel leaned over and reached for Rebecca. "Then come on, little peanut—let's go for a ride and show your aunt our special place."

"She's not my aunt anymore, Dr. Lewiston. She's my new mama."

Daniel's eyes met mine over Rebecca's blond head and he nodded approvingly.

"Let's go, then," I said, and flicked the reins on my horse. I followed Daniel and Rebecca along the levee for a short distance before turning off onto a narrow dirt road, hardly wider than a trail. It bisected a dense pine forest, a thin line of brown against lush green. We dismounted and tied the horses, then followed Daniel into the woods.

It was hard to imagine that we were so close to the river in this secluded place. The only sounds were those of the birds and other small forest creatures who inhabited the tall, scrubby pines. A thick layer of pine needles lay across the path, bristling and cracking underneath our feet. Rebecca held the doctor's hand and I followed quietly, not wanting my voice to ruin the magic of this place.

We soon came to a clearing, where a brilliant white gazebo marked the end of the path. It was large—large enough for a couple to dance the waltz—and the roof had been painted a dark green. A weathered brass hawk perched on the cupola, its eyes bright and penetrating, frightening away any small birds who might come to perch there. In the far distance, a great house rose into view, its unprotected back glaring at us. Half of the roof was missing, the charred walls like blackened bruises on the white house. A flock of sparrows lifted off from what had once been the attic, darkening the sky, and leaving us in the quiet solitude of the ruined mansion.

"Where are we?" I asked, completely lost.

Daniel smiled. "We're at Pine Grove—the King family's cotton plantation. Not that it can be called that anymore, since no crop has been planted in almost five years. It burned in the first year of the war and they left. Nobody's heard from them since."

A frown crossed his face for a moment and I looked away, studying the gazebo. It, too, appeared to be in disrepair, with floorboards missing and paint peeling, and a great sadness fell over me. It seemed that whatever the Yankees had not outright destroyed during the war had been left to face a slow and lingering death. Watching my own house burn to the ground had wounded my spirit more than a bullet to my heart ever could, yet at least I didn't have to watch it slowly fall to the ground as a mother would watch a sick child slowly founder out of this life.

I turned to face Daniel. "It's so quiet here."

He stepped onto the octagonal floor of the gazebo, carefully avoiding a protruding board. Rebecca followed closely behind him, easily stepping over the first board and then skipping with the agility of a child who had made the same movement many times over two more gaping holes before finding a seat on the far wall.

Daniel leaned against an archway and studied me carefully. "Yes, it is. It's reminiscent of so many lives after the war, isn't it? Everything in ruins."

I walked around the gazebo, taking note of the late-fall camellias, the bright, leafy bushes hiding the base of the structure and nearly completely swallowed by brambles and vines. I turned back to Daniel, eager to change the direction of the conversation. I had no wish to remember those desolate days following Robert's return. "I haven't had the chance to ask you what Philip was doing at Whispering Oaks the last time we met."

Before he spoke, Daniel turned to Rebecca. "Go see if you can find any eggs—but stay away from the water until we come, all right?"

Eagerly, the child nodded and skipped off in the direction of a dirt path close to the one we had just been on.

"Is it safe?" I asked, remembering the dangers of our grotto.

Daniel nodded. "She's been there many a time and always stays away from the water—even though it's merely a trickle and can't cause her more harm then wetting her pinafore." He smiled. "She knows not to venture far from the path, and it only meanders into the woods for a short distance. She's perfectly safe and will wait for us until we're ready to come and get her."

I wrinkled my brow. "It sounds like she's been here often."

"Yes—she loves it here. Her mother and I would bring her here quite a bit."

I nodded, remembering Mr. O'Rourke explaining to me the jaunts Elizabeth would take with Rebecca. How desperately Elizabeth must have wanted to get away from that house. She had hated the outdoors with a passion, and had always gone to great lengths to avoid it.

I watched Rebecca disappear and waited for Daniel to answer my question about Philip. The doctor leaned down and picked up a long sliver of wood that had been dislodged from a floorboard and rubbed it between his fingers. Without looking at me he said, "He was there to see you, regardless of what John might think about it. Luckily I was able to persuade him otherwise."

"He wanted to see me? Whatever for? I'm quite sure he understands that his behavior toward my husband the last time we met is completely unacceptable to me. I will not see him."

Daniel's gaze traveled to the neglected camellias, their gentle beauty now hidden under tall grass and weeds. "I told him that, but he seems quite obsessed with you."

"But that's absurd. We've known each other since we were children. It was always Elizabeth that Philip was interested in." I took a deep breath, the memory of the baby that had died with Elizabeth never far from me. "I also gather that their relationship may have continued after Elizabeth's marriage."

A shadow of sadness passed across Daniel's face. "Perhaps. I don't listen to gossip, nor will I speak ill of the dead. But as for Philip, I think it would be wise to avoid him. His antagonism toward John could be due in part to the fact that John's a Yankee; it may have nothing to do with Elizabeth at all. I avoid him simply because he's a member of that rabble-rousing White League." He dropped the scrap of wood, which hit the gazebo floor with an oddly hollow and lonely sound.

"He's threatened John. Philip said that John had taken his most cherished thing from him and now Philip would repay him. He is not the same boy I knew."

Daniel ran his hand along a balustrade, peeling paint flaking off and drifting down onto the camellias. "No,

Philip has changed. He ran away from the war and now is stirring up trouble in the hopes that people will forget his cowardice. But I would avoid him—especially now that he's all but admitted to being obsessed with you."

I waved my hand in the air, dismissing his words. "He was obsessed with Elizabeth and she and I bear a strong resemblance, that is all. He certainly never gave me a second glance all through those summers of coming here to our grandmother's." I said it without bitterness, glad to have been left to my own devices to paint and read instead of worrying about what my hair and dress looked like at all times.

Daniel smiled. "Perhaps Elizabeth's shadow was simply too large for you to emerge from. But now that it is no longer here, we all see how you shine."

I turned away to study the camellias, embarrassed by his words.

He stepped down the gazebo's steps and stood near me. Reluctantly I looked up.

"Are you happy, Catherine?"

He stood so close that I suddenly felt uncomfortable. I shot a glance toward Rebecca, feeling somewhat safer with her nearby. I stepped backward, still smiling, but trying to maintain a distance between us.

With a self-deprecating look, he stepped back, too. "I'm sorry, Catherine. I forget sometimes that we have known each other for such a short time. Perhaps it is your resemblance to Elizabeth that makes me believe that I have known you for much longer."

I looked sharply at him, curious as to how well he really had known my sister.

As if reading my thoughts, he quickly added, "Elizabeth and I were good friends. She needed someone to confide in, and she chose me. I know she confided in Clara, too, but I think that perhaps Elizabeth might have been more reticent in sharing certain things with her than with me. I was her doctor after all."

I nodded, my doubts satisfied. I glanced down at the scarlet camellias, their showy blooms staring out from among the glossy green leaves and the climbing weeds. Taking pity on the vain flowers, I knelt down and began plucking as many as I could fit in my hand. The weeds would soon choke out their beauty, withering their buds. I brought the cluster close to my face and sniffed deeply, the scent reminding me of Elizabeth. Closing my eyes, I felt the velvet softness of the flowers against my chin and thought how these vibrant blossoms were so much like my dead sister. She had been brash and vibrant, yet so vulnerable to the weeds of vanity and the fruitless search for happiness that had finally choked out her life. For a moment I felt only pity for her instead of the anger that had resided in my heart since her death—my anger at her desperate and ultimately selfish act of leaving me completely and utterly alone.

A gentle touch on my arm made me open my eyes, and I saw Daniel's compassionate ones staring into mine.

"Are you well?"

I nodded, then buried my face in the blooms again until I felt Elizabeth's memory drift back into the dark recesses of my mind where they belonged. "Let's go find Rebecca. We need to get back."

We found her crouched in front of a thin rivulet, the water valiantly struggling over mud and rocks, creating a small dripping waterfall that had entranced the little girl. It lay in the middle of an unexpected large clearing. I noticed with delight that the old camellias had found their way into this place and were pushing their heads toward the sky.

Rebecca squealed in delight as Daniel swung her up on his back. I noticed that the pockets of her pinafore bulged and I laughed. "Did you find many treasures, sweetheart?"

She nodded exuberantly. "Oh, yes. No eggs today but lots of pretty things."

I smiled at her childish enthusiasm. "That's wonderful. You'll have to show me everything when we get home."

Daniel added, "We need to leave now—before people begin to worry."

I looked at him with alarm, knowing to whom he was referring. "Yes, let's go. I want to paint Rebecca in this light and I probably have less than an hour before it changes."

Following them down the dirt trail, I glanced at the camellias clutched in my hands, their stems sticking to my sweaty palms. They no longer seemed beautiful to me, but rather were sad reminders of Elizabeth's life and untimely death. They were also one more thing to explain to John, and I had no desire to travel that path.

Slowly I opened my palm and let the flowers fall from my hand, scattering the bright red petals on the dirt path like spilled blood.

Daniel escorted us as far as the lane of trees leading up to Whispering Oaks. As we waved good-bye and watched him ride off for home, I again heard the keening cry of a baby. I shivered as if feeling a breath against the back of my neck.

Rebecca touched my arm, her eyes wide, and then I remembered the glass bottles. Turning in my seat, I spied Marguerite, half-hidden behind a tree trunk, a roll of twine and several empty bottles at her feet. A movement from a low branch caught my attention and I looked up to see Delphine clinging to a branch, a newly tied bottle dangling below her.

Marguerite looked at me for a moment, then turned her head in the direction in which the doctor had ridden. When our eyes met again, hers were all-knowing. Quickly she bowed her head. "Good afternoon, ma'am."

"Good afternoon, Marguerite." I looked past her toward the bottles hanging in the tree and swaying in the wind, their ghostly cries spiraling amongst the gnarled oaks. "Does Mr. McMahon approve of having these here?"

"I don't know. I've never asked him."

"Nor did you ask me, and I don't approve. The sound frightens Rebecca." I looked up at Delphine so she would understand I was speaking to her, too. "I want all of these removed right now and I don't want to see them again."

Marguerite stared at me in silence for a long moment before nodding her head and saying, "Yes, ma'am."

Not wanting further discussion, I picked up the reins and headed toward the house. In the short time since we had left the gazebo, heavier clouds had moved in, obscuring the light and changing my plans for painting Rebecca. I wasn't completely disappointed. I had been battling fatigue for over a week and I was happy for the excuse to lie down while Rebecca napped.

After a quick midday meal, eaten without John, who had remained at the mill office, I slowly climbed the stairs and put Rebecca to bed, barely able to keep my eyes open. When I reached my room, I collapsed on the bed, not taking the time to take off my clothes, and quickly fell into oblivious sleep.

When I awoke, John sat on the foot of the bed, staring at me with a contemplative look. My smile was not returned and he morosely moved off the bed and went to the window, staring out at the pond.

Unease bled through my body, and I wondered if Marguerite had told him of my being with Daniel. I sat up, willing to do battle and defend my freedom and innocence. "What's wrong?"

He didn't look at me when he spoke. "While you were

out with Rebecca, Philip Herndon came to call."

My unease scattered into relief. "What did he want?"

He turned to face me. "I don't know. It was you he wanted to see."

"After our confrontation in New Orleans, I truly have no desire ever to speak to the man again."

Without comment, John faced the window again. "He made the same threats he'd made before, and I told him I'd shoot him if I ever found him on my property again. Not that I think I would. The man isn't mentally stable, I'm afraid, and I need to speak with his parents about seeking treatment for him."

I slid off the bed to stand near him. "Surely not, John. I know you don't want to hear this, but he . . . cared for Elizabeth very much. He is grieving." I touched his sleeve, willing him to look into my eyes. "Let someone grieve for her as she deserved."

He touched my faced with a gentle caress. "You are too kind and loving to people who aren't deserving of it."

"She was my sister, John. That will never change."

He flinched slightly, and I was about to ask him why when the door was flung open. Rebecca stood in the doorway, her underclothing wrinkled from her nap and her unbound hair flying in all directions. She wore a wide smile, given only to those she loved the most, and in her chubby hands she clutched two bright red clusters of camellias.

My heart skidded when I spied them. I remembered her bulging pockets and, knowing her love for flowers, realized it was inevitable that she would have wanted some to bring home with her.

John walked to her and knelt by her side. "These are lovely, Rebecca. Who are they for?"

"For both of you," she said with glee, thrusting out her hand to John.

I stayed where I was, paralyzed, a sick feeling of nausea burning my stomach.

He took them from her and gave her a hug and kiss. "And where did you find such beautiful flowers?"

"Dr. Lewiston took me and Mama to our secret place where these pretty flowers grow. I knew you'd like them so I picked a lot."

An abrupt stillness seemed to fall on John, and Rebecca sensed it, too.

"What's wrong, Papa? Don't you like them?"

He had to clear his throat before getting the words out. "Yes, of course. Now you go find Delphine to help you dress. I need to speak to your mama."

She gave him a loud kiss on the cheek before skipping out of the room, taking all the warmth with her.

Slowly John stood and faced me. "Well?"

I tried to push back the wave of nausea and squared my shoulders. "Well, what? I took Rebecca for a ride and we ran into Daniel quite by accident. He showed us to the most lovely spot and we chatted for a while before returning."

His eyes flickered but he remained silent.

"For God's sake, John! Daniel is your best friend and I am your wife. Do you really think for one second that either one of us would ever betray you? I pity you if you cannot find it in your heart to trust those of us who love you best. And Rebecca was with us. Do you doubt my love for your child so much that you think I could be so despicable as to place her in that sort of situation? Maybe Philip Herndon isn't the only one who is mentally unhinged. Perhaps you both should seek treatment."

He placed his fingers under my jaw, his hand trembling from trying to control his emotions, and brought my gaze up to meet his. His words were harsh. "I can believe the worst of people for a reason. Remember that, my dear wife."

His eyes flashed as they bored into mine for a long moment before he dropped his hand. With great deliberation, he raised his other hand and closed it tightly, crushing the fragile blooms inside, then letting them drift to the floor.

I trembled from hurt and nausea and his coldness, and was glad when he left the room without another word. I barely made it to the washstand before I vomited, taking the last of my energy. Collapsing to the floor, I sat there for a long time, feeling anger, hurt, and grief wash over me in continual succession. When numbness finally seeped into my heart and brain, I stood and cleansed my face. As I slowly dried myself, I spotted the lodestone sitting on my dressing table amidst my brushes and jars of perfume.

Picking it up, I rolled it in my palms, noticing how my touch did not warm it. Instead it remained a frigid, cold lump in my hand, as if my blood had chilled to such a degree that there was no more warmth to give.

Still clutching the stone, I left the room, intent on finding Rose. I was too exhausted to contemplate my next course of action, but perhaps she could help me find my way.

I found her alone in the kitchen, and she looked up as if she were expecting me. The black pot over the stove simmered, creating that oddly pungent odor I remembered from before. She greeted me, then motioned for me to sit while she stirred the pot, whisking the steam toward her face and breathing in deeply. Reaching into a glass jar on a high shelf, she pinched a crimson powder and threw it into the pot, making it hiss and bubble.

Dipping the ladle into the pot, she poured the contents into two tin cups, then handed one to me. I turned away from the bitter brew, the odor making my stomach twist. Looking up, I caught Rose watching me closely, her eyes wide and knowing.

She sat down at the stained wooden table in the same seat she had used before and closed her eyes, the steam from her cup rising in front of her and distorting her face like a reflection in old glass.

When she spoke, her deeply accented voice had once again transformed itself, its grainy thickness calling to mind moist river silt, carrying fertile words heavy with meaning. "Does your husband know your big secret?"

I raised an eyebrow, my breath held. Until this moment I had not even ventured to hope, but now joy leaped inside me and I knew. "No. I wasn't sure . . ."

She waved her hand, her eyes tightly shut in her dark, wrinkled face. "You'll be giving your husband a son." A corner of her mouth tilted up at a vision unseen by me. "That chile will be dark like his father, so Mr. McMahon don't need to wonder no more about your true feelings for him."

I flinched as her eyes flickered open and she stared at me, unseeing. "But there's many bridges for you to cross before you can find that happiness you're searchin' for." She placed her elbows on the table and leaned toward me. "You and that girl chile be in terrible danger. She needs your love and protection now, and you need it more than her. But you need to know who your friends are and who's not your friend."

Her hand crept across the table like a large, dark spider. She grabbed my hand, prying open the fingers. She touched the lodestone and it seemed to burn in my hand. I let it roll off my palm and she replaced it quickly. "You carry this wherever you go. You need it for protection now. And you need to find out who your friends are."

The cloudiness in her eyes passed and she gave me a clear gaze. "There be things you don't know, that people want to keep hidden from you. But you need to know these things so you can understand the true nature of those closest to you." She patted my hand. "You will hurt, but your soul mate—he'll be the one to get you through this dark time."

I cleared my throat. "You . . . you mentioned before two men I share my life with, and one who betrays me. Is there any more you can tell me?"

She sat up and wrapped her fingers around her mug. "No—I only see what I'm supposed to see. It's up to you to figure out what it means."

Nodding, I stood, clutching the edge of the table for support. Leaning heavily on it, I thanked her and handed her a pair of ear bobs Robert had bought for me to show my appreciation. Turning to leave, I felt a touch on my sleeve.

Rose's eyes seemed to flicker in the dimness of the kitchen. "You watch Marguerite. Her power is much stronger than mine. And you carry that lodestone." Her fingers tightened over my hand with the lodestone and squeezed tightly. "You be needin' it now more than ever."

I thanked her again and left, the joy of my impending motherhood mixed inexorably with Rose's dour warnings. Needing fresh air, I walked around the house, avoiding the pond, toward the front. As I passed the side, I looked up, a movement in a window capturing my attention. I realized the window belonged to Elizabeth's old room, and there was no reason for anybody to be in there. Watching closely, I saw an almost imperceptible swinging of the blinds, as if somebody were gently replacing them against the window.

I raced around to the front of the house and took the steps two at a time until I reached Elizabeth's room. The door was shut and I flung it open, waiting for the bang as it hit the wall.

The room lay still and empty, just as Elizabeth had left it, her hairbrush and bottles now gathering dust on her dressing table. I blinked my eyes, noticing something dark and round hovering behind a wooden jewel box. Walking closer, I caught my breath. I stared at the object for a long time before finding the nerve to pick it up. Lifting it toward the light creeping in from the blinds, I examined it closely. It appeared to be a short, thick, and twisted root of some kind, and it emitted an acrid odor, as if it had been soaked in some sort of oil. The object was dark and slick, the roots intertwined with each other and oddly resembling an old and withered face.

Staring at it, I nearly dropped it. Carefully laced in between the sinews of the root was a thin gold chain—my chain, which I had left in the letterbox under my old bed, the key to the empty box hanging from the middle.

My hand shook as I held the gris-gris away from me. I had no doubt who had left it, and it was time to face my husband and his demons and put to rest some of my own. Squaring my shoulders, I left the room, closing the door firmly on the emptiness inside.

Chapter Twenty

I had heard John come in and I knew he was somewhere in the house. After searching the library and his study, I paused in the foyer, listening to distant voices. Many of the windows had been raised to let the cool air cleanse the house, and I realized that the voices were being carried in from outside.

Walking to the back door, I quietly opened it, then stopped. Sitting on the top step was John, his daughter cradled in his lap while he read to her from a book. Her fingers curled on his shirt collar and her head nestled comfortably in the crook of his arm. She laughed at something he read, and when he looked at her, my knees weakened. It was a look so open, so warm, and so full of love that I knew then why I had to be strong and fight whatever forces were pulling me away from him and this place of secrets. His ability to love this child so completely, thus showing his true heart, had stolen my own heart. I loved him, I realized, so fully and utterly it took my breath away. At the same time it instilled a fear so terrifying, I was afraid even to acknowledge it. For I had learned that to love so fiercely could bring loss and grief just as fierce.

Placing my hand over my still-smooth abdomen, I took a deep breath. For the sake of not only Rebecca, but also the child I knew grew inside, I could not give up. The hope of a future with John and our growing family consumed me, giving me something to fight for—something I had not had since Jamie's death.

I tucked the gris-gris in amongst the folds of my dress, unsure as to how to proceed. If John were still willing to keep Marguerite at Whispering Oaks despite the threat she posed to Rebecca, the power she held over him had to be something so awful that I couldn't even consider it.

John turned his head and saw me and my heart lurched. Had I imagined that he looked at me with the same glow in his eyes with which he had regarded Rebecca? If only I could erase all the blackness and doubt that lingered between us—thin and wispy, like smoke, but as impenetrable as a brick wall.

I joined them on the step, sitting close to John. Rebecca reached with her free hand to hold mine and we listened to John's deep voice as he finished the story. By the time he had finished, Rebecca had fallen sound asleep.

Slowly John rose, his daughter gathered in his arms, and I followed him up the stairs to Rebecca's room. He laid her on her bed and I gently covered her with a blanket. We stood there for a long moment, watching her sleep, before leaving.

I waited for him to close the door behind him before I spoke. Touching his arm, I said his name.

He looked at me with shadowed eyes, the emotion I had seen on the porch hidden from my view. Had I imagined what I had seen? Could I truly expect to fight for us and our family if he were not willing to stand by my side and fight with me? I almost blurted out my news then, but something made me hesitate. Perhaps it was the knowledge that if he knew of the baby, I would be tied to him forever, living in this prison of distrust and jealousy.

Silently I held up the root, the gold chain winking in the light from the window.

He sucked in his breath. "Where did you find that?"

"In Elizabeth's room. I know it came from Marguerite, and you and I both know what it is. It's bad gris-gris. And whether or not we believe in it, it is proof that she means us harm in some way. What have I done to her to make her hate me so?"

I heard his slow, deliberate breaths in the silent corridor. "I don't know. Maybe she resents your replacement of Elizabeth. Or perhaps it's simply your resemblance to your sister."

I shook my head in exasperation. "None of that matters now, John. What matters is our peace of mind. Whatever her reasons, she cannot stay here. Let her go. I can accept whatever hold she has on you." I swallowed thickly, searching for the courage to utter my next words. "Whatever she has to say will never change the way I feel about you."

He looked down at me, and for a moment I thought I saw pity in his eyes. He gave an almost imperceptible shake of his head and I dropped my hand, deeply wounded.

I tried to keep the desperation out of my voice. "I cannot live this way—with doubt and suspicion clouding my every move. I told you that before we were married. I can't stay here if things remain the way they are." My voice caught, and I choked on my words, thinking of the child that grew inside, the one thing to bind me here, to this place and to John—if he should find out. "I cannot stay if you continue to make it clear that you distrust me so much that you feel you can't confide in me. I have already survived so much. Surely whatever you are hiding cannot be as devastating to the spirit as that which I have already suffered. I am your wife, John. Treat me as such."

He gripped my arm, and his voice shook. "I am trying to protect you from things you are better off not knowing. Why can't you accept that?"

I pulled away, tears flowing freely down my cheeks. "Because I am not a silly girl who prefers to be coddled. I have faced the worst things life can give—there is nothing that can wound me more deeply than I already have been. Except your distrust. Please, John—tell me. Tell me what secret Marguerite hides."

His dark eyes bored into mine as a fleeting emotion flickered behind them. "I can't," he whispered. Then, his words urgent and low, he said, "Don't leave me."

I looked at him sharply. Were his words a plea or a threat? I thought of Elizabeth, supposedly killed by her own hand, and wondered if her real misdeed had been to threaten to leave her husband.

We stood almost touching in the darkened hallway, the air thick with unspoken words. He sighed, a sound of pain mixed with desire, then bent to kiss me. With all my will, I turned away and his lips brushed my cheek. He stayed there for a long moment, his heated breath teasing my neck, and it took all my determination not to turn back and reach for him. But he had hurt me more than a physical blow would have, and I remained as I was.

Eventually he straightened. Saying my name quietly, he brushed his finger against my jaw, but I remained impassive, despite the warring between my heart and my mind. I didn't turn my head until I heard his boots descending the stairs. I watched him in silence, the joyful words of my impending motherhood stilled on my lips.

He did not come to my bed that night, nor the next, and I did not search for him. My heart and body screamed for him, but my mind clung to reason and I resolved to hold on to that as long as I could, for my sake as much as for the sake of my unborn child.

It had been a long while since I had last cried, but I would wake up in the middle of those desolate nights with a pillow sodden with tears and I would reach for John's warmth, only to feel the cold emptiness of the bed beside me.

On the third evening, he came into the bedroom as I was preparing to dress for dinner at the Lewistons'. I was seated at the dressing table, rummaging through my jewelry box, when he came to stand behind me.

He placed a hand on my shoulder, his finger tracing the line of my collarbone. "You look tired."

I looked at the dark circles under my eyes and wondered if he was mocking me. But when our gazes met in the glass, his expression showed genuine concern.

"Perhaps I can send Mr. O'Rourke with our excuses and we'll stay home tonight."

I shook my head, perhaps too vigorously, knowing how weak my defenses were. I could not give in to my physical desires and hope to cling to my self-respect. "No, Daniel and Clara would be so disappointed. I'll be fine."

A dark shadow clouded his features. Leaning over me, he reached for the pearls nestled in the top tray of the jewelry box. "Then wear these. I miss seeing you in them."

"The clasp is a little loose—I'd like to have the jeweler look at it before I wear them again."

He picked the necklace up and held it to the light, his long fingers stroking the creamy smoothness of the pearls. "The clasp is fine. And it looks lovely with your amber silk gown." With slow, deliberate movements, he wrapped the necklace around my neck and fastened it. His touch and the coolness of the pearls caressed my skin, making me burn. Our eyes met again in the mirror. Before I could move away, he bent and kissed my neck, sending dangerous sparks throughout my body.

Quietly he said in my ear, "I'll be waiting for you downstairs."

I finished dressing, then left the room to go down to the foyer. I moved slowly, my fatigue weighing heavily on me. I was dreading the evening ahead. My mood was not conducive to small talk, nor to Clara's incessant chatter. Nor were my defenses strong enough to fight the inevitable longing for John's touch whenever I was in his presence.

As I approached him, he turned to face me, my wrap in his hands. I swallowed deeply, trying not to show how his mere appearance affected me. His starched white shirt accentuated his skin, darkened by the sun. The black dinner jacket hung on his broad shoulders, outlining their powerful breadth. My mouth went dry as I remembered the feel of them under my hands as we made love.

His gaze swept over me in an appreciative glance; then he moved behind me to set the wrap on my shoulders. I reached for it and our fingers touched. I jerked my hands away as if I'd been burned and stepped toward the door.

Rebecca rushed into the room, Delphine following close behind her.

"Mama, Mama!" the little girl shouted before launching herself into my arms.

I hugged her close and kissed her soft cheek before letting her go. As she ran to her father, I turned to Delphine.

"Remember—you are in charge tonight. Do not let her out of your sight, and I want you to stay in the room with her after you put her to bed until she falls asleep. Do you understand?"

Delphine nodded. "Yes'm."

Confident I could trust the young girl, I thanked her, then allowed John to escort me out the door and into the carriage. I moved over to my usual spot in the far side of the carriage, pressing against the door so as not to touch my husband inadvertently.

Mr. O'Rourke drove and John sat next to me. I fell against him when the coach lurched, and it took all my will to move away. We didn't speak for a long while, and I watched the changing landscape out the window. It was a windless night with a full moon and clear air, the stars brilliant diamonds in the black sky.

I felt compelled to face John and found him watching me closely. His eyes held the same haunting look that they had when we had spoken in the hallway outside Rebecca's room several days before. His words tossed about in my mind, pleading and threatening at the same time: *Don't leave me.* As if reading my thoughts, he said, "It's an appropriate night for All Hallow's Eve, isn't it? Nothing seems quite real."

The carriage pulled up on the levee road, bumping and swaying over the uneven surface. The water seemed so close, too near, and I clutched at my reticule, feeling silly that I had put the lodestone in it but glad that I had done so.

I turned back to look at the water, so calm and peaceful under the light of the moon, its undercurrents hidden under placid ripples. I looked at John and wondered what perilous undercurrents ran through his blood. My hand rested on my abdomen, and I wondered if we might find peace between us so I could share the news that would be only good tidings to both of us.

I was still unwilling to inexorably tie myself to John with so many unanswered questions between us, as if my growing feelings for John and Rebecca had not already done so. But I couldn't help harboring the hope that this child could be the one thing that would erase all doubts and misunderstandings between us, and bring us back to that place of wild contentment that had been upon us in the first weeks of our marriage.

I looked out again at the moonlit water, the unsalty smell of it still so foreign to me. A bat launched itself from a tree on the bank, swooping low and fluttering fast until it disappeared behind the carriage. A metallic click sounded from the outside of the carriage, unrelated to the usual bumps and jars, and I found myself holding my breath.

A feeling of danger suddenly consumed me, making me sick with it, and I pressed myself against the side of the carriage. John reached toward me, taking my arm with one hand as he reached for the door near me with his other.

I looked at his face for a moment, but it was hidden in shadow. His grip on me tightened as I remembered his words in the hall: *Don't leave me.*

I gave a strangled cry as the carriage door swung open behind me at the same time John lifted me out of the seat. The skirts of my gown whipped furiously in the wind outside the gaping coach door, and I clung to John's arms.

Mr. O'Rourke shouted from above, and then I found myself smothered against John's solid chest, the smell of wool and freshly pressed linen heavy in my nose. I didn't open my eyes again until the carriage came to a complete stop.

"Are you all right?" John's voice was thick in my ear.

I nodded, not yet able to speak.

"Thank God. I saw the door opening and knew that one bump in the road would send you out of the carriage. I got to you just in time."

Mr. O'Rourke climbed down from his perch and stood in the empty doorway. Holding a lantern aloft, he said, "The paint's all scratched up—it's like somebody's been tampering with the latch."

John continued to hold me tightly against him. Softly he said, "You're shaking. We should go home."

I shook my head. I felt the need to be with other people besides John. I couldn't help remembering John gripping my arm before we heard Mr. O'Rourke's shout, and I wondered what his true intent had been if the driver had not noticed the open door. His words reverberated again and again in my head, my mind trying to interpret them as plea or threat: *Don't leave me.*

John gave Mr. O'Rourke instructions to continue on, and, after he had fiddled with the latch to get it to stay, the carriage started again. I stayed close to John and away from the door, wondering for the remainder of the journey if I was truly safer in his arms. I wanted to believe it with all my heart, but I couldn't stop myself from thinking of Elizabeth. Had she ever threatened to leave, and was that why she now lay buried in the old family mausoleum?

I turned to look at my husband in the dark interior of the carriage, and saw no malice. He brushed the hair from my forehead and kissed me gently, then gazed out his window, his thoughts hidden from me.

Daniel met us at the door of Belle Meade, an imposing Greek Revival mansion. I noticed the absence of a servant to greet us and take our cloaks, as well as the faded and peeling wallpaper in the grand foyer—both examples of the demise of a way of life that I coldly acknowledged we would never see again.

When Daniel led us into the front parlor, conversation halted as all eyes turned to us, more specifically to me. I felt a flush steal over my shoulders as the uncomfortable silence continued until Daniel took my arm and led me to a chair. As he seated me, he leaned toward my ear and whispered, "You look so much like Elizabeth tonight—it's the way you've done your hair, I think. It's quite stunning."

Self-consciously I reached up to touch the coil of hair

at the nape of my neck, remembering how Elizabeth, after teasing me about my propensity to wear my long hair unbound, had taught me how to roll and tuck my hair in a fair imitation of the style she preferred. After securing it, she had quickly pulled it out again, saying it didn't suit me. But now that I was no longer willing to accept Marguerite's help in dressing or fixing my hair, it was the only formal style I knew how to do myself.

Clara greeted me with a kiss on each cheek, her smile cheerful and warm as she played the consummate hostess with a skill that had been bred into her. Despite the dingy furniture and dusty drapes, she exuded the same hospitality that she would have when her home shone and sparkled and the paint didn't peel from the massive columns across the front.

She wore a dinner gown in a dated style, but the celery-colored silk lifted the usual pallor of her skin, making her eyes shine. When she smiled, as she invariably did when looking at her husband, she was almost pretty. She seemed to flit amongst her guests like a moth around an open flame, but always came to rest by her husband's side. She reminded me of a small child with a favorite toy, afraid to leave it alone too long lest somebody come along and take it from her.

As Clara had assured me, it was a small gathering. Besides the Lewistons, Clara's elderly father, Mr. Brier, and John and myself, Judge Patterson and the elder Herndons completed the party. I was surprised to see the latter until Daniel quietly explained that they were no longer on speaking terms with their son and that he had moved out of their house several weeks prior. They had not seen him since. When Daniel straightened after whispering in my ear, I looked up to see Clara and John watching us closely. Before I could respond, Clara was at Daniel's side, whisking him away to a conversation with Mr. and Mrs. Herndon.

At dinner, as one of the guests of honor, I was seated at Daniel's right side with Judge Patterson on my right and Clara's father across from me. I remembered Mr. Brier's assertion that he had seen Elizabeth in Baton Rouge before we had found her body, and Clara's claim that the old man was not in his right mind. I assumed him to be in his late seventies or early eighties. Stooped and wrinkled, he walked with the assistance of a cane, and one of the servants had to cut his meal into tiny bites. He didn't speak, so I assumed he couldn't, and when he ate, drool fell from the corner of his mouth. But when he looked up, his eyes were bright and clear, and it was obvious that he was following the conversation around him intently.

John sat to Clara's right, putting him diagonally across from me, and every time I looked in his direction, I'd see his dark, brooding eyes on me before I'd looked quickly away.

Conversation at the table seemed strained, as if we were all trying too hard to avoid the obvious topics that would be deemed unsuitable. So we talked of the weather and politics and the recent disappearance and murder of a sheriff in a neighboring parish. But the recent war, the dilapidated house, the missing son, and my dead sister seemed to float behind the dining room chairs like ghosts, unseen but as present in the room as the scarred furniture.

As a young black girl cleared away the dinner dishes and brought out dessert and coffee, Clara addressed me from the other end of the table, ensuring that everyone could hear.

"Catherine, is the food to your liking? You look pale."

It was true that the aromas of food were making my stomach churn, no doubt on account of the baby. I had thought that I had stirred the food up enough on my plate to give the illusion that I had eaten.

"The food is delicious, thank you. I'm just feeling a little tired, that's all."

"Well, it's been almost two months since your honeymoon. Since we're all close friends, I was wondering if perhaps you had some news for us."

I tried to give her a warning look as I answered. "I'm not quite sure what you mean. If you're speaking of my first completed portrait, yes—Rebecca's has been finished and I'm quite proud of it. When you visit us next, you can see it hanging in the library."

Her eyes never wavered from my face. "No, dear. I was hoping you and John might have some more exciting news for us." She lowered her lashes, her composure returned to that of the reserved Clara I knew. Quietly smoothing her linen napkin in her lap, she said, "I'm sorry if I've embarrassed you by speaking out of turn. It's just that I thought—well, I hoped—that we might have something to celebrate this evening. There's precious little good news as it is."

My gaze slid to John. His eyes had darkened and his face had stilled, his hand tightly clutching his wineglass. I turned away and saw Clara, who, remarkably, had her eyes fixed on Daniel, as if to study his reaction.

Clara must have already known the truth—probably from Marguerite. I looked down at my plate, knowing that to lie now would be futile. "Yes, we do have good news. John and I are expecting a child."

There was a call for a toast, and Daniel immediately stood to refill the wineglasses. I noticed how his hand shook as he poured my wine. The sound of broken glass brought our attention to John. The glass in his hand had shattered, leaving spilled wine, shards of crystal, and blood from his cut hand on the crisp white tablecloth.

Daniel placed the wine bottle on the table and hesitated

a moment before approaching John. "Let me take you to my office, where I can make sure there's no glass left in your hand and wrap it properly."

John glanced up at his old friend with darkened eyes and, after a long pause, accepted Daniel's offer. With a bow and an apology, he excused himself, his gaze carefully avoiding mine.

I felt sick to my stomach and was grateful for Judge Patterson's assistance in helping me out of my chair and escorting me back to the parlor. Because of the small size of the group and the absence of John and Daniel, the ladies and gentlemen convened in the same room. I assumed the three remaining men were waiting for the return of the other two before retiring to the library for port and cigars.

Mr. Brier sat next to me on a horsehair sofa. To my surprise, he reached for my hand and patted it solicitously. His hand was surprisingly soft and warm, and I found comfort in his gesture. Still, I felt hot and clammy, almost as if I were suffocating, the need to see John all-consuming. His anger at the table had been palpable and certainly understandable, and I needed to be with him to explain.

The old man leaned toward me. "Don't you pay no mind to my Clara." He pointed to his wrinkled and age-spotted forehead. "Her own lack of children has become an obsession with her. Almost as much as her obsession with Daniel."

After speaking, he immediately sat back on the sofa, closed his eyes, and began to softly snore.

I was soon joined by Judge Patterson. I struggled to stand but he urged me back. "You're pale and need to rest." He fixed a knowing gaze on me. "You let the men work on their own problems—it has nothing to do with you, you understand?"

Numbly, I nodded, not sure I did understand.

He moved closer, so that his words would be heard only by me. "So it would seem that you and John are finding marriage to each other quite suitable."

I flushed and looked down at my hands.

"No need to be embarrassed, child. A good and fruitful marriage is something to be rejoiced over. I know his first marriage was difficult, and it was my greatest hope that you both would find happiness." He knelt down in front of me, peering up at me with a gentle smile. "But I also understand that a new marriage in an unfamiliar place may have bumps in the road. If you ever have need of a friend, please remember that my old ears are still good for listening. You know where to find me."

I looked into his kind eyes and knew I was not alone.

"Thank you," was all I said.

He leaned toward me, speaking quietly. "The old man isn't as senile as Clara would like you to believe."

"What do you mean?"

Before he could answer, there was a loud pounding on the front door. The judge held out his hand, holding Clara back. "You stay here. I'll go see what it is."

As soon as he had opened the door, the sound of a high-pitched, excited voice reached us. With panic tearing at my heart, I raced toward the foyer, recognizing the voice.

"Delphine! What's wrong?"

Her dark skin was streaked with sweat, her clothes damp and disheveled. Rufus hovered in the background, Jezebel flicking her tail behind him, sweat glistening on her flank. It appeared that they had run all the way from Whispering Oaks.

Delphine took several deep breaths before filling her lungs enough to be able to answer. "She's gone, Miss Catherine. Miss Rebecca—she's gone!"

279

Chapter Twenty-one

Spots swam before my eyes, but I held on, convincing myself that I couldn't help Rebecca if I didn't remain strong. I felt a familiar touch on my shoulder, and I melted into John's side, drawing strength from his.

John spoke, his words clipped, his anger and fear held in tight control. "What do you mean, she's gone? Your instructions were to stay with her after she went to bed."

Delphine began sobbing, her words unintelligible. I went to her and brought her inside, asking for a drink of water. A glass was soon pressed into her shaking hands. As soon as she took a sip, I asked her, "What happened, Delphine? Tell us everything so that we may find her as quickly as possible."

She took another sip and nodded. "I did as I was told, Miss Catherine. I didn't let her out of my sight. And I sat in that chair by her bed until she fell asleep."

I pressed on, the urge to bolt out the door and run to

Whispering Oaks nearly overpowering my calm. "Then what happened?"

"I thought she was asleep, but as I stood to go she sat up and asked for a drink of water." She sniffed and brought the back of her hand across her nose. "I told her I'd go get it and to stay in bed. So I went down the stairs and I passed Marguerite. She asked what I was doing and I told her. Marguerite said I'd worked hard enough and that she'd bring the water to Miss Rebecca."

She started sobbing harder and I felt a claw of fear take hold of my heart with sharp talons.

Through sniffs, Delphine managed to continue. "Later I started to worry, since you had put me in charge. So I went back to her room, and her bed was empty." Tears leaked out of her dark eyes as she stared up at me with fear and remorse. "I shouted for her, Miss Catherine, and I looked all over, but she wasn't in the house."

"What about Marguerite? Where is she?" The panic clawed through my words.

Delphine sobbed louder. "I couldn't find her, Miss Catherine. She and Miss Rebecca are just gone!"

John's grip on my shoulder tightened. "Catherine, I want you and Delphine to stay here with Clara and the other women. Daniel and I will ride back to see what's happened and find Rebecca. I'll send Mr. O'Rourke back with news."

I turned to my husband, my hands wildly clutching at him. "No, John. I must come with you. I cannot stay here and worry." Hearing the sob at the back of my throat, I lowered my voice. "Please let me help."

His eyes softened as he regarded me; then he gave a sharp nod. Daniel brought our cloaks and we raced out the door, not bothering with the formality of saying goodbye.

We tore down the levee road, with me clutching John's

arm and staying away from the broken door, while Daniel
and Rufus followed closely behind on their own mounts.
John's hand reached for mine, and I took it, looking into
his eyes and feeling the unity of our spirits. Yes, I thought,
this is how it should be. Together, as one, through all the
good and bad. It went far deeper than trust, and I pulled
our entwined hands to my heart so we could both feel its
beating, and know that it beat for us, for Rebecca, and for
the tiny child growing within me.

When we pulled up in front of Whispering Oaks, I
jumped out quickly without waiting for John's assistance.
I noted the lack of servants to meet us, and I wondered
why until I smelled the smoke. The pungent smell of burning wood was carried to us on the thin air, like thick fists
grabbing us and pulling us around the side of the house.

Daniel saw it first and pointed. "There's fire in the sugar
mill."

"Rebecca!" I shouted, ready to run as fast as my legs and
full skirts would allow me.

Instead John held my arms tightly. "Daniel and I will go
see what we can do. I need you to sound the alarm so the
field hands can come and help us with water. Then go
search the house for Rebecca and let me know if you find
her."

His dark gaze met mine and I nodded, understanding
his meaning. He needed to assure himself that Rebecca
was not in the burning building. Without warning, he
grasped my head in his large hands and pulled me toward
him, kissing me hard.

He let go of me and began running toward the burning
mill. I nearly stumbled as I turned and ran blindly back
toward the house and to the edge of the field, where a
large bell hung in its wooden casing. The evening wind
whipped inside it, causing it to moan into the clear night.
I pulled on the suspended rope, making the bell chime in

a low, monotonous clang, and waited until several men appeared from their quarters to investigate.

I sent one to ride to the neighboring plantations to ask for help, and the remainder to rouse as many people as possible and then to go directly to the well with as many buckets as they could gather. Next I ran for the house, frantically searching for Rebecca. I almost sprawled over a large stump of an oak tree, an ax protruding from its middle where Mr. O'Rourke had left it. Finding my footing again, I continued to run toward the front entrance to the house.

I flung open the door to complete stillness. With the exception of Marguerite and Delphine, I had seen all the house servants outside by the bell. I ran up the stairs two at a time, shouting out Rebecca's name. My lungs pressed against my stays, straining for air that they could not get. Forcing myself to slow down, I took deep breaths as I walked purposefully toward Rebecca's room.

The sheets had been turned down and the pillow had the indentation of a small head, but Rebecca was conspicuously absent. My heart lurched when I spotted Samantha on the floor, facedown. I ran out of the room, my voice near hysteria as I shouted Rebecca's name again and again. She would never willingly go anywhere without her doll.

I ran though the house, opening every door and closet, looking under every bed, and calling her name. I even climbed up to the attic, candle held aloft, searching, but found no trace of the child.

A sick dread settled in my stomach as I caught sight of the growing flames from the mill. What if Rebecca was in the mill? Feeling almost faint from my exertion, I sped out of the house toward the burning mill, where a growing number of men and women had formed lines from the well, transporting buckets of water to overcome the flames. My eyes stung from the smoke as they searched the crowd for John's towering form, but he was nowhere to be found. I asked several of the men hauling buckets, but they hadn't seen him. People swarmed everywhere, the air heavy with smoke, making it difficult to see. My mind screamed, *Where are you John? Where are you?*

Thinking that maybe he had found Rebecca and taken her to the house, I turned back. As my feet fled over the dry grass, I felt a prickling sensation on the back of my neck, and looked up at the house. I thought I imagined a solid thumping on window glass and I stopped in my tracks, small spots of light gathering before my eyes as I struggled to maintain consciousness. A candle had been lit in my art room, and there, silhouetted against the window, was the sweet face of the child I had come to love as my own flesh and blood.

With a strangled shout, I ran back into the house and up the stairs to the little art room off my bedroom. I smelled smoke, as if a candle had just been extinguished, and no light shone under the door. I approached the room cautiously, wondering if I had just imagined Rebecca's face in the window.

I pushed at the door, then watched it soundlessly glide open. "Rebecca?"

The room was completely black, the mixed odors of smoke and paints turning my stomach and making me feel faint. Pressing one hand against the door frame to steady myself, I held my other hand to my nose and called Rebecca's name again.

A small sound came from the far corner of the room, and I approached slowly. "Rebecca, it's your mama. Everything's all right, and I'm here to take care of you. Can you come out now?"

A slight rasping came from the corner again, quickly

followed by the sound of the door shutting behind me and the key turning in the lock.

I spun quickly, my skirts knocking over an easel and dumping the canvas to the floor with a crash. Feeling my way to the door, I grasped at the handle, tugging hard. It didn't move.

"Rebecca? Is that you? Please let me out—somebody, please let me out."

In the inky silence, I heard the rasping sound again, a creeping noise in the far dark corner, and cold perspiration crawled up my skin. *Snake.* I could almost see the black, scaly skin of a cottonmouth as it slithered toward me in the darkness. I knew it wouldn't attack me unless provoked, but I couldn't see it nor avoid stepping on it if it came nearer.

I turned back to the door, banging on it in earnest. "Help me—please, somebody help me. Please let me out!" I thumped louder, feeling the reverberations up to my shoulders.

Again the white spots appeared before my eyes, but I clung to consciousness with every fiber of my being. I had not survived so much hardship to die now—now that so much mattered to me. I banged on the door again with renewed strength, knowing my life depended on it.

I stopped for a moment to listen, but heard nothing except the muted shouts from the mill. Gingerly, hugging the wall, I crept toward the window, hoping to find somebody in the yard below. I nearly sagged with relief as I spied Mr. O'Rourke, the ax from the stump in his hand, walking quickly back toward the fire. I fumbled with the window latch, scraping my fingers until they bled, but was unable to open it. Instead I banged loudly on the glass, praying against all hope that I could break it or that he would hear me banging and look up. I imagined I felt something brush against the skirt of my dress and I pounded even harder.

Mr. O'Rourke glanced up and I waved my hands, hoping he'd spot the movement. I hit my fists against the glass again so he'd realize where I was and watched with thin hope nearly smothered by desperation as he turned back toward the house, ax in hand.

Pressing myself against the wall, I strained my ears, imagining I heard movement from all four corners of the blackened room. The darkness fell all around me, encroaching upon my very mind, but I fought it with my last resources of energy. I placed my cheek against the cool plaster of the wall, concentrating on the reality of it and forcing myself to stay upright.

A pounding sounded from the other side of the door. "Mrs. McMahon—are you in there? Do you need me?"

"Mr. O'Rourke—yes! Somebody's locked me in here—and I need to get out. I think there's a . . . snake in here. Please—hurry!"

"There's no key in the lock. Stand back and I'll use my ax."

I crouched by the window and listened as the ax shattered the door, splinters of wood flying into the room and hitting my bowed head.

When enough of the door had been destroyed, Mr. O'Rourke kicked it in, the jamb fracturing in half. I stood and a movement outside the window caused me to turn my head. Rebecca's back was toward me and she was walking in the direction of the pond, her long white nightgown glowing in the light of the full moon.

"Rebecca!" I screamed at the closed window. I stepped back and felt something smooth and rigid under my foot. A solid force hit the skirt of my gown and I looked down to see the shimmering scales of the cottonmouth in the light of the open door, its fangs buried in the folds of my skirt. Mr. O'Rourke raised his ax and brought it down with a sickening thud, severing the serpent in half. In a daze, I watched as he grabbed the head of the snake and yanked it from my dress, ripping the silk.

I turned to Mr. O'Rourke. "Go get Mr. McMahon and bring him to the pond—now!" Without another word I dashed out of the room, my fingers frantically ripping at my dress and my stays to loosen them so I could breathe— or swim. All I knew was that I had to get to Rebecca before she reached the pond. I could not lose another child. The light that had begun to shine in my soul would surely be darkened forever.

I saw Rebecca hesitating by the edge of the pond and heard her sobs. As I neared her, I heard her voice cry out to me, and it sounded so much like Jamie that my steps faltered and I fell.

"Mama, Mama—where are you, Mama?"

I scraped my fingernails in the dirt, trying to stand, my mind reeling. Was that Jamie's voice? Or was it Rebecca?

I found my footing again and raced toward her, watching in horror as she stepped into the black water.

"Rebecca—stop! Mama's here. Stay there and I'll come get you."

Slowly she turned around and stared at me, her blond hair shimmering in the moonlight like a halo. "Mama?" Her eyes were dreamlike, as if she were walking in her sleep.

I pulled my gown over my head, throwing it on the grass, and stepped out of my underskirts. Reaching out my arms, I walked slowly to her, barely aware of the shouts and running feet approaching from behind.

As if in slow motion, I watched as she seemed to lose her balance, her arms swinging in wide arcs at her side before she fell backward, slowly sinking out of sight within the embrace of the dark, treacherous pond.

My skin seemed stuck to my bones, making me ponderous, lethargic, unable to move. I smelled salt water and heard a seagull's cry. The grass under my feet became warm sand and waves rolled toward me, lapping at my now bare toes. Jamie was just beyond my reach, his fingers stretching toward me before his head fell beneath the waves one last time. I cried out, his name sweet on my lips, my heart heavy with grief.

Then the fear that had remained so elusive in the last year struck me with the force of a human hand, taking the breath from my lungs and jolting my muscles into action. It was no longer the fear of water, but the fear of loss. Without conscious thought, I dove into the pond where I had last seen Rebecca, the chill of the water sending pin-pricks of misery to every pore of my skin.

I dove deep into the darkness, my hands reaching out to grab anything. But my fingertips brushed only the cold water, sending it in ripples down the length of my body. I swam to the bottom, feeling the thick, heavy mud, then kicked myself up toward the surface. I followed the light of the moon, its edges soft and uneven through the water, but still a beacon for me.

I burst through the water, my lungs hurting. I glanced quickly around, ignoring Mr. O'Rourke and those he had gathered, who were now approaching the bank, and looked for any sign of Rebecca. Only the small ripples caused by my movement marred the still surface of the dark water. With a deep breath, I plunged into the dark depths again.

I used the broadest stroke I could, stretching as far as possible, my fingers lonely hunters in the murky coldness. I reached the empty bottom again, pushing aside my despair that I had not yet found Rebecca. Turning on my back, I stared up at the surface, my loosened hair swimming snakelike around my face. I pushed it away and watched as a dark shadow passed above me.

With my toes finding purchase in the silt bottom, I crouched and pushed upward, my fingers reaching for the small flailing hands that seemed to move slower and slower. I skimmed through the water and touched her, then grabbed her around the waist with my other arm before I broke the surface.

Gasping for air, I struggled with Rebecca's limp form until I felt two strong arms grab hold of us and bring us the rest of the way to the bank, where my feet could touch the bottom. Daniel took the child from my arms, and I was at first reluctant to let her go.

John's strained voice shook. "Give her to Daniel, Cat. He needs to get the water out of her lungs so she can breathe."

. With shaking hands I let go, then allowed myself to be lifted into my husband's arms.

We waited until we heard Rebecca's cry, and then she and I were both carried inside the house. I insisted that Rebecca be put in my bed with me. The threat of pneumonia was real, and I trusted no one to watch her as I could. We were dried and dressed in our nightclothes, then bundled into bed with a roaring fire heating the room.

I cringed when I looked at the shattered door to my art room, trying not to remember the cold sweat of fear. Looking up at John, I grabbed hold of his sleeve. "You haven't asked about the door."

He leaned over to tuck Rebecca in, his sleeve brushing across my chest. "Mr. O'Rourke told me. I'll have it replaced tomorrow."

I fell back, trying to read his inscrutable face. I pulled on his arm as he straightened. "It was no accident. I was led there on purpose and locked inside. Now do you believe me about Marguerite? Do you have any doubts about her intentions now? I know I can't prove anything, but there's no doubt in my mind that she means us harm. Including Rebecca."

"Did you see her so that you know for sure? I know that

Philip Herndon was here—my burning mill is proof of that. He is the one who swore to take what was most precious to me. If anybody had a motive to harm you, it would be him."

I pushed myself up, forcing my voice to remain calm. "But what about Rebecca? We know that Marguerite was with her last." I swallowed thickly. "Rebecca could have died tonight."

He flinched, then resumed his stolid expression. "Hush now—you're overwrought. You both need your rest. I've asked Rose to make you a tea to help you sleep. She'll bring it up when it's ready."

He stood and I held on to his hand. To my surprise, I realized it was shaking. "John—please!"

Gently he pulled his hand away. "Go to sleep. We'll talk when you're feeling better."

He bent and kissed Rebecca's forehead and then mine before leaving. I turned to face my art room, as if to make sure nothing would slither out. An unbidden thought crossed my mind—the memory of how I had searched in vain for John at the burning mill before returning to the house, where I had been locked in a room with certain death. *Where were you, John?*

I pushed the recollection aside. He could have been lost in the crush of people attempting to put out the fire, and it would have been easy to miss him.

I watched Rebecca fall asleep while I waited for Rose's tea. It was steaming hot and bitter, but I drank it down, wondering if I would ever feel warm again, and quickly joined Rebecca in oblivious sleep.

The sound of hushed, arguing voices awakened me. The fire had sputtered to a faint glow and a chill enveloped the room. The heated embers were the only source of light, giving me the impression that it was the middle of the night. Something heavy weighed upon my neck, and I realized that my pearl necklace had not been removed when I had been dried and dressed in my nightclothes. My fingers patted it lightly and I remembered the loose clasp, thankful it had not fallen into the water.

After checking Rebecca's slow, even breathing to make sure she was asleep, I slipped from bed and padded toward the door. Opening it a crack, I listened for voices, but heard nothing but the quiet ticking of the tall case clock in the foyer. I was about to close the door again when I heard someone speaking. I recognized the deep voice as John's and I waited for a long moment to hear with whom he was talking.

It was a woman's voice, deep and resonant, and highly distinguishable. *Marguerite.* I heard her laugh, a sound from deep in her throat, and it made my blood chill. I stepped into the hallway and closed the door, locking it with a soft click behind me. Slowly I descended the stairs, gripping the banister to guide my way, following the voices.

A thin light shone from under the library door, thin as if from the light of a single candle, and I walked toward it and placed my hand on the knob. The sound of Marguerite's voice gave me pause.

"You know that if she finds out the truth, she'll leave. She'll go back to where she belongs. Or maybe that's what you've been wanting all along—for her to be gone. Yet you're afraid that she'll take the child with her once she knows."

With my heart hammering wildly in my chest, I pulled my hand from the brass doorknob as if scorched.

I heard the control in John's voice. "You will not blackmail me with this any longer. I won't have it."

Marguerite laughed a bitter laugh. "You stand to lose a lot more than I ever could. When she finds out how you've been deceiving her, she and that child will be gone. Then you'll be left with no child and no one to warm your bed at night." She chuckled again, low and evil. "Maybe that's what you deserve."

A glass crashed to the floor and I jumped back.

"How dare you! Rebecca and Catherine could have been killed tonight because of your negligence, and no amount of threats from you will ever make me ignore that fact."

Marguerite's tone darkened. "I put Rebecca to bed. If the voices of the dead spoke to her, then that's the way of it. There are powers that are stronger than me, and I cannot stand in their way." She gave a low chuckle. "And somebody locked Catherine in that room tonight. Who's to say it wasn't you?"

"Stop it! I should have listened to Catherine and dismissed you long ago. You are a danger to my daughter and I will no longer tolerate your presence here. You are dismissed, and I never want to see you in this house again." Two quick and heavy footfalls sounded in the library, and I pictured him walking closer to Marguerite, towering over her, and her staring defiantly up at him. "Get out. Tonight. And if you ever breathe a word to Catherine, I will kill you. It will be so swift and so sudden that your last living thought will be to wonder how it happened." He lowered his voice further, making me strain to hear him. "I've killed before and I'll do it again. I'm not a man to be thwarted."

Steps approached the door and I drew back into the alcove under the stairs, my eyes mesmerized by the mirror opposite. It seemed to create its own light, casting an ethereal glow that shimmered in the darkness. I clenched my eyes shut, not wanting to see whatever might materialize in its corrupted glass.

The door flew open and John ordered, "Get out."

Opening my eyes, I peered out from my hiding place.

Marguerite turned to John with equal fervor. "I'll do that, but you can be sure that once your precious wife finds out that Rebecca is not your child, she'll know why you married her. And she'll try to leave, just like your Elizabeth. Maybe this wife will be more successful in escaping than her sister." She barked a mirthless laugh. "Maybe you should show her Elizabeth's letters before she leaves. If you don't think they'll kill her. Or maybe that's what you want."

I heard John draw in a sudden breath. "You're lucky I'm not throwing you in jail or worse. Now leave before I change my mind!"

Her voice was insolent as she turned to him on the threshold of the room. "You've got far more to hide than I."

She turned to leave but he grabbed her elbow and pulled her back. "What do you mean?"

Facing him slowly, she turned to smile at him. "I saw Elizabeth before you got to her and took your glove and the gris-gris. Her traveling bag was with her, too, as if she was planning on leaving you. The sheriff would be interested in hearing all about it."

"There was nothing to incriminate me—only evidence that would have destroyed Rebecca's standing in the community."

"It was your glove, remember? And the gris-gris was one for an unfaithful lover. But you know that, don't you?"

"Get out," he said again through gritted teeth, letting go of her arm with a rough gesture.

Her skirts swung in a graceful arc as she turned back to the darkened foyer. I flattened myself against the wall, grasping at the necklace around my neck. *I need you, dear sister. I am so afraid.* Had I finally discovered what she had been so afraid of? Her husband—the man with a known temper and a penchant for violence?

Karen White

I hugged the wall, blending into the darkened alcove to avoid being seen by Marguerite as she walked by. I heard her words again and fear spread like poison through my blood. *Rebecca is not your child.*

Why had John not told me? I already knew about the unborn child Elizabeth carried when she died, so the fact that Rebecca wasn't his either would have come as no surprise. I almost gasped aloud as the next thought occurred to me: He had no claim to Rebecca, a child he loved as if she were his own flesh and blood. The only sure way to keep her with him would have been to marry the child's aunt.

The hope that I had carried inside me, the hope that John had married me for other reasons, turned to ash as quickly as a thin leaf in a flame. John was a willful man. He would stop at nothing to get what he wanted. If I were threatening to leave and knew he had no claim to Rebecca, what would he do to stop me? The same thing that had been done to Elizabeth?

I clenched my eyes shut, pressing my forehead against the wall. Marguerite had gone, but I had not heard John move from the doorway of the library. After a few breathless moments, I heard his slow footsteps walk back into the room and the squeak of his desk chair as he sat.

As I took a step out of the alcove, a loud clattering sound came from the wood floor, as if something had dropped. Not wanting to waste any time to see if John had heard it, too, I fled up the stairs, then hid in the dark corridor above and waited.

John walked out into the middle of the foyer and stopped. "Marguerite? Is that you?" In the stillness of the night, I heard the precise snap of a pistol's hammer and held my breath.

After several long moments, he retreated back into his

library and shut the door, the sound of the lock sliding into place loud and deliberate.

Slowly I made my way back to my room on shaking legs. After turning the key in the lock, I stirred the fire, but the heat was unable to penetrate the bone-chilling numbness that seemed to have seeped into my soul.

I had no hope of sleep, but the warmth of the bed beckoned me, so I slipped between the sheets and snuggled next to Rebecca. *What kind of a man is your father?* I wanted to ask. *He possesses unknown depths of love and kindness in the same soul that harbors so much darkness. And I am afraid. So afraid.*

Too numb to weep, I lay beside Rebecca, absorbing her warmth and keeping my eyes fixed on the ceiling as I waited for dawn.

Chapter Twenty-two

As soon as the light of day touched the windows, I crept from the bed, making sure I didn't awaken Rebecca. I paused by her side and felt her forehead. It was warm, but not overly so, and her breathing was slow and even. Reassured, I stepped back and began to dress. I had been busy making plans all through the long, wakeful night, and I had much to do.

While I sat at the dressing table twisting my hair on top of my head, the door opened and John entered. He was still in the evening clothes he had worn the night before, his hair rumpled. Dark stubble covered his jaw, making him look as dangerous as a knife blade. My traitorous heart leaped at the sight of him. I turned away, focusing on my reflection in the mirror.

He went to the bed and sat down next to Rebecca, watching her as she slept. Then, as I had done, he pressed the back of his hand to her forehead and left it for a long moment. "She's very warm."

I nodded, searching for my voice. "Yes, I noticed that, too. But I think it's just from sleep. We'll see how she is when she wakes."

His dark eyes rested on me for a moment before he went to the fireplace and built up the fire with more logs. Then he came to me and stood next to my chair, not saying anything.

Unnerved by his proximity, I glanced at him. Without a word he fell to his knees in front of me, placing his large hand on my abdomen where our child grew inside.

"The child—he is well?"

A large lump lodged itself in my throat. I remembered his anger of the night before when he had learned of the child's existence and noticed the absence of the words *our child.* Still, his gentleness disarmed me, and I was left floundering. "Yes. Our child is fine. He is well protected in his mother's womb."

He leaned forward and kissed me where his hand had been a moment before, his hot breath moving through the fabric of my gown to my bare flesh. I suppressed a moan and the need to run my hands through his black hair, and instead pushed myself back into my chair.

He lifted his head and his eyes searched mine. "You risked so much last night." His fingers lightly traced my jawbone, his touch heating my blood, until they came to rest on my collarbone. "I remember what you told me of Jamie's death, and I believe I can understand what strength it took for you to save Rebecca."

Tears pricked at my eyes as I realized the enormity of the previous night's occurrences. There was so much unsaid between us, but my uncertainty hovered near. "I love her." There was nothing more I could say.

"So do I," he said, his voice full of meaning. His hand dropped and the light shining in his eyes dimmed. Softly he said, "How lucky Rebecca is to be loved so completely and selflessly that you would risk everything for her."

I longed to fall into his arms and tell him that the love I felt for him was the same, but I could not. The words I had overheard between him and Marguerite had built a strong wall around my heart, one not easily breached.

I turned back to my dressing table and lifted the brush. One by one I picked out the long, dark strands from the bristles. "She is but a child and has been denied the true love of a mother for too long. I am glad that we have found each other."

He rose swiftly, his movements stiff, and I knew that my words of omission had hurt him. He, too, seemed to have expected me to say something else. "You have told me many times that you wish for a loving marriage built on truth and trust. Yet I feel there is something heavy hanging between us—something unsaid. Is there anything you wish to say to me?"

I thought of my questions and accusations—certain he would have answers for me. But not the truth. The lingering suspicion that I could not bear the truth clouded my mind, and I wanted to answer him from my heart: *I want to leave you now—now, before I learn that which I cannot bear.* I shook my head. "I am content," I lied, wishing that he would leave so I would not have to see my own betrayal in his eyes.

His expression hardened before he looked away. With another glance at Rebecca, he turned to leave. "Let me know when she awakens."

I nodded and watched him as he left the room. I turned back to the mirror and stared at my reflection, realizing something wasn't right. My hand flew to my throat and I realized the pearl necklace was missing.

I jumped up and ran to the bed, pulling back the bed-clothes to see if it had fallen off while I slept. Then a sickening realization flooded my veins. I remembered the clattering sound of something hitting the wood floor as I stood hidden in the alcove under the stairs. Uselessly, my fingers swept across the soft skin of my neck, searching for the pearls that now lay abandoned on the wood floor of the foyer.

Quickly finishing my toilette, I sped down the stairs, thankful nobody was there to witness my desperate search. I followed the curve of the banister to the alcove, my heart firmly lodged in my throat. The honey-gold color of the wood shone brilliantly under a new layer of wax. I swished my foot across the expanse of wood, hoping to kick something that I couldn't see, but all I felt under the soles of my shoes was the smooth surface of the floor.

I lifted my head rapidly at the sound of approaching footsteps, making spots dance before my eyes. John stood before me with a questioning look in his eyes.

"Are you looking for something?"

Too ashamed to admit my guilt, I shook my head. "No, I'm just light-headed. I think I need to eat breakfast."

"I'll call for Mary to sit with Rebecca while you eat." He solicitously offered me his arm and I reluctantly took it, understanding the power of his touch and its effect on me. "You need to keep up your strength."

I allowed myself to be escorted into the dining room. John sent for Mary to go upstairs and then poured himself a cup of coffee. He filled a plate with food and put it in front of me before sitting down across the table. I felt my skin flame at the intensity of his gaze.

Forcing myself to remain calm, I returned his appraisal and searched for conversation. The events of the previous night meant I didn't have to search far. "How is the mill?"

"Severely damaged. It's a good thing the harvesting is

done or a lot of farmers would be losing their land over this. It will take a good six months to put it in working order again." I knew that John leased out the use of his mill to local farmers, saving them the trouble and expense of transporting their sugarcane to mills far away. He had acknowledged that he made little profit on the mill but that it was necessary to maintain the local economy.

"Do you know how it started?"

He put his coffee cup into the saucer a little too forcefully, splashing some of the coffee up over the sides. "It was undoubtedly arson and bears the marks of the White League. I have no doubt that Philip Herndon is behind this."

I put my fork down and faced him. "How can you be sure?"

A dark brow rose over one eye. "We have an eyewitness. Rufus said he spied Philip several days ago lurking around the mill and warned him off. Unfortunately, Rufus didn't think enough of the incident to tell me about it." He took a deep breath. "I assume Philip had also been by the coach house to tamper with the latch. I don't think it mattered to him whom he harmed—as long as somebody close to me, or myself, got hurt."

I remembered Philip's threats and felt certain that John's suspicions were not unfounded. "Have they found Philip yet for questioning?"

John shook his head. "No. The sheriff stopped by while you were upstairs. He's sent some men to look for him but so far they haven't found a trace." He picked up his cup and seemed to take a deliberately long sip from it. "The sheriff seems to think Philip had help in escaping. He's disappeared completely; it would have been impossible to do so on his own, especially with his lack of funds."

I placed my hands flat on the surface of the hard mahogany table. "What are you suggesting?"

He stood and kissed me lightly on the temple. "Not a thing, dear wife. Unless there's something you think might shed light on the situation."

Having lost my appetite completely, I slid back from the table. "I have nothing to hide. I have not spoken with Philip since that horrible scene in New Orleans. Believe what you will, but that is the truth."

A dark flush stained his handsome features. "Nothing to hide, Cat? I've noticed that you haven't asked about Marguerite, nor made note of her absence."

Doubt and fear flashed through my mind. I stood, facing him with my chin lifted. "Where is she?"

Leaning close to me, he reached for my hand, sending unbidden shivers of anticipation up my arm. Lifting it, he held it between us and opened my palm. Wordlessly he reached into his pocket and dumped the pearl necklace into my hand.

My fingers closed over the cool beads and I noticed that my hand shook. Slowly I raised my eyes to his. "Is that why you married me, then? To keep Rebecca with you? Surely you know that the law would be on your side. Simply being married to her mother would have made you the child's legal father."

He opened his mouth to say something, then seemed to change his mind. He turned away, his back to me, before speaking. "I'm a foreigner here—a damned Yankee, regardless of my years here or my commitment to the parish. With your friends' and neighbors' help, I'm sure you could have spirited Rebecca away to her rightful family without regard to my legal status."

The small glimmer of hope that I had sheltered inside fragmented like a broken mirror, and I was afraid all the pieces could never be put back. With a drowning sensation in my chest, I realized it was for the best. In the long hours of the night I had made the decision to leave him and his dark secrets. He didn't trust me, much less love me, and I loved him far more than reason dictated.

"And now that I'm your wife . . ." I didn't have the courage to finish the sentence.

"We both love Rebecca. She could find worse parents to raise her."

With a mocking bow he moved toward the doorway.

My words called him back. "If you're not Rebecca's father, then who is?"

He paused and I heard a deep intake of breath. Looking at me over his shoulder, he said, "I do not know. But rest assured, regardless of what man gave her mother his seed, I will never cease to be her father. And I pity whomever may try to separate us."

I listened as his footsteps crossed the foyer to the library, my hollow heart aching. My hand fell to my abdomen. He must have believed for a time that Rebecca was his. But of Elizabeth's second child he'd had no such assumption. Would her second proof of infidelity have angered him enough to be rid of her forever? And what of his doubts about me and my child?

I tried to shut out the insidious thoughts, but they spread through my mind like poison from an oleander petal. It took only a small dose to claim its victim, and I was afraid that I had already succumbed.

A door opened upstairs, quickly followed by the sound of running feet on the steps. I rushed out into the foyer and nearly ran into Mary.

"Miss Catherine—Miss Rebecca's awake. She's asking for her papa."

I looked at the young girl, worry gnawing at me. Her skin was flushed, her freckles standing out in stark relief. "What's wrong, Mary?"

She wrung her hands. "Oh, Miss Catherine, she's burning up, she is. Burning with the fever."

I took the stairs two at a time with John, who had emerged from his study, close behind me. When I approached Rebecca's bed, she twitched and moaned, her face pale and wan. Her bright blue eyes stared at me but didn't seem to see me. I touched her cheek, and her skin nearly burned my hand.

John turned to Mary, who had followed us up the stairs. "Go get Mr. O'Rourke and send him to find Dr. Lewiston and bring him here. Now."

Mary bobbed her head several times, still wringing her hands, then ran from the room, her feet clattering down the steps.

Rebecca clutched at my dress. "Mama, Mama. I'm so hot." Her voice rasped; her lips were cracked and dry.

I sat at the edge of the bed and brushed her hair off her forehead. "I know, baby. I'm going to try to cool you off."

Quietly John said, "I'll go to Rose and have her bring fresh water and bathing cloths."

I looked at him for the first time and saw the tight restraint and despair in his eyes. I wanted to take his hand and offer comfort, but I could not. I simply nodded my head and turned back to Rebecca while I listened as his footsteps faded away down the hall.

Rebecca lingered in a feverish delirium for almost four days. We moved her back to her own room and I began a vigil by her bedside. She could not hold down food, and I spent hours simply squeezing drops of water between her dry and cracked lips from a clean washcloth.

Daniel came frequently, as much to comfort John and me as to tend to Rebecca. He listened to her chest and gave us the promising news that it wasn't pneumonia. He ruled out many childhood diseases, but couldn't determine what was afflicting Rebecca. Her fever remained unabated, regardless of our treatment, and I lived through those nights and days with fear as my constant shadow. I sat transfixed at her bedside, afraid to leave her even for a moment. Jamie had drowned when I had looked away, and the guilt and grief still weighed heavily on my heart. Perhaps I could earn forgiveness if I protected Rebecca in a way that had been denied my beloved son.

On the second night of her illness, while I was bathing Rebecca's forehead yet again with a cool cloth, John silently opened the door. I sensed him before I saw him, my emotions an odd mixture of joy and wariness.

I looked up and saw dark circles under his eyes and a beard growing on his strong jaw. If there had been any doubts before that he loved this child as his own flesh and blood, they would have fled completely now.

He took the cloth from my hand and led me away from the bed. He grasped my hands in his and I felt how chilled they were—as if his lifeblood were flowing out to the child who needed it more than he.

"I want you to go to your room and seek rest. And then I want you to pray. That is the only thing I will allow you to do."

I wrenched my hands away. "No, John. Do not deny me this!"

His hands spanned my waist, his palms pressing against my abdomen. "And what of the baby? You are compromising not only your own health but that of the unborn child." His dark eyes bored into mine. "I will take your place and not leave her side. I promise you that. Can you trust me enough to tend her with all the love and care with which you would?"

I looked back at the frail and flushed face of the child I had grown to love so much and then looked back at my husband. I knew he was right, yet I agonized over the decision. How could anyone care for Rebecca as well as I could? I stared into John's eyes and knew the truth.

Slowly I nodded. "You will send for me if you need anything? Or if she calls for me?"

Relief flooded his handsome features. "Yes. Of course. Now go get your rest. You will need all of your strength."

Reluctantly I stepped back, the warmth of his hands deserting me, and knew that Rebecca would be well tended. I wanted to reach for him, to hold him, and read in his eyes that he felt the same, yet we both stood facing each other, each one holding back our own truth, our own secrets.

I turned away and bent to kiss Rebecca on the forehead, then left the room without a word.

John stayed in her room, nursing his daughter day and night as he had promised. I was allowed in to hold her hand and give her water, and to help change her bedclothes, but John always sent me back to my room to rest. I knew he was right, but I longed to be at his side, watching over our daughter.

On the second day of his vigil I brought his shaving materials and a clean change of clothes. He opened the door at my knock and I barely recognized the disheveled man standing there as my husband.

"How is she?" I asked.

"The same." He opened the door wider to let me in, eyeing the bundle in my hands. "Thank you. I'll be needing them."

I forced a smile to my face that I did not feel. "You'll be needing them right now, I think. What if she awakens and sees you as you are? She'll think you a monster and start screaming." His stomach grumbled, and I added, "A food tray will be brought up shortly."

White teeth showed as he grinned, disarming my resolve completely, and I realized it had been too long since I had seen him smile.

He reached for the stack in my hands and his fingers

touched mine. I let go quickly, almost dropping everything, and he caught it with a quick grab. His eyes sobered. "She'll be fine, Cat. I will it to be so."

My voice was harsher than I intended, my exhaustion and worry no doubt sharpening my tongue. "And no one would dare thwart your wants and desires—not even God."

He said nothing and I reached into my pocket, feeling the cool smoothness of the lodestone. I held it up to him and he took it. "Put this by Rebecca. It's to chase away evil and bring her goodness. She needs it more than I."

Without waiting for a response, I kissed Rebecca's hot cheek and left. I would return to prayer, for that was the only thing I could do for her. Rose was in her kitchen casting spells and offering up sacrifices. I no longer thought of it as pagan, for it seemed a part of this dark, humid place, seeming more at home than Christianity. As long as Rebecca got better, it didn't matter to me what means guided her recovery.

And when she was well, I would take her away. I would bring her home to the bright light that banished the darkness from weary hearts, where the rhythm of the ocean waves lulled one to sleep and kept the nightmares at bay. And where a child could grow without shadows lurking in every corner, where dark secrets didn't obscure the purity of love.

I don't know when I had come to the decision to take Rebecca with me, but even with a heavy heart I knew that I had made the right decision. The walls of this place were steeped in deceit and danger, and I knew she would be in peril if she should remain. Leaving would save both our lives; of that I had no doubt. John would grieve her loss, I knew; his love for her was greater than I had ever seen from a father toward his natural child. But of that broken bond, I could not think. The remembered pain of losing a child weighed heavily on my heart if I did, and I would not carry John's grief for him. If I did, my scarred heart would surely break open, spilling out my resolve to leave, and fleeing Whispering Oaks was the only chance of saving our lives and our very souls.

Rebecca's fever broke on the fifth day. I waited in the hall as Daniel examined her and then reappeared, a shadow of a smile on his face.

"I think she's well on the road to complete health. There seems to be no damage to her sight or hearing, and I expect her to have a full recovery."

Relief flooded my bones, making me shake. I wanted to throw my arms around him, but restrained myself. "Thank you, Daniel, for caring for her."

He put a calming hand on my arm. "I need you to take care of yourself, too. If you show the first sign of fever, you are to call me immediately. I don't think you realize the danger to your unborn child."

Unbidden, my hands went to my bodice. "I will," I promised. I walked the doctor down the stairs, my heart lighter for the first time in over a week.

Daniel paused for a moment at the door, a perplexed expression darkening his brow. "I thought you might want to know that Marguerite is at Belle Meade now. We can't afford to pay her, yet Clara insists that she stay, and Marguerite seems satisfied with a room and food. I hope that doesn't dismay you too much. John has told me of some of the doubts you harbored regarding Marguerite."

I closed my eyes, shaking my head. "As long as she is out of my house, her whereabouts do not concern me, but thank you for telling me. I know she practically raised Clara, so I can't fault either one of them for their closeness."

I opened the door and he stepped out onto the porch.

The late-afternoon sun glinted off his hair and I paused in midsentence, staring at it. It was so much like Robert's— all gentle shadings of gold and yellow. So much like Rebecca's. I grabbed his arm and he turned, his gaze focused on my tight grip.

"What's wrong, Catherine?"

"You, Daniel. You . . ."

I couldn't seem to form the words. I recalled Rebecca's secret place behind the burned plantation house, and how she had disappeared to a secluded place so Daniel and I could be alone. As if she had done it many times before.

He turned to face me, his expression one of worry. "What's wrong? Do you need to sit down?"

I shook my head. "No. No, I don't." I realized I couldn't tell him. I didn't want to acknowledge it. Because then I would have to tell John. Regardless of what I believed John capable of, my heart could not stand the knowledge that he would lose not only his wife and child, but his best friend as well.

His eyes remained guarded. "Are you quite sure?"

"Yes. Really, I'm fine. I'm just tired, I think."

He kissed my hand, his gray eyes warm. "You are so strong, Catherine. John and Rebecca are very lucky to have you." A deep and abiding sadness seemed to cross his face for a brief moment, quickly replaced by his smile. "Take care of yourself, remember. It will take a long time for Rebecca to completely recover and regain her strength. You will have need of your own strength to see her through."

I thanked him, grateful for Rebecca's recovery but concerned over the delay it had caused in my departure. "How long do you think it will be before she's well again?"

He brightened. "By Christmas, I expect. She loves the bonfires along the levee, and she should be well enough by then to join in the festivities."

By Christmas, then. I had plenty of time to finalize my plans. Daniel said his good-byes and I watched him get into his carriage, his hat not completely hiding his hair, the sun glinting off those beautiful yellow-gold strands.

Chapter Twenty-three

With Rebecca out of danger, the darkness that had seemed to be hovering over me lifted, although my troubles were not over. John had been sleeping on a small pallet in her room, but now she no longer needed him there. I could not allow John to return to my bed. His touch had a way of lowering my defenses, of creating breaches in my wall of reason. I wondered how long it would take John to demand my presence in his bed again.

On a chilly November evening, John and I sat facing each other at the dining room table. I forced myself to eat for the sake of the baby, whose presence was now made known by a small mound under my loosened corset. John also seemed to have other thoughts on his mind. From the corner of my eye I saw him eat little but refill his wineglass three times. When I forced myself to look at him directly, I found his black eyes scrutinizing me as a hunter watches his prey.

Whispers of Goodbye

I excused myself before dessert, with plans to change for bed and be fast asleep before John came up. He had begun the habit of retiring to his study for a cigar and brandy, thus giving me ample time.

As I ascended the stairs, I felt a presence behind me and turned, John had followed me and was walking up the steps in my wake. I headed down the hall toward our bedroom, hoping he would go to Rebecca's room. Instead he followed me, even opening the door of the bedroom for me.

I moved to ring for Mary, but John stayed my hand. "I'll help you with your dress."

Knowing I had no choice, I bent my head forward and allowed his hands to unfasten the buttons and slide the gown over my shoulders. Long fingers slid down my chemise, moving forward to cup my breasts, now heavy and swollen from impending motherhood. One hand slid down farther, moving over the mound of my stomach as he moved me against him. I felt his need through the thin linen of my chemise as his lips found the soft skin of my neck.

I wanted to turn in his arms, to forget all that had happened between us, and all my doubts and suspicions, but I could not. I owed it to the child that grew inside me, as well as to Rebecca, to make sure they were safe forever.

I stepped away, pulling up my fallen bodice to cover myself. "Don't."

He looked genuinely surprised. "Why, Cat? I know you miss me as much as I miss you."

"It's . . . the baby. I don't think we should."

Stepping forward, he lifted my chin and stared into my eyes for a long moment, his own eyes dark and secretive. "Is that really the reason?"

I closed my eyes and turned away from him. "Of course it is. I don't want anything to happen to this baby."

He was silent and I crossed to my dresser to remove a nightgown, keeping my hands busy so I would not have to listen to my heart.

He moved so silently that I wasn't aware of his nearness until I felt his hot breath on the back of my neck. I closed my eyes, recalling the passion we had shared for such a short time, and a longing to recapture it pulled at my resolve. He held my heart, for I had seen the goodness that resided inside him. But there was darkness, too, a darkness I fleetingly wished I could cut out the way a surgeon's knife excised a cancer. I had tried, and failed, and now I knew I had to escape the darkness that threatened to suffocate me like a heavy cloak.

For the long years of the war and the time afterward, I had lived under a shadow. Now I would rather die than return to it. Rebecca and the child growing inside me were my light, guiding me through the blackness that encroached, moving me toward the brightness that beckoned at the end of my journey home.

"You cannot deny me, Catherine. It is not the child—there is something else." His soft voice caressed my skin, the temptation pulling at me like fingers in honey. "Tell me."

I straightened, making him step away. "It is the child, John. It is not safe for me to share your bed until he is safely born."

His hands were rough as he forced me to turn and look at him. "I know that is not true." He lowered his face close to mine and I could feel his all-consuming heat. "Marguerite is gone. What is it that you fear?"

I need you dear sister. I am so afraid. The images of Elizabeth's letter, John's glove, and the empty letterbox jumbled in my mind, and I nearly suffocated with the urge to shout out all my suspicions. But I held back, knowing that if I did I would jeopardize all. In the deepest part of my heart, I knew that he would not give me answers. And his reticence would be for reasons that my soul could not bear to contemplate.

I stared into his eyes as they flashed with anger. He dropped his arms but didn't step back. "What about this trust between us that you hold so dear? Practice what you preach, Catherine, and tell me why you suddenly have no desire to share my bed." His lips narrowed as his eyes became guarded, blocking out all emotion. "Have you found someone else who stirs your passions more than I?" His gaze slid down to my stomach, coming to rest on the small mound.

I sucked in my breath, shocked to hear him so blatantly voice his suspicion. I drew back my hand to slap him but he grabbed my wrist. I knew I was being a hypocrite—at least he had the courage to speak of his doubts.

He let go and turned away and my arm fell to my side, useless. He glanced back at me from the doorway. "I don't want you to leave Whispering Oaks without me or Mr. O'Rourke. And if you should leave with Mr. O'Rourke, I want to know about it beforehand."

I took a step toward him. "You want to make a prisoner out of me! I am not a slave or your kept woman with no mind of her own. You can't do this."

He opened the door. "As your husband, I can. It is for your own protection. Philip Herndon has not been found, and I know he has sworn to harm me and those I love." His gaze flickered to the swell of my abdomen once more. "And I will not suffer the embarrassment of having you seek him out."

The implication was clear. My anger, softened by his mention of love, rekindled itself. "Is this why Elizabeth was trying to get away from you? Because you accused her of vile things and then tried to keep her locked in this prison? I am not Elizabeth, though I don't think you will ever understand that. But maybe, finally, I think I can understand why my sister behaved the way she did."

His face paled. Inexplicably, I felt sick with the knowledge that I had hurt him badly. I wanted to go to him, to tell him I was sorry, but my pride, anger, and suspicions held me back.

Slowly he opened the door. "From the first day of my marriage to Elizabeth, I thought that I had married the wrong sister. And now I see it really didn't matter."

Words strangled my throat and my eyes blurred as I watched him walk through the doorway and close the door softly behind him. The last image I had of him was of his eyes—the eyes of a wildcat that had been hunted into a corner, but whose intention was to fight to the death all who threatened him.

I did not see John for two weeks. I learned from Mr. O'Rourke that he had gone to Baton Rouge on business. I slept in our bed, safe in the knowledge that John was far away, and had the pallet removed from Rebecca's room. She was out of danger from the fever but still very weak. Except for this, I told myself, I would have taken advantage of the opportunity of John's absence and fled.

As it was, I did not leave the plantation. The threat of Philip Herndon lingered, although to a lesser degree since he seemed to have vanished. I knew John had hired guards to keep watch over the plantation night and day, and those precautions offered a measure of security. Mr. O'Rourke found excuses to work close to the house, and I wondered if it was for my protection or to keep John informed of my whereabouts in his absence.

Even with John gone, I did not sleep easily. Several times I would lie in bed and imagine I heard footsteps in the hallway. When I'd rise to investigate, I'd find nothing. Twice I thought that I detected the faint smell of lavender, reminding me of Elizabeth. I'd stare out into the hallway, cloaked in night, for long moments, as if waiting for my dead sister to appear. Always disappointed, I'd close my door and turn the key before returning to bed for another restless night.

Two weeks after John's departure, I awoke with a start out of a dark dream in the deepest part of the night. The sound that had brought me awake had been the distinct noise of a door latch snapping into place. I blinked my eyes, trying to identify the dark shapes of the furniture.

Rain pelted at the glass like unseen fingers tapping to gain my attention. I left the bed and moved to a window, pulling aside the curtains and staring out into the rain-clogged fields. As a child I had always loved the heavy rain from the ocean-borne tempests. My father had made a habit of pacing our front porch during storms, as if to guard the house from lightning and wind, and at a very early age I had joined him.

Our waterlogged conversations had created a bond between us, a bond that even Elizabeth couldn't traverse and which was not broken until his death. I pressed my forehead against the cool glass, missing him as suddenly as if he had just died, and feeling more alone and adrift than I had in my entire life.

A movement by the pond caught my attention and I squinted, trying to see through the blur of raindrops. A light, as if from a bobbing lantern, glittered through the rain for a brief moment and then was extinguished. I stared out the window for a long time, not knowing if it had been my imagination. I thought I saw a brief flicker moving toward the pond before that, too, disappeared. My eyes strained to see into the endless darkness of the night, but I saw only the blackness pressing in on me.

My nape prickled, and I realized that the blackness came from within the house as well, as if it were a dark soul whose menacing presence tainted the very air I breathed. I slowly backed away from the window, convincing myself it had been my imagination and pressing away more morbid thoughts. *Will I, too, soon be hearing voices of the dead calling me to come to them?*

I took a lit lamp and walked quickly out of the room and down the hall to Rebecca's chamber. I pushed open the door and held the lantern high, my heart tumbling with relief when I spied her small body tucked under the covers, Samantha pressed against her cheek.

I left the room and noticed for the first time the strong odor of something burning. Moving toward the stairs, I sniffed deeply. It was too strong to be the lingering odors from the burnt mill, and it was definitely not the scent of burning wood. I would remember that smell until the day I died.

Gingerly descending the stairs, I followed the scent to the library. John's pipe sat in an ashtray and I lifted it, feeling the warmth of the bowl. The fire in the grate still burned strong, as if recently tended, and I moved near, seeking warmth.

Putting the lamp down on the desk, I stood in front of the fireplace, my hands outstretched. My fingers straightened and clenched, then stilled as if of their own accord as my gaze rested on the pile of ash under the grate.

I knelt and reached in a hand, pulling out the corner of one of several burned envelopes, its edge raw and sooty. A black slash of ink from a pen formed part of a word, the remainder obliterated forever by fire. The penmanship seemed oddly familiar to me, but there was not enough of it to identify. It gnawed at the back of my mind as I gazed at the heap of ashes, the heat from the fire burning my face.

Grabbing a poker, I scraped out what remnants of letters

I could find, realizing with disappointment that no piece was large enough to be of any use.

I stood, the inevitable question filling my mind: were these Elizabeth's letters? I reached my hand in again, desperate for some word from my lost sister, but my hand got too close to the flame, burning my finger, and I rapidly withdrew.

Stepping away and sucking on my singed finger, I stared into the fire, my mind in deep thought. Grabbing the lamp, I made my way cautiously up the stairs to Rebecca's room. Even without the light from the lamp, my body screamed in awareness of John's presence, betraying my resolve that I remain immune to him.

"Good evening, wife."

His voice held a note of flippancy, but I sensed a deeper, darker emotion—more akin to grief and loss.

"John," I stammered, his presence filling the room and shaking my senses. "I did not know when to expect you back." A brutal gust of wind knocked at the house, jarring me further.

He didn't respond, but leaned forward in the chair, his elbows resting on his knees. Finally he spoke, but his gaze rested on the sleeping child.

His voice sounded tired, and very far away. "When I first saw Rebecca, she was well past the infant stage and already had a look of you about her." He rubbed his hands over his face, the sound of skin against beard stubble rustling loudly enough to be heard over the tapping of the rain.

"And as she grew, she became more and more as I remembered you—the girl you had been when I first saw you. Not so much in the way she looked, but her free spirit and her sweetness and joy in life. She reminded me so much of the girl dancing barefoot on the beach in Saint Simons, her hair loose in the wind. I wanted to spoil Re-

317

becca by giving her all the love and attention that I would never be able to give you."

I fought the urge to go to him, to lay my head on his knee. To touch him. His words moved me, showing me the man I knew lived deep inside his forbidding form. But the darkness lurked within him, too, and I pulled away.

John continued, his voice just loud enough to be heard over the splattering rain. "And then as Elizabeth and I grew further apart and the war took me away, Rebecca became even more important to me. She was mine to love unconditionally, and she freely shared her love with me. It was the first time I had ever experienced anything like it. Even my own mother had not seemed capable of such emotion. All her love seemed to begin and end with my older brother; there were not even scraps left over for me. Which is why I left my home as soon as I could and have never been back. Not even for my mother's funeral." He lifted his eyes to mine, and they shimmered in the lamplight with potent meaning. "I do not take rejection easily."

My heart reverberated in my chest, crying out for this man at the same time my mind reeled with warning. I went to him and knelt before the chair. Tentatively I reached for his hands and he grabbed mine, pressing tightly.

His voice was gruff. "It is not good between us now, is it? And I don't know how to make it different. I thought that two weeks away from you would make my need for you lessen somehow, but it only made it stronger. I've been searching for some trace of Philip Herndon, hoping my mind would be occupied by something other than you." He paused for a moment, the tapping of the rain marking the passing time. "I almost hoped that you would be gone when I returned. Your rejection of me cuts deeper than a knife, wounding my soul. But now that I am back, and I see you here, I know that I could never let you go. Never."

The pressure on my hands increased and I winced, but he seemed not to notice. I stared at him in the darkened room, listening to the rain beat against the house, almost smelling the salt air and the damp cotton of my beloved home, and knowing that to return I would lose part of my soul. Or worse.

I yearned to give him another chance, an opportunity to restore his soul—and mine. I leaned toward him, hearing the urgency in my own voice. "Tell me then, John. The burned letters in the grate. Were they Elizabeth's?"

I felt more than heard his quick intake of air, but he made no move to answer.

"Tell me now, John. I am stronger than you think. There is nothing in her letters that can harm me now."

He let go of my hand and touched my cheek. "You do not know what you ask."

I leaned into his touch, feeling his heat. "Yes, I do. I ask that there be trust and truth between us. For without them we have nothing."

Dropping his hand, he leaned back in the chair, his dark gaze resting on me. He said no more, and my heart and mind receded from him, and I was resigned as to my course of action. His eyes widened as if he could read my thoughts, and I turned away. Slowly I stood and walked toward the door.

"I am sleeping in the master bedroom and I keep it locked at night."

"I know."

The bluntness of his response startled me.

I looked at Rebecca, still peacefully asleep, then back at John. "Good night."

He didn't respond, but I felt his brooding gaze on my back as I lifted the lamp and left the room.

As I took several steps, my foot slipped and I realized that the floor was scattered with small wet spots that resembled footsteps. Curious, I held the lantern high, following the spots for several feet until they dead-ended into a wall. Intrigued, I turned and followed them back in the other direction, realizing with a heavy heart that they led to the master bedroom. Had John's hair and clothes been wet from the rain? I couldn't recall; the emotions he evoked in me had obliterated all other senses. I stared at the small puddles traversing the hallway to my bedroom.

I turned the handle and pushed it wide. I held the lantern high, looking behind me to see if John had followed. Reassured that he had not, I entered the bedroom. The wet footsteps stopped at the side of my bed, and it didn't take me long to realize why.

In the middle of the pulled-back coverlet lay a large black ball of wax. I knew without looking closer that it was a conjure ball. Some were said to contain human flesh, and my own skin shivered at the thought. Smooth pins stuck through the black wax made an even arc over the ball, and stripes of something wet and dark, like blood or paint, were slashed across the side.

My knees trembled as I stared at the ball and I inadvertently cried out. I knew such things were meant to bring death or misfortune to a household, and the fact that it lay in the middle of my bed left me in no doubt as to who was intended to suffer.

I backed out of the room, mentally prepared to grab Rebecca and steal away into the night. But as I moved backward, I bumped into something hard and solid and looked up to find myself staring into the cold black eyes of my husband.

Chapter Twenty-four

I faced John, noting for the first time his wet hair. Quickly I glanced down at his feet and saw that he had taken off his boots. I noted, too, the absence of his jacket and coat. Had he seen them dripping in the hallway and taken them off?

I pushed at his chest, forcing him to step back through the doorway.

He caught my wrist. "What is wrong? I heard you shout."

"Leave, John. And don't pretend you don't know why." My voice shook with hurt, anger, and fear. *Please deny it. Please don't let me believe the worst of you.*

"Let me in." His voice held a note of warning.

My heart sank low in my chest. "No. I've already made that mistake more than once and I will not do it again."

He stood perfectly still, his gaze hard and unreadable. Was he simply warning me with the conjure ball? His voice held no malice. "Then I shall not trouble you again."

Soundlessly he turned away and strode down the corridor toward the stairs.

I closed the door, pressing my back against it, and stared at the insidious thing in the middle of my bed. *I do not take rejection easily.* I thought of Elizabeth, and the price I suspected her of paying for the ultimate rejection of leaving him. My gaze strayed to the lower drawer of the dresser, where I had been gathering things to pack for my journey with Rebecca. His words crept unbidden into my mind. *And I pity whoever may try to separate us.*

I wrapped the evil conjure ball in one of John's linen handkerchiefs, ensuring that my fingers never came in contact with the dreaded object. Dragging a chair in front of the door, I crawled into it and stared at the brass door handle until the morning light touched the walls of my room.

The light of day did little to scatter the dark shadows in my mind. I quickly dressed before cautiously opening my door. With relief, I saw that the hallway was empty and hurriedly crossed the corridor. Slipping into my old room, I placed the conjure ball under the bed, then left the room as silently as I had arrived and headed toward the stairs.

I paused at the top, hearing that ethereal humming sound again. It was certainly Rebecca's voice, so I approached the open door to her room. She was out of her sickbed—her nightgown lay on the floor, so she must have dressed—but she was nowhere in her room.

The humming came to me again, and I turned to follow it out into the corridor. I spied the lodestone on her night table and picked it up as an afterthought. I would be needing it much more than she in the coming weeks.

I stepped out into the hall and the humming abruptly ceased. I paused, listening, and caught sight of Samantha lying on the floor. She was crammed tightly against the wall, and as I stooped to pick her up, I realized that the doll lay in the exact spot where the wet footprints had disappeared into the wall the night before.

Stunned, I pressed my palms against the plaster. I knocked to see if there would be a hollow sound and was surprised to hear someone knocking back, quickly followed by girlish giggles.

"Rebecca? Are you in there?"

I heard a slight click and then a small door opened in the wainscoting. The seams of the door had been perfectly hidden in the woodwork, rendering it virtually invisible. I wondered how many other such doors might be hidden in this house.

Rebecca stuck her face out of the opening, a bright smile on her lips. "You found my secret place, Mama!"

I had to kneel to see past the opening and was surprised to glimpse a set of stairs. Sunlight poured into a high round window. I had seen that window many times from the outside of the house, but it had never occurred to me that I had never seen it from the inside.

I took Rebecca's hands and helped her crawl out. "How did you ever find this place?"

She looked at me with wide blue eyes. "Do you promise you won't be mad at me?"

I nodded, my serious expression matching hers.

Very solemnly, she said, "I spied on my mama. I saw her use it one day and followed her. It goes outside, behind the bushy green plants by the back porch. She used it a lot but she never knew that it was my secret, too."

Smoothing the hair off her forehead, I asked, "Did you ever see anybody else use it?"

She looked down and didn't answer.

"Rebecca, you can tell me. I promise not to be angry."

"I saw my papa. But only two times. Once he followed

my mama. I saw her leave and then he left, too. I thought they were playing a game."

I spoke gently. "You said you saw your papa use these stairs two times. When was the other time?"

She looked up at me with wide blue eyes. "On the same day Papa told me Mama had gone to heaven, I saw him coming back up these stairs with Mama's traveling bag. When she first went away, I saw her with the bag and I wondered why did she didn't have it no more. I was worried because she wouldn't have her hairbrush and how could she brush her hair?"

Small pinpricks of fear dotted the back of my neck. I forced a smile. "Did he see you?"

Rebecca shook her head. "No, I'm too fast to let anybody see me." She plucked at her skirt. "But I wasn't sad. I know Mama didn't want to be here with me. She made me cry."

I watched as her lower lip quivered, and I touched her cheek to soothe her lonely heart, recalling how she would scream when I had first arrived and she confused me with Elizabeth.

"Did you see anybody else use the stairs?"

"Yes, Marguerite used them all the time. She says it's faster to get outside this way."

My fingers trembled as I stroked Rebecca's cheek. *Is this what Marguerite meant when she told John that he had more to hide than she? And if Elizabeth had been running away, to whom had she been running?*

The sands of grief and loss sifted through my fingers again, yet I was afraid to catch them and look closely, unwilling to see the truth. So I let them fall to the ground, unheeded, and occupied my mind with plans to leave. My mistrust and doubts were enough for me. To know more would damage my heart beyond repair and perhaps move me closer to danger than I already was.

* * *

I found Philip Herndon two days later, his bloated body floating facedown in the pond behind the house. I had gone to rid myself of the conjure ball, having decided that whether or not I believed in it, I wanted it out of the house. I was walking, trying to organize my thoughts and to ignore the heavy weight of the ball in my hand, when I spotted something undoubtedly human in the pond.

My heart twisted at the sight, and I dropped the ball, immediately thinking of Jamie. With a small relief, I soon realized that the form in the water was that of an adult. For a moment I thought that it was John and I sank to my knees, unable to fathom the loss or my reaction to it. Someone, possibly Mr. O'Rourke, spotted me and shouted the alarm. Nobody made mention of the conjure ball at my feet, or if they did, I did not hear.

I don't remember much past being led inside the house and registering the news that it was Philip. I sat in the parlor with my feet propped on a footstool and recalled the night of John's return, when I thought I had seen a light by the pond, and then John's wet hair. I felt the sickening realization that my love for John was wrong, that he had undoubtedly unleashed his fury on Elizabeth and her lover, and that I was in mortal danger. I should have realized that a woman as vain as Elizabeth would never have taken her own life. But my love for John had blinded me, and my unwillingness to see filled me with shame and remorse. I gathered my loss and grief around me yet again, finally forcing myself to stare the truth in the face.

John rode to the Herndons' plantation to tell them about Philip. As soon as he disappeared down the lane of oaks, I fetched Rebecca and went to find Mr. O'Rourke to ready our buggy.

He protested at first, but after I explained that the threat of Philip no longer existed, he let me go. I snapped the reins and set off at a brisk trot. When I neared the end of the lane, out of sight of the house, a dark figure stepped out and waved me down.

Instinctively my hand flew to Rebecca, my main concern to protect her. I sighed with relief when I recognized Rose, and slowed to a stop.

"What are you doing out here, Rose?"

"I've been having dark dreams about you, Miss Catherine. You still carrying that lodestone I give you?"

I patted the pocket of my dress, feeling the smooth lump underneath, and felt foolish. "Yes, Rose. I carry it with me wherever I go."

She stepped closer to the buggy. "Good. You need it bad." Placing a hand on the side of the buggy, she stared up at me. "You tell the Herndons they needs to put fresh eggs in Master Herndon's hands, then tie his wrists together before they put him facedown in the coffin. Then sprinkle eggshells on top of his grave and his killer will be revealed." She nodded her head, satisfied that she had told me. "It will work; you mark my word."

"Thank you, Rose. I'll certainly think about it, but I'm not quite sure that Mr. and Mrs. Herndon will take my suggestions. They'll be grieving very much for their son."

Rose patted the side of the buggy before stepping away. "You just do your best, Miss Catherine. If you want the killer caught." Her eyes were full of meaning as she glanced at me one last time before turning away back down the lane toward the house.

I snapped the reins again and felt Rebecca tugging at my sleeve. I had almost forgotten she was with me. "Are you all right?" I asked.

She nodded, then reached over with her pudgy hand and patted the lodestone in my pocket.

I had not been to Judge Patterson's home since my return, but I remembered where it was located. Off the main river road, it was set back on a smaller parcel of land than Whispering Oaks. He had raised oranges and rare birds instead of investing in cash crops, his fortune having been inherited from his father, a shipping merchant. I remembered the exotic screens, vases, and artwork from my visits to his raised cottage as a child. I would always wonder if it was our visits to Gracehaven that had fueled Elizabeth's wanderlust. The Oriental paintings, with their odd black splashes that substituted for our alphabet, and the unique teas and curries we'd dine on always lent an otherworldly feel that would last for days after our visits with our grandmother.

A man came to help us and take the buggy as we approached the single-story structure. The redbrick pillars supporting the white house reminded me of pelicans with their skinny legs standing on muddy banks, their fluffy white torsos perched precariously on top.

The judge greeted us warmly and then, as if reading my mind, sent Rebecca to the kitchen for something sweet. She lifted her face, still wan and peaked after her illness, with a questioning look.

"You may go, but just eat a little. You're not used to eating very much right now. And if you get tired, come back to me." With a bright smile on her pale face she left us, and the judge ushered me into his library.

He rang for tea and then offered me a seat by the fire. Joining me in an adjacent chair, he regarded me with a warm expression. "Forgive me for my bluntness, but you're not looking well, Catherine."

I shook my head, then lowered my gaze to my lap, trying to find my composure. His sympathy was all I needed to lose the control I had so tightly maintained in the last weeks. Finally I raised my eyes to his. "You once offered your assistance in whatever way you could, and I've come to take you up on your offer. I need to leave here—with

Rebecca. And I can't let John know that I'm going."

He leaned forward, resting his elbows on his knees. "I've known you since you were a little girl, Catherine, and I know you're not prone to flights of fancy. But what you're asking of me is very serious, and I need to be sure that this isn't a rash decision on your part. Because once you leave, it would be very difficult for you to return."

I nodded. "I thank you for your concern, but this is a decision that has tormented me for quite some time. I've made up my mind and there's no turning back."

"I see. Does this have anything to do with Elizabeth?"

I looked at him sharply. "Yes—in a way. I . . . I think John may have been responsible for her death. And now Philip Herndon has been found dead." I paused for a moment, weighing my words. "I think we both know that John had a very strong motive for wanting Philip killed."

My hand was shaking, and he put his gnarled fingers over mine; I relished the warmth. The tea arrived and he poured for me; I still couldn't trust my hands to hold a teacup.

"How did Philip die?"

"I found him in the pond behind our house, with a severe gash on the back of his head. But they don't think he drowned. His . . . his tongue had been cut out." I shivered despite the roaring fire in the fireplace.

He took a sip. "Do you have proof of John's involvement in either death?"

"Two nights before, when John returned to Whispering Oaks, I thought I saw lights out by the pond. And then John appeared inside, and he was wet, as if he'd been outside in the rain."

The judge spoke gently. "But if he had just returned from his trip, he would have been traveling in the elements. It wouldn't be inconceivable that he would be wet from the rain."

I nodded. "But he also lied to me. He told me that when he found Elizabeth's body, his glove and an evil gris-gris were next to her. He removed them, telling me that Elizabeth had placed them there to implicate him. He never mentioned her traveling bag—but Rebecca saw him bringing it into the house after she disappeared, and I remember seeing her personal items reappear on her dressing table after her death."

I told the judge about John's pipe in the attic and the buried letterbox with the missing letters and the scent of earth on John's jacket. The old man nodded silently while I talked, his fingers steepled under his chin.

I pressed my cold hands against the cup, trying to warm them. "I know that most of my suspicions can be construed as purely coincidental, which is why I can't go to the authorities. I have only suspicions and doubts—and Rebecca's recollection. It would appear that Elizabeth was intent on leaving John when she was killed." I looked the judge squarely in the eye. "I don't know a great many people who are contemplating suicide who pack a traveling bag."

He nodded. "And the words of a four-year-old would never be accepted in a court of law."

"Nor would I subject Rebecca to such torment. I need to take her far away from here, away from him." I choked back a sob.

"You love him."

I stood, nearly knocking over the tea table. "I can't help myself. There's so much goodness in him, but to know that he's also capable of such violence . . ." I took a deep breath before facing the judge again. "Which is why I need to take Rebecca away. It will kill him to lose her, but I have to think of what's best for her."

Judge Patterson stood next to me and I put a hand on his arm. "And I also wanted to tell another person of my suspicions. My sister is dead, and no matter how she might have provoked him, justice should be served. I will tell you everything I know so that in the future, perhaps you can stand in a court of law and see John McMahon pay for his crimes."

My voice had descended into a whisper, my agony ripping the strength from me. He helped me sit again and handed me back my cup. After I had calmed down, I reached for my reticule. Slowly and deliberately, I pulled out the pearl necklace that John had given me as a wedding gift.

"I want you to sell this for me. I'll need cash for my journey, and this should give me a bit left over, too. I will be going to my mother-in-law's home in Brunswick, Georgia—not far from Saint Simons. Eventually I will want to return to my home, but John will look for us there first. Robert's mother has not spoken to me since his funeral, but I have nowhere else to go. Bringing her funds and an extra pair of hands to help should make us welcome. Since Robert's death, she has been all alone."

I swallowed at the thick cloud of despair that threatened to settle over me. My mother-in-law had become a shriveled, unhappy woman over the course of the war in which she had lost not only her husband, but her three sons as well. I was sure she blamed me for Robert's suicide and the loss of the one child who had had the skill and luck to survive the war but not the strength of spirit to survive the anguish of coming home.

He clasped my hands in his. "When will you need the money?"

"I plan to leave at Christmas—in less than three weeks' time. Dr. Lewiston said Rebecca would be well enough to travel by then."

The judge looked at me in surprise. "Does he know then?"

"No. He is John's friend and I will not jeopardize that." I thought back to the day when the terrible knowledge had come to me concerning Rebecca's father.

"Will you need to stay at Gracehaven until you leave?"

I shook my head. "That would only alert John's suspicions. Besides, he will be gone for two of those weeks on business in New Orleans. For the remaining week I will be very watchful. And I don't intend to be alone for a single moment."

"Surely the child you carry will keep you safe."

I looked down at the ground, my face heating. "John doesn't think it is his."

The judge had the good grace not to appear shocked. "He has never truly recovered from Elizabeth's infidelities. Perhaps that betrayal has driven him mad." He patted my hand. "I will call frequently to check in on you; how is that?"

Impulsively, I kissed his cheek. "I would welcome that under any circumstances. Thank you."

"I don't want you to worry about anything. I will see that everything is arranged for you."

I found Rebecca in the kitchen eating a helping of corn bread heaped with butter, and my heart softened at the sight. She was too thin from her illness, and to see her with an appetite again filled me with joy.

The judge tucked a blanket around us in the buggy to guard against the chill December air, and stood waving good-bye until we rounded a bend and he disappeared from sight.

Chapter Twenty-five

The first week after my visit to Judge Patterson left my nerves on edge and my mind fractured like a war-torn battlefield. John had been aloof, yet attentive. He asked me to accompany him to New Orleans, suggesting that while he was conducting business I could use the opportunity to select fabrics and furnishings for the nursery we would soon be needing.

I had looked away, afraid that my lack of preparations in this area had alerted John to my plans. I had declined, stating my unwillingness to leave Rebecca before her complete recovery. John seemed to accept my answer, but at times I would find him watching me closely, his eyes narrowed and his expression blank, making me feel like a corpse under the measuring gaze of the undertaker.

I continued the pretense of calm serenity, outwardly going about my duties as mistress of Whispering Oaks while in my head I marked the days until my departure. I had not yet told Rebecca. Not only was I afraid that she would be unable to keep the confidence, but I was also afraid that she would not leave her father.

I grieved for her, knowing the depth of her loss and knowing that I could never tell her the real reason why we had to go. I would bear the weight for her and free her innocent soul from the torment of knowing the truth.

Rebecca bristled with excitement over the coming holidays, and I pretended to join in her enthusiasm. The traditional bonfires were to be lit on Christmas Eve, and I would use the noise and confusion of the festivities to disappear under cover of darkness.

Two days before Christmas, while John was still in New Orleans, Daniel called at the house to check on Rebecca. I had just put her down for a nap, so I brought him up the stairs to her room.

By the time we arrived, she had already settled into a heavy slumber. I watched Daniel carefully as he studied the child. He stood by the side of her bed for a long moment, watching her sleep. Reaching out a hand, he tenderly pushed her gold hair from her face.

"She's so much like her mother," he said.

I stepped closer to the foot of the bed. "But not anything like her father." I watched his face carefully.

To my surprise, he showed no reaction to my words. Instead he turned to me. "I used to think that Elizabeth was the most intoxicating woman ever born." He stared at me intently. "Until I met you. But your beauty is deeper than your pretty face. Something Elizabeth could never claim."

Embarrassed, I felt heat color my cheeks. "Really, Daniel. I don't think you should be speaking to me in this way."

He set down his black bag and approached me. "But surely you have guessed my feelings for you."

I looked away from the intensity of his gaze. "We are

friends, Daniel. Nothing more. Nor are we free to pursue a deeper relationship, even if that were something I desired."

He reached for my hand but I pulled away. "Catherine, my feelings for you have grown far beyond friendship. I know it's wrong, but I can't seem to help myself. I want to be with you. Always. And I know you're not happy with John. I've sensed a restlessness in you this last month. He made Elizabeth's life miserable, and now I see he has done the same to you."

I stepped back. "Daniel, I want you to stop this now. Please don't destroy the high regard I have for you. I am not my sister, easily seduced into another man's bed."

He shook his head, approaching me again. "No, you're not Elizabeth. You're much too good, and too beautiful. I suppose it was too much to hope for that you might feel the same affection for me."

"Daniel, you've been a good friend. I'm sorry if any of my actions or anything I've said might have led you to believe that my feelings went further than friendship. I am flattered, certainly, that a man such as you would hold me in such high regard. But you are married, as am I, and I am only in need of your friendship now."

He took a deep breath and regarded me with soft gray eyes. "I apologize if I've offended you. I'm afraid that I've spoken out of turn. It was wrong of me to confess my feelings, knowing that your honor would never allow you to feel the same way about me."

I saw the way his golden hair shimmered in the bright light of the afternoon sun streaming in from the windows. "I am not my sister," I said again.

"No, you are not, and I have been wrong to think otherwise." He started to turn away but stopped, his expression that of a man intent on finding the absolution of confession. "Remember when I told you that I married

Clara because it was love at first sight? I lied. I had seen Elizabeth on my visit with John and I could not leave. So I married Clara to be near your sister. I am so ashamed. My only hope is that you can find it in your generous heart to forgive me."

"Why are you telling me all this now?"

"Because I've been carrying the burden of my secret around for so long. And your forgiveness would be a balm to my soul."

I looked at him wearily. "It is not of me you need to beg forgiveness, but of your wife. She loves you so. And of John."

A flash of anger momentarily crossed his fine features. "I owe nothing to John."

I looked down at the sleeping child, her spun-gold hair shimmering against the whiteness of her pillow. "I beg to differ."

His gaze followed mine, but his expression remained blank. "I did not steal his wife's affections, if that is what you're referring to. She kept those all to herself."

I swallowed, as if digesting his words. "So you're telling me that she never returned your feelings?"

A slow breath escaped him, like the last sigh of a dying man. "No."

I felt relief for a moment in the knowledge that Daniel's infatuation with Elizabeth had remained chaste. Rebecca stirred, and we watched her in silence for a moment. *Then who's your father, sweet child? Was it somebody your mother truly loved?* In my heart of hearts, I wished for it to be true. The thought of a cold and indifferent Elizabeth finding death without it was too hard to bear.

I lifted my eyes to find Daniel watching me intently. I didn't look away. "But you did betray your friendship with John, if only with your feelings for his wife."

His lips curled into a grimace. "It was his own fault. He

could not make Elizabeth happy and he gave up trying. He was like a drought on the flower of her spirit, drawing away all life. He drove her to take her own life. And I see how John has already dimmed your spirit. I fear for you, too."

I turned away, not wanting him to read the secret in my eyes.

"If you are unhappy, let me take you away from here. As your friend, let me help you."

I looked back at him to refuse but he must have seen something in my face, for he stopped suddenly. "You've already made plans to leave, haven't you?"

I started to shake my head to deny it, but the weight of my secret longed to be lightened. "It's not what you think, Daniel. I'm not going with another man. I simply need . . . to get away."

His face colored. "Has he hurt you in any way?"

I turned away to face the window. "No. But I have reason to believe that he is a dangerous man."

"Because of Philip?"

I nodded. "And Elizabeth. Did you know she was leaving John when she was killed? I think she might have been going with Philip, and now he's dead, too."

He looked ashen but kept his gaze steadily on me. "Why do you think it was Philip?"

I closed my eyes tightly for a moment, trying to erase the picture of Philip floating facedown in the pond. "I don't think either one of them tried to keep their affair secret. John certainly knew."

His voice was almost a whisper. "And then she was found dead." He shook his head. "I had no doubts when John said it was suicide. Her mental health had always been frail at best, although she kept it hidden from most. I thought I could save her from her inner torment, but my love was never enough for her. Nothing ever was." Defeat and desolation crowded his words, but I could feel little sympathy for him. "And now you're telling me that John . . ."

I rested my hand on his arm. "I have nothing but suspicion. But I do not feel safe here."

Solemn gray eyes met mine. "Let me do the right thing for a change. Let me help you. I will fight to bring John to justice, but first I need to see you safe."

"How can I trust you, Daniel? You have deceived your wife and your closest friend. How could I be sure that you wouldn't betray me?"

His shoulders slumped in an attitude of defeat. "I need to redeem my soul, and this is my last chance. I could never hope for forgiveness from Clara—and it's already too late for Elizabeth. You are my last chance to rise above this dark hell that threatens me night and day."

My resolve weakened as I stared at this man whom my sister had destroyed. I did believe I could trust him, but I still had other doubts. "Judge Patterson has already offered his help."

He took a step forward. "But the judge is old and feeble. What if John finds out and pursues you? Do you really think the judge is strong enough to protect you and Rebecca from John's fury?"

I looked at Rebecca again, sleeping peacefully with her doll securely tucked under her arm. Daniel was right. The judge would be no match against John, and I would not put an innocent man in the path of John's wrath. Daniel was eager and willing to protect us, and perhaps in doing so, would find his own forgiveness. Pressing back golden hair from Rebecca's face, I rationalized that she might not be as frightened on our journey if she had the doctor with her in the beginning.

Slowly I nodded. "You must swear you will not tell anyone."

He agreed, and I knew I could trust him.

"In two days' time, when they light the bonfires out on the levee, I will need a carriage to take me to New Orleans. I was planning to take one of John's, but if he finds it missing it will be easier for him to search for us."

"Us?"

"Yes. I'm taking Rebecca with me."

His features tightened for a brief moment, but he said nothing.

"She is not safe here." I reached for his hand and squeezed it. "I was hoping you could tell me that she would be well enough to travel now."

"Yes. She's almost completely recovered."

"Good. If you can get us to New Orleans, I have enough funds to hire a coach to take me to Brunswick. Could you do that without arousing suspicion?"

A terrible calm seemed to settle on him. "Yes. I will find a way."

"And if John finds out that you helped me?"

With a determined shake of his head, he said, "He has more to fear from me. From what you have told me, I now have information that implicates him in Elizabeth's death."

He stopped to pick up his bag and I grabbed his arm. "Please tell me that John was not always like that. I still see so much good in him." I choked on a sob.

"Elizabeth changed him—she changed us both. It was for her I betrayed both my best friend and my wife, and I doubt I will ever find forgiveness for either, regardless of who John has become." His eyes were looking inside himself, into the deepest reaches of his heart, and what I saw there saddened me. "But being with Elizabeth, nothing else seemed to matter."

With shoulders stooped with defeat, he faced me. "I will send a message to you as to when and where to meet me.

Have everything ready before the bonfire so we won't be delayed."

"Thank you, Daniel. I'll be ready."

He nodded, placed his hat on his head, then left the room.

I sat on the side of Rebecca's bed and watched her sleep. The back of my neck prickled and I sat up straighter. A slight scratching sounded from what I thought was the wall, as if a fingernail were being slid along the plaster. I bounded off the bed and ran to the deserted corridor.

"Mary? Delphine? Is anybody there?"

There was no answer.

I sped down the stairs to the empty foyer and called out again.

As I stood listening to the deserted house around me, I looked into the old mirror, noting again the irregularities in the glass. I moved to stand in front of it, noticing how distorted my reflection appeared. With a sad grimace, I turned away, thinking how accurate the mirror's portrayal of me was.

John returned from New Orleans on Christmas Eve, in time for the festivities. I was in the library reading when I heard the carriage, but I did not go into the foyer to greet him.

I heard Delphine tell him where I was and he soon joined me, his presence filling the room and drawing me to him before I even looked up from the pages of my book. Having him so near still affected me in ways I could not control, regardless of what I knew of him.

Several parcels tottered in his outstretched arms, and he knelt on the floor beside me, letting the packages slide to the ground. A boyish grin lit his face, making my mouth go dry, and I had to look away.

"I've been shopping," he said unnecessarily.

"I can see that."

He lifted the lid from a small hatbox and pulled out a miniature rabbit-fur hat and muff. "I thought Rebecca might like these."

I nodded, finding it not too difficult to put a smile on my face. His enthusiasm was contagious.

"And this," he said, pulling a slim box from his pocket, "is for you. You can have it now or wait until tomorrow."

I almost said to wait, but instead I closed my book and held out my hand. Something mercenary in me realized that if it were valuable jewelry, I could sell it and use the funds for survival once we reached Brunswick. Slowly I opened the box and gasped. Two beautiful teardrop ear bobs rested on black velvet, the large, round-cut diamonds as big as a thumbnail.

"A diamond for each of our children. I hope to someday give you a necklace full of diamonds."

I felt hot and clammy, the taste of bile thick on my tongue. *What game are you playing?* I wanted to ask him. *These are not the words of a man who doubts his wife's fidelity.* The mixed emotions of betrayal, regret, desire, and loss coursed through me, leaving me empty and shaking.

"Are you ill?" The note of concern in his voice was unmistakable.

"I'm fine. It must have been something I ate." I managed a smile. "These are beautiful. Thank you."

He moved to kiss me, but I turned away. He kept his head lowered, his breath brushing my neck, but he did not speak. Then, unable to stop myself, I leaned toward him and placed my lips against his cheek like the kiss of Judas. I held my face close to his for several heartbeats, smelling his intoxicating scent and my mind reeling at his nearness, then pulled back.

His dark eyes searched mine. "You're welcome," he said before pulling away and standing. "The bonfires will be lit at dusk. I suggest you and Rebecca get ready so we can leave."

"Yes. Of course." I managed to stand on unsteady legs before leaving the room, feeling his brooding eyes on my back as I walked away.

The blazing lights of the bonfires along the levee stretched as far down the river as I could see. The pyramid-shaped wooden log structures towered into the night sky, flames licking upward toward the stars perched on top, an almost pagan ritual to welcome the birth of the Christ child.

Stalks of sugarcane had been piled on top of the wood, creating a rapid succession of shotlike sounds as the steam expanded inside the stalks, causing them to explode. Smoke rose from the tops of the pyramids like the wispy spirits of those no longer with us, their cloudlike arms stretching heavenward.

I kept Rebecca close to me, afraid to get separated in the crowd. John stayed at our side, his presence worrying me. I would have to find a good excuse to leave with Rebecca when the time came.

The smells of roasting pork and burning sugarcane thickened the chilly air, but I could not find my appetite. I made sure Rebecca ate, not knowing when we'd have the chance to stop and eat again. For appearances, I accepted a tin plate heaped with food, although I barely managed to force down more than crumbled corn bread.

John stopped to speak with a cluster of men from neighboring plantations, and I turned quickly to disappear with Rebecca into the crowd. A hand grabbed at my arm and I twisted around in fear, keeping Rebecca behind my skirts. I let out my breath in relief when I saw it was Rose.

She leaned close to me to be heard over the noise of the people and the bonfire. "I sprinkled them eggshells over Master Philip's grave. The man who done killed him

341

will be revealed. My signs say it will be tonight."

Rebecca pulled at my skirts, diverting my attention. "Mama, can I have some saltwater taffy? I promise I won't be messy."

I answered her question, and when I turned back to Rose, she had gone.

Clutching Rebecca's hand tightly, I began to weave in and out of the crowd, hoping to make it difficult for John to spot us. Because of his height, I had no problem locating him, and made sure I stayed far away from him.

I patted the bulge in my skirt pocket, taking comfort in the coins in the leather pouch. Judge Patterson had sold my necklace in New Orleans for a very large sum and had visited Whispering Oaks as promised the previous week to give me the proceeds.

I spotted Rose again and approached her, my question about her words ready on my tongue. As I stood in front of her, her gaze fell behind me, her eyes wide with fear. Pushing Rebecca behind me again, I turned to find myself face-to-face with Marguerite.

Straightening my back, I said, "You are not welcome here. Surely Belle Meade has its own bonfire."

Her green eyes smoldered in the light from the fire, making them seem to flicker with their own internal flame. "Dr. Lewiston sent me with a message for you. He's waiting for you at Belle Meade in his office behind the house. He says you'll know what it's about."

I stared at her for a long moment, wondering why Daniel would have trusted her to deliver the message.

As if reading my mind, she said, "He trusts me not to speak of this to anyone else." She narrowed her eyes. "He says your husband is too suspicious, which is why the doctor didn't come tonight. He didn't want to draw attention to you or to him. He says it's best if you leave tonight from Belle Meade. Take your horse and he'll make arrangements to return her before anyone notices she's gone."

I looked at her closely to see if I could determine how much she really knew about our plans. But her face was inscrutable, the only movement that of her flickering green eyes. "But why would he send you? He could have given anybody a note."

She grinned in the firelight, her eyes receding into shadows. "Because he knew that if John saw us talking, he would never suspect that I was here to help you."

I thought for a long moment. Everything she had said made sense, although I still had misgivings. But if she knew of our plans, Daniel must have trusted her enough to tell her. I closed my eyes for a moment, trying to think, and when I opened them I knew. This could be my only chance to escape, and I owed it to Rebecca and my unborn child to do whatever was necessary.

"All right," I said, keeping Rebecca behind me. "I'll go to him." I took a few steps back to separate us, then turned toward the house without thanking her.

We walked quickly through the grass, one of my hands clutching Rebecca's and the other holding my skirts up so we could go faster. "I have a surprise for you," I said to the child running at my side.

"A surprise?" Her eyes widened with excitement.

"Yes. We're going on a trip. Just you and me."

Her face fell. "But what about Papa? Won't he be lonely?"

I swallowed the lump rising in my throat. "He'll miss you, but he'll be keeping busy with business matters. He'll want you to have fun, though. And Dr. Lewiston will be with us for a little while."

She nodded, but didn't say anything else, her young mind seemingly immersed in thought.

We ran into the house and grabbed the satchel I had packed for the journey, then raced out the back door toward the stables. Jezebel greeted me with a soft whinny as I set about saddling her in the semidarkness. Finally I reached for Rebecca and hoisted her onto the horse, then climbed up behind her. With a gentle kick to Jezebel's flanks, we left the stables, circled around the house, and headed toward Belle Meade.

Chapter Twenty-six

The breeze off the Mississippi picked up, lifting my cape and rustling the leaves beneath us like old voices. I stayed far away from the levee until I was certain we wouldn't be seen by any of the people from Whispering Oaks, then climbed the levee road. The bonfires lit my way, and I kept the hood over my face and my cloak wrapped around Rebecca to keep us hidden. I didn't once look back. I wasn't sure whether I was afraid to test my resolve or if I had no desire to see Whispering Oaks again.

I slowed as we approached the lane leading to Belle Meade. No lamps were lit within the house, nor were torches blazing on the outside of the house and grounds. The windows were dark indentations on the faded white of the house, and the front doorway gaped darkly like an open mouth, lending it the appearance of an empty skull. I shivered, gooseflesh rippling up my arms, and hugged Rebecca close to me.

Long arms of cloud reached around the full moon in a celestial embrace, lighting our way while casting sporadic shadows. Jezebel picked her way across the side of the house with its barren garden to the large brick-and-frame cottage in the rear that housed Daniel's medical practice.

I spied a light in the window of the office with a surge of relief. I slid off the horse, then took Rebecca and Samantha from the saddle. I assumed that we would eventually send Jezebel back home, but for now I tied her reins to a tree. Taking Rebecca's hand, I went to the door of the cottage.

I knocked loudly and waited for an answer. After several minutes I knocked again, but heard only silence. Then, to my surprise, Rebecca turned the latch and opened the door.

A small lamp burned on a table in what appeared to be a waiting room. This was the oldest portion of the cottage and consisted of three brick walls. The fourth wall, part of the newer addition and consisting of frame and plaster, had a wooden door built in the middle, apparently leading to an examining room. A group of chairs were clustered together on a braided rug; a fireplace, devoid of fire, covered an entire side of the room. "Daniel?" I called, my voice loud in the empty room.

Rebecca stepped past me to a large wooden box on a pedestal table. I gave a start of recognition. It was a music box that had been a wedding gift from me to John and Elizabeth. Curious, I walked toward it and opened the lid, startled to recognize the bright, tinny song that floated up to me.

Rebecca stood next to me and began to hum the odd, off-key melody, and it hit a strange chord in me. I thought back on all Elizabeth's doctor's visits, and the drawer full of licorice sticks, and Rebecca's familiarity with this song, and I knew. *Elizabeth wasn't running away with Philip, was she, Daniel? And the child she carried was yours.* I recalled Clara's lamentations of her own barren state, and wondered if she knew about Elizabeth and Daniel—and I prayed she didn't. The knowledge would be too hard for her to bear. I glanced down at Rebecca and tried to see Daniel in her face, but could not.

I noticed a door on the far side of the room and knocked on it, calling Daniel's name. Unease settled in my belly when I again heard no response. I pushed the door open further and it opened slightly, then hit something solid that blocked it. Peering inside the opening, I saw Daniel Lewiston lying on the floor, a thin trickle of blood seeping from his forehead. His body was wedged behind the door, making it nearly impossible to open. *John! How did he find out?*

"Where's Dr. Lewiston, Mama?"

Forcing my voice to remain calm, I said, "I'm going to find out. But I need you and Samantha to sit down in that chair while I look for him, all right? And promise me that you will not go anywhere."

Solemnly she nodded, then settled herself and her large rag doll into a chair.

With all of my might, I pushed on the door and managed to open it a little more, giving me enough room to squeeze through the doorway. The only illumination came from a flickering candle on the desk, casting thick shadows across the room. I knelt by Daniel on the floor and lifted his head.

I called his name and pressed my fingers to his neck. His pulse was faint and erratic, but at least he was still alive. I needed to get help, for I couldn't tend to his injuries alone.

Leaning over him, I whispered, "Daniel, I have to leave you to get help. I promise to be back as quickly as I can." Gently I lowered his head then took off my cloak and put it on him, using a portion of it to pillow his head.

As I stood, I spotted a movement in the shadows and held up my arm in defense. "John!" I cried. To my shock and horror, I saw that it wasn't my husband who emerged from the dark corner of the room.

Clara's eyes were wild in the flickering light. "Your husband won't be able to save you now, Catherine."

I ignored her, not quite understanding yet. "Clara—Daniel is hurt. I must go get help." My voice faded as I spied the mallet in her hand, and it became all too clear as to how Daniel had been hurt.

I barely recognized the voice as coming from the mousy Clara that I knew. "Men are so weak. I knew it was only a matter of time before Daniel would transfer his affection for Elizabeth to you. You're more alike than you think, you know. You attract men like bees to honey. Just like her."

"Clara—you're confused. There is nothing between me and Daniel. He was only helping me escape. . . ." A sick feeling spilled itself in my belly. I was escaping John because I thought he had harmed Elizabeth and Philip and meant to harm me. I gaped at Clara. "You killed Elizabeth."

She threw her head back and laughed an evil laugh I never would have thought her capable of. "Of course I did. She was carrying the baby that was meant for me and taking what was mine, as you are trying to do now. I will never let that happen."

Daniel moaned and I looked down at him. "If you care anything for your husband, then you will let me seek help."

She also glanced at Daniel and her lower lip quivered. "He doesn't love me. He never has. I had once hoped that my love would be enough. . . ."

She looked back to me and the wild cast was in her eyes again. "I wanted you to go away before Daniel noticed you. I tried to warn you away. Marguerite helped—locked you in the attic and put the snake in your room. But *I* put

the doll in the pond. I knew how you let your little boy
die. You all thought I wasn't smart, but I am. Everyone
knows to stay away from oleander leaves—but you never
seemed to understand. If only you hadn't looked so much
like her . . ."

Tumbling images crowded my mind as I tried to make
sense of her words. Acid churned in my stomach as I realized my own folly. In my haste to get away from the one
person who could protect me, I had run straight into the
arms of the one set to destroy me.

I forced my voice to stay strong. "And what of Philip?
Did he have a part in any of your plans?"

"That fool. I told him that we would help him get rid of
John if he'd get rid of you. You're the reason my Daniel
won't love me, and you need to be gone. Like Elizabeth."

I tried to speak rationally with her, make her speak of
her plans in order to get her to calm down. "But why would
Philip agree to such a thing?"

"Greed. It's as deadly a sin as lust. His parents had dis-
owned him and he needed money to leave the country.
Seems he knew too much about some lynchings." She slid
the mallet so that her hands were on the handle near its
head.

Her eyes brightened and she appeared completely normal, her tone of voice no different from when we were
sitting in my parlor and drinking tea. But her words chilled
me to the bone.

"You were supposed to take a tumble from the carriage.
When that failed, he set the fire in the mill to distract everyone and then he waited in the house for you. But the man
was weak like all men and he couldn't harm you. He was
supposed to lock you in the room after Marguerite put the
snake in there, and then stop anybody from helping you.
He'd brought a gun, hoping John would come to your
rescue so he could kill him."

She shook with fury; the knuckles of the hand gripping the mallet turned white. "But he couldn't bear the thought of being responsible for your death. So he left, the coward. I had no choice but to kill him. He was of no use to me if he wouldn't get rid of you. But he knew enough of my plans that I had to make sure he couldn't tell." She grinned a feral smile, her white teeth flashing in the dimness. "I killed him right where you're standing now and where Daniel stood not more than an hour ago. And then Marguerite helped me dump him in your pond, where we hoped you'd find him. That was the night Marguerite laid the conjure ball on your bed, too. And now I shall make sure that its prophecy will come true."

She looked down at the worn mallet in her hand as if contemplating how heavy a blow it would take to fell me. Then her eyes sought mine again. "I know you found the secret stairs in the house, but you never found the hidden rooms. Marguerite and I would hide in them and listen to every word you said. Or pretend to be a ghost for Rebecca. That's how I knew things. But you never suspected, did you? You were too busy trying to get Daniel to fall in love with you. That's how I know that you and Daniel are planning to run away tonight together. But I can't let that happen."

She took a step toward me but froze at the tapping on the door.

"Mama? I'm scared out here by myself. Who are you talking to?"

I threw myself at the blocked door, desperate to keep her away. "Run, Rebecca, run! Go find your papa—anybody. Get help. Now!"

"Mama?" Her voice was full of questions and uncertainty.

Clara moved quickly toward me but tripped on Daniel, falling to her knees.

Frantically I turned back to the partially open door, blocking it with my body. "Rebecca, do it now. Please. Just run—run as far as you can and hide."

"Mama?"

"Do it!"

I heard her run across the room and then fling the front door open before I turned to face Clara. She had regained her balance and was now advancing on me.

"She can't hide from me. Marguerite will find her eventually. But it's you and your lover I must deal with now."

I backed up against the door. "Why would you want to hurt an innocent child?"

Clara's mouth erupted in a bitter laugh. "There's no such thing as an innocent child, is there? Especially not that one. Daniel might not be her father." She shrugged, looking incongruous with the mallet clutched in her hand. "But it's quite certain that John isn't, either."

Fear and despair began winning out over courage and I had to choke back sobs. "Please—please don't hurt her. She's just a child."

"You're not really in a position to tell me what I can and cannot do, now, are you? At first she was merely a means to an end. I thought if something happened to her, surely you would leave. But now . . . she's been here. She knows my voice."

I said a silent prayer that Rebecca had listened to me and had hidden herself far away from the cottage.

"You're making a terrible mistake. Daniel is only helping me escape—he's not coming with me. There is nothing between us."

With a hiss she threw a crumpled letter at me. It hit my shoulder before falling to the rug. "That's a farewell note he wrote to me. He wasn't planning on coming back."

Rage seemed to flood her features as she raised the mallet over her head with both arms. With a grunt she swung at me, narrowly missing my head as I ducked. It slammed the door closed, leaving a splintery scar in the wood panel.

I ran to the desk while glancing frantically around the room for a weapon with which to defend myself, but to no avail. Too late, I looked up to see Clara hoisting the mallet over her head again, its thick end aimed at my skull. Seeing no other recourse, I threw myself at her, my head hitting her forcibly in the chest, pushing her backward and making her grunt. The mallet struck my back with a glancing blow, knocking the wind out of me momentarily.

She fell backward and I on top of her, the mallet hitting the floor behind us with a solid thud. We both grappled to stand and find the weapon first. My hands settled around the smooth wood of the stick before I felt her nails claw into the tender skin at the back of my neck.

Her hands slid down to the neckline of my dress and I heard a loud rending of fabric as my dress tore away. I struggled to stand, surprised at the heaviness of the mallet. Breathing deeply, I said, "I don't want to hurt you. If you cooperate with me and go with me to find help for Daniel, I will see that you get the help you need. You've endured a lot, Clara. There are many people who will understand and will come to your aid."

Her thin brown hair had come loose during our struggle and now hung raggedly over her face and shoulders. Rage and jealousy distorted her face as she came at me again. "I have lost everything and somebody has to pay!" Her fingers flew to my throat and she began to squeeze the breath from me. Still I clung to the mallet, not yet willing to use it. The light began to dim from my eyes, and for a moment I was tempted to let the battle I had been fighting for so long be over. My battle for survival had been a futile, uphill struggle, and I was ready to put the load down and be done with it.

From far away I thought I heard my name being called

and the pounding of hoofbeats. *John.* I forced my eyes open but could barely see the shadow of the woman choking the life from me.

"Catherine!"

It was he, and his voice was like a fire in my blood, awakening every fiber of my being. With my last ounce of energy I shoved at Clara, knocking her away. As I gasped for breath, I blindly swung the mallet, hitting something soft yet solid.

Clara flew sideways, falling into the desk before sliding to the ground. The candle wobbled at the impact and I watched it move from side to side, as if undecided as to what it should do, before finally collapsing and rolling off the desk, the flame catching the long draperies on fire. I watched, mesmerized, as long fingers of flame spread along the length of the curtains, creating a wall of heat that nearly singed my skin.

Dropping the mallet, I grabbed Daniel by the shoulders and tugged with a strength I didn't know I possessed. Maneuvering him out of the way, I swung open the door and pulled him through it. Billows of smoke covered us, making me cough and my eyes sting as I dragged Daniel through the waiting area and to the front door.

My lungs felt as if they would explode, and spots danced in front of my eyes as I searched for air in the suffocating room. I dropped to my knees, no longer having the strength to stand, and found the air clearer near the floor.

As if by my will alone, the door opened, and John stood on the threshold. Strong hands grabbed me, then lifted me. I heard him issue orders for someone else to get Daniel, and then I was breathing the sweet outside air once again.

He laid me on the grass while I struggled for breath and words. I clutched at his coat. "Clara . . . she's still . . . inside."

He uttered a low curse. "I'll find her." With a quick touch

to my cheek, he disappeared in the direction of the burning building. I could find no breath to carry my words of caution to him or to call him back.

Daniel was laid next to me, and I blinked up and recognized the judge and two more men from Whispering Oaks. Daniel had regained consciousness and now struggled to rise, managing to lift himself on his elbows. Relieved to see him alive, I let my head fall back upon the grass, grateful to feel the prickly sweetness of it.

Judge Patterson knelt by my head and brushed the hair from my face. Lifting me slightly, he gave me water to drink from a cup. I drank it thankfully, feeling the cool, soothing liquid slide down my parched throat. "Have . . . you found . . . Rebecca? She's . . . hiding."

As if in answer to my prayer, she came running from behind a large magnolia, the white bow in her hair glowing like a star in the night. She bounded to me and I hugged her to my side, burying my face in her hair. It smelled of smoke and sweat and fear, and I cursed Clara silently for inflicting such harm on this child.

As the judge moved to stand, I grabbed his wrist. "John . . . ?"

He shifted his eyes away for a moment toward the building, which now had flames dancing on its roof and crying out from every window. There was nothing anybody could do but watch it burn.

He turned back to me. "He went around to the back of the house to see if he could get in that way. He hasn't come out yet."

I closed my eyes, remembering how I had felt when I'd heard John call my name, and tried to summon that strength again. When I felt my blood surge, I willed my strength and hope and love to him, and waited. My hand crept to the pocket of my skirt and I found the lodestone, wrapping my fingers around it and squeezing tightly.

The judge spoke, his voice solemn. "I want you to know that I didn't go back on my word to keep your secret. I was approached earlier this evening by Philip's father with a letter Philip had left in his desk drawer before he died. It explained the fire at the sugar mill and Clara's involvement and the reasons for it, as well as some other interesting things I don't want to go into now. And when I saw you leave after speaking with Marguerite, I knew there was trouble. So I told John, knowing him to be innocent of trying to harm you. I hope you will forgive me."

I grabbed his hand and squeezed.

"Marguerite has disappeared into the swamp. We will find her and bring her in to see that justice is served, but I have a feeling that the swamp will serve its own particular brand of justice." I shuddered, recalling the night my carriage had overturned in the swamp, and the sounds of the prowling night predators.

Patting my shoulder, the judge stood and turned toward the house. I held Rebecca's hand in mine, drawing strength from her sturdy little spirit, and taking comfort in her presence. She rested her head on my shoulder and sucked her thumb as the burning house popped and crackled behind us, sending smoke into the sky like an offering. Daniel looked at me for a moment, but the horror and grief in his eyes said more than I could find words for. He turned away, and I stared up into the black sky and began counting stars, keeping the dark thoughts at bay.

I became aware of movement all around me. More men had arrived, perhaps noticing the fire from the levee. Several stopped to check on Daniel and me, and at our request sat us up against a tree. My lungs burned and I still found it hard to breathe deeply. We sat in silence, coughing sporadically, our eyes turned toward the burning building.

A gasp went up from the crowd, all eyes riveted on the

south end of the small cottage. With a creaking groan the wall collapsed, sending sparks and splintered wood toward the onlookers. I stared at the flaming house, then dropped my head onto my drawn-up knees and wept.

Rebecca tugged at my hand, and then let go. I felt her warmth leave my side and I jerked my head up to look for her. Moving slowly, a dark shadow appeared against the flaming backdrop of the cottage. My heart seemed to stick in my throat as I watched the shadow loom larger.

"Papa!" Rebecca ran to him and propelled herself into John's arms. He staggered slightly and did not lift her. Instead he put his arm around her shoulders and walked toward me. A loud cheer sounded out from the gathering men. His face was blackened with ash, and a bleeding cut bisected his left cheek. He stopped in front of us but didn't say anything.

To my surprise, Daniel struggled to stand, supporting himself against the tree. "I'll watch Rebecca. You two have much to talk about."

The two men faced each other, one man's expression wary, the other's impassive. John's voice was deep and hollow, singed from the smoke. "I could not save Clara. She regained consciousness while I was carrying her through the door. She struggled with me and ran back inside. That's when the wall collapsed, and I could not go back in."

Daniel stared at John for a brief moment, his face ashen. "She told me she killed Elizabeth . . . and Philip. I had no idea . . ."

He turned away then and took Rebecca's hand. With slow, halting steps, he walked to the huge magnolia that Rebecca had hidden behind. He settled against the tree, resting his head against it as if still in great pain, and nestled her under his arm.

John collapsed next to me and I listened to his ragged

breath. He coughed, then turned to look at me. "Judge Patterson told me everything. It is beyond my comprehension how you could have believed the worst of me." Anger and pain emanated from his eyes, but he reached for my hand and clutched it tightly, as if making a peace offering. His touch told me that despite the anger, his relief at finding me alive was all that mattered.

The emotions of anger and relief chased each other in a circle in my own mind along with questions yet to be answered. "It's not as if you've always told me the truth. Rebecca saw you on the secret stairs, bringing up Elizabeth's traveling bag. Yet you didn't think it important enough to tell me, and I was left with no choice but to believe the worst."

He let go of my hand and ground the heels of his palms into his eyes. "I did that only to protect myself. I truly believed that she had killed herself and had tried to implicate me. Hence the traveling bag to make people believe she was leaving and to give me a motive to kill her. And, to seal my fate, the placement of my glove and the gris-gris. I shudder to think what would have happened if I had not been the first to discover her body. I knew you would never accept my story if you learned of the traveling bag, so I kept it secret. If I had not heard Elizabeth's threats to kill herself, even I would have had difficulty accepting it."

"But there was also the letterbox and the missing letters. Even though I found your pipe in the attic and the burning letters in the fireplace, you still denied any knowledge of the letterbox. I knew you were lying to me, but you wouldn't tell me the truth."

He sat so close to me that our shoulders touched, our heat nearly matching that of the flickering flames. "I took the letterbox from the attic and buried it. But after I heard you and Rebecca talking about it, I dug it up again to remove the letters. I didn't have the key, so I had to unscrew the hinges and remove the letters before reburying it. I didn't want to risk your ever finding them and reading them."

Tears stung my eyes, and I wasn't sure whether or not they were from smoke. "You should have trusted me with the truth. That's all I have ever asked of you."

"And you should have trusted me to take care of you. All I wanted was to protect you." He took my hands and brought them to his lips. "I want us to start over—far away from this place. We'll go back to Saint Simons, if that is what you want, and rebuild your home. I love you, Cat. I have since the first moment I saw you dancing barefoot on the beach." He closed his eyes, and I could feel his blood pulsing in his hands. "Please give me another chance to make you happy."

I took his face in my hands, using my thumbs to wipe off the dark smudges on his cheeks. "Even when I thought the worst of you, you still managed to claim my heart. I do want to start over—but I want to start with no secrets between us. They're like dark shadows in the corners of our lives, and I can't live with them." I touched my lips to his, sealing my fate. "I need to know what was in Elizabeth's letters."

His hands reached up to cover mine and I felt them tremble. "Don't, Cat. You don't know what you're asking."

I didn't release him. "Yes, I do. I'm stronger than you think."

His dark eyes searched mine, our faces close enough to kiss. "When I tell you, I want you to know that you are not alone. And that you are loved and cherished by me and that nothing else matters."

Fear blossomed in me then—not fear of my own mortality, for I had already faced that, but fear of losing my final innocence. But his touch gave me strength. "Tell me," I whispered.

His hands tightened on mine, and his eyes did not leave my face. "The letters in the letterbox were from your husband, Robert, to Elizabeth. They were love letters dating from before her marriage to me up until the time of his return to Saint Simons after the war."

I started shaking then, as bright bubbles of light seemed to surface and explode in my brain. He continued. "They talked of their intimacy and of a child they conceived when Robert was in Maryland in the army and she visited him there."

Rose's voice came back to me: *There be two men in your life—two men you share your life with. But one of them is not who you thinks he is. He betray you in a terrible way.*

"Oh, God," I whispered, shaking uncontrollably now. Still, he didn't let me go.

"Rebecca is their child."

"No, no, no!" I wanted to scream in denial, but my voice, hoarse from the smoke, deadened my grief. John gathered me in his arms and held me close, his kisses on my hair soft and gentle. I felt as if I were drowning in a sea of betrayal, threatening to pull me under and steal the life from me. He let me cry until I had nothing left inside me, and each tear shed was as cleansing to the soul as a baptism.

When I was finished, John brought my tear-streaked face up to his and kissed me. Grabbing his hands, I allowed him to pull me up out of the darkness. I reached for him, feeling the beginning of my salvation in the beating of his heart. The darkness still tugged at me, as I knew it might always do, but John would bear me up to face it.

Together we walked over to Daniel to claim Rebecca, and then took her home.

Epilogue

Sometimes I come down to the beach and take off my shoes, delighting in the feel of the shifting sand beneath my feet. I can listen to the waves now without hearing the cries of my lost child, and I am more at peace than I ever have been.

I have begun to swim in the ocean again, and John has asked me to teach Rebecca and our son Samuel when he is old enough. We will do so together, John and I, as we have done everything in our lives since the night of the fire.

Robert and Elizabeth's betrayal will always be with me, like a scar from an old wound. The pain is gone, but at times the fingers of my memory touch the ridges of the scar, a medal of survival and a reminder of John's love for me. Forgiveness is an elusive ghost to me still, but I try. Every day I try.

My home and family have become a great tide pool of

my own creation, and my love the dam that protects them from the encroaching waves. I can face the vastness of the ocean now, with the salt wind whipping at my hair and banishing the gnawing of hunger from my soul, and feel only possibility and an overflowing well of contentment.

When I think back on those first tumultuous months of our marriage, I see it as a macabre dance, John and I waltzing around in a circle, with the dark shadow of betrayal lurking in the middle, waiting to consume us. But now the light of my beloved island shines on us, illuminating the corners of our lives and our hearts. We take delight in the building of our house and in the joyful cries of our children. His touch strengthens me, and mine, him. We have waited all of our lives for this, and know that we are blessed.

IN THE SHADOW OF THE MOON

KAREN WHITE

A lunar eclipse. A twentieth-century comet. And suddenly, thoroughly modern Laura Truitt is swept off mysterious Moon Mountain, away from her enchanting Southern home—and over one hundred years into the past. . . .

There, dashing Confederate soldier Stuart Elliott whisks her to his eerily familiar plantation, and his powerful masculinity evokes impossible desires. But the Civil War rages, forging unspeakable danger, threatening to wrench Laura from Stuart's arms. She must await the moon's magic to come full circle. But will it carry her back to the future, heartbroken and alone? Or keep her with Stuart in this passionate, perilous past?

___52395-7 $4.99 US/$5.99 CAN

Dorchester Publishing Co., Inc.
P.O. Box 6640
Wayne, PA 19087-8640

Please add $1.75 for shipping and handling for the first book and $.50 for each book thereafter. NY, NYC, and PA residents, please add appropriate sales tax. No cash, stamps, or C.O.D.s. All orders shipped within 6 weeks via postal service book rate. Canadian orders require $2.00 extra postage and must be paid in U.S. dollars through a U.S. banking facility.

Name_____
Address_____
City_____State_____Zip_____
I have enclosed $_____ in payment for the checked book(s).
Payment <u>must</u> accompany all orders. ❑ Please send a free catalog.
CHECK OUT OUR WEBSITE! www.dorchesterpub.com

Amarantha
Melanie Jackson

'Tis not Robert Burns's legendary elfin knight who greets Amarantha upon her arrival at her folklorist uncle's Cornish mansion, but the dark and wild-haired Tamlane Adair. The Scotsman's languorous movements enthrall her, and the rumors of his nighttime rides across Bodmin Moor only heighten the virile man's mystery. His voice is like satin or silk, sliding over her, clothing her in blissful delirium. Listening, she can almost forget the Jacobite rebellion that has cost her so much. In Tamlane's green eyes, Amarantha cannot help but see the danger of the Cornish coast...and in his arms, its wonderful promise.

___4900-7 $5.99 US/$6.99 CAN

Anne Avery Fire & Ice

It is a huge old mausoleum, a place where p's and q's matter more than people do. Kate had escaped it once, though it still haunts her dreams, along with bitter memories of the boy she'd loved. Now she is back to claim a forgotten legacy, and Elliot is a grown man, no longer gentle but hard and dangerous. People say he is a killer, but the fire between them leaps as fiercely as ever, making Kate wonder whether her mother's bequest to her is the glittering diamonds for which she searches or a proclivity for giving her heart to an ill-fated love.

___52442-2 $5.50 US/$6.50 CAN

Dorchester Publishing Co., Inc.
P.O. Box 6640
Wayne, PA 19087-8640

Please add $2.50 for shipping and handling for the first book and $.75 for each book thereafter. NY, NYC, and PA residents, please add appropriate sales tax. No cash, stamps, or C.O.D.s. All orders shipped within 6 weeks via postal service book rate. Canadian orders require $2.00 extra postage and must be paid in U.S. dollars through a U.S. banking facility.

Name_____
Address_____
City_____ State_____ Zip_____
I have enclosed $_____ in payment for the checked book(s).
Payment <u>must</u> accompany all orders.☐ Please send a free catalog.
CHECK OUT OUR WEBSITE! www.dorchesterpub.com

Moonshadow

PENELOPE NERI

"Lillies-of-the-valley," he murmurs, "the sweet scent of innocence." Yet his kisses are anything but innocent as he feeds her deepest desires while honeysuckle and wild roses perfume the languid air.

"Steyning Hall. It is a cold place. And melancholy," he warns, "almost as if it is . . .waiting for someone. Perhaps your coming will change all that."

Wedded mere hours, Madeleine gazes up at the windows of the mansion, stained the color of blood by the dying sun. In the shifting moonshadows she hears voices calling, an infant wailing, and knows not whether to flee for her life or offer up her heart.

___52416-3 $5.99 US/$6.99 CAN

THE SCARLETTI CURSE — CHRISTINE FEEHAN

Strange, twisted carvings adorn the *palazzo* of the great Scarletti family. But a still more fearful secret lurks within its storm-tossed turrets. For every bride who enters its forbidding walls is doomed to leave in a casket. Mystical and unfettered, Nicoletta has no terror of ancient curses and no fear of marriage . . . until she looks into the dark, mesmerizing eyes of *Don* Scarletti. She has sworn no man will command her, thinks her gift of healing sets her apart, but his is the right to choose among his people. And he has chosen her. Compelled by duty, drawn by desire, she gives her body into his keeping, and prays the powerful, tormented *don* will be her heart's destiny, and not her soul's demise.

___52421-X $5.99 US/$6.99 CAN

Dorchester Publishing Co., Inc.
P.O. Box 6640
Wayne, PA 19087-8640